Beyond This Time

Beyond This Time

CHARLOTTE A. BANCHI

iUniverse, Inc.
New York Lincoln Shanghai

Beyond This Time

All Rights Reserved © 2003 by Charlotte A. Banchi

No part of this book may be reproduced or transmitted in any form or by any means, graphic, electronic, or mechanical, including photocopying, recording, taping, or by any information storage retrieval system, without the written permission of the publisher.

iUniverse, Inc.

For information address:
iUniverse, Inc.
2021 Pine Lake Road, Suite 100
Lincoln, NE 68512
www.iuniverse.com

ISBN: 0-595-28980-0

Printed in the United States of America

This book is for Michael. My knight in shining armor.

Thanks to: Jennifer, Mark and Angela for your never ending support.
The Friday Re-Writes: Peg Lachine and Jeanne Lane.
Couldn't have done it without you.

PROLOGUE

1963

APRIL 05—FRIDAY

The enormous oak roots along Brook Street lifted the sidewalk in so many places, Lettie Ruth Rayson's rusty and dented American Flyer wobbled precariously. Her cargo, lilies for the Palm Sunday church service, sat in the red wagon like royalty. The white bell-shaped blossoms nodded to the passing flowers as they rolled along. Unfortunately, with each sidewalk rut, half the plants toppled over and she had to stop the wagon to sit them upright again.

Lettie Ruth let the handle drop to the ground and blew on her palms to ease the stinging. The blisters, from the constant chafing against the handle, were raw oozing sources of pain. Tiny flecks of rusty metallic paint stuck to the open sores. She needed to find something to wrap around her hands before the wounds became infected.

Knocking on a door and asking the homeowner for several band aids was not an option. One block back she'd crossed the invisible boundary dividing the white and colored parts of town. In fact, by stopping in the middle of the sidewalk Lettie Ruth probably broke three or four rules. People of her color didn't parade up and down in this area, and this was her third trip this morning, hauling lilies from home to the church.

She picked up the wagon handle, grimacing at the pressure. At the next corner she would cut down the alley. With any luck, she might find some discarded newspapers or maybe a car washing rag to use.

It was the cleanest alley Lettie Ruth had ever seen. All the trash tucked inside the aluminum cans, nothing slopped over or littered the ground. Up ahead she spied a cardboard box set out for the Goodwill. That ought to do it, she thought. Bent over, with her head stuck inside the box, she didn't see the three men until they slipped up behind her.

*   *   *

Marlene Stephens found the red wagon filled with lilies when she opened her back gate. She looked up and down the alley, but the only thing moving was a white stake-bed truck turning the far corner. The flowers were pretty, so she pulled the wagon into her back yard. She could give one of the plants to her mother-in-law for her birthday. Exactly what the old biddy deserved—a gift Marlene had found on trash day. With all the money she'd saved by not buying a present, she could go to the beauty shop in downtown Birmingham and have a real manicure.

1

YEAR 2000

MACEYVILLE, ALABAMA
MARCH 02—SATURDAY

Maceyville police officer Kathleen Templeton leaned to the right, which allowed a partial view through the large front window. From the odd angles and disproportional rooms, it appeared someone had laid one house on top of the other. It reminded her of the Winchester Mystery House in San Jose, California. According to legend, Sara Winchester designed the house to fool evil spirits. The structure continued to grow until it had more than one hundred sixty rooms, two thousand doors, ten thousand windows and so many secret passageways and staircases leading to nowhere, even Sara Winchester required a map to find her way.

At the moment, Kat wished for a map of her own to explain what she saw. Curiosity finally overruled caution, and she stepped in front of the window, cupped her hands and pressed her face against the glass. Her hopes that the new perspective would dispel the sensation of being caught between colliding realities, quickly faded. For a second or two the interior looked vacant, then out of the corner of her eye she registered a subtle shift within the shadows. The previously empty room now held two different sofas, which overlay each other. In jerky sequence she saw a stone fireplace appear, then just as quickly disappear. And inches from her nose, a see-through table replaced a see-through rocking chair.

Confused by the conflict between eyes and brain, she felt disoriented. *Physics 101: Two objects cannot occupy the same space at the same time.* Yet wasn't that exactly what she saw? Two objects...same place. Kat backed away and clicked the button on her walkie-talkie, signaling for her partner, Sergeant James Mitchell.

Moments later Mitch, who'd been canvassing the rear of the residence, turned the corner of the wrap around veranda. She gestured toward the house. "You look through the windows out back?"

He stopped several feet away, on the opposite side of the large picture window. "One or two, the place appears empty. Why?"

"Because I've seen more than enough Halloween tricks for both of us. It's three o'clock in the morning and we've caught another prank call. Let's get out of here."

"What are you yammering about?" he asked.

"This house is playin' with my eyes and brain."

Mitch looked at her, his expression shouting he thought his partner had gone round the bend. "Care to expand on that statement, Kat?"

"See for yourself," she said, pointing to the window. "Take a peek through the looking glass, Alice."

He cautiously approached the glass, out of habit his hand rested on his side arm. After several seconds he turned around and shook his head. Kat's hopes plummeted. Apparently she was the only member of the team to see visions.

He shrugged. "Empty." He stared at her for a second longer, then called the station. "Unit 20, 10-8. Clear on that emergency transmission."

✶   ✶   ✶

MARCH 07—THURSDAY

"Maceyville Police Department."
   "Whole peck of 'em raising Cain. Gonna kill me."
"What is your name and address ma'am?"
"801 Mountain View. I hear them out front!"
"Officers are on the way. What is your name?"
"Alice. Alice Carpenter. Gonna burn me out!"
"Ma'am? Hello?...Ma'am can you hear me?"

Kat impatiently punched Rewind on the tape recorder. "Mitch, this time I want you to listen to her voice. Her tone."

"I've already listened to that damn tape four hundred times. I told you, it's another prank call," Mitch said. "In fact, tonight makes a grand total of three bogus calls in six days."

"She sounds scared."

"Kat, it's a snipe hunt. You know, send all the overworked and underpaid cops racing through the streets, sirens blasting while the joker sits back in the shadows and laughs his ass off."

"Yeah, but *what-if,* this one particular call, Alice Carpenter's call, was on the up and up?"

"If that's true, then you explain what we found, or better yet, explain what we didn't find," he challenged.

She shrugged.

"Exactly," he continued. "Based on that call, dispatch sent us to Mountain View and did we find a house burning to the ground? No way, Jose. We found a music recital at the home of a prominent Maceyville newspaper editor. And lucky us, we got to say howdy do to a couple of county judges as well."

"I know all that, Mitch. But if you listen real close, you can hear the woman's fearful. She's got problems and she's spooked. Could be dispatch gave out a different address and I copied it wrong?"

"Nice try, partner, but I already checked, it's a match."

Kat ran agitated fingers through her shoulder length cork-screw curls, then opened her mouth to argue her case, but realizing she lacked the ammo, closed it. Instead of launching another debate, she took the cassette out of the machine and left the room. As she waited for the Property clerk, she fumed over the past six days. The whole mess started on March 2, with the call to that spooky old house on Tenth Street. The caller had clearly identified herself as Gladys Pauley, and reported an intruder.

When they arrived, all Mitch saw was an empty house with a FOR SALE sign in the front yard. Kat got a double whammy, two houses for the price of one. Questioning of the cranky neighbors confirmed the owners had moved out eight months earlier. No one noticed anybody messing in or around the house in the past few hours, nor had they heard anything unusual. But Kat had seen plenty of unusual.

Three days later, on March 5, an unidentified male's garbled message about a white pickup following him home and now it was parked outside his door. According to the caller, the men in the truck were talking loud and taking pot shots at his windows.

En route to 4721 Riverside, dispatch informed them an anonymous caller had just reported an explosion and fire at the same location. This time she and Mitch arrived at a vacant lot filled with overgrown weeds, flanked on the north by a McDonald's, a gas station on the south and the Tombigbee River to the west.

No gunmen. No victim. No burning or exploding house.

Tonight was the *coup de gras*. March 7: 1303 Hours. 801 Mountain View. Unlucky number three. When they rolled up, sirens full on and lights flashing, the circular drive was filled with expensive automobiles. Sweet strains of flutes and violins filtered through the ceiling to floor windows opening onto the veranda. A startled red jacketed valet darted out of the shadows to open Kat's door and politely volunteered to park the squad car. Mitch almost shot the poor man.

At her request, the trembling valet went inside the house and returned moments later with the owner. Mr. Justin Kolsky, editor of the *Maceyville Sun Times*, had been less than gracious to the two police officers in his driveway.

* * *

MARCH 08—FRIDAY

MACEYVILLE SUN TIMES EDITORIAL. Justin R. Kolsky

It has become apparent that the annual budget for the Maceyville Police Department failed to include stipends for up to date city maps. On Thursday evening, March 7, a music recital held at my home was invaded by two armed police officers. When questioned regarding this outrage, they admitted the possibility of having responded incorrectly. In other words, they were at the wrong address!

Fellow citizens, if those individuals sworn to protect and serve are incapable of appropriate response to 911 calls, why should we place our lives, and those of our family's, in their hands?

Police Chief Arlin Smith personally apologized for this inexcusable faux pas, candidly admitting the fiasco at my home was not the first time his department erred. Nor the second. It was the third such incident—by the same two officers! When questioned as to the outcome of the prior two false responses, no one in the Maceyville Police Department could provide this editor with any information. No follow-up to a crime report? Are those poor folks that made the 911 call still awaiting the arrival of *our peace officers? Waiting to be rescued from danger?*

To the Maceyville P.D. I say: Go out and get yourselves a current map. Learn your way around our city. Do your job.

Like the old tale about the store manager who was reprimanded by the big boss, who then yelled at the clerk, who in turn went home and yelled at his spouse, and being dead last on the totem pole, the spouse kicked the living crap out of the dog.

Thus, Chief Arlin Smith yelled at his two officers.

James Mitchell and Kathleen Templeton stood at attention in his office, subjected to an angry diatribe in response to the morning editorial. For a good half hour the chief expounded on their less than accurate procedures and how they'd embarrassed a distinguished citizen. He went on to upbraid them for showing up at Kolsky's home with siren wailing and weapons drawn. Then for good measure, he dragged in the damage their gung-ho style inflicted upon the reputation of the entire department.

"Hell fire, y'all. Your heads ought to be hanging lower than a spotted hound dog's right now," the irate chief concluded. He lit a cigar, pleased that he'd effectively shifted the blame for the less than flattering editorial onto his two officers.

Due to Mr. Kolsky's influence with the mayor and city council, and the fact it was an election year, Mitch received two weeks desk duty in Verification of Employee Records. Kat was assigned to the Computer-File Entry Section. All because they interrupted a music recital.

2

MARCH 09—SATURDAY

"A good evenin' to you, Officer Templeton," said Dreama Simms, as she wheeled the cleaning cart into the Computer-File room.

Kat smiled warmly at the petite grey-haired woman. "Hey, Miss Simms. How you doing tonight?"

"Lordy, my lumbago is acting up, child. How 'bout yourself?"

Kat shrugged and gestured to the files scattered across her desk. "Shift number three, with eleven more to go," she said, referring to her two-week assignment. "I suppose I really shouldn't complain, at least the chief didn't fire me." The first night on the job, she'd defiantly demonstrated her displeasure by refusing to wear a proper uniform and informed all who would listen, 'If I'm going to be a secretary, I'm sure as hell going to dress like a secretary!' This declaration, in addition to the red leather miniskirt, earned a second reprimand for her file. Tonight Officer Templeton wore the proper uniform.

"Well, I liked that red hot outfit," Dreama said. "You looked good, girl."

"Good don't necessarily mean professional," Kat said, mimicking Chief Smith's nasal twang.

"Assigning you to this cellar is a pack of silliness if you ask me," Dreama snorted.

"Politics is more like it," Kat grumbled. "But I thank you for the kind words."

Dreama nodded and returned to work. Kat sorted through the manila folders and entered the information in the computer, punching the keys with force. She hated the job. This was not her idea of police work. It was bad enough to be taken off patrol, but the Computer-File night shift was humiliating.

However, her current assignment offered one bonus, private concerts by Miss Simms. In the late fifties and early sixties she'd been a star performer in black night clubs all over the United States. Her record albums adorned store windows and one achieved the Gold status. The reasons for the abrupt end to a very promising career remained a mystery, because Miss Simms discouraged anyone from prying into her past.

As Kat worked through the mountain of paper work, Miss Simms plugged in an old portable record player and gently placed an LP album on the turntable. With the first note, Kat closed her eyes, spellbound. Dreama Simms recorded voice was smooth as Kentucky bourbon. The silky notes melted into each other, filling the cavernous dungeon with rich melodic sounds.

"You know," Dreama said, interrupting the heart wrenching *Angel Eyes*. "I recall another house set afire on Riverside."

This statement caused Kat to sit up in her chair. "You mean there's been another one? When?" The second prank call she and Mitch caught had been for Riverside. What was going on in Maceyville?

Dreama chuckled. "Child, I'm talking about way back in the springtime of 1963. 'Round the time of all that civil rights trouble up in Birmingham."

Kat knew what Dreama Simms meant by 'the trouble in Birmingham'. Her own parents had been active supporters of Martin Luther King's campaign for equality. Her Pop had taken part in demonstrations at the Woolworth five and dime stores to integrate the lunch counters and even been arrested and jailed because of the Birmingham sit-in. Her mother had been hosed by the Birmingham police as she left the 16th Street Baptist Church. Kat often wondered, if in the same circumstances, she'd have had the courage her parents displayed. By comparison, the bouts of racism she encountered today were minuscule.

"That was almost 40 years ago," Kat said, bringing her thoughts back on track. "What on earth made you think about that house tonight?"

"In the springtime my memories get all stirred up. Been happening for years." Dreama gently raised the record needle and turned off the player. She leaned against her cart and stared into space. "I was barely thirty and already been working the clubs for nearly twelve years when I ended up in Maceyville. That March I was going around with a handsome devil named Maximilian Devore. Seem to recall it being early in the month when it all started. On that night, my man come down to The Blue to ride me home after work. As we come up to that fork on Riverside and Azalea, we saw the house explode. Girl, the whole sky lit up like Christmas morning. Everyone was running all over the streets in their night clothes."

"What happened to the folks in the house? Did they get out safely?"

The cleaning woman shook her head. "Everybody tried to help put out the fire, used garden hoses and buckets...but it didn't help none. That place burned to ashes in no time. I often thought if we'd only got there a little bit sooner, 'stead of stopping along the way for a kiss or two, things might have turned out different for that poor man."

Kat's skin prickled. The similarities between Miss Simms story and her own experiences were eerie. On March 5, she and Mitch caught a shots fired call on Riverside, male complainant. Shortly before they arrived, a second report had been transmitted about an explosion at the same address. "Do you by any chance remember the victim's name, Miss Simms?" she asked.

"I remember. I remember them all. His name was Dilmer Richards, honey," Dreama said. "I knew him from the church choir. Officer Templeton, they never caught up with the men. Now that I think on it, a few days before there'd been another house fire in the east Hollow, on Tenth Street. That time a woman died."

"Gladys Pauley," Kat whispered. "Her name was Gladys Pauley."

Dreama Simms laid down her dust cloth and stared at the officer. "That's right, child. But how come you to know that?"

Kat cleared her throat and gestured to the computer. "I've been transferring lots of old files lately. Her name must have stuck in my memory."

"There was a great deal of burning back then," Dreama said sadly. "I reckon you'll be coming across it in your work. A few days later it happened all over again. This time on my own street, Mountain View. I lived in a duplex along there until the city moved us out so they could tear them old buildings down. 'Course that was long before you got borned. Nowadays that area is full of fancy custom-built houses. No more shanty town. No more colored folks." She gave a mighty shove and the heavy cart rolled through the doorway. "See you tomorrow night."

Kat nodded absently, her thoughts elsewhere. Tenth Street, Riverside and Mountain View. Three crimes, same locations, yet separated by almost forty years. A silly coincidence? It couldn't be anything else, she told herself. But the hairs on the back of her neck curled and her arms broke out in goose bumps.

* * *

An hour later Kat gave up all pretense of working and brushed aside the stack of manila folders. The stories Miss Simms shared kept interfering with her assigned job. What were the odds of the dates, names and addresses duplicating themselves? Sure there were dozens of Jones' and Smiths in town...but how many Pauleys were around?

Determined to sort out the mystery, Kat cleared the NEW FILE screen and entered her security code. Five years ago the department began converting hundreds of outdated files into a data base. The cases went as far back as the late 1950s, which allowed Kat the luxury of pulling up information with a few keystrokes rather than crawling around the dusty spider-infested basement. Besides, she would have to be crazy to spend a lot of time searching the old records because of something this silly. And in a few minutes she'd have unraveled this impossible thread linking the year 2000 to 1963.

She doubted Miss Simms' memory would be wrong about the date. A series of house burnings in your own neighborhood wouldn't be easily forgotten. So she requested: March-April, 1963 ARSON/FATALITY.

The computer went to work, its hard drive whirred and clicked as it scanned nearly forty years of stored data.

Within seconds the screen came alive:

MARCH-APRIL, 1963 ARSON/FATALITY

03-02-63	Pauley, GladysN	#23476	01:25 A.M.
03-05-63	Richards, DilmerN	#23477	12:11 A.M.
03-07-63	Carpenter, AliceN	#23478	01:03 A.M.
03-10-63	DeCarlo, MattieN	#23479	01:30 A.M.
03-17-63	Beason, Harold	#23480	06:50 P.M.
03-29-63	Peterson, Abel	#23481	02:15 A.M.
04-01-63	Jefferson, TyroneN	#23482	05:05 A.M.
04-02-63	Spencer, LeroyN	#23483	05:20 A.M.
04-05-63	Doe, JaneN	#23484	12:45 A.M.

MARCH-APRIL, 1963 ARSON/FATALITY (Continued)

| 04-10-63 | Block, GriffinN | #23485 | 02:00 A.M. |
| 04-12-63 | Norton, Richard | #23486 | 07:00 P.M. |

Kat pulled the patrol notebook out of her handbag and compared the information. Three names: *Gladys Pauley, Dilmer Richards and Alice Carpenter*. Three dates: *March 02, 05 and 07*. Three duplicates of the calls she and Mitch answered.

Kat's finger lightly traced Alice Carpenter's name on the screen. Thirty-seven years ago, at 1:03 A.M. on March 7, this woman had reported a group of men threatening to burn her out. And March 7, 2000, *another* Alice Carpenter had reported the same incident, on the same date and at the exact hour. How could this be? There must be a logical explanation. An error in the record.

Kat hit the EXIT key to return to the previous menu, where she selected: LOCATION.

MARCH-APRIL 1963 ARSON/FATALITY

2789 10th	03-02-63	Pauley, GladysN	#23476	01:25 A.M.
4721 Riverside	03-05-63	Richards, DilmerN	#23477	12:11 A.M.
801 Mt. View	03-07-63	Carpenter, AliceN	#23478	01:03 A.M.
5429 Park	03-10-63	DeCarlo, MattieN	#23479	01:30 A.M.
109 Blodgett	03-17-63	Beason, Harold	#23480	06:50 P.M.
900 Grant	03-29-63	Peterson, Abel	#23481	02:15 A.M.
7643 Elm	04-01-63	Jefferson, TyroneN	#23482	05:05 A.M.
654 Azalea	04-02-63	Spencer, LeroyN	#23483	05:20 A.M.
3449 Brook	04-05-63	Doe, JaneN	#23484	12:45 A.M.
2987 Oak	04-10-63	Block, GriffinN	#23485	02:00 A.M.
387 Riverside	04-12-63	Norton, Richard	#23486	07:00 P.M.

Tenth Street. Riverside. Mountain View. Once again she'd hit three-for-three on the addresses. Kat reached across the desk and dialed Mitch's home number. What would her Yankee partner have to say about all this?

When she'd first signed on with the police department six years ago, Kat had endured several difficult months. She was breaking new ground, not only as the first female officer, but also as the first *Black* female officer in the department.

She'd anticipated the rookie jokes, and the gauntlet she must run before being accepted. However, she was unprepared for, and didn't expect to encounter so much resentment and distrust because of her gender. Or her color.

Kat had come close to quitting the department all together. Then James Mitchell, a well-respected thirty-five-year old, eight year veteran, changed everything. Although born in Alabama, Mitch had left the South early on, spending his formative years in Pennsylvania. Growing up in the North weakened the prejudicial attitudes that so effectively bound many others and one day the six-foot three-inch, 250 pound mountain, with ginger-red hair and a multitude of freckles, asked Kathleen Templeton to be his new partner.

His request only opened a small crack in the door, and Mitch told her, "It's up to you to prove yourself, Kat. Do that and then you can kick the door wide open." His assessment had been accurate. Over time, the crude remarks and negative attitudes subsided and she was judged on performance alone. No gender. No color. The door hung by its hinges. Before long, Mitchell and Templeton were known as 'The Red and Black Unit'. And as an exceptional team.

They worked well together because each brought different skills to the job. Gifted with flawless logic and a knack for negotiation, Mitch's calm demeanor worked wonders with hysterical and frightened individuals.

Kat operated from a different perspective, mostly instinct and attitude. Her strong and reliable street sense, enabled her to quickly analyze a developing situation for potential violence.

On their first anniversary as partners, Mitch gave her a little cowboy boot-shaped pin, made of copper and silver, with a brass spur. He said it served as a reminder that sometimes she might have to kick the door in. She wore it every day, either pinned inside her uniform or on public display. It was her good luck talisman. Like the copper and silver, she and Mitch were the ideal blend.

She hoped their chemistry would be strong enough for him to buy into her latest scheme.

* * *

Mitch glanced up from the computer printout. "What's this letter 'N' all about? It's only next to certain names."

"It stands for Negro." Kat said. "Personally, I've always found that tidy little Southern euphemism to be insulting."

"Then do something about it."

"Maybe I will."

Southern traditions were slow to change because the folks kicked and screamed, fighting it every step of the way. But eventually the changes had come. To be honest, Kat knew some degree of racial tension still simmered beneath the moist earth, but it seldom erupted with the force seen in the turbulent sixties.

Yet, in spite of all the progress, from time to time the old South reared its ugly head, and when that happened, she wanted to grab a sword and slice it off. Humming *We Shall Overcome* she glanced at Mitch, then moved the blinking cursor to the *N* and hit DELETE eight times.

"After chopping off all those ugly heads, I sure do feel a whole lot better," she said as the last *N* disappeared. "How about you?"

He grinned and gave her the thumbs up sign. "Now, regarding this other business. Kat, there is no way these arson cases are connected to the crank calls we caught."

"I know it sounds a little crazy," her voice dropped to a conspiratorial whisper, "but they *are* connected. How else do you explain names, dates and addresses that match?"

Mitch quickly responded. "A twelve-year-old smart ass computer hacker got into the system and played the department, and us, for fools."

She shook her head. "I don't think so. It's too pat. My instinct tells me this is for real. Plus, you've got all the things Dreama Simms said."

He pushed away from the desk and walked over to the coffee corner. He poured a cup and added a liberal dose of creamer and Sweet n' Low.

Kat joined him at the coffee pot. "In the five and half years we've partnered, have I ever steered you down the wrong path? Trust me."

He held his hand up. "Stop. This isn't about trust and you know it. You're a great partner and friend, I just wondered where this instinct of yours is coming from."

"It's my New Orleans blood rising to the surface."

"Mumbo jumbo," Mitch muttered.

She could tell from his face she was losing ground. She should have known better than to discuss anything so undisciplined as instinct with 'Only the facts, ma'am' Mitchell. Her partner didn't have one drop of instinct in that barn sized body of his.

"Okay," Kat said, knowing she had to try another route or give up the entire ball game. "Maybe instinct is a poor choice of words. You're probably right, some kid hacked into our files and pulled our chain. But," she paused and held one finger in the air. "This type of 911 is dangerous. If these idiots keep on tying up the lines, and the street patrols, someone could get seriously hurt."

When two small lines appeared between Mitch's eyes, Kat silently rejoiced. That was his 'I'm listening' frown. Which meant she'd made a first down.

"Good point, Kat," he said. "We can't let a bunch of whiz kids run the department ragged."

"I have an idea."

His cornflower-blue eyes narrowed suspiciously. "What idea? You got a crystal ball stashed in your pocket book? Want to hold a seance, New Orleans Voodoo Woman?"

"Hardee-har-har. My partner's turned into a stand-up comic."

He bowed to the empty room then treated her to his flawless Elvis impersonation. "Thank you, thank you very much."

Kat rolled her eyes and snapped the paper in front of his face. "Look at the printout, see where I've highlighted? On March 10, 1963, Mattie DeCarlo died at 1:30. *Another* arson fatality." She pointed to the clock on the wall. "It's eleven-thirty now."

Mitch ignored her and hummed *Are You Lonesome Tonight?*

"In thirty minutes it will be March 10, Mr. Presley," Kat continued. "I think we should be waiting in front of the house on Park Street at exactly 1:30 A.M. to see if another call comes in."

"So *what-if* it does?" Elvis asked. "Those kids aren't gonna make the 911 call from Park Street."

"No, but they might show up to watch the fun. When they do, we're already on the scene and can catch them red handed."

"I don't know, Kat. Correct me if I'm wrong, but I see a close resemblance to the situation that got us the desk duty in the first place."

"There's not one little ole thing to bother about," Kat assured him.

"I'm not bothered, partner. I'm wondering how to explain our ghostly rendezvous with Mattie DeCarlo to the chief."

"I'll do all the explaining."

"You bet your ass you will."

"Okay, grab your jacket and let's hit the street." Kat smiled. Fourth down and goal to go.

Mitch poked a finger in her dimpled cheek and grinned. "I love a take charge gal."

"I'll drive, big guy. Look on the bright side, you might get a chance to see The King of Rock and Roll in concert."

"Think he'll be wearing that cool white jump suit with the eagle on the back?"

"I'm sure of it. And while you're waiting for him, I'll buy you a dozen Krispy Kreme doughnuts too."

"Thank you, thank you very much," Elvis commented.

3

"Elvis believed in ghosts, you know," Mitch informed her, as he tossed the empty red, white and green Krispy Kreme box into the back seat.

"That is most enlightening. What time is it?"

He pushed the button on his watch to illuminate the dial. "The witching hour is upon us, Voodoo Woman. It's 1:20 in the A.M., only ten minutes to go. And Elvis believed he could contact his mother, Gladys Presley."

Kat didn't respond to his baiting, she concentrated on the road as her red Honda bounced along the weather worn east Hollow asphalt. The rains continuously eroded the poorly maintained roadway and left crater-size pot holes. The citizens had repeatedly voted down road improvement bonds, not wanting any increase in their property tax. One of these days they'd figure out it cost a whole lot more to replace a set of shocks every six months than spending two or three dollars a year in extra taxes.

She pulled over to the curb directly opposite 5429 Park Street. She rolled down the window to study the blue trimmed house. During the construction boom in the mid-seventies, the east side of Maceyville, called 'coon hollow' by a few rednecks, evolved from tar paper shotgun houses into compact single story L-shaped dwellings with separate garages.

Without entering the house, Kat already knew what the floor plan would be. Her Aunt Della still lived in a similar house a few streets over.

"At the beep, the time will be 1:25, m'lady," Mitch drawled as he slid down in the seat. "Be sure wake me if Casper DeCarlo shows up. *Definitely* let me know if Elvis pays us a visit."

"Uh-huh," Kat mumbled. Physically she sat next to her partner, but mentally she was in the front room across the street. The hardwood floors were shiny as a new penny from repeated hands and knees waxing and buffing. Straight through the door and into the kitchen. The cast iron skillet permanently rested on the stove top, blue and white checked curtains at the window, potted herbs on the sill. Kat could almost smell the cornbread as it baked in the oven. Beyond, a single bathroom and a bedroom filled with heavy dark mismatched pieces of furniture.

Her partner's noisy snoring broke her trance. She glanced his way. His slouched posture, chin touching his chest, all indicated his conversion to sleep mode. She returned her attention to the street. In her brief absence a light fog had crept into the neighborhood and now muted the street lights. An odd occurrence on such a clear warm night, she thought.

Suddenly materializing out of the fog, a man veered off the sidewalk and onto the narrow strip of grass next to the street. He squatted near the front bumper, pulled a bent cigarette out of his shirt pocket and shoved it in his mouth. He scraped a fingernail across the fat head of a kitchen match. In the flickering light, Kat caught a glimpse of a narrow mean face, the details shadowed by the brim of his baseball cap.

He stared at the house across the street, seemingly oblivious of both the automobile and the two passengers inside. He shifted slightly and she saw the glass jug, with a ragged strip of cloth sticking out of the top.

He stood. Kat blindly tapped Mitch's arm to rouse her sleeping partner, her eyes trained on the dangerous stranger. "Can't let him fire bomb that house," she whispered. She withdrew the .38 caliber service revolver from her holster, but kept it low on the seat, out of line of sight. She could bring it into firing position in less than a second, if necessary.

She held her breath when the man started walking, convinced he would hit the right fender. But instead of banging into it, he moved through the car and into the street. Kat rubbed her eyes, it was late and she must have imagined his impossible feat. She'd bumped her shins and been rewarded with purple bruises too many times to actually believe a person could walk through a solid object.

She reached overhead and switched the dome light off. "Let's go," she said to Mitch, as she eased the driver side door open and slipped out of the car. Nearing the middle of the street she sensed she was alone in her pursuit of the mystery man. Where was Mitch? Annoyed by her partner's slow response, she stopped barely across the center line of the road and waited, foot tapping, hands on hips. After several seconds she sighed out of frustration and glanced over her shoulder, prepared to read him the riot act.

A wispy mist stood between Kat and the red Honda. And Mitch. She jerked to attention. What in the holy hell was he doing in the car? Why didn't he get out? They were partners, he should be covering her six not sleeping in the freaking car. But there he sat. She could vaguely make out his silhouette. The light fog had turned into heavy wet curtains hanging in the air.

It took several seconds for Kat to process the visual input. Her car was softening, almost melting into the early morning gloom. Suddenly, an unseen hand drew the miasma drapery across the deserted street. And the car was gone.

"Mitch calls this the witching hour. I think he's right," she whispered.

Having lost sight of the mystery man in the fog, and unsure of the situation, Kat reversed course. Once she crossed back over the center line, the mist dissipated and she could see her car again. She hurried around to the passenger side and reached for the chrome door handle, then hesitated before closing her fingers. A dozen of Mitch's annoying what-if questions rattled around in her head. She constantly nagged and complained about his habit of what-iffing a situation to death. And now she was guilty of the same sin. Well, *what-if*, the chrome handle wasn't really there? *What-if*, her hand passed through the door the same way the man had passed through the fender?

"Hells bells, Kathleen," she muttered. "You're being ridiculous." She wiped sweaty palms on her uniform trousers, took a deep breath and grabbed hold of the metal, then chuckled with relief. Of course it felt hard and damp. Perfectly normal. What did she expect to find? Sometimes she could work herself up into such a frenzy.

She opened the door and squatted. "Mitch," Kat spoke in a sharp demanding voice to get his attention.

"What?" He sluggishly turned in her direction, his cornflower-blue eyes groggy.

She tugged on his arm and pulled him partially through the door. As he climbed out, his foot slipped off the edge of the curb, legs buckled under his weight and he fell face down on the grass.

"Are you okay?" Kat asked.

"I'm in great shape," he grunted. He used both hands to push his torso off the ground, then regained his feet. He leaned against the car, allowing the steel to support his flesh and bone frame as he muttered obscenities under his breath.

"Let's take a little stroll, partner," Kat said.

"Where are we going?"

"To the middle of the street."

Mitch placed an arm around Kat's shoulder. "That sounds like more fun than Mardi Gras."

"Believe me. This will beat it all to heck." They crossed the broken white line and Kat stopped.

"May I ask why I'm standing in the middle of the street?"

Kat turned him around. "That's why," she said, and pointed to her red car. It was the same as before, there, yet not there. A backdrop of trees and houses could be seen through the fading Honda.

"What the devil's going on?" Mitch growled.

"The same thing that happened before."

"Before?"

"Yeah. When I followed the man."

"Man?" His eyes jumped from the empty space recently occupied by Kat's car to her face. "What man?"

"The one who was standing next to the car. You didn't see him?"

Mitch shook his head. "The last thing I remember is telling you the time. It was 1:25."

A cold shiver dashed up and down her spine. "What time is it now?"

He pressed the small button to illuminate the read out on his watch dial. "1:30."

Kat stared at him. "Only five minutes later? That's impossible, Mitch, it's been at least ten minutes since I first saw him."

"Shee-itt!" He pointed down the street. "Look at what's coming our way."

✶   ✶   ✶

"Mitch, we've got to talk about it," Kat said, breaking the long silence. They sat in the back corner booth of the Daisy Wheel café, surrounded by fluorescent lights and red vinyl. "Mitch," she repeated.

He avoided her gaze by drawing designs on the white Formica-topped table with his water glass. Even though he felt silly, the Park Street incident had struck a nerve deep inside him. This business was too damn close to his own nightmares. In those dreams he'd call out to Lisa and she'd turn to him. He would hold his arms open. But every time, she walked right through him. The same way the firemen had walked through him earlier. As though he had no substance. As though he'd never existed.

He met Kat's eyes and spoke for the first time since leaving Park Street. "We saw things that aren't possible," he said quietly, hating the quivering timbre of his voice.

"I know," Kat whispered. "But we—"

"Stop it right there. We're not rehashing this nonsense."

"Yes, we are," Kat insisted. "You and I stood in the middle of that road and watched my car completely disappear. Then everything around us altered. I mean, the trees grew smaller, houses changed color. Cars that weren't visible a split second before, 1959 Ford Fairlaines and beat up old Chevys, suddenly popped up in driveways or along the curb." She reached over and gave his hand a reassuring squeeze. "We *both* saw the red-orange flames licking out through the windows. Felt the heat. Jesus, Mitch, look at your own arms, the hairs are singed. The Maceyville Fire Department showed up. We saw their trucks, the flashing lights, heard the sirens. Damnit, we saw it all."

"But nobody could see us!" he exploded.

"There's an explanation for all of this, and we can figure out. But first we have to talk it through."

"There isn't any explanation." He reached across the table and touched her cheek. "It's like UFOs or ESP. You can't explain any of that stuff, Kat. And if you're smart, you'll ignore everything that just happened."

"You are dead wrong, Mitch. It can't be ignored. I was meant to see those things tonight. You hear what I'm saying? I tell you it wasn't an accident or random event."

"Listen to yourself, Kathleen Templeton. Are you telling me New Orleans voodoo spirits called you to Park Street tonight?"

"Maybe…I don't know. But you have to admit we saw *something*."

Mitch slid out of the vinyl seat and stood next to the booth. "No, Kathleen, I don't have to admit anything. I'm heading home and you best forget all about it."

4

MARCH 10—SUNDAY 6:00 A.M.

James Andrew Mitchell sat on a metal folding chair in the middle of his living room. Elbows on knees, he stared at the boxes and crates lining the walls. He'd been in this apartment for almost six months, one of these days he would have to unpack and buy some decent furniture. For the time being, he was content with a mattress on the bedroom floor, a refrigerator and card table in the kitchen and a T.V. in the living room.

    The apartment was Kat's doing. She'd been the one to decide he should sell the little brick house and get on with his life. "What life?" he asked. He worked twelve hour shifts and headed the call list for Sunday and holidays. Given that kind of schedule, what did it matter where or how he lived?

    Forcing himself off the chair, he ambled into the kitchen. He took a bottle of orange juice out of a refrigerator that was also Kat's idea. She claimed no human could exist without one, and just to prove her point, once a week she dropped by with several items requiring refrigeration. He'd grudgingly accepted the ice box, but balked when it came to acquiring a stove. He never cooked, in fact he didn't even own real dishes. No, that wasn't exactly the truth. In one of the sealed boxes stacked along the wall in the living room he could find a set of dishes. Still wrapped in silver or white paper printed with wedding bells or doves.

    Unpacking could wait.

    Familiar images of Kat and her Pop, the Reverend Alvin Rayson, took up space in the corner of the kitchen. He saw them seated at Lisa's bedside, holding her hand and whispering words of comfort to the dying woman. They never wavered in their vigilance nor devotion as the months elapsed.

    By contrast, he'd wandered around in a fog-shrouded daze, unwilling to accept the inevitable conclusion. The only woman he'd ever loved was going to die. Maybe not today or even tomorrow, but soon. A twenty-seven-year-old woman did not die of a brain aneurysm.

He remembered screaming those foolish words in the doctor's face, his heart bending and twisting under the weight of the sorrow and terror of his future. Wondering what it would be like to spend the rest of his life alone. Without Lisa. Unable express these feelings, his grief turned into a sullen silence and the silence ultimately became anger. Anger poured from him like sweat on a hot afternoon, spilling on everyone around him. Before long most of his friends dropped from his life, like the apples off a cold November tree, leaving him bare and isolated.

No one knew how to comfort the bridegroom. What could you say when the bride collapsed in the doorway of the church? When the wedding couple left the ceremony in an Ambulance, rather than a limousine.

Mitch clenched and unclenched his balled fist. A year after losing Lisa, he still remained furious with the unfeeling emergency room staff. He'd carried her into the hospital himself, refusing to allow the paramedics to touch her, and gently placed her on the gurney. People wearing blue scrub suits had shoved him aside, and cut her beautiful wedding gown into tattered bits of lace. Later, once they'd finished with their medical hocus pocus, they'd thrust the plastic bag containing her dress and personal items into his hands with a curt, "Sorry, sir."

What did those words really mean? Was the nurse sorry she destroyed the wedding gown? Was the doctor sorry he couldn't save Lisa's life? Were they sorry he'd waited in the hospital hallway in a rented tuxedo, Lisa's wedding band, the one she never wore, still in his pocket?

Through it all Kat stood by his side. Her strength had been his anchor. And now, when she wanted him to listen, he'd cut her off. Turned his back like a frightened child.

*   *   *

By the time Kat reached her home, the sun was busily climbing the low hills surrounding Maceyville. But sleep was the last thing on her mind, so she started a pot of coffee and while it brewed took a shower.

Kat closed her eyes and allowed the hot water to beat against her body, hoping to drive the knots of tension from her neck and shoulders. Suddenly she felt someone—or something—enter the room. An icy hand squeezed her heart.

Her eyes popped open. Clouds of steam filled the small yellow bathroom, obscuring the familiar. She instinctively reached for her revolver, but her hand only slid down a soapy thigh. Opaque steam tentacles curled around her feet, her ankles, then reached up, pulling her to the shower floor. All of Kat's strength followed the gurgling path of water flowing toward the drain.

Colored lights flashed all around her and suddenly she found herself walking along an empty street. The sidewalks were wet. Puddles of rain water reflected the red-yellow-green-red-yellow-green pattern as the traffic lights marched through their sequence.

Her first impulse was to run, but an invisible force kept her to a steady even pace. She didn't like being jerked around like a stringed puppet, so she tried to come to a complete halt. It didn't work. Kat had no control over her actions. Whatever force that wouldn't allow her to run a few seconds ago, now wouldn't let her stop. The force pushed her past the small dress shops, shoe stores, banks, a Woolworth five and dime.

As though a hand had yanked her leash, she came to an abrupt halt in front of a dimly lit display window. The sign above the store read: Parisian. She recognized the name of the well-known business that had been owned by the Hess family in downtown Birmingham since 1920. What on earth was she doing in Birmingham?

The prim and proper pasty white mannequins, in shirtwaist dresses and high heels seemed to mock her confusion. Clustered in twos and threes, she imagined their hushed comments as they gossiped their mean little secrets. Kat looked into the painted eyes and saw displeasure at her presence.

Uneasy, she peered down the street. A warning whispered in her ear and brushed across the back of her neck. Like a wild animal she lifted her head to the wind as though she could smell the approaching danger.

A peripheral shift caused her to gasp. She whipped her head to the left, and a reflection in the Parisian's display window followed suite. The movement startled her, because she would have sworn on a stack of Bibles, there had been *no* reflection before. She raised her arms and the mirror image copied her actions, playing a bizarre game of Simon Says.

Even though Kat knew it had to be her own reflection, the clothes were out of sync. Like the house on Tenth Street, two realities overlapped. She looked at her arm, then touched her sleeve, relieved to feel the familiar coolness of her favorite red silk blouse. Khaki trousers encased her legs, athletic shoes on her feet. But the woman in the glass wore a light-colored suit with a knee length straight skirt. Three large buttons and black fur collar accented the matching short jacket. A small pill box hat perched jauntily on the reflection's straightened page-boy styled hair.

"Lord, have mercy," she said quietly. "She looks like a black Jackie Kennedy."

The ringing telephone broke the eerie spell. She turned from the window trying to locate the source. The sound originated from a booth halfway down the block. Urgency crawled around inside her belly. Deep down, in a place beyond logic or reason, she knew she was expected to answer. She took off at a trot, stumbling as she raced to reach the booth before the incessant jangle stopped. She yanked the receiver from the cradle.

"*Kathleen*," a weak, static ridden voice filtered through the phone line.

She trembled, her teeth chattering like a wind up toy. She took a deep breath and forced confidence into her voice that she didn't feel. "Yes."

"*Dangerous for you. Stay away. Don't cross.*"

The colored lights flashed once again, and as quickly as she'd arrived on the deserted street, she was back on the shower floor. No mannequins. No blinking streetlights. No phone booth. Just ice cold water drumming against her bare skin.

*   *   *

Mitch stood on his tiny balcony and stared across the Tombigbee River. If he squinted just so, he could almost make out Kat's yellow frame house on the rise. He imagined her curled up and snoring away, untroubled by the craziness of a few hours ago.

"Dang that woman," he muttered. Maybe she did have several pints of New Orleans voodoo blood in her veins after all. She certainly knew how to burrow under his skin like a tick. And the harder he tried to pull her out, the deeper she dug.

What did all this nonsense mean?

Why did he give up cigarettes? And more importantly, why did he quit drinking? Right this minute a tumbler filled with Jack Daniels and a good smoke would be just the ticket to settle his mind. Earlier he made an attempt to sleep, but after an hour of wrestling the bedcovers like a swamp gator, he gave up on the idea.

Determined to sort it all out, he headed for the carport. He generally did his best thinking while tinkering on his 1962, 409-cubic-inch 380 hp, four-in-the-floor Chevy Impala SS. The jet black vehicle, with red interior and full wheel cover spinners, once belonged to his father. Billy Lee Mitchell claimed to have purchased the car on his wedding day and in his excitement, almost forgot the ceremony. Mitch didn't put much stock in the story, but it never failed to get a rise out of his mother, which was most likely the reason his dad continued to spin the tale for so many years. He shook his head, thinking about his parents, still mystified as to why a sweet Pennsylvania girl—attending the University of Alabama—had married the miserable SOB. Billy Lee Mitchell had been a racist, a drunk and mean as a wet badger.

On Mitch's fifth birthday his father hauled the family down to the annual Ku Klux Klan rally. The hate spewing speeches, burning crosses and hooded men in robes terrified the kindergartner. When a very drunk and belligerent Billy Lee decided to anoint his son with the white hood, Mitch ran away and hid in the woods. There had been hell to pay when the old man finally located him hunkered down in a rotted out log.

One year to the day, his mother, worn out from constant battles to keep Mitch from turning into a redneck racist, packed one suitcase and took her six-year-old son north. Other than the court ordered two week summer visits with Billy Lee, Mitch spent the next twelve years on his grandparent's farm in Lebanon, Pennsylvania.

Thanks to his mother, his life turned out good. He'd never expected to end up right back where he started, but maybe sometimes a person follows a predetermined course. If not for the full ride football scholarship to the University of Alabama and his mother's fondness for her alma mater, Mitch would never have returned to the Heart of Dixie. Fate? Or stupidity?

Even though he'd lived in Tuscaloosa during all four years of college, which was only 30 miles from Maceyville, he never contacted Billy Lee. Mitch wondered if his father ever knew his son had played for the Crimson Tide, or later on, six years of pro-ball with the New Orleans Saints. The old coot probably stayed too drunk to have recognized Mitch if he did happen to see a Monday night football game.

Pamela Mitchell had been proud of the son she raised alone, even if she didn't remember. He missed being able to talk with her, several months ago a stroke had taken not only her ability to walk and speak, but her memory as well. A sad end to a sad life.

When Billy Lee died of cirrhosis of the liver, Mitch had inherited his kudzu-covered farmhouse, decrepit barn and the Impala. His father's possessions weren't all that impressive. Billy Lee had never taken very good care of himself or the farm, and both had died early from neglect. Mitch let the place stand for eight years, then when he and Lisa set a wedding date, they decided instead of spending money to make the house inhabitable, they'd have it razed and sell the land. The amount they'd received had made a nice down payment on the brick house in town.

"At least you didn't kill the car, you old boozer," he mumbled. The only noteworthy thing Billy Lee had ever done in his whole pathetic life was to have a good time. Of course, his father's idea of a good time involved ferrying bootleg whiskey all over the county. His long running game of chase with the ATF agents and the State Patrol, had resulted in numerous wrecked transmissions and burnt out clutches. To this day, if Mitch tried to push the Chevy beyond 65 mph, she'd choke, smoke and then die in the middle of the road.

He tried to remember when the Impala's quirky engine behavior began. He recalled Billy Lee complaining it started around Christmas 1962, shortly after he'd bought it. As the story went, his father had been trying to outrun a carload of ATF agents on the old highway the first time she quit on him. Billy and his sidekick, some idiot named Barnes, ended up celebrating the holidays in the Maceyville lock up.

Prior to raising the hood, Mitch ran the soft buffing cloth over the automobile body, periodically scrubbing at microscopic dirt specks. His face, reflected in the high gloss wax job, captivated his attention. He appeared haggard. The dark circles ringing his eyes made him think of a raccoon. Agitated, he ran his hand through his ginger colored hair.

"Mitchell," he told his twin, "you closely resemble a carcass my dog once dragged home."

He looked like an old man with one foot in the grave. Or one foot in the past. Images of dried up Egyptian mummies, which would blow away with the slightest breeze, raided his brain. He'd seen those prune people in the museum, and he didn't look one whole hell of a lot better right this minute. Could his brief foray into 1963 have altered his biological clock? Going back and forth in time, no telling what might happen to your body.

"That settles it," he muttered. If a single jaunt screwed him up this much, it would take a whole army and then some to get him to try it again. Oh yeah, he knew exactly what Kat would propose the next time he saw her: Another trip back in time. She'd drag out that damn computer print-out, point to another name on the Arson/Fatality list and play the sympathy card. 'But Mitch,' she'd say, 'if we can prevent so and so's murder, then we are morally obligated.'

Bull pucky! Any Tom, Dick or Harry who died that long ago ought to stay dead. What business did he have traipsing through the past, stirring up Lord knows what kind of mischief?

"I'll tell you this, Kathleen Rayson Templeton," Mitch shook a finger in his partner's imaginary face. "We've got more than enough criminal activity on our plate in the here and now. There is no reason for us to go looking for more."

Mitch fished in his pocket for the car keys. He'd go see Kat and tell her exactly what was what. When he withdrew his hand, the crumpled computer sheet fell to the ground. He stooped to pick it up. Bent over, hands on knees, he froze, holding his breath. Laying there all balled up, it made him think of a coiled rattlesnake. If I touch it, the damn thing will bite me, he thought. Bite me so bad no one will be able to save me. Suddenly a puff of wind rolled the paper several inches closer to his feet; it began to unfold like a flower.

Childishly, he began to bargain with the monster hidden within the paper. "Here's the deal, if you open up any more I promise to take another shot at Park Street. On the other hand, if you stay wadded up, I'll forget all this nonsense. What do you say?" The paper lay silent, as though considering his offer, then it crinkled and another crease opened, revealing one name: Jane Doe.

"Forget it. I'm staying right here. There's too much of this voodoo shit in the air."

*   *   *

The comforting aroma of chicory coffee filled the yellow shiplap house. Kat leaned against the counter and waited for the water to complete its journey through the machine innards to the glass decanter. Her sense of time was all screwed up. How could she have showered, and taken the weird trip to la-la land, before ten cups of water filtered through the pot? It made no sense. But then, the past few hours weren't exactly stellar examples of the sane and normal.

She grabbed the pot from under the drip spout, not caring as the final drops skittered and danced across the heated surface, she needed a jolt of reality. And nothing was more real than the bitter taste of chicory.

Icy fingers wrapped around the steaming mug, she pushed through the screened door and walked out to the back yard. She sat in a small patch of early sunlight, pulling the soft terry cloth robe tighter and tighter against her trembling body, hoping the warmth could drive the dark chill away.

Like an excited child in a toy store, her mind raced from one event to another as the sun climbed in the sky. Back and forth, from the disappearing Honda to the man on Park Street. The display window. The phone call. On and on she whirled, until an exhausted terry cloth bundle fell asleep in the bright morning light.

As the sun dropped below the horizon, Kat retreated inside, carefully locking the door behind her. She traveled from room to room, turning on every light and closing the curtains at each window. Her nest secured, she curled up on the sofa and pulled her mother's favorite blue afghan up to her chin. However, the old blanket, a cherished friend that had given her comfort since childhood, did little to assuage her fears.

She'd had her fill of bodiless voices and phantoms. She wanted and needed the company of a real live person with red blood coursing through their veins. A person with warm skin and a beating heart. The question of with whom to share all her fears and mixed up thoughts loomed like a specter in the waning light.

Logic dictated she should select Mitch as her number one choice. After all, he'd been on Park Street and seen the same things. But he'd taken himself out of contention early on. After partnering for five years, she knew better than to expect him to change his mind. He'd made it painstakingly clear he intended to ignore the early morning events. To him, nothing had happened. And if he refused to acknowledge those things, he certainly wouldn't be receptive to hearing about phone calls from a shower head.

She loved Mitch, but sometimes he could be a royal pain in the pahooty. And right now she needed an open mind to listen and acknowledge her theories were possible, if not wholly credible. Unfortunately, her partner failed to meet those qualifications. One name remained on a very short list, her father, Alvin Rayson.

Kathleen Ruth, was the only child of Alvin and Dolores Rayson. When she was six, her mother, the Switzerland of the family, the neutral ground on which her opinionated husband and equally stubborn daughter met, died of ovarian cancer. Without Dolores, and her peace making skills, the years that followed were often stormy and always dramatic.

Shortly after high school graduation—in yet another grandiose display of her independence—Kathleen Rayson met, married and divorced William Templeton all within six months. Her short-lived marriage set off World War III between Kat and the reverend. Pop so intensely disliked the smooth talking, arrogant and sinful William Templeton, that he isolated himself. His one man cold war lasted as long as her marriage did. With the ex-husband gone, the father and daughter relationship resumed its stormy course.

After a brief lull, their battles once again escalated. They finally reached epic proportions the day the twenty-two-year old Kat announced, after three years at Howard University, that she intended to switch her major from History to Police Science. And as a footnote added, "After graduation I'm applying to the Maceyville Police Department." This Sunday dinner proclamation had ignited a series of high voltage debates which resulted in a polite truce between parent and child.

The Reverend Alvin Paul Rayson, minister of the Demopolis Hope and Glory Baptist Church, maintained the position, in no uncertain terms that, "Violence—or, God forbid, taking a life—was WRONG. Wrong because the Bible said, 'Thou shalt not kill'. Period."

Six years after graduating from the police academy, Kat still fervently worked to convince him law enforcement didn't always mean violence or killing. But their opinions were so diametrically opposed, she doubted common ground would ever be reached. And she did not foresee any great changes in the near future.

In spite of all their skirmishes, they maintained a loving relationship. When not on Sunday duty, Kat drove the twenty miles to Demopolis and sang in the Hope and Glory Baptist choir, then cooked dinner for her father. And no matter what, she could always talk to him.

5

MARCH 17—SUNDAY

It took a full week before Kat had calmed down and her mind organized enough that she felt capable of sharing what had happened on Park Street with her Pop. On Saturday night she fried chicken, made potato salad and baked beans to take to Demopolis. She wanted to talk to Pop, not have to worry about cooking after church.

She drove over for the church service and then invited him to a backyard picnic. Braced by his rip-roaring sermon, she eased into the subject during the meal.

Understanding Pop's misgivings and worries each time she put on the uniform, Kat deliberately excluded some facts. Such as failing to mention why she and Mitch had gone to Park Street in the first place—the stakeout for a serial arsonist—and the weird 1963 connections. She simplified things by saying they'd been driving by the house when they noticed a strange man lurking in the shadows.

Pop had grown unusually quiet during her tale, but she was grateful for the interest reflected in his honey-colored eyes. When his silence continued as they packed up the remains of their picnic and moved indoors, Kat began to panic. Then she began to what-if. *What-if,* he thought the whole thing sounded like a ghost story designed to scare the britches off junior high girls on a stormy night? *What-if,* he didn't believe anything she said? Once he'd settled on the sofa with his coffee, she couldn't stand his silence any longer and blurted out, "So what do you think, Pop?"

"It reminds me of some things I heard back in 1963 when I worked at a church in Maceyville. My sister lived there then, and we sure spent good times together. Lettie Ruth was a rare gem, Kathleen. Filled with laughter and a never-ending supply of energy. I've always felt you were cheated a little bit that she couldn't be around once you come along. You two would have gotten along like greens and cornbread."

"She's the sister that up and disappeared, right?" The Lettie Ruth mystery had been Kat's childhood obsession. Of course she only became obsessed because no one in the family would talk about the woman, or why she'd disappeared.

The topic had been so hush-hush and top secret, that ferreting out morsels of information became all the more tantalizing. Unfortunately, Kat continuously ran head on into a brick wall of adult silence. The subject was taboo, and no amount of snooping or whining ever generated any new data or enticed one single relative to spill the beans. In twenty-nine years all Kat ever learned was that Lettie Ruth Rayson had never married, had been a nurse and lived in Maceyville. Then in 1963, vanished without a trace. Period. End of story. *Finis.*

"So how come the family doesn't speak about her, Pop?" Kat probed. After all these years plus her time and effort, she'd be darned if she'd miss out on a rare opportunity to garner one more a tiny scrap of Lettie Ruth trivia.

He tilted his head to the side and rubbed his chin. "I suppose because it hurts too much."

Since her Pop tended to be up front about most everything and loved long detailed explanations, she found his evasiveness peculiar. Her police antenna wiggled in the air as she wondered what information he hid. She also found it annoying, especially now that she was all grown up. "Come on, Pop," she cajoled. "You know something. You just admitted you were there."

"I was indeed." Rayson's eyes glazed over.

She'd seen that faraway look before. As a girl she often found him in similar states when he mined deep into his own thoughts regarding Lettie Ruth. In the wee hours of the morning he would sit in the front room, holding his sister's picture and crying. Kat always wondered what horrible memories he carried around inside his head.

"Pop?" she said quietly, fighting the urge to physically yank him away from his secrets. Right now he was as far gone from this time and place as her aunt. And it frightened her.

He shook his head and smiled. But she recognized the falsity of that smile when his dimples, so like her own, failed to show. His mouth must be rigid as steel for them to remain unseen, she thought. Kat knew from personal experience their dimples were impossible to hide. She'd spent most of her childhood trying to keep the sink holes from forming in her cheeks each time she smiled or laughed. Eventually she came to realize the futility of the task. Like Pop, she'd been blessed—or cursed—with the 'what-darling-dimples-you-have' syndrome.

Kat tucked her arm through his and gave a little squeeze. "Are you all right?"

"Of course I am," he snorted. "You are a bigger worry wart than your momma."

"It's not worrying to be concerned about someone you love."

"I hate causing you to fret so. I'm getting older, Kathleen, and on occasion I get caught up in the past."

"Is the past where you went this time?"

"Yes," he said. "To 1963. I was twenty-seven, fresh out of the Army and ready to start at the seminary come fall. And so full of myself I barely fit in my britches." Rayson chuckled and his ample mid-section jiggled.

"How old was Lettie Ruth?" Kat asked, bringing the conversation back on point. And keeping her fingers crossed the question didn't trigger another backward slide.

"Thirtyish," he said vaguely.

"Did she disappear from New Orleans?"

"No, from Maceyville."

"When…exactly."

"On April 5. The Friday before Palm Sunday," he said quietly. "The rest of the family still lived down in New Orleans, so I called them with the bad news."

Pop looked so sad and haunted Kat wished she never broached the subject. "I'm sorry, Pop. I didn't mean to bring all this unhappiness down on you."

"I'm fine, child. I like talkin' about my big sister. She was a wonderful person." He glanced over at Kat. "Sometimes I see Lettie Ruth in you."

"How so?"

"Like you, Sister leaned toward an independent life. She left home to attend nursing school at Fisk University up in Nashville, and never came back to New Orleans. Instead, she moved to Maceyville and worked with Doctor Timothy Biggers."

"Did she have her own house?"

"No, the doctor ran a clinic out of his home and she moved into some extra rooms on the third floor. It was during this period that she and a girlfriend got involved in all sorts of civil rights things. The Freedom Riders, lunch counter sit-ins, the voter's registration campaign, why those two women even marched along side Dr. Martin Luther King. My big sister was a bonafide civil rights activist before she disappeared," he said proudly.

Kat hated to burst his happy bubble, but the words *civil rights activist* and *disappeared* set off bells in her head. The two were not compatible. "Pop, in those days activists didn't just up and disappear. They were out right murdered."

"What do you know about that, child?" His body suddenly sagged as though someone had dropped a load of cement on his shoulders.

"I've read the books, Pop. They teach classes on the movement in college."

"But what do you *know*?"

"I know about the dogs and fire hoses. I know about the beatings and lynchings. I know the next year, in June 1964, three Freedom Summer Project volunteers were shot in the head by Ku Klux Klan members," Kat declared.

"I knew them," Rayson said, his voice took on the respectful hushed tones of a funeral parlor. "They were good boys. Andrew Goodman came from Queens College, James Chaney, a twenty-one-year old black out of Mississippi and Michael Schwerner, a New York social worker."

"Do you think Lettie Ruth met a similar end?" If her aunt got involved in the movement, she probably ruffled a few feathers. And the local Klan wouldn't hesitate to teach an independent black woman a lesson or two.

"Some things are for the knowing, and some for the telling, Kathleen."

"What's the big secret?" she snapped. "I'm a card-carrying Rayson, Pop. And I'm certainly not a child anymore. I deserve a straight answer."

"And you'll get one by the by," Rayson said sharply. "But right this moment we're goin' to keep on discussing your experience…not Lettie Ruth."

Kat, recognized the stubborn set of his chin and settled for a simple nod. She'd let it pass for now, but they would return to this subject.

Rayson cleared his throat then began. "As I said, I came up from New Orleans to help out at church in Maceyville. Soon as I stepped off the bus I seen Lettie Ruth was all worked up. She started jabbering away about some fool notion of studying up on the spirit world."

"Spirit world?" Kat asked. "Don't you think that's strange interest for a thirty-year-old woman? And a civil rights activist," she added, still annoyed at the abrupt end to the Lettie Ruth discussion.

He laughed. "She was just full of fun and had an ornery streak as wide as the Mississippi River. I learned as a child to go along for the ride and enjoy it. She claimed to have heard about several folks interacting with the spirits. Her idea was for us to meet with them, afterwards we'd decide whether or not we believed in ghosts."

"So what did you decide, Pop? Do you believe in ghosts?" Kat asked, jumping to the chase, her patience worn thin.

"Kathleen, some questions can't be answered with a yes or no. I'll tell you the stories we heard, then you make up your own mind."

Kat drummed her fingers on the sofa cushion. "Pop, my mind is already made up. But I am curious as to what you believe."

"My personal beliefs have nothing to do with what happened to y'all on that street."

"Sweet Judas, Pop, can't you give a body a straight answer? Do you believe in ghosts?" If he didn't believe in ghosts, then her theories about the man, and especially the phone call, didn't have a prayer.

Rayson frowned. "Don't be pulling attitude on me, girl."

"I just asked a question."

He put his arm around her shoulder and pulled her close. "Yes, I do believe in ghosts, Kathleen. But that's not the real question you're askin' me."

Kat pushed her annoyance away and stuffed it between the sofa cushions. Any argument at this time would be less than productive. "And what might my real question be?"

"You're asking if I believe your tale," he said.

"Well, do you?"

"Of course I do, child. You're not prone to lying. And I've seen plenty of strange things over the years. Now as I said, Lettie and I met the folks on their back porches," Rayson said, easily picking up his rhythm as though there had been no interruptions. "In kitchens, sometimes under oaks or magnolias and listened to incredible tales.

"Miss Mattie De Carlo, the librarian, called him her Dancing Ghost. Prior to this encounter, she'd been in a wheelchair for ten years, the result of a fall down a flight of stairs."

Although she could see Pop's mouth moving, his voice disappeared in the roaring sound in her ears. *Mattie De Carlo* had died on Park Street in 1963. Kat's nerve endings tingled. Her instincts were right. The connections did exist.

"Apparently this Dancing Ghost first appeared the previous Fall," Rayson was saying.

"Do you remember where she lived?"

"The ghost?"

"No, Mattie De Carlo."

Rayson thought for a moment, then shook his head. "Somewhere near Aunt Della's place I think. Why?"

"Because we were parked in front of—" Kat stopped herself. If she said they'd been waiting outside a nonexistent house from 1963, all the weird occurrences would come out. And she didn't think he was quite ready to hear the rest of her theory. "Just go on with the story," she said.

Rayson squeezed her shoulder and resumed his tale. "That particular evening, while reading in her wheelchair, a shadow suddenly fell across the page. She told us she knew beyond doubt she was wide awake, and even recalled the exact hour 'cause the mantle clock struck the hour, seven in the evening. Glancing up, she was quite startled to find a handsome young man standing beside her chair."

Kat listened, impatient to hear how this ghost tale related to her own dilemma. Thirty-seven years in the pulpit had shaped his conversational style so much that he'd become a master at weaving life's experiences into a tapestry. A tapestry with a point. Pop preferred to let his listeners discover the parallels between his rhetoric and their situation. She hoped some form of enlightenment would eventually show its face.

"Without speaking," Rayson was saying, "the ghost placed a record on her old Victrola and cranked the handle. A beautiful waltz filled the room. He extended his hand, inviting her to dance. Miss De Carlo initially withdrew from this apparition, fearful of any contact. But the Dancing Ghost, not easily discouraged, stepped closer. With an engaging smile and a gentle tug, he pulled her out of the chair."

"She touched him?" Kat asked, thrilled by the first inkling of a connection between this story and her own experience. She remembered how the man on Park Street passed through her Honda as though he was without substance. *What-if,* she'd reached out? Would she have touched a flesh and blood man?

"Oh yes indeed. Miss De Carlo mentioned being surprised by his warmth. Well, to get on with it, her reluctance dissolved and she soon waltzed gracefully around the room. Suddenly, without warning, she found herself back in the chair, book in her lap. A soft chiming sound echoed in the room, she glanced to the mantle clock. It read seven o'clock. The hour hadn't budged one second. The clock was still chiming off the same hour as when the ghost had first appeared."

"Mitch and I noticed the same thing. It's like we got stuck at 1:25 A.M. That's when our ghost man first appeared outside the car. And it happened again in the shower, when I was transported to Birmingham. Maybe that's the explanation for why the coffee didn't finished dripping even though I must have been gone long enough. At least long enough for the hot water to run out."

Rayson nodded. "Some folks say time has no meaning in the afterlife."

"Sort of a time continuum?"

"If you're meaning everything grinds to a stop, then I reckon so."

Kat laughed and patted his chubby ebony cheek. "Pop, you gotta get out more, go to a few sci-fi movies. Even watch a couple of episodes of *Star Trek*, they're very entertaining."

"Kathleen, the good book is plenty entertaining."

"So are Darth Vader and Obi-Wan Kenobi," Kat muttered like a grumpy little girl.

Rayson cleared his throat, the prelude to resuming his oration. "Now, Boyd Turley, that's an entirely different matter. For some years his family lived apart, divided. One side of the bunch claimed the other stole a whole peck of money their late daddy intended to be equally divided between his two boys. Boyd assured everyone he never found the money and if he did, he most surely would give his brother an equal share."

"This is real helpful," Kat complained.

"You might be surprised how helpful, if you hushed up and listened," Rayson responded.

At this point Kat surrendered. Pop had no intention of speeding up the process. He'd get around to addressing her questions in the 'by and by'. She sighed and snuggled against his chest, comforted by his familiar aroma of Old Spice and Ivory soap. Listening to the steady rhythm of his heart, for the first time in days she felt safe.

"Strange things began happening to him around Easter. The first thing, noises. Not the banging or clanking you'd expect from any self respecting ghost, more like rubbing. Sometimes from the front room, other times the bedroom. This went on close to two weeks. One morning, just before he crawled out of bed, the whole room switched around on him. The furniture, bedspread and curtains took on different colors. Suddenly the walls were painted, not wallpapered. It looked like his folk's old bedroom all over again. He said this image only lasted a few seconds, and later on he figured he went back to sleep and dreamed it all up."

"I can surely understand his thinking," Kat said. "I keep asking myself the same thing, could I have been asleep and dreamed it all. Especially now that I think about how those old tupelo trees along the road shrank and out of date cars appeared and disappeared. It was like a magic show."

"You want to hear the rest of my story or not, Kathleen Ruth Templeton?" he interrupted.

"Sorry, Pop. Please go on."

Rayson grunted, then nodded solemnly. "He was sittin' in the front parlor when he seen his daddy cross the room carrying several rolls of wallpaper. Naturally curious at all these goings on, Boyd followed. He watched from the doorway of the bedroom as his daddy unrolled the wallpaper and began applying the paste. To his amazement, his father placed dozens of twenty and fifty dollar bills over the paste. Then, proceeded to paper the walls. When Boyd ripped into the paper later on that same day, he found the missing treasure hidden beneath the delicate rosebud patterns."

"That story didn't help me much, Pop. Especially since I'm not searching for missing treasure."

"Are you seeing people that ain't there? You told me about the man and the firemen doing things they already done. And that's the same thing."

Properly chastised, Kat mumbled an apology, "Sorry, sir."

"The last story I will share is the most closely related to your situation."

"Then why didn't you start with that one?"

"Don't be pulling attitude on me, girl," Rayson snapped. "Now, this whole incident appeared to be triggered by a school outing. The day before the trip, a little school girl received a phone call. The caller used her proper name and warned her to not go. Claiming it would end tragically, and if she went along, she would die."

"What happened?"

"That gal was so spooked she stayed home, is what happened. And sure as molasses, the school bus run off the road and a good number of children did perish."

Kat sat up and twisted around to stared wide eyed at her father, her heart flipping somersaults in her chest. "That's like my phone call. The voice very clearly warned me not to cross over. To stay here."

"*Not* to cross over?" Rayson's brow wrinkled. "I thought you and Mitch already—"

"No," she interrupted. "No, on Sunday morning we barely stepped over the Park Street center line before turning back. We never went all the way across."

"So what is your thinking on the meaning of your phone call?"

"Even though the voice said not to cross, I have a deep down feeling I'm meant to go all the way."

"Why do you say that?"

"I wouldn't have seen and heard those things otherwise. Pop, I just know something's waiting for me on the other side. Something important."

"What about the warning?"

"I don't know."

"Are you positive the things you saw, the people and those fire trucks, were from another piece in time?"

Kat hesitated, her earlier omission just sneaked up and bit her on the behind. She should've told him the whole story. And so she did, explaining how everything pointed to 1963—the prank calls, the computer printout with the matching names, dates and times. Concluding with Dreama Simms' recollections.

"I've known Dreama since I was a boy. She and Lettie Ruth ran around together in New Orleans, got into trouble together too."

"Then you must know what happened with her singing career?"

"I do. But we ain't gonna talk about it."

"Pop!" Kat's frustration peaked. Not only would her aunt remain a mystery forever, now Pop had added Dreama Simms to his 'Ain't gonna talk about it' list.

"If she wanted folks knowing her business, I imagine she'd do the tellin'," Rayson said.

"How about a hint? Just a baby-sized clue about why she gave it up."

Rayson rubbed his hand across his throat, his eyes far away. "She can't sing anymore," he said. "And that's all you'll be hearing from me."

Kat got up and stomped into the kitchen. She took her annoyance out on the ice trays, banging them on the counter with such force the cubes jumped out and skittered across the floor.

"When you're done beating my ice trays to death, come on back in here," Rayson called.

She ground her teeth to keep from responding with a caustic remark. If Pop knew how completely frustrating and annoying she found his behavior, he'd be delighted. She was convinced he only lived to aggravate his daughter.

When she returned to the living room, instead of finding an impish glimmer in his eyes, she saw something else. She sat beside him and placed her hand on her father's cheek, turning his head until she could see his face.

Frightened eyes stared out of his face. "Don't be afraid, Pop. I know this is right. You do understand I have to go?"

"I understand, child." He took a shaky breath. "But it was such a hard period here in Alabama that I fear for you. Lots of good folks got hurt…or worse."

"Good folks like Lettie Ruth?"

"You thinking she's what this is all about?"

"Possibly. You see, she's my only connection to 1963." Could the static ridden voice on the phone really belong to her missing aunt? Did Lettie Ruth open the door between 1963 and 2000 as an invitation? One way or another, her aunt had reached across time by offering Kat a tantalizing glimpse of the past and beckoning her to step closer; or as the voice warning her to stay away.

Go or stay? Move backward through time or forget the whole thing and go forward? This was the same as asking a child to choose between eating their dessert or vegetables. Kat's dessert was the thrill, the adrenalin rush of having the opportunity to jump back in time. A chance to make things right so Pop wouldn't have to suffer so much.

On the vegetable side, whatever happened to Lettie Ruth could come full circle and trap Kat as well. The warning—*Don't Cross*—might be the one truth in all of this.

Yet another part of her couldn't ignore the possibility the warning was only a ruse to prevent her interference in a long ago event that maybe should never have taken place.

"What should I do, Pop?"

"I don't suppose you'll know until you get there."

6

At this rate, she and Mitch would stand eye-to-eye, nose-to-nose, and toe-to-toe until the sun came up. He'd arrived on her doorstep minutes after she'd returned from Demopolis and they'd been at it ever since. Crawling through the pros and cons of the time journey across Park Street, until the topic resembled a well-plowed field.

Sighing dramatically, Kat broke the stand-off and moved to the sofa. She glanced over her shoulder at Mitch, still rooted to his space in the middle of the room. "You're a hard headed Pennsylvania Yankee, James Mitchell. You can't think past your own opinion."

"That's because the only other opinion is complete and unadulterated lunacy."

"See there, that's exactly what I'm talking about." As she spoke, a small part grudgingly admitted there might be a bit of truth in his assessment. A trip through time did sound ludicrous. What exactly did she hope to accomplish once she'd arrived in the past?

As though tuning into to her thoughts, Mitch asked, "Why do you want to go back anyway? Is there a reason you haven't told me?"

He looked so worried Kat almost canceled the whole project johnny on the spot. But the reason she felt so compelled to return to that turbulent period was personal and beyond Mitch's understanding. This was a rare instance where race divided the Red and Black unit.

Mitch had never experienced discrimination because of his ginger-red hair and freckles. He'd never been shopping in a department store and had every step shadowed by store security because of his color. His family, friends or neighbors weren't beaten or shot or hung from a tree branch because they drank out of the wrong water fountain. In other words, he'd never been black.

No white male, or female for that matter, could truly grasp the significance of the civil rights movement. To Mitch, the sixties were historically interesting. To Kat, they heralded the dawn of self-awareness for African-Americans. For the first time, blacks united to demand the same rights taken for granted by white citizens. The right to vote, to eat at a lunch counter, to attend the school of choice, to be allowed in a dressing room in a department store. These rights were what Lettie Ruth fought and died for.

"I have to go back," Kat said, answering his question after several moments of soul searching. "I'm doing this for my family. For Pop. He's lived with Lettie Ruth hanging over his head for years. Not knowing what happened to her is eating him up on the inside."

"If no one figured it out in the last thirty-seven years, what makes you so certain you'll be able to do any better?"

"I'm a trained police officer, I know how to investigate. If I'm there when it goes down, I can help to put the pieces together."

Mitch stared into her eyes, into her soul. "You're going back so you can stop the whole thing."

Kat remained silent to avoid lying to him. Of course she would try to stop Lettie Ruth from disappearing forever. She would be entering the picture forewarned of a horrible event that could be easily averted with a few cautious steps. How could she be expected to do otherwise? Could Mitch? Given the identical circumstances, she knew he would respond the same way.

"Have you considered the ripple effect from messing with the past?" Mitch asked. "You know the old joke about preventing your own birth? It may not be so farfetched, partner."

"Mitch, I promise not to marry my father," she said, trying to lighten his mood.

"Don't get cute. This is serious stuff. With serious consequences. Remember, action equals reaction. And I guarantee saving Lettie Ruth will change Alvin's future. *What-if,* your interference prevents him from meeting and marrying your mother? Who knows, he could hook up with some sassy New Orleans gal and you'll dissolve in a puff of smoke."

On the surface his ideas sounded a bit silly, but underneath lay a very solid foundation. By moving one particular chess piece at a crucial moment, the outcome of a game was set. However, if a different piece were moved, and in a different direction, the game changed. A new winner emerged. *What-if,* Mitch's theory about all the past, and trying to change it, was right?

"Scouts honor." She held up three fingers in the Girl Scout salute. "I won't try to change anything." Even as she mouthed the words, Kat knew this promise would be broken. "I'll investigate afterwards."

"Fat chance of that," he growled. "No way in hell are you going to stand back and wait until Lettie Ruth goes missing. You'll step in."

"Don't be so sure, mister. I am quite capable of determining what should and shouldn't be done."

"What makes you such an expert on should and should not?" Mitch challenged. "Your aunt was involved in issues and situations you've only read about in the history books. I'm willing to bet once you're running around in 1963, you'll find a lot of silt muddying the waters. And without a play book, Kat." He stopped and looked her in the eye. "You won't be able predict how a particular action on your part will turn out. Keep in mind, just by *being* there, your presence will have altered the future."

Kat buttoned her sweater all the way to the neck, fighting the chills invading her body. He laid it all out in front of her, like a buffet of disasters. And it frightened the living daylights out of Kathleen Templeton.

"You'll be occupying a space that was either empty prior to your arrival, or you'll replace someone else," he continued. "Let's take a look at a couple of what-ifs." He began to pace the room, slipping into his lecture mode.

Kat cringed. She absolutely hated his What-if lectures. Mainly because they usually ended up making sense. And right now she didn't want his logic to mix in with her emotional objectives.

"*What-if*, you're riding down the road with Lettie Ruth on your way to a civil rights shindig, and get run off the road by a gang of good ole 'Bama boys? Are you willing to die, Kat? Die because you're in the wrong place at the wrong time? You can't predict the what, where or when of that wrong place."

"Mitch," she protested, hoping to derail his speech long enough to make a getaway.

He ignored her and marched on. "And *what-if*, you discover Klan members plan to torch Lettie's house or your Pop's church? Are you going to call the cops and wait for a squad car? Think again, m'lady, they'll throw your tail in the slammer first. You cannot go back and make things right, Kathleen. All you will do is get yourself hurt. Or killed."

"I *can* change one thing, Mitch. I can stop my aunt from—"

"No, you can't!" he shouted, raising his voice for the first time. "It's stupid to think so. Want to know why?"

"Sure, why don't you educate this dumb little black girl."

He whirled on her, his face turning scarlet. "That's a cheap shot, Kat. Don't turn this into a black versus white issue. I'm talking about problems that could arise if you tinker with the past. Step outside your emotions a second and listen to me," he pleaded. "Lettie Ruth disappeared, and because she did, certain events have followed. Things changed for Alvin, and for dozens of other people as well. If you alter one detail, one minute factor, no telling the repercussions that will follow."

"If you've dragged the boogy man out from under the bed to scare me, it ain't working."

"It's not an imaginary monster under the bed, Kat. This is a reality check."

"I don't see how my presence in 1963 can screw up the entire world."

"Example. You told me how Pop met your mother *after* Lettie Ruth went missing."

"True. Mom came over to Dr. Biggers' clinic where Pop was staying. She brought him her famous sweet potato pie. He said he lost his heart and stomach to Dolores Townson sitting on that front porch."

"Allow me to pose this question, if Lettie Ruth doesn't go missing, will Alvin still meet Dolores? Will she still bring him that sweet potato pie? If she doesn't...will they fall in love, get married and have a beautiful baby girl named Kathleen?"

"That's absurd. Of course they will," she argued. She didn't like the tone of their conversation. Mitch was beginning to make points.

He pointed to the phone. "Call Alvin and ask if he's willing to risk the life he's led for the past thirty-seven years." He stopped pacing and squatted in front of her. "Kat, there will be stuff going on in people's lives that you know nothing about and maybe shouldn't."

Kat shook her head so hard her hair fell across her eyes. She brushed it away and glared at Mitch, driving daggers into his mouth to shut him up.

Mitch stood and resumed pacing. "With Lettie Ruth back in the picture, his life will take a different course. It has to. And it is possible your parents will never meet."

"He wants me to go."

He stopped pacing and turned to stare at her. "Alvin said that?"

"Yes. He asked me to try and prevent Lettie Ruth's murder." Kat looked away, she'd fudged the truth a little. Pop's actual words to her had been '*you won't know until you get there.*' Which in her zeal she may have interpreted as '*Go*'.

"Oh, suddenly your aunt's been murdered instead of disappeared? When did her status change? What information is Alvin holding back?"

Her temper flared. "Are you suggesting Pop hasn't been one hundred per cent up front?"

"I'm suggesting antecedent events," Mitch answered.

"What's that supposed to mean?"

"An antecedent event, a preceding event or cause."

"For God's sake, Mitch, I know what the word means."

"Excuse me all to hell and gone. I only meant to be clear. *What-if*, he forgot…or sugar coated, the details? One small, seemingly unimportant fact could be a major player, with regards to your safety. A possibility which concerns me. A lot."

"Then you come along and keep me out of trouble," Kat countered. If he was so worried about her safety then he ought to jump at the invitation. "We can work the case together. Double the manpower and cut our time in half."

"Thank you no. I've seen as much of 1963 as I care to."

"Come on, Mitch, it shouldn't take more than a couple of days to sort through everything and get it squared away."

Mitch sighed and sat on the sofa. "When are you going?"

She unfolded her copy of the Arson/Fatality printout and spread it on the coffee table. "Like I said, *three hours ago*, I believe this Jane Doe entry, dated April 5, to be Lettie Ruth. So I took vacation days starting April 1. I'll go then."

"Four days before anything happened? Isn't that too early to show up, especially if you have no intention of interfering?"

"Interfering or not interfering isn't the issue," Kat said. "The reason is very simple. If I don't leave on the first, then I don't go at all."

Mitch ran his hands through his hair. "April 1 or never? Elaborate."

"I've gone over to Park Street three times since we were there last Sunday," Kat admitted.

"And?"

"And, on two of the trips I could have walked back and forth across Park all day and night without going anywhere, except to the other side of the street."

"No shrinking trees or magic cars?"

"Nope."

"That's an interesting little side bar to all this," Mitch said. "Got any theories on the how's and why's nothing happened?"

"I think it's all linked to the deaths," Kat said. "The first time we were able to step into 1963 because that's the morning Mattie De Carlo died." She pointed to the printout. "Look here, see Harold Beason's name on the 17th? That's today. So on my way home tonight I decided to test my theory. I tried again, and it worked just like the first time."

"You did it?"

"All the way into 1963. I only took a few steps, but it definitely worked. Since nothing happened the other times, I figured the window or doorway was closed. That's when I decided passage was connected to a death."

Mitch ran his finger down the list of names on the printout. "Hey, there's another door opening on April 2. You could wait another day before leaving."

"One day doesn't make all that much difference. Assuming my theory is valid, the door should open again at 5:05 in the morning on April 1, when Tyrone Jefferson died. And that's when I'm goin'."

Mitch's color paled and the paper in his hands trembled slightly. "This business spooks the hell out of me."

"Mitch, I'm not so sure you were ever supposed to be part of this. From the get go I've been dragging you along on this adventure. Otherwise…"

"Otherwise, I wouldn't know about the doorways. Or for that matter, about any of this stuff."

"Right. So maybe this is the way it's supposed to go down."

"Once you get there, where will you start?"

"Right there," she said, tapping the print-out. "The Jane Doe address."

Mitch bent over the papers and read the address out loud, "3349 Brook Street. Residential or commercial?"

"I drove by yesterday and it's a strip mall now. I don't know what was there in 1963."

"You sure this Jane Doe is your aunt? Dead on sure?"

"Maybe not dead on," she hedged, dreading the beginning of another lecture.

"So you're working from a purely speculative base. Maybe it's her. Maybe it's not. Maybe she went missing on this date and time. Maybe she didn't. Maybe, maybe, maybe!" As he spoke his voice gradually rose until the last word was delivered in a shout and he was back on his feet.

"If you feel this way, just go on home and let me tend to my business."

"That's the first smart thing you've said all night."

* * *

From across the room the wrinkled and smudged computer printout stared at Mitch. It wouldn't leave him alone.

Agitated by the way things had turned out with Kat, he couldn't stop throwing stuff around. A good thing he didn't have any real furniture in his apartment or he'd probably end up tossing it off the balcony as well.

What was going on in Kat's mind? No amount of talking, cajoling or yelling could deviate his hard headed partner from her course. Convinced unless she went be-bopping to 1963, her Pop would crumble into a thousand pieces, made reasoning with her impossible.

For nearly forty years Alvin Rayson had lived with the knowledge something bad happened to his sister that April. The old man knew how things were back then. Hell, the entire state of Alabama knew what went on in those days. Lettie Ruth Rayson had been ass deep in the civil rights movement. She'd probably pissed off every KKK white knight within a twenty-mile radius of Maceyville. Of course she'd been murdered.

But for Kat to believe that she alone could change her aunt's fate made him want to puke purple. A person didn't mess around with history. What a crock. If everybody started sticking their fingers in the 'once upon a time' cake, the world was done for.

"Which makes no sense," he shouted to the bare walls.

7

APRIL 1—MONDAY

One hour before sunrise, Kat Templeton stepped off the curb and began the journey out of her own time. In preparation, she'd spent all her off duty hours at the library, studying old newspapers and magazines, immersing herself in the early 1960s. She memorized details, little bits and pieces of trivia. It would be imperative to avoid drawing attention to herself. Chances were high she would encounter people she knew. The only advantage she held was that they wouldn't know her.

She took one final look over her shoulder, knowing full and well if her resistance lowered one itsy bitsy inch she'd turn tail and run. The notion of time-travel seemed extraordinarily feeble minded as Kat neared the point of no return. What could she be thinking? The only reason she stood at this very odd doorway was because of voices and visions. Merry Christmas! Like Joan of Arc, Kathleen of Maceyville was setting out on a crusade to change things for the better.

Mitch's rational arguments against this venture continued to fight against her own emotional need to intervene. She slowed her pace, then came to a complete halt a foot from the white dividing line as she recalled yesterday's conversation with him. At the moment it seemed such a long time ago...

She'd been loading her backpack while a highly agitated James Mitchell drove her antique French rocker in short furious spurts. For the umpteenth time her partner hammered the facts home. Lettie Ruth Rayson's fate had been determined nearly forty years ago. Anything Kat did to alter that, could have serious repercussions.

"Repercussions?" she shot back. "Since when is saving a life considered a repercussion?"

"You know what I mean," Mitch said, his calm tone grated on her nerves. "Action equals reaction."

"Are we going to get into another time-travel tussle here?"

"Fictional time-travel is different from reality, Kat. Once in motion you won't have the option of going back and rewriting the script. Could be you'll dabble in dangerous waters, little girl."

His little girl comment raised Kat's hackles and she had to consciously resist the urge to grab the rocker and dump him head first onto the floor. Instead, she busied her hands by stuffing a third, then a fourth set of unnecessary clothing in the pack. Which she immediately removed because any extra clothes she required could easily be purchased at her destination.

Kat removed her driver license, credit cards, library card, photographs from her wallet and placed them in the desk drawer. Her police identification and .38 were in a safety deposit box at the bank. Remembering the scene in the movie, 'Somewhere In Time' when Christopher Reeve's character discovered a penny with a future date and was yanked back to the present, Kat made certain all her folding money dated pre-1963.

"I won't dabble in anyone's business, Mitch. If I've told you once, I've told you a hundred times, I only want to try to find out what happened to Lettie Ruth."

"And once you get it all figured out? Are you going to confront the good ole boys down at the Klan hall? Get the local law to arrest them?"

Kat sighed loudly, annoyed with his unending supply of sarcasm. "Okay Mr. James 'I-Know-Everything' Mitchell, what do you suggest? Lettie Ruth's disappearance has haunted Pop for 37 years. I remember waking up in the night and finding him sittin' out in the front room with her picture in his hands. His body would be shaking, his cheeks dripping with tears. This thing has been nibbling away for years, Mitch, and if I don't do something, it's gonna eat clean through him."

By the time she finished her speech, the rocking chair stood motionless. Mitch sat like a stone statue, his blue eyes saying much more eloquently than words how he felt. "Knowing is sometimes worse than not knowing, Kat. You feel up to rubbing noses with the rock hard truth about Lettie Ruth? Are you sure your Pop wants to know?"

"I think we already know the truth."

"Then why in Sam Hill are you risking getting caught up in that same net."

Kat herself had spent several days wrestling with that particular question. Family obligation? Old fashioned curiosity? It made no difference either way, she knew if she passed on this opportunity she'd be the one sitting up all night looking at a faded photograph.

"I have to go," she told him.

He sighed, an indication the argument was over. "When will you come back?"
"There are two entry doors. April 10 and 12."
Mitch gave her a bear hug. "Come home on Wednesday the 10th. It's sooner."
"I'll see you in ten days, scouts honor."
"I'll be waiting on Park Street at two o'clock sharp, partner," he'd told her. "Don't be late."

Time to go.

*   *   *

1963

Kat hitched the backpack higher on her shoulders and focused on her destination. As she stepped over the line, the fog turned thick as gumbo, with little chunks of 2000 and 1963 floating around together. As though cued by an unseen stage manager, the L-shaped houses were replaced by tar paper shacks and ramshackle shotgun houses. The trees lining the street began to shrink, or completely disappeared. Neat yards turned to weed and dirt plots littered by an assortment of broken furniture, tires and all around junk.

Things even smelled different. Instead of honeysuckle and sweet jasmine, rotting garbage and rancid sewage permeated the air.

Although it had taken less than a minute, by the time she reached the other side she was exhausted and walking around on spaghetti legs. Unwilling to immediately dip into her limited cash, she opted for a secluded patch of grass in a nearby vacant lot rather than a hotel room. And because of that decision, nosy fingers were now poking in her chest.

Kat kept her eyes closed, waiting for the scene to play out. She prayed the prying digits belonged to a curious child rather than an adult.

"Don't touch her, Virgil. She's dead."

"Tain't neither. Lamar, see how her girl things are a movin' up and down."

At the sound of the young voices discussing her anatomy, the tightly wound coil of tension in Kat's stomach loosened. She could handle a couple of kids. Her eyes flew open as she grabbed the chocolate colored wrist poised above her breast. With a roar she sat upright, determined to teach the little stinkers to keeps their hands to themselves. The stunned expression on the boys faces made her laugh. She'd succeeded in scaring the bejesus out of them.

Kat released her grip and stood. She brushed the loose grass from her jeans and tee-shirt, periodically shooting the boys her best Maceyville cop glare. "Didn't your mommas teach you any manners?" she demanded.

"Yes'um," they answered in unison as they shuffled backwards.

The boys were like two antsy colts, ready to jump the coral fence at any second. Unless she wanted to draw a whole peck of attention down on her head, she needed to keep them low keyed and calm. Otherwise they'd high tail it out of here and spread the news all over the east Hollow of a strange woman sleeping in the bushes. Not a very auspicious beginning.

"What are your names?" Kat asked, softening her glare and tone slightly.

"I'm Virgil," answered the chunky owner of the prying finger. "And that there's Lamar standing off yonder under the tree."

"Pleased to meet you, Virgil. My name is Kat." She turned to the second boy. Unlike the short and pudgy Virgil, he was tall and skinny as a rail post. His skin was such an exact color match to the bark, he practically disappeared into the tree trunk. "Come on over here, Lamar. I won't bite."

Virgil took a couple of sideways steps, reached out and grabbed Lamar by the shirt sleeve and yanked him closer to Kat. "Me'n him is cousins," Virgil announced. "And we was borned on the very same day."

"The same day, huh? How old does that make you guys?" Kat asked.

"Thirteen-years-old come Friday," Virgil said. "April 5."

Kat drew a shaky breath. The pieces were already beginning to connect. On April 5 her aunt Lettie Ruth Rayson had gone missing. She forced a smile and asked, "I know you boys are only twelve, but that should be old enough to find your way around here without getting lost. Right?"

Lamar nodded.

"Sure 'nuf. I been on most every street in the east Hollow," Virgil bragged, his wide chest puffed out like a proud peacock.

Kat picked up her dusty pack and slung it over one shoulder. "Then you're just the man to help a lady out. I'm looking for Brook Street."

"Ma'am?" Virgil asked. "Why's you dressed in britches and your daddy's undershirt? You planning on doing field work today?"

Her eyes widened, surprised by his question. She'd been in 1963 for less than five hours and already made a whopping mistake. Women her age did not wear jeans and tee-shirts and go tromping through downtown.

"You're a smart boy, Virgil. Field work is exactly what I planned," she said. "But now that I see what a fine day it is, I'm thinking about shopping instead. I bet y'all know where I can buy a pretty dress."

Virgil pointed down the street. "Three blocks thatta way."

"Then turn right on Webster Avenue," Lamar added, jumping into the conversation for the first time. "Miss Jane's is right beside the Waffle Shop. And Brook Street is by the river, so stay on Webster then go left on Grant, and you'll run across it."

"You give good directions, I shouldn't have any trouble," Kat said as she headed in the direction indicated.

"Hey, Miss Kat," Lamar called.

She turned back to the boy, his tree bark brown face too serious for one so young. "What is it, Lamar?"

"You best be careful in town. Some white folks down there ain't too nice to coloreds."

"I appreciate the advice." The boy sounded like someone who'd run into trouble downtown. And that scared her. Lord almighty, what had she gotten herself into?

8

YEAR 2000

APRIL 1—MONDAY

Mitch didn't know how long the phone rang before the noise penetrated his sleep-deprived brain. He considered ignoring the demanding jingle-jangle, but he was enough awake he doubted he could get back to sleep.

He grabbed the phone and barked an unfriendly greeting into the receiver.

"Sergeant James Mitchell? This is Dr. Emmerson, at Maceyville Memorial Hospital."

"Yeah?"

"I'm trying to contact Kathleen Templeton." The doctor went on to explain when his efforts to contact Kat proved unsuccessful, he had contacted the police station. They gave him Mitch's number thinking he might have information regarding his partner. "Do you know where she might be found?"

"Afraid not, she took vacation time. What's the problem?"

"It's her father. Alvin Rayson suffered a heart attack early this morning."

"How bad? Will he be all right?"

"The prognosis isn't good, Sergeant."

* * *

Mitch stood in the Cardiac Care Unit and stared through the glass partition. Alvin Rayson was surrounded by enough medical equipment to supply an entire hospital wing. Ghostly white figures hovered around his bed, some adjusting dials, others fiddling with the pastor's assorted tubes and wires. The beeping heart monitor and the gentle stream of oxygen were the only sounds in the room.

Three hours later the CCU nurse finally gave him the okay to enter the room. Alvin's eyes were open and he moved his hand slightly, motioning for Mitch to come closer.

He bent over the bed and took the preacher's hand. "Hey, Alvin. Looks like they got you wired for the Internet."

"I don't do Windows," Rayson whispered.

Mitch chuckled. "Me neither. How you getting along? Is there anything I can get for you?"

"Kat," Rayson wheezed.

"Pop, I can't get in touch with her."

"James, you gotta cross over too."

"I think it would be better to wait, she'll be back soon," he said.

Heart attack notwithstanding, his opinion on time-travel remained the same—not a good thing. Alvin was as stubborn as his daughter and Mitch knew the pastor wouldn't head for glory without telling Kat goodbye.

"Things I didn't tell her. Bad things gonna happen."

"What things?" A brief flicker of anger burned in Mitch's eyes, the man in this hospital bed told her to go. Her own father, so tied up with his own personal drama that he never considered his daughter's safety.

"About the day...about what happened before."

A dark and ugly feeling stirred deep inside Mitch's gut. As he feared, Kat had taken off without knowing the complete story on Lettie Ruth. He should have listened to his own instincts and hog tied her rather than allowing the time-traveling act.

"Tell me, Alvin. What does Kat need to know?"

"Troubles started before Lettie. On the day she—"

The heart monitor gave a high-pitched shriek and Mitch was shoved aside as a team of doctors and nurses went to work on Rayson.

Mitch paced back and forth in the small CCU waiting area, his emotions creating a crazy quilt in his head. Without Alvin's information was Kat's life in jeopardy? He wondered how much the reverend held back. Before he could work his way through the conflicting maze, the doctor found him.

"You should try to locate Mrs. Templeton," the doctor said. "Reverend Rayson's condition is extremely critical. I don't know how much longer he'll last."

"Critical? You mean he could..."

"He's in bad shape, Sergeant Mitchell. Find his daughter."

* * *

1963

Miss Jane's Dress Boutique would be hard to miss even on a dark night, Kat thought. The building stood out like a big pink flamingo on a snowy white beach. And the bright yellow Waffle Shop next door lent a carnival look to the right side of the street.

It seemed half of Maceyville decided to go shopping today. All the parking spaces along Webster Avenue were filled and entire families sat in, or on, their cars to watch the people parade. As she walked down the street a sad looking cur dog, near a shoe store, stopped biting and scratching fleas long enough to let out a growl, then returned to his scratching.

Several stores down from the dress shop, three men took up space on the barber shop's bench where they alternated talking trash and spitting tobacco juice into coffee cans. Their feet were sticking so far out on the sidewalk Kat's path was blocked. She gave them a cursory once over, then lifted her leg and stepped across the first set of outstretched legs. She was straddling the second pair when the dark-haired owner raised one foot high enough to rub against her crotch. Without thinking, she clamped her thighs around his muddy work boot and twisted sideways. The man landed on the sidewalk.

Before she took another step, a wiry blonde, with a strawberry birthmark spread across his right cheek, shot up off the bench and grabbed her by the hair.

"What the hell you doin', coon?" he snarled. "Got no right jerking Floyd down like that."

The words were barely out of his mouth before he drew back his hand and slapped Kat so hard she nearly bit her tongue in half. Her mouth filled with blood, but he stood too close for her to spit without hitting him. So she swallowed, gagging on the metallic taste.

"I'll handle this, Little Carl," the man on the ground said. "She ain't nothing but an uppity nigger bitch that needs taming."

Kat's spine stiffened, she didn't want any more trouble from these clowns, but she refused to put up with their insults or physical abuse. More angry than afraid, Kat reached for the badge she no longer wore. Understanding struck home when her hand closed on the empty space. She'd come face-to-face with the anything goes Southern mentality regarding African-Americans. People of her color were considered sub-human, to be toyed with whenever it suited the 'true' sons of the South. What on earth could she have been thinking to stir it up with these boys?

The dark-haired Floyd clambered to his feet, his eyes coal-furnace hot. "Next time you pass this way, jungle bunny, you step off the walk." He used his hand to wipe away the tobacco juice dribbling down his chin. His mouth stretched in an evil grin as he looked from the brown juice to Kat. He spit a wad of tobacco into his palm, then quicker than a snake, grabbed her breast. He squeezed hard enough to make her gasp. He laughed at her pain then released his hold. But he'd left his mark, a slimy brown hand print decorated the front of her tee shirt.

Kat's honey-colored eyes narrowed as her temper rose to the surface like a mighty whale. "You lay another hand on me, *Floyd*, and I'll slap your ass in jail so fast you'll be asking your buddies where it went."

As soon as the words were out, she realized her error in responding to his taunts. If she wore her police uniform no one would question the propriety of her response. But she didn't have a uniform, and more importantantly, she wasn't in her own time period. This was 1963 Alabama. Kathleen Templeton didn't have rights.

"Floyd, why you letting a nigger get away with such sassy talk?" goaded the third man, a fat hunk of lard who remained glued to the bench, too lazy to move. But apparently not too lazy to offer his two cents worth.

"Shut the hell up, Louis," Floyd hissed. "This coffee colored split tail ain't gettin' away with a fucking thing."

The strawberry-marked Little Carl's hand shot out and cupped Kat's crotch. He snorted and pawed at the ground like a deranged jackass. "I just love that nappy patch, don't y'all?" he asked.

Floyd and Louis, brayed in response. By this time a small crowd ringed the sidewalk and the few white men, in the predominately black audience, tittered obscenely. Embarrassed by their own inability to intervene, all but one of the black faces looked away.

The elderly man, wrinkled and black as an old piece of used carbon paper, stepped forward. "I thinks you gentlemen best be leaving the girl be."

Louis spun around, his fat belly jiggling. "That you, Tupelo Josephs?"

"Yes sir, Mr. Louis. And I said for y'all to stop messin' with that girl."

"Jesus, Tupelo Joe, how old you niggers got to be before you learn to mind your own damn business?"

"I turned 90 in February," Tupelo Joe said.

Louis shook his head. "And you ain't learned a damn thing. Tell you what we're gonna do here—" he stopped mid-sentence when a boy, with a shock of white blonde hair flopping across his eyes, burst through the crowd.

The boy stopped in front of Louis. "Hey, Daddy," he said, panting like a hot puppy. He bent over at the waist and gasped for air. "Momma said get your fat ole butt back to the car, she wants to get to the Piggly Wiggly before the on-sale weenies is all gone."

The obese Louis grabbed the back of his son's tee-shirt and yanked him upright. "Arlin Smith, tell your momma I'll be there when I'm damn good and ready," he snarled. "And tell her I said, don't be sending you to fetch me no more."

Kat stared in amazement. This dirty tow-headed kid was Arlin Smith? Thirty-seven years from now he would be the Maceyville Chief of Police. Just goes to show you, she thought, like-father like-son. The old man was a jerk and the Chief had turned out to be an even bigger jerk.

Arlin squeezed through the crowd and disappeared down the street. With the boy out of sight, the elder Smith turned his attention back to the old man. "Now, Tupelo Josephs, I don't want to have to get on you about this. So just be on your way."

Tupelo Joe stepped closer. "No, sir. This time you gonna listen to this here old colored man." He grabbed Louis' fat arm just above the elbow and squeezed. "I said to leave her be," he commanded, his voice low and threatening.

Floyd snatched a bottle off the ground and swung it against the bench seat. The broken bits of glass made a tinkling sound as they hit the concrete. The silent crowd parted, as he moved toward Tupelo Josephs. The remains of the bottle, clinched in his hand, glinted in the sunlight. "Shouldn't done that, nigger." He raised the bottle waist high, then thrust the jagged point into Tupelo Joe's hand. He smiled when the old man cried out in pain as he slowly drew the sharp glass downward. Josephs' hand blossomed a bright red and he let go of Louis.

Being cornered brought out Kat's survival instincts. Seeing the brave old man assaulted brought out her police instincts. She fought hand-to-hand combat with the urge to take Floyd down. But she knew such a response would not be very smart. In this scenario, the smart move was to get away. Floyd had just crossed the line into a dangerous new level of harassment, and Kat didn't intend to stick around and see what cruel games he would invent for her transgression.

She back pedaled until her rear end rammed the parking meter. Her eyes swept the street, it would be fool hardy to take off without a clear and safe destination point. She saw Miss Jane's Dress Boutique less than thirty yards. She could make it without breaking a sweat. These farm boys didn't have the brains God gave a turnip and she'd be long gone before they uncrossed their eyes.

The second time Floyd made a grab for her, Kat ducked under his arm, pushed through the crowd and sprinted down the uneven sidewalk. The men's taunting remarks nipped at her heels like stray dogs.

* * *

The little gold bell tinkled daintily as Kat raced through the door into Miss Jane's Boutique. In her haste she tripped over the rubber floor mat, crashing head first into a three-tiered display of cardigan sweaters. She got tangled up and ended up face down on a pile of soft Orlon. She sat up and stared in horror at the lumpy gobs of tobacco her tee-shirt had deposited on a pearl-white sweater. The last thing she needed, in her current predicament, was a white sweater, but from the look in the clerk's eyes, Kat felt it wise to produce a fist full of cash in a hurry.

"Get yourself off my merchandise, girl! You get that skinny behind off those things right this second!" The ear shattering command heralded the arrival of Miss Jane herself, an ebony Humpty Dumpty with wildly flapping arms and a shocking pink beehive.

Kat did as ordered and quickly jumped to her feet.

Miss Jane picked up the damaged sweater and waved it accusingly in Kat's face. "This is downright nasty, girl," she shrieked. "What got into you? Running in here and tearing up my goods. You ain't got a lick of sense."

Stunned by the decibel level of the attack, Kat said the first thing that popped into her head. "I'm sure it will wash out."

"Warsh? Warsh out? Nobody's gonna buy no warshed out sweater."

"I'll buy it." Kat fished in her pocket and pulled out a handful of green, hoping to assuage the furious egg-shaped woman. If her morning got any further out of control, she could only imagine what the afternoon held in store. Even as a curious and rowdy child she'd never stirred up this much trouble in such a short period of time.

"Ain't that the gospel truth, girl. You is gonna buy it, *and* you is gonna clean up this mess," Miss Jane declared. She stood with both hands on her ample hips, her head bobbing like a pink chicken with each word.

Kat squatted, and ever so carefully, gathered the scattered pastel cardigans. She made certain they remained a safe distance from the brown stain on her shirt. She picked up the stack and held it out to the shop owner. An offering to the thundering goddess of Orlon.

Miss Jane accepted her offering, then proceeded to scrutinize each individual sweater, searching for further signs of abuse. Slightly mollified at finding them unharmed, she turned her microscopic eyes on Kat. "Why's you dressed for cotton picking?"

Judas Priest, Kat thought, is everyone in town obsessed with my appearance? She promised herself on the next time-travel adventure, she'd plan her wardrobe with greater attention.

"I was on my way to your store to buy a dress when I ran across a glitch."

"Gulch?" asked Miss Jane. "Ain't no gulches 'round here."

Kat smiled in spite of her fear of the woman. "Not a gulch," she explained. "A glitch. You know, a trouble spot."

Miss Jane inclined her head toward the street. "You mean them damn fools up by the barber shop?"

Kat nodded. "Now there's a trio for you. All of 'em put together barely got the brains of one little ole June bug."

"For sure they is stupid as stumps. But they is also mean, child," Miss Jane warned. "You best not mix in with them."

"I don't plan on it," Kat said.

"Good." Miss Jane nodded approvingly. "Now, let's see to getting you some proper town clothes. Might ease your way a bit."

"I'm more than ready to have my way eased."

"You been traveling far?" Miss Jane asked, as she sorted through a rack of dresses. Ever so often she pulled one out and held it up for further inspection, then either slung it over her broad shoulder or shoved it back on the rack.

"A goodly distance," Kat hedged.

"Where 'bouts?" the store owner asked, eyeing a blue flower print dress.

Like the Reverend Alvin Rayson, Miss Jane refused to accept half answers. Kat needed a believable response to stop the inquisition. "I'm up from New Orleans."

Miss Jane held the blue dress a little closer to Kat, but still maintained a safe distance from the tobacco stained tee-shirt. "You got folks in Maceyville?"

Now that was a loaded question. What was she supposed to say? Yes ma'am, my Aunt Lettie Ruth lives here, but she doesn't know me from Adam; and I don't know her from Eve because I haven't been born yet.

"I'm just passing through," Kat said. "Looking for work." She instantly regretted the spontaneous ad lib. Which most likely, would only cause more trouble.

"Work you say?" Miss Jane handed her an armful clothing and pointed to the dressing room.

"Uh-huh," Kat mumbled and quickly moved toward the back of the store.

"I know somebody what wants a girl that can type real good," Miss Jane called out. "You ever work one of those electric typewriters, honey?"

9

A little less than an hour later, Kat stepped out of Jane's Dress Boutique wearing a new denim skirt and red and white-checked blouse. She also carried a shopping bag filled with two dresses, including the blue flowered one, and the dirty white sweater. Her jeans and the tee-shirt, with Floyd's hand print emblazoned on the front, were rolled and stuffed inside her backpack.

At Miss Jane's insistence, she accepted the slip of paper with the name of the man needing a typist. The pushy woman also told her, not suggested, to talk with Pastor Gordon down at the Webster Avenue Freedom Methodist Church about a decent place for a single woman to stay.

"Y'all got to be careful nowadays," the shop owner cautioned. Kat tended to agree, sleeping under a bush again didn't seem a very good idea, especially after meeting Floyd and his pals.

She paused in the shade under the hot pink awning. The bench in front of the barber shop was empty, free of the riffraff that only came to the east Hollow to kick up trouble. She felt relieved the three stooges had tired of their idiotic games and returned to their own part of town.

She took off down the street enjoying the late morning, thankful her ensemble drew little attention from passerbys. According to Miss Jane, the church would be a mile or so down Webster. The red brick church, several blocks beyond the business district, lay across the informal boundary separating the black east from the white west Maceyville. In Kat's own time, the Freedom Methodist church no longer existed, replaced years ago by a fried chicken take-out and a gas station.

Many things were the same, but ever now and then something popped up and caught her by surprise. For example, the sawed off wooden barrels of colorful begonias evenly spaced along the curbs and the old fashioned globe street lamps. Too bad they're gone, she thought they prettied up the district.

As the temperature warmed, the humidity rose several notches and before long her blouse was sticky with perspiration. Nosy insects buzzed her, periodically swooping in to land on sweat slick arms and bare legs. Kat lifted her shoulder length curls and dabbed the beads of moisture on the back of her neck. She wished for a breeze to cool her down, but the sprawling live oaks, their branches festooned with Spanish moss, remained motionless.

Her hand brushed against the cowboy boot pin adorning her new blouse and for at least the twentieth time since crossing Park Street, she wished for Mitch's company. She would like to share this glorious day with her partner. Even the humidity couldn't diminish the early Spring beauty. The earth, pleased to have survived another cold winter, celebrated with a myriad of colors and scents. As she passed from the business district into the residential area, she admired carefully groomed yards showcasing hydrangeas, black-eyed Susans and yellow jessamine.

She could imagine the activity in the woods surrounding Maceyville as the cane and kudzu fought for territory. Thickets of blackberries and huckleberries would be working hard at making the fruit for summer jam.

What am I doing here? The thought shot into her head and ricocheted around like a wild bullet. Walking in the bright sunlight, this whole exercise seemed foolish. Who would ever believe Kathleen Templeton, time-traveler extraordinaire, had crossed one narrow pot hole filled street and wham! ended up 37 years in the past. Jiminy Christmas, she must be out of her mind.

More aggravating, the reason for her trip somehow got mislaid along the way. Was she here to prevent Lettie Ruth's death? Or did another purpose lie beneath all the smoke and mirrors? The voice on the phone warned her not to cross over, so naturally she'd done the exact opposite. And now Kat didn't know what her next move should be. She couldn't exactly march up to her aunt's door and announce herself or her mission.

And she couldn't go home for nine more days.

Caught up her thoughts, Kat failed to notice the white stake-bed pickup idling in the alleyway until it lurched forward, blocking her path. By the time the occupant's identity registered, she'd been hog-tied and thrown into the back of the truck.

Little Carl's strawberry birthmark glowed like the setting sun as he shoved the filthy rag in her mouth. He pushed her face down on the hot metal truck bed. "We got her, Floyd," he yelled, and banged on the cab. "Take off."

Clouds of dirt billowed over the sides as the pickup gained speed. Kat struggled for a breath, but the wad of flannel prevented her from inhaling fully and the disgusting taste caused her to gag. She turned her head to the side, hoping to dislodge the rag before she choked to death on her own vomit.

"Scoot on over and let me get a look, Little Carl," a voice above her whispered harshly.

Rough hands grabbed Kat's shoulders and flipped her over. Louis stared hungrily, like she was a cake in a bakery window. He wiped the sweat off his fat face and ripped open her blouse, dodging the flying buttons. He shoved her bra above her breasts. "Got a pair of tits on her that oughta give three or four gallons of chocolate milk."

"Don't you boys be startin' without me," Floyd hollered from the driver's seat.

"We're just makin' sure this here nigger's equipment is in the right place," Little Carl said.

"It damn well better be in the right place when I get to her," Floyd threatened.

"Aww, Floyd, we ain't doing nothing," Louis whined.

A type of fear Kat hadn't experienced since her childhood nightmares reared its ugly head. Thick oily waves of terror surged through her veins. As though she'd suddenly flipped a switch on a synthesizer, her heart beats picked up speed, hitting with such force her entire chest vibrated.

Control. I have to get under control, she told herself. I can't go on wallowing in fear. To do so would be a sure fire death warrant. She'd foolishly publicly humiliated their leader and now these boys were out for blood. Her blood.

This bore all the markings of a gang rape unless she could shift the odds around. Faces of the rape victims she'd counseled clustered behind her closed eyes. All the comforting words she'd spouted, all the psychology—disappeared like puffs of smoke in the gale force storm brewing inside her.

A fleeting thought of Lettie Ruth streaked across her mind. Is this how life ended for her aunt? Did three country boys throw her in the back of a truck and carry her off? Sweet Jesus God, Mitch was right. She'd walked right into a spider web spun thirty-seven years ago and got tangled up in the sticky strands.

Action equals reaction.

Like a knight in shining armor, Mitch's favorite slogan rode into her personal hell. Instead of lying here like a wilted Magnolia blossom, she must react to these men.

Kat knew how to defend herself, but in order to utilize those skills, she must have freedom of movement. Trussed up like a Christmas goose, she didn't have a prayer. Ignoring the hands roaming her body, she arched her back slightly, creating space between her spine and truck bed so she could manipulate the rope cinched around her wrists. Her sweat slick hands allowed a tiny bit of movement within the confines of her bonds. Only a little, but a little was always better than nothing.

Action. She worked her hands back and forth.

Reaction. With each twist, the fiber strands stretched a fraction of an inch. Things were reacting, but not fast enough. Before long, this wild bumpy ride would end and she would be forced to deal with multiple attackers. God in heaven, help me, she prayed.

Take the offensive. The police academy self-defense instructions echoed in her head. *Go after them one at a time. Start with the closest attacker. Don't hesitate, cause immediate serious pain and damage.*

Unless she freed her hands soon, the only one suffering any serious pain and damage would be Kathleen Templeton. She fought for the control necessary to systematically assess her situation, a feat which couldn't be accomplished in a panicked state of mind. She concentrated on her breathing until it leveled off and her mind settled enough to function rationally. Floyd appeared to be the self-appointed leader of this mangy pack, which meant: incapacitate him first. Without the Alpha Dog's influence, the other two might turn tail and run.

The truck came to a sudden halt and a suffocating blanket of dust enveloped them. The high-pitched screech of metal on metal as the tail gate was lowered caused Kat to momentarily freeze. All the players were present and the contest about to begin. Unfortunately, her game piece wasn't in position.

Floyd jumped out of the cab and hurried around to the back end. He grabbed her ankles and with a mean chuckle, hauled Kat down the length of the truck bed. Her new denim skirt rode up around her waist and his intrusive hand snaked inside her panties. Still hog-tied, she had no choice but to endure the humiliation.

Her head rode a scant quarter inch off the ground as Little Carl and Floyd half-carried, half-dragged her into the field several yards off the road. Sharp cotton bolls snagged on her blouse and cut into her bare arms and legs.

Where was Louis? She had to keep track of each man, the last thing she needed was to be blind sided. Kat let her head fall back until it dragged the ground. There he was. Louis trailed behind, panting like a winded hound as he maneuvered his bulk down the narrow row.

Without ceremony, Little Carl and Floyd suddenly released their hold. Kat's head and back hit the ground. At the moment of impact her fairy godmother must have waved her magic wand, because the rope binding Kat's wrists fell away.

"Shit! The nigger's free," screamed Louis, kicking at the coiled rope lying across his boot as though it were alive.

"Hells bells, you can't tie a knot worth a damn," Little Carl scolded.

"Louis, grab hold of her hands," Floyd ordered.

Louis did as instructed, sitting on Kat in the process. His weight made it even more difficult for her to breathe. Wheezing sounds escaped around the rag filling her mouth.

"For Christ's sake, he's so fat he's gonna squash her like a bug," Little Carl complained.

"Get your big ass off my nigger bitch," snarled Floyd, giving Louis a mean shove.

"Who gets first go at her?" Little Carl asked, greedily looking from Kat to Floyd.

"That coon's pussy is mine for sure," Floyd announced. The bulge beneath his dirty jeans a clear indication of his intent. "Now git off her, Louis!"

Still down on all fours, Louis lifted one sausage hand and one leg, as he clumsily rolled off Kat. Grunting like a hog stuck in a mud hole, he got onto his feet.

Posturing for the other men, an overly confident Floyd motioned for them back off as he straddled Kat. "I'm gonna have you six ways to sundown...and then some," he promised, removing the saliva-soaked wad from her mouth. He leaned forward and pinned her arms above her head, his face only inches away. "We're gonna set this ole cotton field on fire, bitch."

Kat held her tongue. Two things must occur before Floyd could set anything on fire. One: unfasten his jeans. Two: he must release one of her hands to accomplish number one.

She allowed a squeak of triumph to escape when he let go of her left hand to unbutton his fly. Floyd chuckled, stupidly mistaking her response for sexual excitement.

Action. Kat grabbed the back of his neck with her freed hand. Elbow close to her body for more control, she pulled his head down toward her left shoulder.

Reaction. Thrown off balance, Floyd instinctively released her right hand to stop from toppling over. Kat went on the attack. She pressed her right fist against his temple and drove her thumb into his left eye.

His screams carried across the cotton field. Out of the corner of her eye she saw Little Carl and Louis step away from the unfolding drama.

Kat continued to increase the pressure to his eye as she turned his head away. As expected, Floyd's body followed. She bent her right knee, planting her foot securely on the ground, then rotated her hips. Without releasing her hold, she rolled right along with him.

They now lay on their sides, face-to-face. Her left hand around his neck and her right thumb firmly embedded in his eye. For good measure, and because she was pissed off, she gave his head a couple of hard bounces on the ground. Sensing Floyd's loss of desire to set the field on fire, Kat shoved him away. She quickly sat upright and pivoted, making sure to keep her feet between them.

When she finally looked over her shoulder, Little Carl and Louis stood behind her.

10

YEAR 2000

Mitch drove from the hospital directly to the station house. He took the fire stairs to the file room to avoid running into anyone he knew. But he didn't have to worry, since it was after five he found the lower level deserted.

He rapidly gained access to the old records and printed a copy of the 1963 Arson/Fatality sheet. He ran his finger down the page and sighed with relief. He didn't remember two doors opening today, but there they were in black and white. The first, Tyrone Jefferson, which Kat had used at 4:05 this morning. The second, Tupelo Josephs would open Mitch's door at 6:12 this evening.

He glanced at his watch: 5:30 P.M.. He stared at the name and date, here was his chance. He had about 45 minutes...if he chose to use it.

Mitch broke out in a cold sweat recalling his nightmares of Lisa walking through him because he didn't exist. On Park Street, the firemen had walked through him. *What-if,* he arrived in 1963 and no one could see him? *What-if,* when he returned to the year 2000 no one could see him?

With trembling hands he folded the printout and shoved it in his pocket. He couldn't ignore the strange premonition that this single decision would forever alter his life.

* * *

Pushing his fears to the back of his mind, Mitch returned to his apartment to pack his gym bag. He concentrated on the objective; with military precision he planned the mission. After consulting the list once again, he calculated the shortest amount of time available for him to locate Kat. On the other side, he should be able to easily find his wayward partner within the allotted ten hours. In spite of her protests to the contrary, he knew where she would go. She would seek out her aunt. Once located, he and Kat would wait out the clock…wait for Leroy Spencer to die at 5:20 A.M., April 2, 1963. Mitch closed his eyes when the callousness of his plan registered.

Acting as judge and jury, he'd sentenced the unknown Mr. Spencer to death. But the idea of stepping in and changing things wasn't an option. If he did, he and Kat couldn't return to the year 2000. Of course, all they had to do was wait until the next name popped up, then cross. He buried his face in his hands, what kind of a monster had he become to consider someone's death a ticket to the E-ride?

The god-like power over life and death was difficult to comprehend. Did James Mitchell have the right to decide between Alvin Rayson's life and Leroy Spencer's? He believed Kat should be given the opportunity to see her Pop one last time. But if the doctor's predictions held true, the preacher was going to die with or without his daughter's presence. Mr. Leroy Spencer's death was another matter. If he and Kat were correct about a serial arsonist being responsible for the deaths, a phone call to the people listed would alter the past. Who said because someone's name turned up on a thirty-seven-year old list, he absolutely must die?

Forever the optimist, Mitch reminded himself for each problem, a solution could be found. All he had to do was design an alternative method of opening the door between the years. Before 5:20 tomorrow morning.

* * *

1963

Mitch paused, right foot suspended above the white line dividing Park Street. "Thank you, Mr. Tupelo Josephs," he whispered. And lowered his foot.

It took only a single step for Mitch to travel from April 1, 2000 to April 1, 1963.

He slowly crossed the scraggly patch of half-dead grass, wide eyed and mouth hanging open like a trap door. The scene unfolding around him brought to mind a book he'd owned as a child. When he rapidly flipped through the book, the characters drawn on the pages did a jerky dance. And the constantly changing landscape all around him displayed the identical frenetic quality. Objects underwent rapid fire alterations as an invisible hand flipped through the pages of time.

Suddenly a big tupelo tree popped up in the same place he occupied and he rammed his nose into the rough bark. From that point on, Mitch made certain to remain dead-center on the sidewalk. He thought it unlikely another tree would be lying in ambush on the concrete path.

"This is spooky as all get out," he said, mainly to see if he sounded normal. At the rate things were shifting he wouldn't count on anything being normal.

When he arrived at the fork of Riverside and Azalea, he sighed with relief. The familiar neon sign still turned the front of The Blue into a buzzing blob of colored lights. The bar had been his refuge from the world for eight years. Whenever he dropped by, he could always hook up with a couple of fellas looking to put together a trio. Mitch enjoyed the impromptu jam sessions, and his skill on the piano guaranteed him a seat.

The Blue's owner, Dean Broodman, was too cheap to pay for live entertainment and thus initiated one of the first open-mike establishments in Alabama. Mitch couldn't recall exactly when the old skinflint took over the place, it seemed he'd been clomping around behind the bar since the dinosaurs roamed the earth. Of course, this being the past, if Broodman was around at all he would be in his late thirties.

He shoved open the perpetually squeaky door, which obviously hadn't seen an oil can in well over forty years, and felt like he'd come home.

The Blue was a long rectangle, constructed from three double wide railroad boxcars hooked end to end. The small tables, haphazardly arranged near the door, thinned out toward the back to make room for three pool tables. The stage, as Broodman called it, was nothing but upended wooden flats resting six-inches off the floor.

Although Mitch didn't know the two guys making music, one blowing a real sweet sax and the other fingering the guitar, no matter the year, he wasn't going to be shy about making himself at home on the piano bench.

Mid-way to the stage the hairs on his neck began to squirm, stirred by something he couldn't put his finger on just yet. Until he'd accounted for his unease, he decided to stay close to the exit and veered left toward the bar.

He climbed on the brown leather stool and tried to catch the bartender's eye. Within ten seconds, everyone seated along the counter had relocated, leaving Mitch alone. After the mass exodus the low murmur of conversation dwindled off and the two guys on the stage stopped playing. The whole building was tomb silent. Every head in the room was bowed, all eyes trained on the floor.

Had he inadvertently crashed a private party? He glanced around, but didn't see any banners proclaiming Happy Birthday or Good Luck. But there was definitely something out of kilter. Nobody looked like trouble, if anything they were too well dressed for a neighborhood bar. Suits and ties for the men; the women in dresses. Orderly.

And Black.

The realization hit like a truck load of bricks. The familiarity of The Blue had temporarily blinded him to the fact his was the only white face in the building.

"'Scuse me, sir."

At the sound of the soft voice, Mitch nearly jumped off the bar stool. If a crystal chandelier had hung above the bar, he'd have been dangling from it about now. He gripped the edge of the counter to keep his hands from shaking and turned to the speaker.

"Yes," he croaked. His stomach had crawled into his throat.

"You be lost, sir?" asked a skinny old man about a hundred-years-old. He stood behind the bar, fidgeting and twisting a white towel nearly half to death. "You see, Sir. This…here's…a Negro…'stablishment," he pronounced each word individually, as though Mitch were an extraterrestrial recently landed and didn't speak English.

* * *

Kat lay face down on a cotton plant. Her left hand, folded beneath her naked body, was useless because of the three broken fingers. Using her good right hand, she clawed at the loose dirt, dragging herself down the long row. She hurt from the inside out, and from the outside in. But she wouldn't die in a tacky cotton patch. Ripped and torn during the brutal attack, her body screamed louder with each passing second.

"If I don't get out of this field I won't make it through the night," she whispered hoarsely. Seeking comfort, Kat reached for the boot pin from Mitch. She needed to touch her good luck totem, to draw strength from the much loved piece of jewelry. Instead of metal, her hand brushed across a bare breast and she winced. With a feather-like touch she traced the bite marks, smearing the oozing blood across her chest.

Floyd. Little Carl. Louis. The men had passed her around like some blow-up doll at a stag party. Once they used up all their testosterone, they'd beat the living hell out of her.

Anger quickly replaced her pain. And the anger that flowed within her was red. Red as the blood seeping into the Alabama soil. "You son-of-a-bitches ain't getting away with it," she told a nearby cotton boll. With determination forged from strong Rayson blood, Kat pushed up onto her knees. Light headed, due to a wicked concoction of internal injuries, concussion and blood loss, she knew better than to try and rush it. Instead, she slowly shifted from one position to another, resting between the minute movements.

Once upright, she staggered through the rows like a Saturday night drunk. Ever so often she saw double images or everything faded until only blurry shadows remained. But she refused to give in. Refused to lie down and let the white man win.

Less than six feet separated the field from the dirt road when gravity took over and pulled her to the ground. The shadows around her deepened until nothing remained but night.

"Open your eyes, honey."

The lazy butterscotch voice sounded sweet as a choir of angels. Kat felt her lips move, yet no sound emerged.

"Wake up, girl. You can't lay here in the clothes God give you."

The rumbling baritone caused Kat to twitch, as her body remembered the abuse at the hands of three men with similar voices. "Give it back," she mumbled. "It's mine."

"What you want?" Baritone asked.

"Honey, what you say?" Butterscotch whispered. "What is it you be wantin'?"

"Boot. My little boot," Kat struggled to be understood. Of all the things wrong at this moment, the missing piece of jewelry seemed the most paramount. "They stole it."

"I'll look 'round for your boots," Baritone promised. After a few seconds he said, "I don't see nothing laying on the ground. Let me turn her over, maybe she's on top of them."

"Lordy mercy, Taxi, you ain't got a lick of sense. Don't be touching that child 'till you throw something over her."

"What you expects me to use?"

"Take off your shirt," Butterscotch ordered.

"Dreama Simms, this here is my brand-new catalog shirt. Look at her, she's bleeding all over the ground."

"Maximilian Devore, you cover that girl up right now!"

"I puts this on her and it's spoiled forever."

"Taxi."

Like a summer breeze, the fabric fell across Kat, shielding her from the rapidly cooling twilight. A gentle hand smoothed the hair away from her face. Murmured words of encouragement penetrated the final wall of her foggy state. She opened her eyes, relieved to see two black faces staring at her.

"Don't hurt me," Kat whispered.

"That's all right, sugar. Just take it easy," Butterscotch cooed.

"Need him." Kat grabbed the man's hand. "Please."

"Who you be needing?" Baritone asked.

Kat's eyes filled with tears. She hurt so bad and wanted her sweet Pop to come and take her home.

"Taxi, we gotta carry this girl to town, and get Timothy to take a look."

"Hos...hospital." Kat's voice sounded foreign, husky and ragged around the edges. She must make them understand the importance of her request. "Rape kit. Evidence."

"I knows, honey, I knows. Don't be worrying 'bout that now. Me and my man will take good care of you."

Two strong arms picked Kat from the ground. She closed her eyes and rested her head against the man's bare chest, reminded of the way her Pop had carried his sleepy little girl to bed. Safe.

She felt safe.

*   *   *

Kat's eyelids fluttered open. Waves of excruciating agony pounded her body. Her thinking was clouded by bits and pieces of flotsam. What happened to her? An accident? Was Mitch okay? The last thing she remembered was riding in the patrol unit. Or was that a dream? If thoughts were tangible, hers would have been flopping around like catfish on a river bank. Annoyed by her inability to remember clearly, she waded through the confusion, sorting and categorizing the clutter in her head.

Eventually her addled brain began to cooperate. She remembered meeting two boys, Virgil and Lamar. An altercation in front of the barber shop. Miss Jane. Pink hair and a white sweater.

A white stake-bed truck.

The cotton field.

The fear engulfed her so completely she couldn't breathe. Kat struggled for air. Did they bring her here? Did the men wait beyond the closed door? Wait to rape her again? She lay paralyzed, body rigid, eyes rolling around in her head like a trapped animal.

She shifted her weight and her bare buttocks landed in a cold moist depression in the mattress. She gingerly slid her good hand underneath, and withdrew it. Blood. The towel she rested on was saturated. She became aware of the steady warm trickle. Her life force pumped from her body with each beat of her heart.

"Move, Kathleen. You gotta move," she commanded, angry with herself for being so weak. She tugged on the sun-dried sheet tucked around her body until she could sit up. Someone had swaddled her like an infant and she didn't much care for it. The restraint made her nervous. She yanked harder and her broken middle fingers, splinted with wooden tongue depressors and white adhesive tape, throbbed painfully.

She released her hold on the fabric and it fell around her waist. She wore a faded hospital gown, only the slit opened in front instead of in the back where it belonged. "Oh no," she groaned, as the smell of Ivory soap and antiseptic escaped from beneath the covers. She'd been bathed and doctored. All the evidence washed away. No rape kit, no photographs or nail scrapings. Would the district attorney bring charges without evidence?

Kat snorted in disgust at her silly delusions. Charges? What a stupid thought. Those men left her in the field on purpose. They hadn't treated her wounds or moved her to a nice clean room so she could sic the police on them. Nobody cared if a black woman got raped and beat up. She was a nonperson. A creature to be tolerated. A servant. A nigger.

They'd kidnaped her off the street in the middle of the day and abused her because they knew they could get away with it. And they made certain she suffered so there would be no misunderstanding about her place in this world. They hurt her—hurt her bad, all because her skin happened to be dark.

Even in the dim light cast by the small table lamp she could see the numerous indigo bruises decorating her arms. She separated the two sides of the gown, shuddering as the fabric rubbed across her wounds. Kat touched the bite marks on her breasts, instantaneously reliving the moment fat Louis inflicted them. Her stomach contracted and she rolled to the edge of the bed, trying to avoid soiling the pretty bedspread.

The simple movement caused hot claws to dig into her wounds, twisting and pinching until she cried out in pain. Not even the physically fit body of a twenty-nine-year old policewoman could withstand the brutality she'd experienced today.

She drifted into a restless demon filled sleep until her own screams woke her. Howls of terror bounced off the blue flowered wallpaper. Once again she fought her attackers, swinging wildly at the phantom images floating in the air. The water glass on the night table became the first casualty as it hit the hardwood floor and broke into large pieces. Desperate to escape, Kat eased her legs over the side of the bed and planted her foot squarely on a sharp edge.

The pain ignited a hidden reservoir of strength and determination. She would no longer be a victim. She intended to take control of her life and of her body once again. She hobbled across the room, a bloody trail of footprints followed close behind. She struggled with the window, trying to raise it high enough to crawl through. But no matter how hard she pushed, it wouldn't budge. The nails holding it in place allowed only three or four inches of movement. She whirled around, searching for something to break through the glass panes. Before she located anything of use, a black cloud of gnats swarmed in front of her eyes, blanking out her vision. She began to tremble and her knees buckled.

* * *

Lettie Ruth Rayson nearly jumped out of her skin when she found her patient lying in a heap on the hardwood floor. Not until she saw the terror in those honey-colored eyes did Lettie realize she still held the big cooking fork. She lowered her hand and dropped it on the floor, then kicked it out into the hall. No sense giving this half crazed girl a weapon, she thought.

"It's all right." Lettie Ruth held out her hands, palms up, in what she hoped would be interpreted as a peaceful gesture. The woman jumped as though Lettie had stabbed her with the fork. The frightened patient scrambled backwards, her bloody bare feet slipping on the polished floor.

"Nobody's looking to harm you." Lettie Ruth kept her voice soft and without emotion. She'd worked the Psychiatric Ward during nursing school and knew how little it took to send a frightened patient over the edge.

The woman continued to scoot backwards until she hit the wall. She drew the ragged old hospital gown across her trembling body and raised her head. Her eyes were clear and Lettie Ruth could see a lot of fight left inside.

"Where am I?" she demanded.

"You're at Dr. Biggers' clinic. I'm his nurse and we fixed you up." Lettie Ruth took a step toward the woman, testing the waters. If she could get closer, this whole little drama might wind itself down to nothing. Meeting no resistance, Lettie continued to edge in until she stood directly in front of the woman.

"You got a name?" Lettie Ruth asked softly.

"Kat."

"Pleased to meet you, Kat." She pointed to the bloody floor. "How's about letting me take a look at those feet of yours?"

Kat studied her for several seconds, then nodded. As she struggled to stand, Lettie Ruth stepped aside. She would hate to jinx things by moving in too fast. The woman had some difficulty, but from the stubborn set of her jaw and determined expression, Lettie Ruth figured she could make it on her own.

While Kat continued her slow and painful journey back to the bed, Lettie Ruth prepared the solution to clean her feet. She made a quick trip down the hall to the bathroom for warm water. When she returned, she found her patient seated on the edge of the bed.

Lettie Ruth smiled. She'd been right about this one, Kat still had some spunk left. She poured the pitcher of water into her Grandma's porcelain washbowl and added the hydrogen peroxide solution. She carried it over to the bed and sat cross-legged in the floor. She gently raised Kat's foot, then lowered it into the wash basin. As she used tweezers to remove the glass shards, Lettie Ruth kept up a stream of light chatter, trying to draw out her mysterious patient. Unfortunately, Kat seemed reluctant to reveal any information other than the fact she'd been attacked by three white men.

There was something so familiar about the girl, and Lettie Ruth kept staring, trying to place where she might have seen her. She finally decided since they were near the same age, they may have gone to Fisk together. Kat was a pretty thing, kind of a creamed-coffee color, with shoulder length curls and striking honey-colored eyes like Alvin's. Lettie thought she must be at least five-feet eight-inches tall, because the bed was high and she didn't have any trouble sticking her feet in the basin on the floor.

As Lettie pulled a large hunk of glass out of her heel, Kat jerked her foot back so hard her knee nearly hit her own nose.

"Sorry," Kat mumbled, eyes skipping around the room. "It's been a piss poor day."

Laughter erupted before Lettie Ruth could catch it and tie it down. Belatedly she slapped a hand across her mouth and looked apologetically at Kat. "Girl, I am so sorry."

Kat attempted a smile, dimples digging holes in her cheeks. "It's okay."

"Those big ole dimples you got are sure fire man pleasers," Lettie Ruth commented. "My little brother has dimples just like yours. Doesn't seem fair for a boy to get all the good looks in the family."

"My Pop has dimples too," Kat said. "When I was little he used to tell me they were contagious."

Lettie Ruth let out another whoop. "Jumping Jesus! I forgot all about my chicken. By the way," she shouted, as she raced out of the room, "I'm Lettie Ruth Rayson."

* * *

Kat's mouth dropped open. Lettie Ruth Rayson? Much like Humphrey Bogart's character Rick in the film, *Casablanca*, she wondered how, out of all the houses in Maceyville, she'd ended up in this one.

Some of Mitch's what-if arguments must have taken root, because Kat knew she had to distance herself from her aunt. And her father. She remembered Pop's story of the Spring he'd spent with his sister hunting ghosts. And here she was, smack dab in the middle of *that April*, which meant Alvin Rayson could walk through the door any second.

What-if, she happened to say or do the wrong thing? Something to change the previous pattern. The ripple effect from her interference could wipe out Kat's future. As soon as she could move, she had to get out of this house and away from her family immediately. Later on she'd figure out how to protect her aunt from the approaching danger.

11

Kat Templeton took a small bite of fried chicken, gagged and spit it out. This made her third attempt to eat something. Chicken, mashed potatoes, green beans. No matter what went in her mouth, it tasted nasty. It tasted like the men in the field.

At first only her hands trembled, soon the tremors spread throughout her body. She shook so hard the brass headboard rattled against the wall. The white sun-dried sheets rippled like an ocean. Memories of the attack flooded all her senses. Once again she saw the blue spring sky above as she lay on the ground. She felt the sun warmed dirt against her bare back. Smelled their sweaty bodies. Heard the grunts as they pounded and punished her body, invading every opening.

Now they leered at her from the shadowed corners. Fat Louis stood beside the dresser, her blood smeared across his mouth. Little Carl peeked out from the closet, his tobacco stained teeth glinted yellow in the semi-darkness. Floyd, in the corner by the door, unfastened his jeans.

Kat couldn't hold back the terror. Screams bubbling from a molten pool within her soul erupted with volcanic force. Her fear and rage filled the pretty blue and white bedroom, contaminating everything.

"Shhh, baby, shhh. Lettie Ruth is with you. Things gonna be fine."

Kat curled up in a ball. A tiny ball could hide from the white men. If she could only make herself small enough, they wouldn't be able to find her under all the covers.

"Kat, you come on back now. Quit screaming, child. Open up your eyes."

Cool hands gently brushed her forehead. Good hands. Black hands. "Is that you, Momma?" she asked the hands.

"No, baby, it's not your momma. It's Lettie Ruth. Come on now, open those pretty honey-brown eyes and look at me."

Kat shook her head. She didn't dare to allow even a sliver of light to enter her dark hiding place. If she opened her eyes, the men would be able to see her. The only safe place was in the dark.

*   *   *

Mitch brooded about the incident at The Blue all the way to the *white* side of Maceyville. But the fact he'd been sitting in an all-black bar wasn't the burr rubbing under his saddle. However, the discomfort his presence had generated among the Blue's regular customers kept digging under his skin. Until he'd walked in there, his understanding of Maceyville, Alabama—1963—had been naive at best.

Thanks to his grandfather Paddy O'Connor's guidance and strong influence, Mitch had learned at twelve, to never make a judgement based on a person's race. To him people were people. Some good and some bad. Color didn't carry much weight on either side. But his white skin definitely counted for something in this particular here and now. And he would be wise to remember it. This world depressed the living hell out of him.

And his present surroundings, Bubba's Julep Junction, did little to lighten his mood. He wouldn't be in this joint except The Blue, was coloreds only and off limits to a ginger haired freckle-faced Irishman.

He thought Bubba's smelled like the belly of a hog. In a childish display of temper he shoved the enormous pile of peanut shells at his elbow onto the shelf behind the bar. He didn't figure anyone would care, if they even noticed.

This whole mess was Kat's fault. Neither of them should be in this here and now. At least he didn't have to search the whole damn town for her. He knew where to go. No matter how much she denied it, the first thing she would have done is contact her aunt Lettie Ruth. All Kat's rigamarole about not interfering wasn't worth a plug nickel. He knew his stubborn, hard headed and impossible to control partner.

Disgusted, Mitch tipped his beer bottle and finished off the last lukewarm drop, then grimaced. Although he preferred draft, he'd ordered bottled because he seriously doubted Bubba washed the glasses. And instead of eating a big juicy Blue burger—with cheese and extra onions—he'd dined on bottled beer and peanuts. Of course Bubba's offered food, but eating anything in this joint that didn't come in a natural wrapper was completely out of the question.

Pissed off at the world, he swivelled around on the tattered stool and studied his fellow white patrons. The folks down at the Blue were a whole level above this crowd. This bunch looked like charter members of the redneck Welfare club. And all of them getting drunker than a skunk on a Monday night.

He noticed Bubba's well-defined sections, reminiscent of a high school cafeteria where the jocks and nerds never shared a table. The booths along the wall were staked out by old farts that probably sat in the same damn seat every day, drinking themselves into oblivion. At the middle tables sat the married guys, who spent the whole night trying to peek down the bar maid's blouse or pinch her butt every time she delivered a round. The shellacked bar, from now and until the end of time, would remain the domain of the born to raise hell crowd.

Mitch's cop instinct zinged. The trio down at the far end were a nest of vipers just looking for trouble. When they'd busted through the door earlier, carrying on and congratulating themselves on some great escapade, his skin began to tingle. The fat one seemed especially pleased with himself and kept snapping his teeth at the air like a deranged hound dog. Every time he went through his pantomime, the other two guffawed. Mitch failed to see the humor, but then again, he sat too far away to catch all the nuances of their conversation.

After several minutes of watching, curiosity got the better of him and on his return trip from the men's room, he relocated within earshot, taking the stool next to the dark-haired man.

The boys were slapping each other on the back as they boasted of their sexual prowess. "Jumping Jehosaphat," he muttered after a few minutes of eavesdropping. They thought their dicks were the greatest thing next to sliced bread.

As though picking up Mitch's disparaging thoughts, the dark-haired one reached down and massaged his crotch. "And then she says, y'all ain't got nothin' in those britches to cause me harm."

"But you sure showed that nigger's twat a thing or two, Floyd." The one with a strawberry mark on his cheek, giggled nastily.

"Hell, Little Carl, once she got a taste...I reckon she up and changed her mind." Floyd cackled, then thrust his pelvis forward several times for emphasis.

"Lots of uppity talk came out of that big hole in her face. Downright disgustin'," Little Carl said.

"Told me she's a po-lice-man," the fat one spat out, along with several good size peanut chunks.

A bad feeling washed over Mitch. He gave them his full attention. What were the odds of another black woman running around Maceyville claiming to be a cop? Even though he and Kat discussed how she would have to be on guard all the time and how to behave, he wouldn't put it past his cocky partner to get into an argument, then flash her badge.

Sometimes Kat didn't have anymore sense than God gave a turnip. But she was far from ignorant about how things worked in the sixties. She knew better than to act out. On occasion she displayed a lot of attitude, which Mitch didn't fault. A tough attitude went hand and hand with law and order. The cop's weapon of choice. However, to get her back up and flash an attitude in this segregated racist society *would be* dumb.

"A nigger woman cop," Louis repeated, shaking his head.

"That's a bald face piece of shit," Floyd snorted.

"Ain't never gonna be no nigger cops in Maceyville," Little Carl declared.

"Well, boys, if that cunt wants to play cop, she can frisk me any ole day," Floyd said.

"Appears to me she done frisked your Johnson," Louis giggled.

"That porch monkey bitch can…" Floyd stopped mid-brag when he noticed Mitch's interest. "Hey boy, this conversation's private," he said.

Mitch didn't respond, instead continued to stare into the mirror. He would kick his own butt if he could reach it. He'd been thinking how stupid it would be for Kat to get involved with this bunch and by jingo he'd stepped in it. For God's sake, a stranger in a bar never trespassed on this type of bull session. In all fairness, Floyd et al weren't broadcasting their conquests to the world. They'd kept their voices pitched low and if Mitch hadn't gotten nosy and moved from the opposite end of the bar, he'd been none the wiser.

"Did you see how those dimples were working me?" Louis said, unaware of the brief exchange between Floyd and the ginger-haired man.

"Shut it up, Louis," Floyd growled. He took a deep swallow of beer and redirected his attention to the interloper. "You got something on your mind?"

Mitch shook his head but didn't make eye contact. "No harm, no foul," he muttered, activating his best Elvis Presley drawl. He figured it was a whole lot safer to sound like The King of Rock and Roll than a Pennsylvania farm boy.

Floyd's hand landed heavily on his shoulder. "Best tend your own business."

"The whole damn world's got a shit load of business what needs tending," Mitch replied, allowing alcoholic cadences to coat his words. He could gather more information faking a drunken stupor than by out and out confrontation.

If Floyd believed Mitch had partaken of the devil's brew one too many times, he might back off, or at least relax his guard.

Floyd studied him for a few seconds then smiled, revealing crooked tobacco stained teeth. "Sure buddy, you go on tending to the world."

Mitch nodded, and for effect, swayed a bit on the stool. "I got me lots of business."

"Had some business ourselves earlier today. Right boys?" Floyd asked his friends.

"A whole plate full," Little Carl said.

Louis snorted and a nose full of beer sprayed the counter. "And it tasted like a creamy chocolate pie."

"Not dark chocolate, mind you," explained Little Carl, "creamy milk chocolate."

"I like chocolate pie." Mitch's words came out as though his mouth was filled with mush.

"Git this boy some pie!" Floyd shouted. The other two joined in the chorus.

"Yeah," Mitch added. "A big fat piece."

Little Carl leaned across Floyd and whispered to Mitch. "Our piece wasn't big and fat. But it sure was juicy."

"Juicy?" Mitch contorted his face into a mask of confusion.

"She was wet and ready," Little Carl confided.

"Another round for us and our new pal," Floyd shouted to the barkeep. He stood on the rungs of the stool and reached across the bar so he could steal a fistful of maraschino cherries. As he moved backwards, his shirt pocket snagged on the spigot and a copper and silver jewelry piece clattered onto the counter.

Mitch scooped up the little boot. He rubbed his thumb across the star-shaped spur, blinking back hot tears. Any lingering doubts regarding the 'chocolate pie's' identity went down the toilet. He'd given this pin to Kat on their first anniversary as partners, telling her to use it to kick the law and order door wide open. She'd worn his silly little gift every day since then, even when in uniform she pinned it to the inside the blouse. When asked why, she laughed and said 'Because a girl never knows when she'll need to kick a little ass'.

Mitch rested his head on the bar and closed his eyes. He gripped the pin so tightly the metal cut into his palm. His temper boiled just below the surface and he fought the urge to rip these guys into a thousand bloody hunks of flesh.

The ugly knowledge that all their dirty talk had been about Kat crawled around in his belly.

When the beers arrived, Little Carl raised his in a toast. "Here's to that piece I ate this fine spring day."

"You betcha," said Louis. He took a long pull from the bottle then belched loudly.

"Here's to our very own pussy," Floyd crowed. "And I'm ready for seconds."

Mitch's freckles popped out on his face like a bad case of measles. His eyes flashed blue lightening. In one fluid motion, he knocked Floyd off the stool and sent him sailing over the tables in the middle of the room. In a split second, Little Carl and Louis were all over him like a rain squall. Mitch shrugged off their blows like so many drops of water. It would take a whole lot more than these ineffectual little assholes to do any damage.

Bubba's clientele, at least the ones that weren't knocked out of their seats by Floyd's head-first landing, grabbed their beers and side stepped the fracas.

Too stupid to give up, the three kept coming after Mitch. As a single, or in a pack, he didn't care. Time after time his knuckles connected. Blood speckles decorated his shirt and the nearby walls.

Peripherally he saw the bartender raise the baseball bat and the beginning of its downward arc before the room faded to black.

12

APRIL 02—TUESDAY—1:00 A.M.

Shapes. Mitch concentrated on focusing, but similar to extreme close-up photographs, all he could initially identify were the individual features. A pair of dark eyes. A twitching nose. A pair of whiskers. He blinked at the enormous rat sitting on his chest. The creature displayed equal interest in the human. Since his visitor appeared more curious than contemplating his next snack, Mitch rolled onto his side allowing the furry creature to slide off his chest.

No wonder I woke up with a King Kong size rat squatting on my chest, Mitch thought, as the rodent scurried away. Bubba's store room resembled a trash dump. The corner where the rat vanished was a heap of rubbish and used food containers. Overflowing waste bins perfumed the air.

Mitch pressed a palm to the floor, the first step in rising from his prone position, and felt the rough texture of wool. He rolled his head to the side, faded stenciled letters: USAF, hugged the ragged edges of the blanket. He wondered who'd been thoughtful enough to throw it over the filthy floor before depositing an unconscious James Mitchell. That same thoughtful whoever, also cleaned him out. His pockets were turned inside out, what cash he'd carried long since gone. He congratulated himself on having had the foresight to leave his police badge and gun at the Yellowhammer Inn. He didn't mind losing a few bucks, but having Floyd's wild bunch in possession of his department issued weapon and identification would be worse.

The door creaked open and a shadowed face appeared in the crack. "You doin' all right, boss?"

Mitch tensed, expecting a re-enactment of the earlier brawl. To his relief, a tall muscular black man around his own age slipped in the room. Mitch tried to speak, but his throat was so dry words were impossible. The man knelt beside the blanket, then raised Mitch's head so he could drink from a glass.

The water tasted cool and sweet, bathing his parched vocal cords. "Thanks," he croaked.

"You best be getting on out of here," the man advised. "Them boys ain't too happy with the licking you give out."

Mitch chuckled. He cleared his throat and allowed Elvis to enter the building once more. "The licking I gave out?" the King drawled. "You better take another look, buddy, I'm the only one flat on his back in here."

"That's only cause Mr. Bubba hit you over the head."

Mitch smiled at the use of mister and Bubba in combination.

"Before he done that, you was winning," the man praised.

"No, before that I was stupid."

The man stood and brushed at the knees of his dark trousers. "I thought you be real brave to call 'em out on account of that woman."

Mitch propped himself up on his elbows so he could see the man's face. "You know who they were bragging about?"

The man dropped his eyes and shuffled backwards a few feet. His expression indicating he clearly wished he'd kept his mouth shut. Odds on Mr. Bubba wouldn't hesitate to beat the living crap out of this good Samaritan for bringing Mitch a glass of water. He could only guess at the punishment for talking about rape.

This looked like a good time to hit the trail before he did any more damage. Mitch didn't have any more business being in this place and time than his partner did. And speaking of his partner, he seriously doubted those boys got much of a chance to do any real harm. They may have stolen her boot pin, but nothing more. Kat was capable of defending herself. She possessed the moves and skills needed to send them to the nearest hospital. He must have been suffering from time-travel lag to have considered the possibility she could ever be a victim. She would never get into that kind of situation.

What should he do? Realistically, he figured he'd be of more use keeping Alvin Rayson company until Kat returned than wandering around like a fool in 1963. There was no way in hell of finding Kat before the 5:20 A.M. door slammed shut. So it looked like he'd be traveling home alone.

I don't have anything to worry about, he told himself, she's fine. As his brain argued with his emotions, an early morning conversation with his Pennsylvania grandfather, James Patrick O'Connor, interjected itself into the middle of the whole discussion. His grandfather had been as honest as the day was long, and not given to casual talk. When he did speak, Mitch had learned to listen.

On that particular morning they'd been in the barn, ready to start the milking, when old Paddy kicked his three-legged stool over to Mitch and pointed, meaning take a seat...

"I hear you had a bit of trouble, son."
"Don't know what you mean." *Although he knew Paddy was referring to yesterday's schoolyard brawl, his twelve-year-old brain believed he could outfox his grandfather.*
"I meant school."
"School's going fine, Grampa Paddy. I got a B on my—"
"You gave Peter Toland a split lip."
"That's a damn lie."
"James, I want to know why you jumped him."
"He called Samuel a nigger."
"And he called you a nigger lover."
Mitch jumped on the stool so he could stand eye to eye with the old man. "I ain't no nigger lover, Grandpa Paddy. Daddy says coloreds ain't no damn good."
"Your daddy says a lot of things. Are you in agreement with him?"
"Course I am. He's my daddy and he says coloreds are God's trash."
"What about Samuel? Is he God's trash?"
"Well..."
"Or is Samuel your friend?"
"He's a nigger!"
"Didn't you get into a fight because Peter Toland called Samuel a nigger?"
"Yes."
"But now you're saying coloreds are no good? That they are God's trash?"
"Well, Daddy said—"
"If you believe Billy Lee, why did you defend Samuel?"
"Toland needed a beating."
"The only reason for the fight was because you dislike Toland?"
"He's a jackass."
"What he called Samuel had nothing to do with your actions?"
He stuck his chin out. "Nope."
Grandfather Paddy pulled a second stool over and sat beside Mitch. "So you're Samuel's fair weather friend?"
"What's a fair weather friend?"
"A person that befriends another only if they have nothing to lose."
"Oh."

"So, is Samuel your friend?"

The question, asked by this old grandfather wearing shabby work clothes and a straw milking hat, revealed a new truth to the twelve-year-old. Mitch nodded. "He already cost me one after school detention," he grumbled. "And I suppose there'll be another one. Toland doesn't know how to keep his mouth shut."

"Are you saying Samuel is your friend?"

"Yeah. And I suppose that makes me a nigger lover." Speaking the ugly words aloud finally freed him from the racist cage Billy Lee erected around him. The walls, built of slurs and epitaphs, crumbled.

And now, this situation with Kat reminded him of Samuel and Peter Toland all over again. He could play it safe, temporarily push their relationship into the closet and turn out the light. A fair weather friend.

Or he could stop screwing around and do something.

His feet tangled in the blanket when he tried to stand and the man grabbed his arm, saving Mitch from cracking his head on the concrete floor. "Thanks," Mitch paused, how could he talk to this guy if he didn't know his name? "What's your name?"

"What you want to know for?" The man looked ready to rabbit.

"Because I find it difficult to carry on a conversation with a fellow unless I know who he is."

He nodded. "Name's Maximilian Devore, boss. But they call me Taxi."

Mitch wanted to asked how he'd evolved from being a Maximilian to a Taxi, but this didn't seem an opportune moment. "Pleased to meet you, Taxi." He held out his hand. After several indecisive seconds, Taxi briefly touched his hand, not a shake exactly, but a start. "Folks call me Mitch."

"Pleased to make your acquaintance, Mister Mitch."

"The woman that Floyd and the others were bragging about, could be a good friend of mine," he said, hoping it was a local woman rather than his partner. He shook his head, ashamed for wishing ill will on someone he didn't know.

He read the disbelief in Taxi's eyes before the words soaked into the walls. The statement must have smelled like a pasture full of cow manure. How many white men in Alabama openly admitted to a close friendship with a black woman? In 1963, social exchanges between adult whites and blacks fell in two distinct categories: nonexistent or clandestine. And Mitch's admission had shattered any possibility of a clandestine relationship into a million pieces. Another mistake.

How many errors in judgement were necessary before he learned how to behave in this society? He should have known better than to plant his butt on a stool in a *colored's only* bar. And he sure as hell shouldn't drag a black man into the middle of this mess.

But he needed information, and Taxi held onto it like an ace in the hole. Mitch knew he could turn on the cop, talk tough and shove him around a little. Under those conditions, Taxi would talk, or clam up so tight it would take a pry bar to open his mouth. Mitch couldn't afford the latter. If Kat had met up with the three goons in the other room, she could have been seriously injured. It would be smarter to find another tactic, something besides rough and gruff, to convince Taxi to trust him enough to speak freely. And he better be real convincing or his source would back completely out of the door.

"My friend's name is Kathleen, but I call her Kat. See this?" He opened his hand to reveal the cowboy boot pin. "I gave it to her. And that son-of-a-bitch Floyd had it in his pocket. I know he took it by force, because she'd never give it up voluntarily." Mitch blinked rapidly, clearing the moisture from his eyes. Pictures of what Floyd had so vividly described intruded into his thoughts.

Taxi reached out and took the pin from his hand. He rubbed his thumb across the copper and silver boot. "She asked 'bout a boot when me and my woman carried her into town," he said softly.

Mitch's stomach clamped down on his beer and peanuts as he struggled to overcome the nausea. "Where did you take her?"

"Cain't say."

"Can't say...or won't say?" Anger sparkled like ice crystals in Mitch's eyes. Finally accepting the probability Kat *was* the victim of a rape, he had neither the time nor inclination to baby Maximilian Devore. He wanted straight answers.

Taxi backed away, shaking his head. "I won't be mixing in a white man and a Negro woman's affair. Besides, your kind don't never go visiting in the east Hollow."

Mitch smelled the sickly sweet odor of fear emanating from Taxi, and immediately shoved his impatient anger away. The strong-arm approach would only drive him further away, and without his help Mitch didn't have a prayer of locating Kat.

"Taxi, she's my friend," he said, turning down the pressure. "And after the ruckus, I'm pretty sure those fools will be looking for her."

"She's in a good place. Ain't no harm goin' to come her way."

"Don't bet your paycheck on it. They aren't completely stupid, they know she's a star witness for the prosecution."

"No need to worry on that count, Mr. Mitch. She knows better, she won't be talking to nobody about them."

"Kat isn't like the other women in the east Hollow. She's…well, she's more progressive."

"She still be colored."

"We can stand here until the cows come home and never reach middle ground on this point," Mitch said tiredly. After only a few hours in the old South, he longed to shove his fist in the face of the nearest good ole boy. "The bottom line is that I need help. Your help."

"I done told you, I cain't be taking you over there."

"I don't want you to take me anywhere." Mitch pointed to the pin in Taxi's hand. "Will you give that to her? Ask Kat where she got it. Then ask if she wants to see me. Can you do that? Please. She's very important to me."

Taxi took his time answering. "I reckon I can ask a couple of question, Mr. Mitch."

Mitch smiled, getting word to Kat was half the battle. Now he needed to find out where Taxi stashed her. And since the *black* east Hollow appeared to be off limits, he would require an escort.

"What if I wait for you to bring me her answer at the bus station?" he suggested, knowing he couldn't stay in Bubba's store room. The depot would have both a colored and a white waiting room. Neutral ground. Taxi could freely come and go without being questioned.

"I suppose that's a good a place as any," Taxi said.

13

Taxi Devore got as far as the Webster Avenue Freedom Methodist Church before his hands got to shaking so hard he couldn't hold onto the wheel and had to curb the De Soto. He sorely wished somebody would come along and tell him what to do. It seemed to him that he'd been making this same wish over and over again his whole life. He'd not so much been raised, as growed up, and nobody much cared how. His momma ran off early on, and from then on his daddy moved from one girlfriend to the next, leaving Taxi and his seven sisters to get along on their own. But he always wished for a shove in the right direction.

Tonight he'd opened a door on a stinky swamp filled with all sorts of dangers. What kind of a colored girl got herself mixed up with a white man? She ought to know enough to stick with her own kind. Helping Mr. Mitch find his woman would bring the devil right down on top of Maximilian Devore. Yes sir, right on top.

"What am I doing?" he asked. While waiting for an answer, he picked at the loose skin around his thumb. "Should of known better, Maximilian," he mumbled around the thumb in his mouth. "Got to stay clear of white boy business. Cause the only thing to come out of that's my Negro ass in a sling. No doubt 'bout it. No sir, no doubt."

He wiped his thumb on his trousers then pulled the shiny little boot from his pocket. The street lights reflected off the delicate squiggles on the copper toe. He couldn't help but wonder why Mr. Mitch gave a colored girl such a fine gift. Must be for a reason. Most likely a bedroom reason. Shoot, he and Dreama Simms had been together for close to a year, and all he gave her was that pair of red glass earrings from the five and dime. And that was for her birthday.

The longer he held the boot, the more it seemed to kick him in the back of his brain. "All the banging in my skull reminds me of a surly jackass that wants out of the barn stall," he muttered, rubbing his aching head. "Not gonna involve myself," he told the boot. "The woman's doing just fine at Dr. Tim's clinic. Lettie Ruth knows all about nursing the sick."

Besides, if Dreama found out about Mr. Mitch she'd pitch a fit to beat all. She didn't take kindly to Negroes that took up with whites. Male or female. Ever since those boys got a hold of her several months back, she couldn't see the good in white folks no more. Taxi had friends living on both sides of town, and no matter what Dreama wanted, he wouldn't stop seeing any of them.

Taxi shoved the jewelry piece in the glove box, thinking maybe if he kept it a little distance away the jackass in his head would quit kicking. No sense getting involved in other peoples woes. When he didn't turn up at the depot, Mr. Mitch would figure his girlfriend didn't want nothing more to do with him. And that would be the end of it.

"Nope, ain't gonna drive to no Greyhound depot this time of morning," he said. With the decision under his belt, Taxi cranked up the car engine and headed to The Blue. Dreama ought to be in the middle of her second show now.

* * *

THE BLUE

Hard as he tried, Taxi couldn't shake his mind free of Mr. Mitch's face. It kept pestering him like a white ghost floating all around the room. He couldn't let it go. Might be because of the way the man had looked when he said her name, *'Kathleen, but I call her Kat'*. Or the awful sadness in his eyes when he said, *'Please'*.

The woman from the field was on the mend, he was sure of it. Dr. Tim and Lettie Ruth had patched her up good. And no need to worry about Mr. Floyd finding her in the east Hollow. Shoot fire, those boys wouldn't waste their time searching for a beat up Negro girl.

But when he thought about the brawl in Bubba's bar, he just had to smile. Whoopee, but Mr. Mitch ripped into those miserable excuses for people. Taxi had listened to their bragging and seen them puff out their chests like scrawny roosters fresh out of the hen house, wondering about the kind of men that felt pride in taking a woman by force.

Thinking about all this business didn't do him no good. He couldn't go getting soft in the head about a white man. This Negro intended to mind his own *p*'s and *q*'s.

Taxi directed his attention to Dreama. His beautiful angel sat at the piano, in a pretty pink spotlight. The green dress hugged her curves something bad. He got short of breath thinking about what hid underneath all that silky material.

He whistled and cheered as Dreama tossed her head and made the old piano sing. She pounded the keys so hard, all her parts started wiggling and jiggling. As she beat out a hot rendition of *Bill Bailey*, she caught his eye and gave him the high sign. Four quick nods meant one more song and she'd be heading out the back door.

His woman had a real problem about folks seeing them together, which Taxi did not understand. They were of both well over the legal age for drinking and for doing what men and women did to each other. And they'd done it all. But Dreama still refused to hold his hand in public.

Crazy woman. Last week she near ripped his arm off when his hand slid a little too low during a slow dance. You can bet he'd kept a safe distance ever since, it would be hard for a one-armed man to find work. Of course, once they got in his car later on, Dreama nearly jumped his bones in the front seat. It made no sense.

Maybe he ought to buy her something pretty like that shiny boot pin. Could be she might treat him a little better. Or give him a kiss on the dance floor.

*   *   *

Dreama Simms struggled to keep her stage show upbeat, but to her ears, the music sounded flat and lifeless. The Blue crowd didn't seem to notice her lackluster performance, clapping and hollering after each number. But she felt the difference.

Trying to chase away her low blue funk, she jumped into *Bill Bailey*. Unable to fully concentrate she felt it would be best to stick with a number she could pick out in her sleep.

The cause of all this distraction was the wounded little bird she and Taxi found at sundown. All beat up and bloody. Barely alive when they'd stumbled across her in the field. Dreama had cradled her like a newborn babe all the way to Timothy Biggers clinic, worried sick a body hurt so bad wouldn't make it into town alive.

Dreama had been hit plenty in her 30 years, starting in with her daddy—who'd been real big on slapping the whole family around. And a few men since those days hadn't been shy about using their fists, but she'd never been hurt that bad. Even when she'd dangled from that tree branch. And those awful bite marks. Only animals wearing people clothes could do something so cruel. Mean, low down men dogs done that. And they liked it.

She gave her head a shake to get rid of the ugly pictures inside and let her hands kind of dance across the keys. Thank God it was near closing time. Sometimes two o'clock in the morning came way too slow. As soon as she finished, she'd get Taxi to carry her to the clinic and check on the little bird. More than anything she wanted to talk to the woman and get the low down on the who's and why's of her beating. Dreama Simms did not intend to let this crime go by like so many others.

For several months she'd been collecting statements and sworn affidavits from colored victims and witnesses of white attacks. She sent these reports to the Alabama State Police, the FBI and two Congressmen. Her carefully written accounts of the brutality inflicted on Southern Negroes made it harder for the local law boys to claim nothing happened. In addition, a friend that worked for a newspaper up North printed them too. Newspaper accounts of the goings on made good reading all over the country. Any day now another batch would be ready for the mail and she wanted to include the information about the woman from the field.

* * *

The Yellowhammer Inn had opened for business in the 1860s. A handprinted sign in the lobby explained how the Inn had been so named to honor the Alabama soldiers who'd fought and died in the War Between the States. These men had trimmed their gray Confederate uniforms in yellow, which resembled the wing patches of the yellowhammer woodpecker. A second sign explained the woodpecker was the state bird and source of Alabama's nickname: The Yellowhammer State.

All that might be true, but in Mitch's estimation, the Yellowhammer Inn was not a state hotel. He conceded the room did have slightly better furnishings than his own apartment, at least here the mattress sat on a box spring and frame instead of the floor.

Other than the goose egg on the back of his head, the free for all in the bar left him no worse for the wear. He didn't even have a black eye or split lip to prove to Kat how heroically he'd fought for her honor. Without tangible evidence, she wouldn't believe his magnificent victory. At least he'd been victorious until Bubba cold cocked him from behind. Maybe he should leave that part out.

The Yellowhammer Inn was two miles from the Greyhound depot, and Mitch was acutely aware of the clock ticking toward the 5:20 A.M. window for their departure. Without a car, he couldn't waste much time. He quickly stripped of the bloodied shirt and jeans and showered off the debris collected during his eventful visit to Bubba's Julep Junction. Luckily, he'd stuck an extra shirt in his gym bag. He'd chosen the plaid short sleeve sport shirt because he didn't think it wouldn't mark him as a tourist—or time-traveler. He hadn't thought to bring another pair of jeans, so he settled for shaking the dust off. His key ring flew across the room and he jammed it back in his pocket, hoping he wouldn't loose it thirty-seven years in the past.

The only part of his ensemble that worried him were the Millennium Special Nike athletic shoes. The city council had ordered a pair for each officer in the department as a thank you for a job well done. Of course, that occurred before the Red and Black team's fiasco with newspaper editor Justin Kolsky at the music recital.

He looked down at his feet and grimaced. Too late now. Fancy leather athletic shoes certainly weren't available thirty-seven years ago. Hopefully, people would be too sleepy to scrutinize his footwear.

He retrieved his Maceyville police I.D. and the Smith & Wesson .38-caliber revolver he'd wedged between the slats and cloth sheeting on the underside of the box springs. He strapped the ankle holster in place and positioned his weapon. After the run in with Floyd and his pals, he felt a little extra leverage might be called for in future encounters. He knew they'd seek him out, demand retribution to rebuild shattered egos. The when and where yet to be determined.

He glanced at his watch. He must be at the depot when Taxi arrived. If Mitch wasn't standing on the doorstep, the man would disappear forever. He grabbed his gym bag and headed out the door. If things worked out, he and Kat would cross over in three hours, no more tinkering around in the past for either of them.

* * *

Dreama pulled out of Taxi's arms and smoothed the wrinkles from her green silk dress. His hands were busier than a whole herd of octopuses, she thought, can't let my guard down one second without having to peel some part of him off my body.

"Taxi, you stop that," she scolded, slapping his hands away. "And cool off, boy, I got important business to tend to right now."

He groaned and leaned his head back against the headrest. "You ain't a kind woman, Dreama Simms. Get a man all heated up then say, I got something important to do. Ain't Christian."

"Start this car and drive me over to the clinic," she ordered. "I want to see Lettie Ruth and talk to that woman we picked up."

"You in the business of giving out orders all a sudden?"

"No, I'm in the business of knocking you up aside your head if you don't get this car moving. I told you, I got to talk to her. I can't be playing with you all night."

He rolled his eyes and folded his arms across his chest. "I been hearing enough talk about her the past few hours. I ain't a happy man, Dreama. No sir, ain't happy at all."

"What you mean hearing talk? Who you been around?"

"Don't get your tail feathers all riled up."

Dreama turned sideways in the seat and took a good look at his face. Taxi was a sweet man but he couldn't lie worth anything. And right this second her man was lying up a storm. She just knew he'd been flapping his gums—or heard somebody else flapping theirs—about the woman. And she intended to find out what had been said.

"Maximilian Devore…" she paused for dramatic effect, allowing the unspoken threat to hang in the air. "What did you hear? Is some low down going around telling uglies about her? Or did you spread the gossip yourself?"

Taxi's fingers beat out an agitated rhythm on the steering wheel. "Some fellas over at Bubba's were shootin' off, that's all. Not me. No, ma'am, not me."

"Who then?" The words burst out with enough force to cause him to flinch. Dreama scooted closer and rubbed his neck. "Baby, I'm not mad at you," she crooned. "Just need to know who's been saying what."

"White boys," he mumbled. "Bunch of no good white trash bragging on their deeds."

Dreama's stomach churned. She didn't care for the scared feeling running high speed inside her. White boys, Taxi said. White boys with an 's' on the tail end, meant more than one. Letting folks know about the rape would surely open the cellar door on all sorts of payback time for Dreama Simms. And now, she had to worry about the trouble coming from three different directions on account of that 's'. "You for sure they were talking about our wounded little bird?"

"One hundred per cent for sure."

"Out in the open?"

Taxi nodded. "They didn't give much mind to who all might be listening. And believe me, they should of cared." Taxi chuckled.

Her fur stood on end and her tail feathers twitched when she heard his low chuckle. "You find their actions amusing, Mr. Devore?"

"No," he said, raising his hands to fend off expected blows. "They ain't the least bit funny."

Dreama fluffed her hair and stared out the front windshield. Her patience, already frazzled from the sunset discovery gave out. "Take me to Lettie Ruth," she said through gritted teeth. If it had been winter instead of Spring, he could have chipped ice off the car roof.

14

DR. BIGGERS' CLINIC

"She won't talk," Lettie Ruth told Dreama Simms and Taxi Devore, as she came down the stairs.

"I thought she be talking to you by now," Dreama said, following her friend into the waiting area.

Lettie Ruth made herself comfortable in an overstuffed arm chair. Dreama stretched out on the sofa and Taxi leaned against the door jamb, looking decidedly uncomfortable.

"It's to be expected," Lettie Ruth explained. "She'll come around in a few days. Until then, I want to keep her calm and quiet. Give her a secure feeling."

"And that means no men company," Dreama said, pointing an accusing finger at Taxi lingering in the entry hall.

"Woman," Taxi sputtered. "I got no need to see her. I only came along cause you made me."

Lettie Ruth smiled at him. "You're a good man, Taxi. I'm certain Dreama didn't mean you specific. Did you?" She glared at the other woman. Although she and Dreama had been best friends since they were children playing in the streets of New Orleans, Lettie never much cared for her mean streak. The girl's tongue was sharp enough to cut through a beef steak, and she used it on a regular basis. But picking on Taxi for absolutely no reason seemed vexatious.

Dreama looked shamed. "No, I know you wouldn't harm her, Taxi honey. Come on over here," she said, patting an empty space on the sofa.

He went over and took a seat beside her. "I would never do that. I seen what those boys done to her." Taxi shook his head. "shames me to be a man."

"You is a good man, Maximilian Devore," Lettie Ruth repeated. "And we all know there's a whole wide world of difference between you and them."

Dreama nodded in agreement and climbed into his lap. "And I'm sorry to be gettin' on you like that. But I do believe she'd be better off without seeing people that need to shave first thing every morning."

"You feel that way too, Lettie Ruth?" Taxi asked. "Feel Kat don't need to see no man?"

His eyes seemed to be asking another question, but for the life of her, Lettie Ruth couldn't figure out what he wanted to know. What difference could it make to him whether or not her patient wanted to see any men?

Suddenly Taxi jumped up, dumping Dreama on the floor as he crawled over the back of the sofa. He peeked between the Venetian blind slats. "Turn off the lights!" he yelled. "Get 'em off now."

The women didn't argue with him. Dreama scrambled to her feet and Lettie Ruth popped out of the chair. They ran in opposite directions and soon the only illumination came from the headlights of two vehicles idling in the driveway.

"What's going on?" Lettie Ruth whispered, stepping to where she could see out the window. "Who's outside?" A truck had pulled up close to the building and a dark colored sedan sat cockeyed, half on the driveway and half on the grass yard. Cat calls and unintelligible shouted words filtered through the partially open clinic windows.

"It's those men from the bar," Taxi told her. "The ones who hurt Kat."

"How you know that?" challenged Dreama, peeking around his stooped shoulder. "And how come you know her name?"

"I knows, Dreama. I just knows. Don't be asking me questions all the time."

"You think they'll come in here?" asked Lettie Ruth. Her heart had stopped beating several minutes ago and she'd probably keel over dead any second.

Taxi shook his head. "They ain't drunk enough yet."

"What do they want with us?" Lettie Ruth asked.

"They want to scare us into keeping our peace," Dreama said. She slipped her arms around Taxi's middle and leaned her cheek against his back. "They want to make good and certain we don't tell anyone important what happened in that field."

"You sure called that one right, honey," he said. He reached around and patted her behind. "They've been forced out into the daylight and the boys are getting skittish."

"What are they up to now?" asked Lettie Ruth. She could see three shadowy figures moving around beside the truck. They took several steps toward the clinic door, then backed off. After a low voiced discussion, they threw several empty bottles against the sign out front then jumped back in the pickup.

"That'll be it for now," Taxi assured them. He let the blinds slip into place as the vehicles squealed around the corner. He turned and took Dreama by the shoulders. "You stay here with Lettie Ruth. I got business to see about."

"What kind of business you got at this hour of the morning?" Dreama demanded. "It's going on four o'clock, sun ain't even up."

"Got to make a run over to the depot. You two stay inside and keep the lights low until we get back." Taxi gave Dreama a quick kiss and hurried out the back door.

"Did he say *we?*" Lettie Ruth asked.

Dreama shrugged. "I ain't got no idea what that man is talking about."

* * *

"All right, Lord," Taxi prayed as he pulled away from Dr. Biggers clinic. "No need for you to hit me over the head. I planned on going to see Mr. Mitch. Just soon as I got Dreama settled down."

Taxi clucked his tongue. It didn't do him one bit of good to lie. That Man upstairs had all the answers. Knew everything about everybody. He knew, that Maximilian Devore planned on leaving Mr. Mitch to see out the rest of his days in the Greyhound waiting room. But it appeared the Man didn't much care for that. He wanted Taxi to get his butt shot off. Yes sir, that's exactly what He wanted.

"Is this gonna make you happy, Lord? Watching this colored man drive this old beat up green De Soto all the way to the depot in the early morning hours while a pickup full of whites is out looking for him?" He cocked his head, and could swear he heard heavenly laughter. "That's what I figured. Well, I'm for sure hauling my black butt cross town to fetch him. And why? So that white man can bust in on Lettie Ruth and Dreama and scare the dickens out of them. And you know how my woman's going to like that. She won't be speaking to me, or doing anything else to me, for a long time. Yes sir, a long, long time."

As he pulled into the back of the depot, Taxi realized he'd never asked Kat about the cowboy pin or seein' Mr. Mitch. His whole story could be nothing but lies. "If I'm dead wrong, and he belonged to that other bunch, the ones that raped her...oh Lordy."

* * *

GREYHOUND BUS DEPOT—4:00 A.M.

Mitch wiggled around on the hard wooden bench until the feeling returned to his lower half. The boarding area left a lot to be desired when it came to comfort, cleanliness and odor control. In fact, it smelled as though someone had taken a good long piss underneath his bench. Mitch guessed he should be grateful that's all they'd left behind.

After spending the better part of two hours staring at the sign mounted on the wall: WHITE ONLY he decided it was the stupidest thing he'd ever seen. What made some people so afraid? Did they really think black skin pigmentation would rub off if they got too close? Did African-Americans carry a contagious disease, and the only way to protect yourself was by total segregation?

If that was true, then all the time he'd spent riding in a patrol car next to Kat it was a wonder his skin hadn't turned pitch black by now. Or, on the flip side, it's a wonder Kat wasn't white and freckled. The mental picture of their altered appearances made him smile.

The steady tapping on the glass partition drew his attention to the far side of the room. Taxi, looking ready to bust a gut, stood on the opposite side of the wall in the COLORED ONLY area.

Mitch's heart did flip-flops when he saw him and a thousand watt smile lit his freckled face. He glanced at the clock mounted above the ticket counter: 4:00 A.M.. He and Kat still had one hour and twenty minutes to get to Park Street before the door closed.

He hurried toward the dividing wall, but Taxi waved his arms warning him off. He reminded Mitch of the workers on the airport tarmac as they moved the planes in and out of the gates. Once again he'd come close to making another major gaffe. Why couldn't he get it through his thick Irish skull, white and black neither sat together or spoke publicly. He nodded in understanding and an obviously relieved Taxi motioned him outside.

* * *

"You and Alvin still messing around with that ghost business?" Dreama asked softly. She and Lettie Ruth had moved to the second floor after Taxi left and now sat on wooden chairs outside Kat's bedroom. At the moment the patient appeared to be sleeping soundly, but as a precaution, they'd left the door open in case she awoke.

Lettie Ruth shuddered. "Those stories folks been telling me make the hairs on my neck stand up."

"You believe in ghosts?"

"Not when all this started, but I tell you, girl, I'm about to the place where I gotta say yes I do."

"You ever seen one?"

"No, but when Delores Townson was a girl a ghost called her on the telephone. Told her she ought not to go on a school bus trip. Said it would end bad."

Dreama's eyes widened and she rubbed at the goose bumps on her arms. "What happened?" she whispered.

"She stayed home and the bus crashed."

"Oh my Lord. That must've scared that sweet child."

"Maybe. All I know is she says she ain't never going out to no cemetery for funerals ever again. Not ever."

"Speaking of Delores, she still studying teaching?"

"Been at Fisk this term. She come home for Easter and Alvin got a look. I think he's got his eye on her. Caught him sneaking peeks during choir practice on Thursday. He's gonna miss her, she and her family are going to New Orleans tomorrow, to see family." Lettie chuckled.

"Oh I got to get on him about her. Is that good looking brother of yours here?" Dreama asked.

"Brother's sleeping down at the church." Lettie Ruth smiled. "Did you know he's preaching for the first time this morning, at the county wide Ladies Prayer Meeting? He hasn't been in a pulpit since his Army Chaplin days."

"I think he mentioned it the other day. He'll do good, got fire in his voice." Dreama's brow wrinkled. "You say he's sleeping at the church?"

"Alvin and Timothy both been sleeping down there for the past week. Pastor Gordon's been getting threats from somebody saying they's gonna torch Freedom Methodist. It's getting so scary tonight Timothy carried that big ole M-1 rifle along."

Dreama shook her head. "Been way too many fires this month. Gladys Pauley, Dilmer Richards, Alice Carpenter, Mattie De Carlo. The list is long, Lettie Ruth. A lot of good people lost forever."

"I fear there will be more fallen soldiers before our battle is done. And now poor old Tupelo Josephs," Lettie said. "They found him in that little shack of his out by his garden last night all burned up. I heard he mixed it up with some white boys down by the Waffle Shop."

"It don't pay to get into any kind of business with white folks today," Dreama said. "You know, me and Taxi saw that house explode up on Riverside and Azalea last month."

"Dilmer's place?"

"Uh-huh. A sweet, sweet man that never hurt a soul. Pastor Gordon's feels they went after Dilmer on account of the meetings up in Birmingham."

"What meetings?" Lettie Ruth asked.

"Dr. King and the Southern Christian Leadership Conference called meetings to train a bunch of folks about nonviolent protesting."

"About that protesting, I know I promised to take part in the Birmingham lunch counter sit-in tomorrow. But with Kat here and all..."

"You ain't backing out now? Alvin's gonna drive and I already put our names on the paper at the church."

"What paper?"

"The one folks sign before going to a protest. You have to sign back in when it's all over. That way we keep track of everybody. If someone don't sign in at the end, we go looking for them. And they expect you and me in Birmingham tomorrow."

Lettie Ruth shook her head and gestured toward the bedroom. "I'm not leaving that child alone. She needs my help a whole lot more than any lunch counter sit-in."

Dreama made a face. "That's only an excuse to stick your head in the sand. Can't hide if you want changes, Lettie Ruth. You gotta get out there and fight for your rights."

"I'm too tired to listen to another soap box speech, Dreama Simms. I'll try and go on Palm Sunday." Lettie took her hand. "And you got my word, I'll be walking beside you on Good Friday when Dr. King leads us marching and singing all the way to the city hall. I'm gonna make me a sign to carry that says 'Freedom has come to Birmingham.'"

"Get me a pad of paper." Dreama laughed. "I'm going to get those promises in ink." She pretended to write in the air. "Palm Sunday, April 7 and Good Friday April 12. I got you down now, girlfriend. Oh and, Lettie Ruth, it would probably be best if you left the singing part to me. You can just hum real soft like."

Lettie Ruth playfully slapped at Dreama's shoulder. "Why don't you go down and start some coffee boiling?" She stood and stretched. "And leave the doctoring to me. I'll be along after I check on Kat."

Lettie Ruth tiptoed into the room, not wanting to disturb her patient. Kat lay on her side, right arm tucked under her cheek and her left, the one with broken fingers, hung over the edge of the bed. The covers were a tangled mess around her legs.

As Lettie Ruth leaned forward to brush the wiry tendrils of hair off her patient's moist forehead, Kat's eyes flew open and her left hand shot up from the side of the bed. In spite of the broken fingers, she grabbed Lettie's wrist in a vice grip. The wooden tongue depressors dug into Lettie's skin and she pressed her lips together to keep from crying out.

"Don't touch me," Kat snarled.

"Hey, honey," she said softly. Although Kat's eyes were open, they had the dazed look of a sleepwalker. She rotated her hand to loosen the iron grip.

With a jerk, Kat sat up and twisted her arm backwards. The maneuver forced Lettie to her knees beside the bed.

"I warned you," Kat growled.

The light slanting in from the hall fell on the upraised arm. Lettie Ruth recognized her Christmas money sock and heard the distinctive jingle of coins as Kat swung at her head. The first blow landed on her shoulder, temporarily numbing her free arm. The second hit her temple. Shooting stars…then a black fog filled the bedroom.

✶ ✶ ✶

Dreama sat at the kitchen table and rested her head on folded arms, her energy level all used up. If Taxi's skinny butt didn't waltz through the door in the next few minutes, she was going to drop in her tracks. She generally managed to stay on her feet after a show until three o'clock or so, but it was after four now and this girl wanted to go to bed.

The thumping noises from upstairs were loud enough for Dreama to open her eyes, but not loud enough to raise her head or get up and investigate. Most likely just Lettie moving around and helping Kat. Her eyes drooped, no way she could stay awake another minute.

*   *   *

Within minutes of leaving the Greyhound depot, Mitch reached the decision that Maximilian Devore's 1946 green De Soto barely met the lowest standards to still qualify it as functional transportation. The seventeen-year-old car had enough smoke coming out the tail pipe to be mistaken for a coal burning train. Every time Taxi hit a pot hole, which seemed frequent, Mitch had to reattach the rusty coat hanger holding the rear passenger door shut. When the De Soto plowed through a Grand Canyon-sized crater, Mitch's head bounced off the interior roof like a ginger red basketball off a felt-covered backboard.

"Judas Priest! You learn to drive at a demolition derby?" Mitch immediately regretted his outburst. Taxi had placed his own life in jeopardy by helping out, the least he could do was behave in a cordial manner. "Hey, don't get me wrong, I really appreciate everything you're doing. Thanks," he said, trying to make up for the brusque words.

"It's okay, Mr. Mitch. I knows this ain't the best vehicle."

"It's a whole lot better than what I'm driving."

Taxi chuckled, as he guided the car through another round of bone shattering bumps.

The main route would've been a whole lot smoother, but Taxi had suggested they keep to the back roads. Mitch agreed. They were like two vampires hiding out from the sun. He knew it would only take one busy body to get them in enough trouble to last a lifetime, plus ten years.

"Sorry 'bout the ride, boss. But folks won't take kindly to us going around town together."

"Probably not," Mitch agreed. It wasn't exactly against the law for white and black to be in the same vehicle, but then again, it wasn't the 1963 accepted norm either. Under the circumstances, the last thing he wanted was to be rousted by the White Citizen's Committee or the Klan. The thought of those hooded bone heads prancing around gave him a twinge of unease.

In turn, that twinge set off bells and whistles. His cop switch flipped on and he scanned the street, alternating his gaze from right to left. For the third time in less than a minute, the same twinge prompted him to lean over the seat and stick his hand out the front passenger window—permanently frozen in the half-raised position—to adjust the exterior side mirror. The pair of headlights that jumped into view sent his stomach rocketing into his throat.

"We've got company," he said, taking care to use a detached cool tone to avoid rattling the driver's already frayed nerves. "Of course a pair of headlights doesn't necessarily indicate trouble." He leaned over the front seat again. "You know, it's getting close to 4:30 in the morning, and lots of folks are headed for the early shift at the Demopolis dam."

"Or the railroad yards and steel mills in Birmingham," Taxi added, his voice hopeful.

"Sure," Mitch said, as the speedometer eased up to 50 miles per hour.

"They still back there?" Taxi asked, glancing over his shoulder.

"Now, don't get all worked up. These back roads get their fair share of traffic, it could be nothing more than someone traveling between home and work."

"Don't mean no disrespect, Mr. Mitch, but them lights don't appear to be falling back none and I done speeded up twice."

Mitch twisted around in the seat and took a hard look, trying to estimate the distance between the vehicles. On this narrow and poorly maintained road nobody should be traveling more than 25 mph, yet the headlights remained a steady two lengths behind. Which meant the other car was moving at the same speed, around 50 miles per hour.

"Taxi," he kept his voice pitched low because a crazy idea the people tailing them might overhear danced in his head. The eavesdropping theory wove in and out of his logical thought processes, a conga line that wouldn't give up. In fact, Mitch believed about half of his rational senses had already joined the dance party. He needed to get a grip on himself before an innocuous situation escalated into a full-blown alert. "Let's take a left at the next corner." He pointed down the road. "Once we're on Smithson, you floor this crate. I mean, push this mother to the limit."

"This ole mother ain't got much fire in her belly, Mr. Mitch."

"Do the best you can, Taxi. What I'm interested in is discovering if those fellas riding our ass are after us or on their way home for breakfast."

"I think maybe they plan on having you and me for breakfast," Taxi said.

"I'm not in the mood to be anyone's eggs and bacon today. How about you?"

"Me neither, boss. Y'all hang on, now."

The heavy old De Soto sped down the road and slip swung around the corner like a fuel injected race car. The tires grabbed the asphalt and the car barely fish tailed before shooting east down Smithson. The four lane street ran parallel to the Tombigbee River, a route with gentle curves and very enjoyable on a Sunday afternoon drive, but dangerous for high speed racing. Mitch barely had time for a breath before the headlights bounced back into view. That pretty much settled the issue as far as he was concerned, he and Taxi were most definitely the foxes in this hunt.

As Mitch plotted a way out of their current predicament, Taxi maneuvered the boat of a car around the curves, increasing their speed in tiny increments. How long could the engine last? The car was seventeen-years-old and probably clocked at a minimum, 100,000 miles on the odometer. Oil changes? Tires? He wouldn't give odds on regular maintenance. Those factors, plus the three loud backfires in a row, caused him to severely lower her life expectancy.

When he twisted around to get a better look out the rear window the edges of his badge folder dug into his hip. On his way to the bus depot he'd stopped by the Yellowhammer Inn and retrieved both gun and badge. At the time he didn't know why, but maybe one of Kat's New Orleans voodoo spirits had latched onto him, guiding him as well.

"Taxi." Mitch tapped him on the shoulder. "Think you can shake them for thirty seconds?"

"We got a side street comin' up fast, boss. It winds crooked between some warehouses."

"That sounds good. Try to get a street or two ahead of them, then you and me are going to switch places."

"Switch? But I'm driving here, Mr. Mitch."

"Don't tell me you've never played this game. I'll climb in front, grab the wheel and then you shimmy over into the back seat."

Taxi nodded. "I knows the game. I just don't see no point to it, boss."

"Trust me on this, there's a damn good point."

15

The seat maneuver went smoothly, and by the time the tail car caught up Mitch was ready to pull his Ace. He tapped the brakes, hoping the tail lights functioned, otherwise the sedan would plow into them. Luckily everything seemed to be in working order and both vehicles began to slow. Mitch picked his spot, the intersection of Grant and Laurel, and pulled over. He exited, then walked until he stood in the middle of Grant. He wanted to draw their attention away from Taxi, who'd refused to leave the pseudo-protection of the locked De Soto.

The sounds of slamming doors and footsteps echoed off the brick buildings along the street. Three men in baseball caps clambered out of the pursuit car with all the grace of a herd of rhinos. Their identity didn't surprise Mitch.

In pack formation—Floyd, Little Carl and Louis moved in, snipping and shoving at each other like wild dogs spoiling for a fight. They split off and circled around the green car, banging on the roof and trunk, screaming at Taxi inside. So much for diversionary tactics.

If this exact moment had been captured in a comic strip, Mitch would have been drawn with a big light bulb over his head. Their posturing and bravado were facades, like a fancy paint job on an inferior product. With the clarity of a ten-point diamond, he saw the truth behind the ridiculous segregation rules. Taxi, and all he represented, scared the shit out of these folks.

During Mitch's epiphany the guys had grown bored banging on the car, so Little Carl hawked up a lugey and spit it through the open window. Once their enjoyment in this childish display wore off, they egged each other on until Floyd finally unzipped his fly and urinated on the front windshield. Lewd comments equating Taxi with human waste fouled the early morning breeze.

Mitch longed to inform them that the man they were tormenting had demonstrated more class and courage in the past few hours than they ever could hope to achieve in a lifetime. But he settled for name calling.

"Hey, assholes," he taunted.

The pack turned in toto, ready to expand their dominion. They came together in the middle of the street then moved forward, three abreast. Mitch withdrew the Maceyville Police Department badge from his back pocket and held it out in front of him.

They skidded to a halt, three dogs on a short leash. Their 'I'm gonna beat the shit out of you' grins dropped to the ground. Mitch took a step closer and gave them his infamous evil eye.

A sound several feet away caused him to look past them to the black Impala SS. If asked, he'd be hard pressed to say which he recognized first—the car or the man seated behind the wheel. Mitch took a faltering step backwards as Billy Lee Mitchell opened the door and slithered off the red vinyl seat. At that moment he heard Taxi's frightened squawk, and didn't blame him one iota. The man moving toward him was the monster in many of Mitch's nightmares.

In a single heart beat he became a terrified five-year-old again, trembling as his father approached. Any second he expected to hear the ridicule in Billy Lee's words and voice, the ugly shouted curses. He flinched with each slap of his father's boots on the pavement, reliving the blows delivered with closed fists. Or open handed. Or with anything the angry man could swing.

The driver stopped less than five feet away, fists clinched and a 'go to hell' look in his mean eyes. Billy Lee Mitchell reminded Mitch of a dark avenging demon. Six-feet of bad boy attitude, with a coal-black razor crew cut and deep brown-black eyes that burned with unrighteous fire. His unbuttoned denim work shirt revealed a muscular chest. Tight jeans and steel toed boots completed the ensemble. Billy Lee snorted and cocked his hip. The streetlights glinted off the brass knuckles on his right hand.

Mitch could see his father ached to get into it, wanted to draw blood. But Billy Lee might be surprised at the outcome. This time his opponent wouldn't be a scared five-year-old. His opponent would be a full-grown man. A *large* man. Mitch still carried his pro-football 250 pounds and at six-foot three-inches, he had the immovability of a stone wall. By comparison, Billy Lee, who weighed in at around 170 pounds was three-inches shorter and more closely resembled the schoolyard bully than the ogre Mitch remembered.

"You want some of this, white boy?" Billy Lee asked, gesturing over his shoulder at Taxi.

"Nope." Mitch flashed his badge a second time. "You and your home boys go on, leave this man to me."

"Well, well. Listen to the Yankee boy givin' out orders," Billy Lee said.

Mitch groaned inwardly. He'd forgotten to use his Elvis voice, and his Pennsylvania accent had given Billy Lee a nit picking point. "This Yankee's got a badge and a gun, pal. I suggest you get your 'Bama ass in gear," he ordered.

The other three looked at Billy Lee, awaiting their cue. Mitch mentally crossed his fingers. This confrontation did not bode well for a time-traveler. All the dire predictions he'd laid on Kat about making contact with her aunt were now reversed. Maybe he should listen to his own lectures some time.

A cold smile crawled across Billy Lee's face as he flexed his fingers, making certain Mitch could see the brass knuckles.

Then again, Mitch thought, *if I stuck my whole damn arm in the history pie, would it make any real difference? Would the world stop spinning if, just once, I beat the living crap out of Dad?*

As soon as he decided to take the old man on, a whole army of What-Ifs marched through his head, banging on drums and blowing bugles. *What-if*, he pulled his gun and shot Billy Lee right between his mean eyes? Would James Mitchell cease to exist in that instant? *What-if*, Billy Lee killed him first? Would Mitch still be born in 1965? He rubbed the back of his neck. The strain of trying to figure out all the ramifications of this reunion settled into a big muscle knot.

"Why you riding in that nigger's car?" Billy Lee challenged.

"I'm driving the car, not riding in it," Mitch shot back.

"Makes no difference where you sit, Yankee. Y'all is still together."

"See this?" He took two steps forward and shoved his badge within inches of his father's nose. "This is a police badge, punk. And that means I can ride in any damn car I feel like. And I can ride in that car any damn time I choose. *And* with any damn person I want. You got that straight?" Mitch asked, poking him in the chest.

"I got it," Billy Lee said, his tone incredibly surly. "We was only checking out the situation. No one knew y'all was on police business."

Mitch turned to the other three men. "Now that you got it, climb back in that piece of shit Chevy, that won't go over 65 mph, and get out of my face." Mitch wished for a camera to take a picture of his father's face when he heard the crack about 65 mph. He allowed himself a small smile as the men scrambled back in the Impala. In less time than it took to flush a toilet, they were gone.

Taxi called out the window, "How come you don't sound like Elvis Presley no more?"

Mitch walked over and leaned back against the side of the car. "I'm working undercover, don't tell anybody I'm not really from Memphis."

"My mouth is shut tight. Mr. Mitch, you a real policeman?"

"Yes I am. Just not in this particular Maceyville."

"Mmm, then it's good them fellas didn't look close at that badge, boss. I seen that dark one before and he's got a hard on when it comes to Negroes."

"I did notice something along those lines, Taxi." Mitch wrinkled his nose at the stench of the drying urine on the windshield. "We'll need several buckets of water to wash down your car."

"It don't matter, Mr. Mitch." Taxi removed the coat hanger and shoved open the squeaky back door. "Not much paint left on her anyway."

"She really stinks."

"My momma always says a little ammonia is good for washing windows, Mr. Mitch."

"Hey, Taxi will you do me one more favor?"

"What's that, Mr. Mitch?" Taxi asked as he crawled out of the car.

"Drop the mister." He stuck his hand out. "My friends call me Mitch."

Taxi took his hand. "I reckon I can do that, Mitch."

* * *

Kat shoved her arms through the sleeves of the navy blue sweater she'd found hanging behind the TV room door. The man's shirt, from the laundry basket in the bathroom, wrapped around her body twice, but the trousers were a pretty close fit if she rolled the cuffs up. Unable to locate any street shoes, she'd settled for a sad looking pair of maroon house slippers abandoned under a chair in the waiting room.

The women didn't fool her. All their sweet talk was a lie. Kat was a prisoner. Why would they sit outside her door for such a long time unless they were on guard duty? They'd only pretended to be her friends so she would lower her guard. What plans did they have after she'd relaxed? She heard them talking about burning houses and churches. Did that mean they would hand her over to Floyd so he wouldn't burn their house down?

She needed to escape. Kat fumbled with the stubborn door latch, wasting precious minutes working the rusty bolt free.

The early morning light painted the neighborhood with a surreal brush. Shapes blended together, undefined edges softened by shadows. Kat hurried down the sidewalk, thankful no cars traveled past her. She had to put as much distance between herself and the clinic before Floyd returned.

Headlights bounced down the street and she dove for cover in the nearest yard. Huddled behind the overgrown rhododendron, she watched the green car stop in front of the clinic. Two men inside, one black and one white. *Floyd!* The women had sent someone for Floyd. Now he'd hunt her down like a blood hound. She sprinted for the alley behind the house.

* * *

"That girl sure knows how to hit," Dreama said, examining her friend. A nasty looking bruise decorated Lettie's shoulder and lump was growing on the side of her head.

Lettie Ruth pressed the ice pack against her temple. "She's just scared, didn't mean to do me any real harm."

"I'd be hatin' to see what you be lookin' like if she'd meant to hurt you."

"She's near crazy on account of what those boys done to her," Lettie Ruth said. She pulled her blouse over the bruise and worked on the buttons. "We need to go after her."

"You want to bring that wild cat back here?" Dreama shook her head. "If she'd been beatin' on me, I'd let her be."

Lettie frowned. "I'm not going to let her be. She needs help. Yours and mine."

Dreama rested her hands on her hips. "She needs to be locked—" A knock on the door interrupted her thought. "We'll be discussin' this when I get back."

"No discussion. We're going after her."

"Lettie Ruth Rayson, you ain't got to take in every stray you run across." Dreama glanced over her shoulder when someone pounded on the door.

"She ain't a stray. That girl's special. I got a feelin' about her."

"Well, she ain't family neither, so quit actin' like a mother hen."

* * *

Mitch rested his head against the car window and closed his eyes, torn between depression and fear. The door to the year 2000 had banged shut twenty minutes ago. Now he and Kat were stuck here four more days, until April 5th—the day Lettie Ruth Rayson would disappear. No, that's not right, he corrected, recent experiences and seeing the hatred whites held for blacks, had shed new light on the past. Lettie Ruth wouldn't disappear on Friday. She would be murdered.

When the car stopped, he opened his eyes. The address painted on the porch post caused a sharp pain to shoot through his head: 3449. The Jane Doe, assumed to be Kat's aunt, had disappeared from 3449 Brook Street. "What the name of this street?" he asked.

"Brook Street. And this here is Dr. Tim's clinic."

Everything has come a full circle, Mitch thought. And I don't like the shape of this particular circle.

They climbed out of the car and hurried to the door. Taxi glanced nervously over his shoulder at the silent neighborhood, then knocked. "They better get this door open. I don't care to be standing here letting the neighbors see our business."

Mitch tried to keep most of his freckled body tucked into the shadows, but he was a big man and the porch wide open. A white man in the east Hollow at daybreak wasn't the norm. His presence would draw unwanted attention and if someone happened to mention seeing his red hair it would only be a matter of hours before Floyd and his crew arrived.

"Are you sure she's still here?" he asked.

Taxi answered by giving the door a good pounding.

"The doctor could be out on an emergency call," Mitch suggested, when no one responded to the horrendous beating Taxi inflicted on the door. "Or maybe Kat got worse and he took her to the hospital."

"Ain't no colored hospital close by. All the doctoring we got is right behind this here door. Besides, Dr. Tim don't go hauling his stuff all over town. You get sick, you over come here."

When Dreama Simms opened the door Mitch took a step backwards. Thirty-seven years and an equal number of pounds were gone, but there was no way to disguise the saucy expression or her familiar high energy smile.

Within a split second the smile faded and the future Police Department housekeeping manager stared at him with distrust.

She stepped aside enough to allow Taxi to squeeze through the narrow opening, but before Mitch could get one foot across the threshold the door slammed in his face. He was still rubbing the sore spot on his nose when Taxi opened the door and yanked him into the house.

An indignant Dreama stood with arms folded and foot tapping. Her volatile expression dared Mitch to say one word. He offered a smile. She snorted and marched out of the room.

"What's wrong with her, Taxi?"

"The woman's gone and got herself an attitude, that's what's wrong."

"You didn't tell her about me," Mitch accused.

"Things heated up around here before I come to fetch you, Mitch. No time to get into it."

"So what happens now? With that thunderstorm expression she's wearing there's no way she'll let me see Kat."

Taxi squared his shoulders and hitched up his pants. "I'll be taking care of that little thunderstorm right now. Yes sir, right now," he declared and followed Dreama.

Mitch took a seat in the waiting room, and waited. His experiences were growing more bizarre by the second. First he'd run head on into his father. And now Dreama Simms. He dreaded what lay ahead. Good thing he hadn't been born yet, because he wouldn't be the least bit surprised to meet himself this afternoon.

The voices coming from the other room rose and fell as the argument escalated. Mitch did his level best to keep from eavesdropping, but with his name repeatedly mentioned he couldn't help but tune in.

"Dreama honey," Taxi said. "I'm tellin' you, Mitch is her friend."

"What you mean 'her friend'? And why you keep on calling him Mitch?"

"He asked me to do that. Mitch ain't like them others, baby. He's good white folk."

"How you know he's good? He could be one of them from the field. You consider that?"

"He ain't part of that bunch. I seen him beat 'em up at Bubba's."

"Well there you go, Taxi. You tell me he beat on someone and that's supposed to make him good white folk?" Dreama asked, sarcasm dripping off each word.

"Baby, you not hearing me. No sir, not hearing at all."

"I'm hearing fine. You expect me to step aside and let that man at Kat? Let him do any ole thing he pleases on account you can call him plain Mitch, instead of *Mister* Mitch."

"Now settle down."

Mitch paused in the kitchen doorway and cleared his throat. He'd entered enemy territory to rescue his fellow soldier, who, at the moment, appeared to be getting the living crap kicked out of him.

"Ma'am?" he said, tense and on guard in case she took a swing at him. "I couldn't help but overhear, and you're wrong about me. I *am* Kat's friend and I've been looking for her."

"And if my man could've kept his lips from flapping, how was you expecting to find this friend?"

"By searching every inch of Maceyville," Mitch said, challenging her hostile attitude.

"Well, she ain't here no more," Dreama said, a cruel smile played around her mouth. "So's you best get your walking shoes on, there's lots of inches in Maceyville."

Mitch stared at her, unnerved by both the information and the cruelty with which she delivered it. He'd never done anything to her and didn't deserve to be treated like scum. "You listen to me, Dreama Simms, Kathleen Templeton is my friend. And you and your racist attitude can go directly to hell." Having said his piece, he turned on his heels and left the room. The front door slammed hard enough to rattled the windows.

16

APRIL 02—TUESDAY

The too large maroon slippers flopped around on Kat's feet. Half the time her soles hit the asphalt alleyway rather than the tattered felt lining of the shoe. Although the awkward footwear slowed her progress some, she'd managed to put at least a half mile between herself and the white man in the green car. She took some small comfort in knowing Floyd didn't know where to look. Which gave her a temporary advantage. She wasn't foolish enough to believe she could outrun him forever. Slowed by a battered body and on foot, it wouldn't take him long to catch up with her. And he would be looking hard. He'd raped a police officer. Assault on a law enforcement personnel was a federal offense, which carried a substantial jail sentence.

Sensing danger close on her heels, she picked up the pace. Only one more house until the alley intersected with a major thoroughfare, Webster Avenue. She could see the steady line of cars parading by, folks heading off to work. Kat paused at the street and looked both ways. She needed to be on the alert for Floyd's pickup. It wouldn't do to walk into another ambush.

"I have to remember," she muttered, struggling to recall pertinent details that would set his white stake-bed truck apart from the dozens on the road. "Think, Kat. Think."

She remembered several large rust spots on the right door. A broomstick handle, with a confederate Southern Cross flag attached, tied to the left rear fender. And something on the radio antenna flapped in the wind as they drove. She closed her eyes, trying to bring the image into a clear focus. Her eyes spilled over with frustrated tears when she couldn't do it.

"Hey, Miss Kat!" The boisterous greeting carried easily across the street.

Virgil and Lamar, the boys she'd met yesterday morning, darted across Webster Avenue, dodging the traffic and ignoring blaring horns. Instead of striped tee-shirts and jeans, today they wore their Sunday's finest: long sleeve white shirts with skinny black ties, dark trousers and polished leather shoes. All the little boy dirt had been scrubbed from their faces and hands.

"Whoa, Miss Kat." Lamar whistled. "What happened to you?"

Before she could respond, the inquisitive Virgil bombarded her with rapid fire questions.

"Why you got ice cream sticks on your fingers? Is that a black eye? I ain't never seen a colored woman with a black eye. What you be doing in this alley?"

Kat ignored his first two questions and answered the last. "It's a short cut," she explained.

"A short cut to where?" Virgil asked.

"Miss Kat," Lamar interrupted, looking closely at her clothes. "Couldn't you find Miss Jane's dress store yesterday?"

Virgil poked Lamar in the side and pointed to her feet. Kat looked down at her stolen men's clothing and the sad looking maroon house shoes. "My new outfit got ruined yesterday," she said.

The boys glanced at each other, silently communicating. "You come along with us, Miss Kat, my house is close by and we'll get you some girl clothes," Lamar offered.

"That's real kind, honey, but I can't take clothes from your momma."

"His momma won't care," Virgil said. "She be dead."

Kat looked at Lamar and he nodded. "She's been gone a long while now. But Daddy keeps her dresses in a box in the closet. He won't mind if you take one."

The boy looked so eager to help, Kat didn't have the heart to turn him down. "I'd be proud to wear your momma's dress, Lamar."

He smiled and offered his arm, a true Southern gentleman. Virgil, not to be left out, put his arm around Kat's waist, and the threesome walked down the sidewalk together.

* * *

A green blanket of kudzu almost buried Lamar's long and narrow shot-gun house. A few early purple blossoms added a splash of color to the weathered ship-lap. The gravel walk pointed the way to the front door, and Lamar lifted up the tangle of drooping vines engulfing the small porch so Kat could pass underneath. She stumbled slightly because of the silly looking house shoes.

Her hip banged the wringer washing machine, perched on a bleach spotted wooden pallet next to the top step. Lamar gently took her elbow and helped her to the door.

He knew the outside of his home would look better with a coat or two of paint, but no one could find fault with the immaculate interior. The hardwood floors didn't have a high wax sheen, but first his momma, and now his daddy mopped them so many times they looked like soft velvet. The window panes sparkled, because that was one of Lamar's regular Saturday chores, and the living room glowed with spring light. He thought the overstuffed sofa covered in patchwork made the room look like somebody was ready to have a party.

Lamar rubbed his hand across the fabric. It reminded him of Momma. He remembered when she sewed it all together, taking pieces from her dresses, his too small clothes and from shirts his daddy had stained so bad he couldn't wear them on Sunday. The piece from his momma's favorite dress covered the sofa arm. When nobody was home, he rested his head in that very spot. Sometimes he could even smell Momma's rose water perfume.

A worn red velvet recliner and arm chair pretty much filled the rest of the skinny room. But his daddy had magically squeezed in a cabinet television and a water marked coffee table, and still managed to leave a narrow passage to the next room.

"Her clothes is back here," Lamar said, as he led the way through the kitchen and into a bedroom at the rear of the house.

Kat hesitated in the doorway and looked around. "Lamar, is this your daddy's bedroom?"

"Not now. He been sleeping in the front room." He dragged a large cardboard box from the closet and slid it across the floor to Kat. "He says he don't like comin' in here no more, now that Momma's gone." Lamar didn't like sleeping back here either. It was so lonely and sad without Momma's things around. He'd been pretty mad when his daddy packed everything up. It didn't seem right somehow. Like he wanted to forget her.

"Is he home?" Kat asked.

She looked so scared, Lamar felt glad his daddy wasn't home. "You can come on in, he's down at the church, getting ready to preach to the Ladies Prayer Breakfast."

"Yeah," Virgil interrupted. "Me an Lamar is suppose to hand out programs and help the old ones to their seats."

"It's okay, Miss Kat," Lamar said, noticing her frown. "Once I explain to him, he'll say we done right. Shoot he might even preach about how we was good Samaritans."

Kat took a couple of steps into the bedroom. "Preach?"

"Yes, ma'am. He pastors Webster Avenue Freedom Methodist," Lamar said proudly, hoping his daddy being a preacher would make her feel better. He didn't know nobody that was scared of a man of God.

"My Pop's a preacher too," she said softly.

"Do you like having a preacher man for a daddy?" Lamar asked.

"Sometimes yes, and sometimes no."

Lamar nodded. "I feel that way too. Especially when I got to go twice on Sunday and then to Wednesday night bible class. You know he makes me get up in front and sing?"

"And, Miss Kat," Virgil confided. "Lamar can't sing worth beans."

Lamar was glad to see the small smile on her face. She looked so sad. Not talking like before. Yesterday she'd been a happy lady, kind of smart mouthed but he liked her a lot. Today her eyes looked funny, like all sorts of bad thoughts were spinning around inside her head and ever so often stopped to peek out through her eyes. He wished he was older, then he'd know how to help her.

"Hey, Miss Kat, how about this one?" Virgil held up a slinky black dress with sequins sewn around the scooped neck line. "It's real pretty."

"Virgil, I swear you don't got the brains to boil water," Lamar scolded. "That's Momma's party dress."

"I know that. But it's a real pretty party dress."

"Virgil, it's too fancy for my needs," Kat said.

The boy looked disappointed, but laid the dress aside without argument.

Lamar's held up a pale yellow shirtwaist with pearl buttons and a Peter Pan collar. "This one okay?"

"I seen shoes the same color somewhere in here," Virgil said, as he dug around in the bottom of the box. A few seconds later emerged with a pair of yellow sandals.

She nodded and held out her hand. "If y'all will pass them on over, I'll see if they fit."

When she closed the bathroom door, Lamar leaned over to whisper in Virgil's ear. "Something's wrong with Miss Kat. She's all quiet."

"I seen a woman beat up like that once when she come to over talk to Daddy. She sure cried a lot."

"Lordy mercy, I hope she don't start cryin'," Virgil said. "I hate when ladies carry-on."

Lamar shook his head. "I don't much think Miss Kat is one of those crying kind of ladies. She got something inside that makes her strong."

"Well what we going to do with her now? Can't let her walk around all beat up. The police will put her in jail for sure."

"I'll take her over to see Daddy. He'll know what to do." Lamar held his finger to his lips when the lock on the bathroom door clicked open.

As Kat stepped through the door, Virgil whistled appreciatively.

Lamar thought she looked real pretty in his momma's dress. But he knew one more thing that she needed. "Miss Kat, can you wait one second?" He dug around in the bottom of the box until he found a pale yellow satin ribbon. "Momma always tied this in her hair when she wore that dress," he said and handed her the ribbon. "I'd be proud if you would too."

* * *

Mitch, scrunched down in the front seat of the De Soto for the last half hour, popped his head over the window frame when he heard the clinic door slam. Seeing Taxi on the covered porch, rather than an angry Dreama Simms, he stuck his hand out the window and wiggled his fingers.

Taxi hurried down the sidewalk. "You all right?"

"It's a heck of a lot safer in the car than it is inside," Mitch grumbled. He'd never met anyone as irritating or judgmental as Dreama. He found it hard to equate the furious whirlwind he'd sparred with and the woman he saw every day at the station. He got along fine with the *other* Dreama. He liked her. Liked her a lot. And she like him.

"No doubt about it, Dreama's got a sharp tongue at times." Taxi shoved his skinny brimmed pork pie hat to the back of his head and scratched his forehead. "Been cut up myself on occasion. Most usually she don't mean half what she says."

"Half is more than adequate for me."

"Aww, don't pay her no mind, Mitch."

"It's not in my best interest to keep making enemies, I need all the friends and help I can get. And that includes her."

"Well, now I wouldn't be counting on her help just yet. She got strong opinions when it comes to white folks."

"I'd take another shot at changing her mind about me, except I'm on a tight schedule. We need to get back home because Kat's Pop had a heart attack yesterday. They're not sure he'll pull through."

"So you been looking so hard for that girl cause her daddy's sick?"

"Yep. She needs to be with him, not on some crusade." And she'd be at the hospital, right now if I'd stuck to my guns, he thought. I should have done something two days ago instead of spouting theories and what-ifs. Now that those predictions had become reality, he felt more like crying than throwing an 'I told you so' party.

"I'll do my best to smooth things out," Taxi was saying. "Oh, if you reach in my glove box I got somethin' belonging to you."

Mitch popped the catch and saw Kat's boot pin. He picked it up and squeezed it. "Guess you never got a chance to return it to her."

"She'll like it better if it comes back to her through you. Now come on inside, Lettie Ruth got breakfast ready."

Mitch sat up so fast his head hit the roof of the car. "What did you say?"

"Lettie Ruth Rayson works here at the clinic with Dr. Tim and she fixed us breakfast."

"Jesus, Mary and Joseph," Mitch whispered. As if things weren't already messed up enough, somehow Kat had ended up in the same house with her mysterious aunt.

"You be acting mighty peculiar, Mitch. Something wrong?"

He opened the door and climbed out of the car. "Taxi, so many things are wrong I can't begin to list them all."

"Well then, I say we get us some breakfast and do a little talking 'bout that list of yours."

*   *   *

The four people seated around the table ate in silence. Mitch kept his eyes on his plate and fervently wished someone would say something. As the minutes crawled by, other than the tinny clink of a fork against a plate or a slurp when one of them took a sip of coffee, the room might well be inhabited by ghosts.

"This is foolishness," Lettie Ruth said, breaking the sound barrier. "It's high time to speak our minds."

Mitch cleared his throat and three pair of dark eyes jumped to his face. "Let me start by thanking Miss Simms and Taxi for bringing Kat to the clinic. And you, Miss Rayson, for taking such good care of her." Lettie inclined her head, silently acknowledging his gratitude. "If you don't mind, would you please tell me what happened to her?" he asked.

"Why you want to know?" Dreama asked, her tone sharp.

"Because I'm worried, Miss Simms. I've heard talk and I want to sort the truth from the fiction."

Lettie Ruth studied his face, after a few seconds she appeared to have reached a decision. "She was beat and raped, Mr. Mitch," she said quietly.

"White men treated her no better than an animal, then tossed her aside," Dreama said. Undisguised anger radiated from her words.

Mitch's chin dropped to his chest and he closed his eyes. Everything Floyd and his pals had bragged about was the gospel truth. Once again guilt reared up and pawed the air. If he'd only reacted to her pronouncement about returning to Park Street, rather than passively sitting on his butt. He may have failed her once, but not a second time. He'd do everything in his power to right this wrong.

"Will she be all right?" he asked without looking up.

"In time she will get better," Lettie Ruth answered. "But she won't ever be all right again, Mr. Mitch. A woman can't endure this much violence and not come out changed."

He raised his head and looked at the three people at the table. "Is there some way to make it easier for her? I'll do whatever you tell me."

"I don't think she wants your help, Mr. Mitch," Lettie Ruth said.

"Because I'm a man?"

"Because you're a *white* man," said Dreama Simms.

"That's a load of bull shit," he said heatedly. He took a deep breath and slowly released it. He couldn't let her get under his skin. His number one priority was to find Kat and take her home before it was too late. He didn't know how Pop Rayson was doing, but in the worst scenario he couldn't hold on much longer.

"It's the way things is around here," Dreama said. "Your kind ain't all that welcome. And you wait and see, Kat will be tellin' the same once you two hook up."

He chewed the angry words filling his mouth into bits and pieces before they ricocheted all over the kitchen. Focus, he told himself. When it didn't work, Mitch pushed away from the table.

Mitch stared out the waiting room window as Dreama's comments replayed in his head. *Because you're a white man.* Would her cruel words prove prophetic? Would Kat refuse his help based on his color?

"Mitch?" Taxi stood in the doorway. "I'm sorry Dreama answered you so mean, but it's probably the truth. Your friend don't want nothing to do with white folks right now."

"I'm not white folks," Mitch snapped. "We've spent twelve hours a day, five days a week together for the past five years. That ought to count for something. But now I'm beginning to wonder if I should even try."

"Of course you should. Just gotta give her some space for a little while. Your Kat's trapped with one foot half in and one foot half out of hell right now. Soon enough she'll be wanting a good friend to help show the way out."

"It will take a better man than I am to show her the way."

"Women got lots of peculiarities, Mitch, and one is being able to know the good and bad in a man. It's like they can see right through your skin, into your heart. I reckon Kat seen the good in you. And between us men," Taxi glanced at the kitchen door then lowered his voice. "I bet it don't matter to her if you be colored or white."

More than anything Mitch wanted to believe color didn't matter. But could she emerge from this unscathed? Taxi could talk from sun up to sun down about how Mitch differed from Floyd, but at the end of the day he still had ginger-red hair, blue eyes and freckles. He couldn't get much whiter than that.

If their situations were reversed, and he'd been the one attacked, his perceptions and attitudes toward blacks would probably be forever altered. Right or wrong, that's how it worked. Humans hauled around cart loads of prejudicial bull shit for lesser reasons.

Segregation was a prime example. It provided a method for uneducated white Southerners like his father to cope with the emerging Black-Awareness. Those from the east Hollow had worked hard to improve themselves and their community and welcomed the changes. In the opposite corner, men like Billy Lee swaggered and threw threats around in a desperate attempt to hold on to their self perceived superiority.

But they were scared, and maybe a little jealous of any changes in their narrow strip of the world. Scared because they'd never dared to dream of a better life. Those boys didn't want anything except what they already had—a six pack of beer on Saturday night, welfare checks each month and a woman to bed or beat when the mood struck.

The crux of the matter was respect. The bigots didn't respect themselves, and the only way they could feel worth anything was to shove their frustration down a black throat. Forcing strong men like Taxi to bow and scrape, proved to all the Billy Lees and Floyds that they were still better than the dumb ass nigger with a high school education and a full-time job.

White Only. Colored Only. How much longer before it dawned on people that white was a color too? Mitch brushed the hair off his forehead, embarrassed by his mental speech making. Judas Priest, he'd been preaching to an audience of one. He thought he kept his mouth shut, but from the strange look on Taxi's face, he wondered how much he'd spoken out loud.

17

"If you ask me, this relationship between her and *that gentleman* shines a whole new light on everything," Dreama said, as she wiped down the kitchen counter.

"What are you hinting around, Dreama Simms?" Lettie Ruth asked.

"Maybe Kat didn't get dragged out to no field. Could be she wanted to be with those boys."

Lettie Ruth shook her head. "You ought to be shamed. You and Taxi found her, and you know she didn't look like she'd gone out there to have fun."

"It's true I found her, but I also got ears. That white man seems mighty fond of a Negro woman. Nothing good *ever* comes from that."

"Why do you act this way, Dreama?"

Dreama pulled down the high collar on her green dress. The scars across her throat glistened in the morning light. "You know how I got this…and why. So don't be lecturing me on *good* white folks." She turned away and looked out the window, her eyes glistening with angry tears. Last year a group of *good* white folks had tied a rope around her neck, then hauled her up a tree because her manager was their color. Not hers…

She'd told Harvey coming down South would be a mistake and they ought to stay in Detroit. Record the new album in a studio. But he pushed, and pushed so hard for the concert tour she finally gave in.

Their long bus was filled with musicians and equipment. The boys partied all the way from Detroit, while Dreama sat in the back and chewed her fingernails. None of them understood the rules, but once they crossed the Tennessee state line they'd learned. Slashed tires, rocks thrown through the windows. The Klan disrupted almost every concert. When Harvey asked her why this happened, she pointed to her band. Her white band. "This sort of thing don't work down here," she said. "Negro and white live in different worlds."

Harvey dismissed her explanation, poo-pooing it as total nonsense, and the bus rolled into the Heart of Dixie.

Dreama Simms ended her concert tour just outside Birmingham, hanging from a tree. Her larynx crushed. Her singing career over.

"What they did to you was wrong," Lettie Ruth said. "But's that's only a tiny handful of folks out of the whole big world. You can't mistrust all whites on account of them."

Dreama wiped her eyes with the dish towel. "Name three of those pale ghost people you trust."

"I trust Timothy."

"And?"

Lettie Ruth shook her head. "And you got me so worked up I can't think straight."

"You ain't worked up girl. You got no names 'cause there ain't no good ones."

"Did you lose every ounce of ability to see the good side of white folks the minute you started in with that NAACP bunch?" Lettie Ruth asked. "They teaching you how to hate at those meetings?"

"They teach me to think twice before believing every word out of a white mouth. I'm learning how to stand up for my rights."

"What about Kat's rights? Seems she has a right to be friends with Mr. Mitch if she's a mind to."

"Yeah, lot of those type friendships down at Miz Rita's parlor."

"I'm not talking about no whore house friendships, and you know it. Just because a woman got a white man friend, don't mean something dirty's going on." Lettie Ruth glared at Dreama and propped her hands on her hips. "Timothy Biggers is white, you think cause I live in his house he's jumpin' me?"

Dreama fought to keep the smile off her face. The very idea was plain old silly. The doctor didn't have time for women, much less a colored one. "Forty-three ain't so old, honey," she said. "And he's good looking for a white man, reminds me of that movie star, Gregory Peck." The comments were only meant to tease her friend, but from the fire in Lettie's eyes, maybe she'd touched on something.

Their relationship had always intrigued Dreama. They worked closely together and put in long hours, which was to her understanding, the reasoning behind Lettie Ruth movin' in with him. Of course they lived in separate parts of the house—Lettie upstairs and Timothy down—but it was still under the same roof. And the arrangement raised more than one eyebrow at the Freedom Methodist church.

When it came to Timothy Biggers, the gossips didn't have far to look for a juicy bit of trash. He'd been the talk of Maceyville for going on ten years. Tongues started wagging the very day he opened his clinic in the east Hollow and dared the west side of town to do something about it. He showed no preference, doctoring everybody equal, long as they came through his door. And another thing, his waiting room wasn't split up into colored and white sections. Biggers ignored the segregation laws because he simply didn't give a good goddamn.

As for the Ku Klux Klan, hard as they tried, those boys couldn't scare him off. One run-in between the doctor and the Kluxers ended with three white knights stretched out on the tables in his exam rooms. As a World War II veteran and medical doctor, Biggers had known where to shoot them, without killing anyone. He'd sewn them up afterwards. Rumors held that he sent everyone of those boys a bill, and added a little extra on account of all the aggravation they'd caused him. Nowadays they pretty much ignored his goings on. Occasionally they tore up the flower beds or painted his sign out front to read: DR. NIGGERS CLINIC, instead of Dr. Biggers Clinic.

"Well?" Lettie Ruth was asking, her tone sharp and demanding. "You think I got some sort of arrangement with Timothy?"

"Of course not," Dreama answered. "What a foolish notion."

Lettie Ruth looked ready to tear the head off a live chicken and Dreama thought better of airing her suspicions. If the nurse wanted to play doctor with the doctor, they'd best keep the window shades down and the lights off. If word of a love relationship started circulating around Maceyville, there would be hell to pay from both the east and the west sides of town.

"And it's equally foolish to assume something beside friendship is going on between Kat and Mr. Mitch," Lettie Ruth lectured. "If you're so curious, why don't you go find her? Then ask her all those questions burning so bright inside your head."

"Maybe I'll do that."

* * *

After their heart to heart in the waiting room, Mitch and Taxi returned to kitchen. Lettie Ruth greeted him politely and didn't seem to bear any ill will, but Dreama was a whole different set of circumstances. The second he entered, she gave Mitch a look hot enough to dry up the entire Gulf of Mexico. Mitch decided it would be in his best interest to make one more try at peace negotiations.

"I want all of you to drop the mister, just call me Mitch," he announced, pulling out a chair and sitting down.

Dreama snorted and tossed her head. "We may live in the east Hollow, *Mister* Mitch, but we ain't too dumb to wonder the reason why you ask us to do that."

"Dreama's right," Lettie Ruth said quietly and without anger. "Do you know what happens to coloreds in Maceyville that don't show white folks proper respect?"

"I've got a pretty good idea, Lettie Ruth. But I don't see it as disrespect," Mitch explained. "Kat sure as hell doesn't call me Mister Mitch. Never has and never will."

"And that's another thing," Dreama snapped. "Why is you all tangled up with her?"

"She's just as tangled up with me," Mitch countered, as he worked to come up with a plausible explanation for their relationship. He couldn't tell them he and Kat were police officers from another time zone almost forty years in the future. And he couldn't bring up Kat's relationship to Lettie Ruth or Alvin Rayson. Luckily, Dreama pushed on with her argument and he didn't have to respond.

"Ain't no reason for a Negro woman to get all tangled up with a freckled white man," she declared. "That girl struck me as having better sense."

"Well, she doesn't," he snapped. It was a childish comeback and Mitch knew it, but whatever he'd said would have been wrong. Dreama already hated him. In fact, she carried such a large chip on her shoulder it would take a bulldozer to knock it off.

Lettie Ruth clapped her hands sharply, effectively ending the bickering between Mitch and Dreama. "Y'all take it out in the yard, or hush it up," she ordered. "I'm fixing to go look for that girl, any of y'all coming along?"

"I'm comin'," Taxi said.

"Count me in," Mitch said, as he rose to his feet.

"Me too," said Dreama. "I ain't letting him out of my sight."

Lettie Ruth sighed, reminding Mitch of a weary mother. "Fine, then you two can travel together in the car and keep an eye on each other. Me and Taxi will go on foot."

"Lettie Ruth!" Dreama shouted.

"Hey! No way," Mitch shouted.

Lettie Ruth and Taxi looked at each other, shrugged and walked out of the room, leaving the bickering duo alone.

"Well?" Mitch asked.

"I'll be doing all the drivin'," Dreama declared.

"Fine by me."

* * *

WEBSTER AVENUE FREEDOM METHODIST CHURCH

Alvin Rayson stood before the Ladies Prayer Breakfast participants. This was the first time he'd preached to a full church since the Army, and his knees trembled. He'd sweated through his undershirt during the choir number, his Sunday white shirt during the scripture reading, and now was working wetting down his suit coat. Pastor Gordon cleared his throat, a gentle nudge for Alvin to get on with his sermon.

"In Paul's letter to the Romans 12:19 it says: *'Dearly beloved, avenge not yourselves, but rather give place unto wrath: for it is written, Vengeance is mine; I will repay, saith the Lord'.*"

Rayson soon found his rhythm and began to relax. Somewhere in the middle of verse 20, he saw Lamar and Virgil sneak in and take their seats in the back row. A pretty young woman, wearing a yellow dress, sat sandwiched between them in the pew.

Throughout his fiery sermonizing his eyes were repeatedly drawn to the woman. Her attention never wavered, even when he wandered off the subject. When she smiled at one of his pulpit jokes, his heart soared. He got the feeling his message fell on fertile ground and all the hours he'd devoted polishing today's lesson weren't wasted. God knew this woman would be in church this morning.

Before long he was preaching, beseeching, cajoling and scolding the church in the time-honored style of a revival tent preacher. He got so worked up at one point, he slammed his hand down on the pulpit so hard the wooden cross nailed on the front panel crashed to the floor. Always the showman, Reverend Alvin Rayson knew when to shut up. And he did.

After the invitation and benediction, he slowly worked his way through the congregation keeping his eye on the woman in the yellow dress. He took the time to speak to each woman by name, graciously accepting handshakes and praises, even though he would have preferred passing through the crowd unhindered. But he knew better than to try and rush the Prayer Breakfast sisters.

When he finally reached Lamar and Virgil's guest, he saw the severely swollen and blackened eye. Bruises covered her face and arms and he wondered if she'd been in a car accident or if someone had inflicted the damage. If the latter turned out to be the cause, although he'd just spent over an hour preaching against seeking vengeance, he wouldn't mind getting his hands on the person handing out such beatings.

"Lamar, I don't believe I've met your guest," he said.

"Pastor Rayson, this is my friend Miss Kat," Lamar said.

"Glad to have you at Freedom Methodist, Miss Kat," Rayson said as he extended his hand. His welcome hung empty in the air. The woman wouldn't meet his eye, much less shake hands. In the few minutes it had taken him to move from the pulpit to the back row, she'd erected a full size wall between herself and the world.

"She don't feel so good today," Virgil explained.

"A person don't have to feel good every single day, Virgil," Rayson said. "Why don't you boys escort our guest into the fellowship hall for cake and coffee."

Not knowing exactly what to do, he simply watched as Lamar took Miss Kat's arm and guided her down the length of the pew. He thought about her behavior, avoiding eye contact and flinching when he'd offered his hand. She was afraid and he didn't have any idea what she feared. His years in the seminary hadn't prepared him for this type of situation.

* * *

Kat immediately felt at home in the chaotic fellowship hall. The aroma of fresh coffee and cinnamon spice cake, the hum of competing voices and outbursts of laughter reminded her of Sundays at Hope and Glory. Momentarily forgetting where she was, Kat turned in a circle, eyes sweeping the crowd for her Pop's robust figure. He must be nearby, she could hear his deep rolling laugh. She spied Miss Jane's pink beehive over in the corner and quickly ducked behind several women. The last thing she needed was a discussion with the shop owner regarding her bruises and the borrowed yellow dress.

Laughter drew her attention across the room. A young and slender Alvin Rayson stood near the piano bench, surrounded by a harem of single women. Without missing a single syllable he forked spice cake into his mouth and kept up a running dialogue at the same time. She watched him devour his cake and cheerfully accept another slice. Now she knew the source of Pop's Santa Claus belly—the Sunday coffee fellowship. No wonder he refused to discontinue the practice, the man was a sweets monster.

When the pretty young woman shyly approached the handsome pastor, with yet another piece of cake, Kat saw a smile on Pop's face she'd almost forgotten. The special one he'd bestowed only on her mother, Dolores Townson. From across the room she watched her father and mother take the first steps on a path, which in time, would lead them to the altar and a daughter named Kathleen Ruth. So much for Mitch's theories about a sassy gal from New Orleans stealing Pop's heart, she thought. Looked like her parents would still get together, only a few days earlier than before.

She felt a little ache when she thought about her partner. She missed him and regretted not listening when he warned her about the dangers. She'd foolishly brushed off all his dire predictions and ended up in a cotton field. If Mitch were here, he would surely yell at her for being so stupid. But he would also wrap her in his big arms and dare the world to hurt her again.

She swiped at the tears on her cheeks and blew her nose on a napkin. She wanted to go home right now, not in four days.

Hearing Pop preach today had helped clear her thinking. As the panic subsided, she realized how foolish she'd been to attack Lettie Ruth and run away. Neither her aunt or the other woman would ever to do anything to harm her. As for the white man she saw getting out of the car, her reaction had been over the top. Good heavens, it was a medical clinic and he'd probably come to see the doctor. She needed to go back and make her apologies.

*   *   *

Alvin Rayson kept a close watch on the yellow dress, his heart filled with sorrow. She appeared so lost he longed to hold her in his arms and protect her fragile soul. Underneath all the bruises, her looks reminded him of the pretty Delores Townson. And in some way, also of himself.

He caught Delores' eye and suddenly his head filled with images of the future. He saw their wedding. A little white house with roses bushes under the front window. In the middle of his daydream, Miss Kat appeared, and he immediately recognized her as their child. His daughter. He saw the three of them, walking side by side down a long road.

He gave his head a shake, what a flight of fantasy. But then, after studying ghosts for several weeks, anything seemed possible. He took one more look at his guest. She did possess Delores' beautiful coffee coloring and the deep Rayson dimples and honey-colored eyes. He supposed anything was possible.

18

"This ain't a good situation," Floyd told Little Carl. The two men sat on the hood of his pick-up watching the fire ant procession in and out of a cone-shaped mound near the river bank. One hundred feet away, the Tombigbee River rode high, threatening to overflow its banks. "Billy Lee says our gal is holed up in Dr. Niggers clinic."

Little Carl took a swig from the whiskey bottle in the brown bag. "Then we got to go over to there and drag that coon out by her Brillo pad hair."

"You and what army?" Floyd sneered."Remember what happened a few years back? Biggers shot those boys to hell and gone."

"Lucky bastard. Betcha he couldn't do it again."

"You the only one in your family without a set of brains?" Floyd asked, thumping Little Carl on the back of his head. "Biggers fought in the war, for Christ's sake. Got himself a star for bravery. I seen it pinned on his uniform when he marched in the Veteran's Day parade."

"Shitfire, I can go down to Ollie's pawn shop and pick up one of those for two bucks. Betcha his ain't real."

Floyd smacked him on the head again. "It's real, you horse's ass. You ever hear of a place called Iwo Jima?"

"Yeah, and I seen the movie too, John Wayne starred in it. Now there's a man that can really kick the shit out of people."

"Biggers was a real goddamn Marine, Little Carl, not a Hollywood actor. And you can bet a month's pay, a *real* Marine knows how to shoot. He could hit you right between the eyes at 100 yards."

"Only if he can see me."

Floyd turned his head slightly, and a blurry Little Carl came into focus. "What's that supposed to mean?"

"I hear the docs been sleeping with the rest of the niggers down at Webster Methodist lately. So if he's there, then he ain't at his clinic."

"And if he is?"

"Then we blow his head off with some TNT before he can grab his rifle."

Floyd rubbed his chin. "If he's gone, his bitch will still be guarding the door." After a couple of run-ins with Lettie Ruth Rayson he knew she wasn't a shrinking violet. Last time she'd given him a lot of sass and it came real close to being embarrassing. "Maybe I ought to teach her a lesson too," he said smiling broadly.

"You mean his nigger nurse?"

"Yeah, Lettie Ruth. I'm thinking she might make a fine doormat for my boots." Floyd slid off the hood. "Let's get back and talk to the King Kleagle. We got us some strategizing to do."

* * *

Mitch didn't know which he disliked more, riding in the back seat or the way Dreama Simms drove Taxi's car.

"Uh, Miss Simms?" he said, when the light three blocks ahead turned yellow. "You might want to ease off on the gas a little, you have a light coming up." He knew from first hand experience that the De Soto, like a jet plane, required a long runway to stop.

"You just leave the driving to me, *boss*. I got plenty experience behind this wheel."

He clamped his mouth shut and reached for the seat belt. Of course there wasn't one, so he used both arms to brace himself against the front seat. No way in hell could she make a smooth stop. They were too close. Twenty yards away, the light hung in the blue sky, an angry red cyclops staring down on them. The sound of screeching tires confirmed Mitch's original theory, Dreama couldn't drive worth a damn. And no goddamn seat belts in the hunk of junk car.

"See there," she said, fanning the air to erase the burning rubber smoke. "No need for concern. Here we be, sittin' at the light, all in one piece."

"What about Taxi's tires? Think there's any tread left? Or did you burn it all off in your Indianapolis 500 braking maneuver?"

"For a white boy, in my back seat, you sure got lots of opinions," Dreama threw back. "How you plan on getting around town once I kick your butt out this automobile?"

"Alive," Mitch growled. "I'll get around town alive."

When the light turned green she stomped on the gas and the car shot through the intersection. An inch past the crosswalk, she curbed and cut the engine. "Time you and me get it all out in the daylight," she said, turning around to face him. "Appears we don't have much likin' for each other and that's not likely to be changin'."

"Not for another thirty-seven years anyway," Mitch muttered.

"What are you mumbling about?"

"Nothing. Go on, we don't care for each other and…?"

"And, that brings to mind several questions I want answered."

"Fire away."

"What's the story with you and Kat? We talkin' love here?"

Mitch laughed. "Miss Simms, why is it so hard for you to accept we're only friends? Don't you have any men friends?"

"Of course I do. *Negro* men. Not a freckley white face in the whole bunch."

"So your problem is because Kat's a black woman and I'm white man."

"A *black* woman? I'm not so sure I like the sounds of that word. It's insulting."

"Wait a few years, and you'll be shouting 'Black is beautiful'."

Dreama narrowed her eyes and looked at him as though he'd grown a second head. "Black is beautiful? What's it supposed to mean?"

"You'll figure it out. I thought you wanted to talk about me and Kat."

"Me and Kat. Might cozy sounding."

"You mean because we're not a matched set, not both *colored* and not both *white*, the only kind of relationship we can share is of a sexual nature?"

Dreama's dark eyes locked on his, boring deep into his soul. Exactly what Taxi had described earlier, she was looking into his heart. Searching for the good and bad in James Andrew Mitchell. He maintained the eye lock, waiting for her verdict.

A subtle change in her expression told him for better or worse, Dreama Simms had reached her decision. He held his breath, hoping and praying she could overcome her own racial bias and see him as a person. A color free person.

* * *

Kat Templeton shut the door and leaned her head against the stained glass oval. She listened as Lamar and Virgil moved down the sidewalk chattering like a couple of magpies. The boys had insisted on escorting her back to the clinic, and no amount of talking on her part could dissuade them. After all was said and done, she'd been grateful for their company. Her self confidence eroded to such a point she needed a microscope to find enough courage to go to the ladies room. Which pretty much ruled out any walks from the church to the clinic without escorts.

She turned from the door and moved toward the kitchen, a tall glass of iced tea sounded good after the long walk. As she reached the foot of the staircase, she heard a squeak at the top of the landing. Her eyes slowly rose upward, climbing each individual step until she reached the top. She didn't recognize the man descending the steep staircase and the rifle he carried did little to erase her fear. Unable to scream or run, she gripped the newel post, praying for enough strength to rip it out of the floor.

He's white…white…white. The word reverberated in her head, a dying echo in an empty room. All the knowledge and skill she'd possessed as a law officer had deserted her in a head long rush. The months at the Police Academy, all the courses in self-defense and weapons, six years of proving she deserved to wear the silver badge. All of it disappeared the moment the white man took his first step toward her.

Kat wrapped both hands around the post and tugged, but it had been set deep in the flooring and wouldn't even wiggle. She took a quick inventory of the waiting area—old tattered magazines, sofas and chairs—nothing she could use as a weapon. She released the post and raced toward the kitchen. She only needed a few seconds to find a carving knife.

Frantic, she flung open the cupboards. Nothing. She moved on to the drawers, pawing through the contents. Forks, spoons, pot holders, paper sacks. *Where are the knives?* One drawer, shoved crookedly into its slot, stubbornly refused to open. She stopped battling long enough to listen. The stairs squeaked three times in succession as the man descended. *Hurry.* She tightened her grip on the chrome handle, convinced this single drawer held a treasure of knives, and yanked. The container took flight, sailing across the kitchen. Gadgets rained down on the linoleum and table until it collided head on with the wall-mounted clock.

The last utensil clattered noisily to the floor and in the ensuing silence she heard a heavy tread approaching the open kitchen door. *Time.* She needed more time. Standing in the middle of the disarray, her lips moved in a silent prayer. Her eyes filled with frustrated tears. A person could not cook without knives. Vegetables must be chopped, meat sliced and diced. She knew they were here, secreted away, out of the reach of distraught patients. "Like me," Kat said. "I'm a distraught patient. I need to protect myself."

"Protection from what?" The man casually leaned against the door jamb, his empty hands hung at his side. "You know, I'm the one that put the splint on your fingers. Remember?" His soft drawl marked him as a Southerner. A white Southerner.

Kat stared at her bandaged hand then at his face. She didn't remember anyone except Lettie Ruth. It was a lie. He didn't belong here. He was like the others. Unarmed, and handicapped by a broken body, the only option she had was to put distance between them. She shuffled backwards across the kitchen until she bumped into the wall.

Her eyes traveled from his head to his toes. White male, 35–40. Six-feet, black hair and brown eyes. Unshaven and wearing a pair of ill fitting trousers and a wrinkled dress shirt. The dark circles under his eyes indicated a lack of sleep. He reminded Kat of the derelicts she and Mitch had rousted from the city parks, yet his calm demeanor belied his appearance. She looked into his eyes, searching for the instability of a drug addict or the disorientation of the alcoholic.

He reached into his back pocket. Kat grabbed a kitchen chair and raised it above her head, prepared to launch it at him if he so much as twitched.

He tucked the wallet under his arm then held his hands out in front, rotating them, palms up then palms down. "You can put the chair down. I'm not armed."

"Who are you?" she asked, hoping he didn't hear the quaver in her voice. She must keep her fear hidden. Project the image of total control. Make him believe she was someone he didn't dare mess with.

The man kept his eyes on her face and raised his right arm until the wallet fell to the floor. He kicked it across the kitchen. "If you look inside," he told her, "you'll find a picture ID and my medical license."

She used one foot to rake the wallet closer, her eyes still watchful. "Medical license?"

"I'm Dr. Timothy Biggers. You're a patient in my clinic." He offered her a small smile. "In fact, you're *my* patient."

Squatting, she picked up the brown leather square and flipped it open. True to his word, she found an Alabama driver license, issued to Timothy David Biggers. The man in the photograph was better groomed than the one standing across the room from her, but it was the same person. On the opposite side, the promised medical license.

Kat stood up and glared. "How do I know this is real?"

"I guess you don't. If you prefer, we can stand here until Lettie Ruth gets home from church, then you can ask her if it's real."

Her legs buckled and she slid down the wall until she was sitting on the floor, the wallet clutched to her chest.

In three steps Timothy Biggers closed the distance between them. He knelt beside her, and without asking her permission, began the medical routine of pulse taking and shining a light in her eyes. "You'll live," he pronounced, as he replaced the penlight in his shirt pocket.

"But you're not black." Kat hadn't expected a doctor working in the east Hollow to be white.

"Okay, I'll play. Simon says, you're not white."

Kat smiled at his response. She found it difficult to equate this rumpled man and his casual airs, with a physician. He resembled a gardener more than a doctor. Tall and lanky, he constantly brushed at the dark hair falling across his forehead. His brown eyes were kind, yet behind the gentle caring, lived a mischievous twinkle.

"Pleased to meet you, *Dr. Biggers*," she said.

He inclined his head. "Likewise, Miss...?"

"Templeton. I'm Kat Templeton."

"Well, Miss Templeton, I do believe we've covered the social amenities, so you head upstairs and get back in bed." He gestured to the mess surrounding them. "Soon as I put my kitchen together, I'll see to our lunch. You like peanut butter and banana sandwiches?"

* * *

Lettie Ruth and Taxi's pace had slowed as the temperature and humidity climbed. They'd already canvassed dozens of streets in the east Hollow, talking to the folks watering their yards or sitting on porches, but had come up empty. She knew her runaway patient was too pretty to be overlooked by any man under the age of ninety. And the women most surely would have sized her up as possible competition. Someone must remember seeing Kat. They just needed to find the right one.

"There's one more house up the road a piece," Taxi said. "Want me to hurry on ahead and see what they got to say?"

Lettie Ruth pulled the pink blouse free from her blue print skirt and flapped the bottom in the air. "It is a miserable day, and I thank you for the offer, but I ought to finish the job I started."

She pushed down the fear gnawing away at her insides. Kat's disappearance had rattled her more than she'd let on. Rednecks were a dime a dozen around Maceyville, and Lettie was scared to death her patient would cross paths with another bunch. If they got to her again, she doubted the girl could survive. Or would want to survive.

Taxi fanned his face with his hat. "Lettie Ruth, you got any idea where she's gone?"

"Her whereabouts is as big a mystery as that Russian satellite circling above our heads."

He squinted up at the sky. "What they callin' it? Sputnik?"

"I believe so." She tugged on his arm until he looked away from the sky. "Taxi, what do you think about Mitch?"

"I think he's a good white man. Yes sir, a good man."

"And the thing he's got going with Kat? Is it a good thing too?"

"I don't got opinions when it comes to men and women. All I know is, he seems mighty worried if all they got between them is a bed sheet."

Lettie Ruth nodded. "I reckon they share something more than a bed. Me and Timothy been friends for a long time, so I know it's possible for a Negro woman and a white man to get along." She grinned. "And me and Timothy sure ain't got no bed sheet between us."

Taxi laughed. "Aww, Lettie, please don't let Dreama know. Shoot, finding out you and Dr. Tim is just friends would break her heart. You know, she's got all sorts of theories about y'all."

"Don't I know. And I've heard every single one of them more than once. Between us, I think your woman needs to occupy her time some other way besides minding other people's business."

"She does like tellin' folks what to do. And she spends a heck of lot of time minding my bizness, that's for sure." They reached the last house and he opened the rickety gate that separated the yard from the dirt-packed road. "I don't know the family living here. Do you?"

"While back it belonged to the Basteen's, but they couldn't keep up the payments. I never heard who took it over from the bank."

"Well, from the looks, they ain't got much pride in the place."

She agreed. The house badly needed painting and the yard wasn't anything but a pile of dirt. Come the first hard rain, and the whole thing would turn into a mud hole. A couple of scrawny chickens pecked at the ground, but she doubted they would find anything to eat. Bugs liked to live in green grass, not brown dirt.

Taxi stepped up on the tilting porch just as someone shoved the screen door wide open, nearly knocking him to the ground. He regained his balance and politely removed his hat.

"Get the hell off my property, nigger," the obese man standing in the doorframe ordered. A mean junk yard dog scowl covered his face. "And take the bitch with you," he said, pointing to Lettie Ruth.

"Sorry to be bothering you, boss." Taxi backed down the steps, his eyes glued to the ground. "Friends of ours used to live here."

"Cain't you see this ain't no nigger's house, boy?"

"Yes, sir," Taxi mumbled. "I can see it sure ain't."

"Then git!" Having said his piece, he turned and re-entered the house. A second later the door slammed.

Lettie Ruth and Taxi didn't linger. They hurried down the road and several minutes passed before either spoke. "That cracker ass back there is named Louis," Taxi whispered, then glanced over his shoulder as though he feared the man could overhear them.

"You say Louis?" The name sounded familiar and Lettie Ruth frowned. It took her a second to make the connection. When she did, a shudder ran through her entire body. Kat had said the one doing all the biting was named Louis.

Taxi nodded. "Yep. I heard him and the other two bragging down at Bubba's. The fat one back yonder," he jammed his thumb over his shoulder, "is a real mean sumbitch."

Lettie Ruth stopped and turned back to face the house. "You got any names for the other two?"

"Honey, you and me both know you ain't gonna be able to do nothin'. They is white. Nobody never pays no mind to what they do, least not in this town."

"Maybe it's time someone paid some mind," Lettie Ruth said.

"You're startin' to talk like Dreama and that kind of talk always kicks up a whole mess of trouble."

"Trouble or not, I don't see myself letting this one pass. No woman should be thrown in with a pack of worked up males like a bitch dog."

He glanced nervously at the house, then tugged on her arm. "We can't be standing here gawkin', he's bound to be watching us out the window."

Lettie Ruth sighed. "I know, Taxi, I know," she said sadly. "I'm just so tired of the way things is down here. I'm beginning to think Dreama's right."

"Right about what?"

"About changin' things in Maceyville. About it being time for us Negroes to get treated like human people."

"It's been that time for a long time. But if Dr. King can't keep folks worked up, you and me ain't gonna see nothin' new."

"You know those protests planned for Birmingham? Alvin told me he personally signed up more than fifty from Webster Avenue Methodist alone."

"Yeah, I'm planning on goin' to one or two myself. You on the list for Palm Sunday?"

"Dreama took care of that." She shielded her eyes and pointed at the dust cloud down the road. "Somebody movin' our way mighty fast."

Taxi didn't hesitate, he grabbed Lettie Ruth around the waist and flung her into the drainage ditch. Half a beat later he lay beside her. They ducked as the white stake-bed truck rumbled past sending a storm of pebbles and dirt raining down on them.

Lettie Ruth peeked over the edge of the drainage ditch. The pickup skidded to a halt in front of the last house. Two white men got out and stomped up the porch. After a second the door opened and they went inside. She turned to Taxi. "Are those the other two?" She didn't have to hear for his reply, the tight wad in her gut had already answered.

"Uh-huh. That's Floyd with the black hair. The other one, they call Little Carl." He climbed out of the ditch first, then reached down and hauled Lettie Ruth onto the hard packed shoulder of the road. "I think we ought to be movin' along. This road's a bit crowded," he said.

"Let me get straightened out first." Lettie Ruth brushed at her blouse, but the dirt, combined with the sweat soaked fabric had turned her clothes into caked brown layers. She gave up on the blouse and worked on her shoes. Balanced on her right foot, took off her left shoe and shook the gravel and loose soil free. Then reversed the process. Engrossed in her grooming activities, she failed to see the white truck pull away from the house.

Taxi, likewise occupied with the gravel in his shoes, also missed the action at the end of the road. By the time they were alerted by the rattling pickup it was too late for a stealth getaway. All they could do was to jump back into the ditch, then claw and scramble up the other side.

"Gotta get into the corn," Lettie Ruth panted. If they could reach the field then they might have a chance. It was still early in the growing season, but there'd been enough rain and warm days for the corn to be knee high. And that should be tall enough to discourage the truck from driving into the field.

At the edge of the corn they took off down different rows, running zig-zag patterns. The men would be carrying shotguns or rifles, and they didn't want to make easy targets.

Thirty yards into the field Lettie Ruth tripped over a rock, and sprawled face first on the ground. The fall knocked the wind out of her and it took several precious seconds to get back on her feet. Unable to draw a deep breath, the best she could manage was a slow trot. She shot a glance over her shoulder. The men weren't far behind. She heard their shouted threats and the laughter.

Three rows over, and several yards ahead, she saw Taxi moving fast, his knees pumped so hard they nearly hit his chin with each step. He had a good lead on the men and with her help could get away. Lettie knew if they caught her she had a fair chance of coming out of this alive. But if they got a hold of Taxi, it would be a death sentence for sure.

So Lettie Ruth stopped running and turned to face her pursuers.

19

The men surrounding Lettie Ruth were like her daddy's old hunting dogs. As a girl she'd watched the dogs move in on coons and possums. In a pack, they'd circle the prey, then one at a time they'd dart in and nip at the trapped animal. The prey always lost, but each time the little creatures had impressed her with their courage and fight.

Like a spoke in the middle of a wheel, she slowly turned until she'd made eye contact with each man. She hated the sound of her ragged breathing and tried to stop gulping down the air. These dogs were waiting for the first sign she was failing, and then they'd move in for the kill. She allowed herself one last deep lung full of air. She preferred dying from lack of oxygen to showing them any weakness.

She stood erect, her head held high. This time, the *coon* would be walking away alive.

Little Carl took a step closer and sniffed the air. "This girl smells like something dead."

"She does put out a powerful stink," Floyd agreed. He flicked the hem of her pink blouse. "Got mud and shit all over her clothes. Whatcha think, boys, this gal in need of a bathing?"

Louis nodded. "I got a big ole wash tub up at the house. And some wire scrub brushes."

"How about we give you a bath?" Floyd asked.

Lettie Ruth pressed her lips together and remained silent. They were already looking to harm her, so why speed things up by shooting her mouth off.

Louis placed both hands on her shoulders and pushed Lettie Ruth to her knees. "Maybe you'll feel more like talkin' after you eat something."

She watched his pudgy hands work the fly on his jeans. When he reached inside, she closed her eyes.

"Looouisss!" The voice carried the quarter mile from house to field without losing one decibel.

Louis jerked as if a jolt of electricity had ripped through his body. He wheeled around and faced the house. A woman in a red dress stood on the porch. "Whaatt?" he hollered.

"Git back here," the woman ordered. "Got work for you to do."

"Put yourself back inside your britches before Marie gets a look," Little Carl whispered.

"Jesus, oh Jesus," Louis whispered, fumbling with his shriveled genitals.

Floyd shook his head and snorted. "Why are you two morons whispering? That cow's a good quarter mile away. She can't hear you."

"Oh yes she can," Louis said as he stuffed himself back into his pants. "Marie's got ears like a goddamn bat."

"Bats don't got no ears," Little Carl declared.

"Do so," Louis argued.

"Don't either."

Thanks to the woman hollering down the road. Most of the danger had passed for Lettie Ruth Rayson. And she was tired of listening to their stupid argument. She looked up at Little Carl and said, "You're wrong. Bat's have ears. They can hear, but they're blind. That means they can't see."

"Shut it up, nigger bitch." Little Carl kicked at her leg. "And get the hell out of here."

"But plan on seein' us real soon," Louis promised, then glanced over his shoulder at the woman still standing on the porch. "Be right there, honey pie!" he yelled.

Lettie Ruth stood and brushed at her skirt. She looked from man to man, memorizing their features. "Good afternoon, gentlemen," she said, then turned and walked toward the road, head high. Several feet behind her she heard Little Carl's whiney voice.

"Did you know bats was blind, Floyd?"

The sound of flesh hitting flesh made her smile.

*   *   *

Dreama Simms didn't speak for almost an hour, and Mitch wasn't sure what to make of her silence. Either she'd decided he wasn't worth the time of day or she just didn't have anything to say. Being the eternal optimist, Mitch decided to go with the latter. It seemed plausible Dreama would prefer concentrating on the search rather than engaged in polite conversation.

Feeling momentarily invincible, impervious to her salvos, he tapped her shoulder. "Miss Simms? Looks to me like we've run out east Hollow. You plan on canvassing the west side now?"

"I plan on heading back to the clinic," she said. "We ain't gonna find that girl riding around in this automobile. I got to get out and talk to people. That's how you find somebody."

"You're right. Nothing better than one to one questioning."

"Why would she run off like that?" Dreama asked.

For a moment Mitch wondered if she'd spoken to him or to herself. Still wearing his impervious to sharp tongues cloak, he replied, "The same question has been on my mind. Did you talk to her much before she left the clinic?"

"She wasn't in no shape for conversation when we dragged her out of that field. Then when me and Taxi came back to the clinic after my show, Lettie said Kat don't feel up to talking."

Dreama's detailed answer surprised Mitch. She'd provided information and been civil about it. The hot anger she'd allowed to simmer all morning seemed to have evaporated. Or at least cooled down several degrees. But he hesitated to make any assumptions with regard her new attitude, civility and trust were two very different cans of worms. For the moment he'd settle for civil. He'd work on the trust later.

"You have any idea what she and Lettie Ruth may have discussed?" Mitch asked.

Dreama glanced over her shoulder. "Why?"

He heard the ice in her single word. What now? No matter what he said, he couldn't win. "I only asked, because if she talked about a particular place or mentioned a name, it might tell us where to look," he explained.

"Best I know Kat don't know nobody in Maceyville, except for you. And I ain't got any idea about her family ties. Course, you'd be the one knowing the answer to that, seein' how y'all is such good friends."

Since he didn't want to mix it up again, he decided to ignore the last part of her statement. "Her folks are down in New Orleans," he said, omitting Lettie Ruth and Alvin Rayson. Technically, at this time, neither one was related to Kathleen Rayson Templeton, since she hadn't been born yet.

Dreama tapped her fingers on the steering wheel. "Well, if you got any ideas where we ought to be looking, go ahead and speak up."

Encouraged by her response he forged ahead. "Could we go to the field where you found her? I'd like to check it out. See if I can turn up something to help nail those three bastards."

"Taxi told me you was a policeman. You gonna investigate?" she asked, almost smiling.

"Yeah, I'm going to investigate."

And that's not all, he thought. I'm going to put those boys on trial, tie the noose around their beet-red necks and then throw the fucking rope over the tree myself.

"Good," Dreama said. "You investigate. Then when you get all done…tie that rope real tight."

Mitch could feel his face getting hot and knew he'd turned a nice shade of embarrassed crimson. Apparently Dreama Simms was another Voodoo Woman, capable of reading his thoughts.

Before long they left paved city streets behind and bumped along hard packed farm roads. Mitch rolled the back window down, breathing in the Spring air. Varying sizes of green shoots poked through the rich damp soil in the fields on each side of the road. Ragtag scarecrows stood guard, but the crows weren't intimidated. In fact, most of the strawmen only provided the scavenger birds with a place to roost.

The farther they traveled from Maceyville city proper, the bigger the trees. Sprawling canopies of live oak and cypress now shaded the lane. Huckleberry and blackberry bushes crawled over the split rail fences along the shoulder of the road. The clusters of berries were still hard and green, but Mitch thought it would be a good harvest come August and September. In his own time, most of the trees and roadside brush had been cleared to make room for television cable lines. No more summer berries

A little way past a recently burned house, Dreama pulled over and stopped at the rutted intersection of two unmarked dirt lanes. She stuck her hand out the window and pointed. "When we come across her, she'd crawled to the edge of that field over there."

Mitch climbed out and rested his arms on the roof of the car and studied the cotton patch. The recently cultivated soil would make it almost impossible to determine the exact location of the assault. Any blood, signs of struggle or footprints would have been obliterated. Even though he didn't expect to discover anything, he needed to try.

He'd gone forty or fifty yards into the field when he heard the bleating car horn. Dreama stood beside the De Soto, pointing down the road. The sleeves of her green silk dress shimmered in the late morning sun as she waved her arms.

Mitch stood on tiptoe and squinted, he saw two figures coming toward them. A man and woman. From Dreama's reaction he decided they were her friends and none of his concern. He resumed his search. A second later she shouted. Mitch glanced over his shoulder and saw her running full speed, her high heels kicking up little clouds of dust. He'd been a cop too long to ignore these actions. First the horn honking, then arm waving, shouting and now the running. It all blended together in a 'something is wrong' stew.

Now it was his turn to run. He reached the car the same time as the trio arrived. The crisp clothes Lettie Ruth and Taxi were wearing the last time he'd seen them, were caked with dirt and mud. Scratches and blooming bruises decorated their faces, arms and legs. "What happened to you two?" he asked.

Taxi and Lettie Ruth exchanged a look. "Took a spill off the road," Taxi said.

He knew a lie when he heard one and the fact it came from Taxi hurt his feelings. He'd considered the man to be a friend, and now Taxi had shut Mitch out of the secret clubhouse like the new kid on the block. *The new white kid*, a voice in his head mocked.

"It must have been one hell of a spill," he said, not caring if he sounded petulant. Taxi twirled his hat around in his hand and nodded. Lettie Ruth wouldn't meet his eyes, apparently her lying skills weren't as fully developed. "You spill off that same road, Lettie?"

"Got my good skirt and new pink blouse all dirtied up," she complained.

"Uh-huh. Where did all this dirtying and spilling take place?"

"Over yonder," Taxi said, waving his arm in no definite direction.

"Bull shit. This is all bull shit and you both know—"

"Y'all need a cool drink and some food," Dreama interrupted. "Let's head home." She hustled Lettie Ruth into the front seat and climbed in beside her. Taxi slipped in behind the wheel and started the engine.

"Climb on in the back, Mitch," Taxi said.

Mitch was so busy being pissed off that he got in the car without argument. The 'something is wrong' stew had turned into a damn five course meal.

* * *

"Pleased to meet you, Dr. Biggers." Mitch tried to erase the surprise from his face as they shook hands.

Biggers laughed and patted him on the shoulder. "It's okay, I get that reaction quite often. People don't expect a white man, seein' how I live and work in the east Hollow."

"You did kind of catch me off guard," Mitch admitted. "And I thought I'd met my quota on surprises already."

"I think there's one or two left in the bag."

Mitch whirled around at the comment. A smiling Kathleen Templeton stood at the top of the stairs, her dimples bigger and deeper than ever. "Hey, partner." The two words were the most he could get out.

He took the stairs two at a time until he reached the top then scooped Kat in his arms and carried her down to the waiting room. When he placed her on the sofa she wouldn't let go of his neck until he sat beside her.

"I wanted you to come," she said, as tears filled her eyes. "I prayed and prayed."

He kissed her cheek. "I'm here, kid. I'm here."

Mitch heard someone sniff and looked up in time to catch Dreama wiping tears off her cheeks. Their eyes locked and she nodded, as close to an apology as he would get.

Kat gasped in surprise. "Is that…?"

Mitch jumped in before blurted out something about the future housekeeping manager. "Kat, I'd like you to meet, Dreama Simms. And that's Taxi Devore over by the stairs. These two brought you to Dr. Biggers clinic."

"Holy shit," she muttered, as the couple crossed the room.

"You looking a whole lot better than the last time I seen you," Dreama said.

"And you're looking a whole lot younger than the last time I saw you," Kat responded, then jumped slightly as Mitch poked her in the side.

"Taxi and I met last night at Bubba's Julep Junction," Mitch said, trying to cover her *faux pas*. "He's been a real help locating you."

Kat turned to him. "Bubba's? But you always go to The Blue."

"Dreama works at The Blue," Mitch interrupted. "She plays the—"

"That's right," Kat said to the woman, "you're a singer."

"Not anymore, honey," Dreama said quietly. "Not anymore."

"Now she's the best piano player east of the Mississippi," Taxi said proudly. "None better."

Dreama reached for Taxi's hand. "Thank you," she whispered.

"Hey, I don't know about the rest of y'all," Biggers said, interrupting the awkward moment, "but I'm hungry."

"Then get out there and fix yourself something to eat, Timothy," Lettie Ruth said.

Biggers moved toward the kitchen. "You'd think I'd get a little respect around here," he grumbled. "It is my house and my clinic."

"Then you ought to be doin' the cooking," Lettie Ruth declared.

The knock on the front door waylaid Biggers' next salvo and he yelled, "I'm closed!"

"You can't close," Lettie Ruth scolded. "This is a doctor's office and you're the doctor."

"I'm always closed on Tuesday's. Besides, you're the nurse."

"What's that 'pose to mean?"

Biggers plopped down in the arm chair. "It means go get the door."

Lettie Ruth clucked her tongue and gave him a sharp look. "You behave yourself," she whispered, as she opened the door. "It's only Alvin, so you can relax."

Biggers grinned and kicked his shoes off. "Howdy, Preacher," he called over his shoulder.

Mitch felt Kat stiffen when her father walked into the room. He was equally on edge. He'd been through more than enough family reunions lately.

Alvin Rayson glanced around the room. His gaze settled on the two people seated on the sofa. "Good to see you again, Miss Kat." He walked over and extended his hand to Mitch. "Alvin Rayson."

Mitch stood and took his hand. Slightly taken aback at the young Pop, he was at a loss for words. "Mitch...James Mitchell."

"Miss Kat came to the Ladies Prayer Breakfast this morning," Rayson announced. "By the by, I didn't see anybody else in this room sittin' in the pews."

"Alvin, me and your sister heard you practicing that sermon so many times we could of got up and preached it ourselves," Dreama said.

"It wouldn't have been near as good," Kat said, her voice catching.

Rayson's chest puffed out. "About time we got somebody around here that knows what they's talkin' about."

"That's cause she don't have to sit and listen to you all the time, Alvin," Dreama said.

"Food," Biggers croaked, feigning imminent death by starvation. "I need food."

Lettie Ruth grabbed him by the arm and hauled him to his feet. "Then get your lily white butt out in the kitchen. On second thought, stay right where you are." She gave him a little shove and he fell back in the chair.

"This mean you're gonna cook for me?" Biggers asked, as she turned and walked away.

"No, I'm cooking for everybody else," she said over her shoulder. "You can go down to the Daisy Wheel Café."

He turned to the group for sympathy. "Y'all think she ought to be able to kick a man out of his own kitchen?"

"Don't know if she ought to," Taxi said. "But I'm on my way to that kitchen to help out before I end up at the Daisy Wheel."

"Mitch?" Biggers pleaded.

"Don't know nothin' about cookin', Miz Scarlett," the King of Rock and Roll said.

Kat groaned.

"I heard that, Mitch," Lettie Ruth yelled. "You go right along with Timothy, both y'all can eat at that tacky café."

20

APRIL 03—WEDNESDAY

After sleeping until almost noon, Mitch felt half human for the first time since leaving his own Maceyville. He spent the early afternoon helping out in the clinic, or as Lettie Ruth called it, 'getting in her way.' An hour ago she'd dismissed him from medical duty and sent him outdoors to 'play.'

He came out the kitchen door and found Kat in an Adirondack chair. The back yard was hidden behind a screen of tall junipers so he felt it safe to join her. As he crossed the lawn his eyes wandered over the three-storied clapboard, admiring the roses blooming on the trellis. Now he knew where Lettie Ruth had gotten the fragrant flowers he'd seen in nearly every room.

The doctor had told him the clinic had once been the Heart of Dixie Hotel. When Biggers' began to remodel, he'd left the lobby intact so he could live in the manager's quarters behind the front desk. The large rectangular dining room, across the foyer from the lobby, he'd divided into four examination rooms. The original kitchen, at the rear of the building and accessed by walking down the narrow front hall, he updated with modern appliances.

On the second floor, four of the six guest rooms—three on each side of the open U-stairwell—served as a hospital. Of the remaining two rooms, Biggers converted one into an office, the second into a TV room and medical supply storage. He said he'd blown most of his budget on the bath at the head of the stairs. He'd gutted the old bathroom and rebuilt from the ground up, equipping it with a large sunken whirlpool tub and a separate shower.

Lettie Ruth lived alone on the third floor, where she had her choice of six bedrooms and a private bath. No whirlpool.

"Did you know we're staying in the former Heart of Dixie Hotel?" Mitch asked as he made himself comfortable in the empty Adirondack chair.

Kat whistled. "Heart of Dixie, huh? Sounds kind of upscale for the east Hollow."

"I don't think an east or west Maceyville existed in the 1800s. If there had been, I'm sure the city council would have moved the boundary lines to accommodate the hotel."

"I noticed a lot of land attached to this place," she said. "Must be two or three acres."

"In our time this whole area is a run down trailer park."

She pointed to the elaborately landscaped lawn. "How does Biggers pay for the upkeep on all those bushes?"

"No upkeep. A few patients pay off their medical bills by doing the yard work."

"I wish somebody would offer to do my gardening in exchange for policing their neighborhood."

"In your dreams," he said. "We're lucky to get a free cup of coffee on Christmas."

She laid her head back on the chair and closed her eyes. "This trip didn't exactly turn out the way I'd planned," she said, wincing at a sudden pain. "About the time I think I have a handle on the rape, I go into a tailspin."

Mitch stared at his partner. The bruises and black eye were ugly reminders of what had happened to her and he found it difficult to keep up the light banter. He didn't know what to say. He felt as helpless as he had when the doctors diagnosed Lisa's brain aneurysm. All the time Lisa spent in the hospital, he'd never said the right thing. He'd sat beside her bed like a mute, a living ghost no one could see or hear. He didn't exist. And now someone else needed him. He prayed for the right words.

"It will take time, Kat. No one expects you to act like nothing happened," he said, knowing his response didn't come close to what he wanted to say. Or what she needed to hear.

"I thought I would be a stronger person." She opened her eyes and stared across the gently sloping lawn. "Everything scares me now. A floorboard creaks outside my room and I imagine the boogie man. Yesterday, two twelve-year-old boys walked me home from church because I couldn't do it alone."

"Once we're home, out of this crazy place, things will get better."

"No, they won't, Mitch. I'll be carrying these bruises until the end of my life. Nothing will heal them except seeing those three bastards in jail."

Mitch agreed. Unfortunately, given the time and place, he knew their crimes would go unpunished. He also suspected Kat knew this as well, which provided the fuel for her fears. "I'll never know what you went through," he said. "Or what you are going through now. But I'm willing to listen, and help in anyway I can."

"Then start helping by taking me home."

The next few minutes weren't going to help his partner. They would probably do the exact opposite, but there was no way around it, she had to know. "I've got a couple of things to tell you, before we get into all that."

Kat sat upright in the chair, her honey-colored eyes frightened. "What's wrong?"

She knew him too well. She'd already read the bad news message in his face. He took a deep breath. "Pop had a heart attack yesterday morning." Mitch knew his approach lacked diplomacy and tact, but there was never an easy way to deliver bad news.

"Is he…is he okay?"

"The doctor said it's bad, honey." Mitch looked at his shoes. The anguish he saw in her face broke his heart.

"I never considered the strain my coming back here would put on him. He sat right beside me, his arm around my shoulder and told me how bad things were in 1963." She shook her head. "But I didn't listen."

"But he's been talking this way for years. His heart attack was just a matter of time, you know how he eats. It's not your fault."

"Thinking about Pop lying in a hospital all alone, with no family around to comfort him, is crushing the life out of me," she said, rocking back and forth.

He reached across the space between their chairs and squeezed her hand. "Don't do this to yourself. He knows where you are and Alvin understands why you're not with him."

She brushed a tear off her cheek. "You know, yesterday I thought the only reason you were here was because we're partners and you were going to watch my six. The Red and Black team live and in person in 1963."

"God, Kat, I wanted to come with you. But I didn't have your courage. I kept sensing something really bad would happen to me if I went with you."

"Then why did you put yourself in the middle of all this?"

Mitch shrugged. "Hey, bad voodoo or not, when you need me I'll always be there for you."

"Thank you."

"'Tis nothing m'lady." He took her hand. "I talked to Alvin yesterday, and I guess there are a few things he forgot to tell you. He was worried."

"Then I'm right, his heart attack *was* triggered by my stupid trek into the past." She took a deep breath. "What did he forget?"

"I don't know. His machines started beeping before we got a chance to talk about it, and the doctor kicked me out of the CCU."

Her grip tightened on his hand. "We have to go home, Mitch. Go home today."

"Can't go today."

"Then when?"

"Let me check." He pulled his hand free and took the tattered Arson/Fatality computer printout from his back pocket. He studied the names and times. "Looks like we aren't going anywhere until Friday."

"This is so wrong," Kat said. "Pop's in the hospital and I'm thirty-seven years and three days away from him."

"You have zero control over this issue, Kathleen. We came through at a certain time and we have to leave at a certain time."

"He needs me, Mitch."

"Your Pop's a tough old bird. He knows the score, he'll still be there on Friday."

"That's April 5. Mitch. The same day Lettie Ruth..." Kat's voice dropped off, her thoughts unspoken.

A gust of wind rattled the paper in his hand. "We still have time to make some changes in the past. It's not too late for Lettie Ruth."

"Right now I'm more concerned with Pop's future. Besides, the past has already changed."

"What do you mean?"

"You and me, Mitch." She waved in the direction of the clinic. "We weren't part of their lives before. But what happened to me has drawn this group together."

"They weren't total strangers before you came along. Their relationships were already established."

"Those were different relationships. Now they have new ones."

"I don't know. Things seem pretty much SOP around here. Everyone seems to have followed through with the whatever they were doing, or planned to do, before you and I showed up." He said the words, recited the litany but in his heart he knew better.

Kat shook her head. "Wrong, partner. I can name three changes since our arrival."

"Like what?"

"Like how Lettie and Dreama *didn't* go to the Ladies Prayer Breakfast yesterday. You really think my aunt would have missed hearing her brother preach the first time if not for me?"

Mitch grunted and picked at a mosquito bite on his arm.

She held up two fingers. "I've heard Pop tell the story of how he and Lettie Ruth took part in the Birmingham lunch counter sit-in *on this date* and got arrested a hundred times. But they didn't go today and he's been here all afternoon. Mitch, he's suppose to be in jail."

"That's a big change."

"Glad I got your attention," Kat said. "And the third thing, because they were out looking for me, Lettie Ruth and Taxi ended up in the wrong part of town this morning and got jumped."

Mitch's freckles popped out on his too red face in response to her last statement. "Rein it in, boy," she cautioned. "We've had our share of troubles with that bunch, don't stir it up."

"Damn it!" He roared, jumping out of the chair. His long legs got tangled in the arm rest and as he shook them free the chair flipped over. "I've had enough of this racist shit. What in the hell is the matter with the people in this town?"

"That's just the way things are. It's 1963, Mitch."

"1963 sucks big time."

"No argument on that point." Kat drew up her knees and pulled the yellow dress skirt over them then patted the end of the chair. "Sit down here and listen to me."

"Don't feel like sitting," he grumbled.

"Sit, stand. I don't care what you do…as long as you pay attention. This is not our time, Mitch. We don't belong here and our dumb mistakes will bring a world of hurt down on these people."

"Where are you going with this?"

"We have to let the past remain the past," she said sadly.

"That past include Lettie Ruth?"

She nodded. "Remember your speech about making a ripple in the pond? Well, our ripple is turning into a tsunami. If we change what originally happened, we could end up getting more people hurt."

"I don't see anything like that happening," he argued. "Missing a church service and one sit-in doesn't fall in the disaster category. Nobody has gotten hurt."

"All right, then what about the car full of rednecks that chased you and Taxi? Would that have happened if you'd been asleep in your apartment early yesterday, instead of getting into brawls down at Bubba's Julep Junction?"

"I handled the situation. Taxi won't have any more trouble out of them."

"Oh yeah? I'll bet next month's pay those boys will be looking for his green De Soto for a long time to come."

"Come on, Kat. They don't have any reason to go after him again."

"They don't need a reason. Taxi is a *Negro*. Not a black man. Not an African-American. But a Negro. And that same Negro got caught ridin' around in a car with a white man. That dog don't bark down here."

"They could've chased him any time. Doesn't mean it's my fault." Mitch felt like a fool, but he couldn't let her keep thinking along these lines. She'd been through enough without adding the rest of the world's troubles to her load.

"If I'm willing to take my share of the blame, you should do the same," she lectured. "Yesterday morning Lettie Ruth was supposed to be in church, not on a road with Taxi. And she and Pop were supposed to sitting at a lunch counter in Birmingham this afternoon. Hear me on this, none of these things happened before."

"Who's to say we're the catalysts?" he argued.

"Stop it, right now," she ordered. "You know we're at the heart of these changes. We have to leave the past alone. Otherwise, we'll create a bigger mess. Now, what time can we leave on Friday?"

"On Friday," he ran his finger down the names. "we can leave at—Shit."

"No." Kat grabbed his wrist. "Please, Mitch. I don't think I can stay here much longer."

He shook free of her grasp and held up his hand. "Lettie Ruth's death has moved back two days. From this Friday, to Sunday. And other names have been added since we started this conversation."

She buried her face in her hands. "I told you we were the carriers of death."

21

"Listen to me, Kat." Mitch pulled her hands away from her face. "You cannot fall apart now. I know you've been through hell, but if you don't get a grip, the hell is going to start all over again." He watched her struggle with her demon emotions. After a few minutes the lines smoothed as her facial structure was reshaped into a mask of strength.

"All right," she said, smoothing the wrinkles out of her dress. She met his eyes. "Explain yourself." The hysteria was gone, her voice calm and determined.

Impressed by his partners incredible willpower, he felt immediate relief. Could she keep it together once she learned the latest twist in their nightmare? "A few minutes ago we had a green light to head home at 12:45 A.M. on Friday." He handed her the printout. "Take a look at this."

She read down the Arson/Fatality names. "Sweet Jesus," she whispered. "The 5th isn't even on the list now. How can it change?"

"I guess we're having a much more interesting discussion than I thought."

Kat stared at him. "But *how?*"

"Voodoo." He ran his fingers through his ginger hair. "Hell, I don't have the answer. All I know is Jane Doe is gone and Lettie Ruth has been added. Along with three brand-new victims."

She shook her head. "Not three, Mitch. Count again. There are four new names on that damnable list."

"Four? There were only three names when I handed it to you." He walked over to her chair and knelt in the grass. "Show me," he said, pointing at the paper with a shaky finger.

MARCH-APRIL 1963 ARSON/FATALITY

2789 10th	03-02-63	Pauley, GladysN	#23476	01:25 A.M.
4721 Riverside	03-05-63	Richards, DilmerN	#23477	12:11 A.M.
801 Mt. View	03-07-63	Carpenter, AliceN	#23478	01:03 A.M.
5429 Park	03-10-63	DeCarlo, MattieN	#23479	01:30 A.M.
109 Blodgett	03-17-63	Beason, Harold	#23480	06:50 P.M.
900 Grant	03-29-63	Peterson, Abel	#23481	02:15 A.M.
7643 Elm	04-01-63	Jefferson, TyroneN	#23482	05:05 A.M.
6780 South	04-01-63	Josephs, TupeloN	#23483	06:12 P.M.
654 Azalea	04-02-63	Spencer, LeroyN	#23484	05:20 A.M.
119 Webster	04-07-63	Devore, MaximilianN	#23485	09:45 P.M.
119 Webster	04-07-63	Gordon, LamarN	#23486	09:45 P.M.
119 Webster	04-07-63	Rayson, Lettie RuthN	#23487	09:45 P.M.
119 Webster	04-07-63	Templeton, KathleenN	#23488	09:45 P.M.
119 Webster	04-07-63	Smith, Louis	#23489	09:45 P.M.

"These last four, not counting Lettie Ruth," Kat said, touching each name as she read them aloud. "*Maximilian Devore. Lamar Gordon. Kathleen Templeton. Louis Smith.*"

"This is a very weird piece of paper," Mitch said, taking the list out of her hand. He got up and began to pace in front of her chair. "It all goes down on the 7th now. Let's run it through and see what turns up."

"You mean a connection to us?"

He ignored her question and said, "Besides Lettie Ruth, we have Maximilian Devore."

"Which is Taxi," she said. "And we know him."

"What about Lamar Gordon?"

"Lamar is the Webster Avenue preacher's son. I met him on Monday." Kat choked back a sob. "Jesus, Mitch, he'll be thirteen on Friday…but because of our chance meeting, he's gonna die on Sunday."

"Hold on a minute. You saw him once and only for a few minutes." He shook his head. "There's no way to connect that brief encounter to his name on the list."

"If I'm right, and we're the eye of this storm, the more we interact, the greater the danger."

He stopped pacing and trapped her honey-colored eyes with his blue ones. "You just negated your own argument. You're not interacting with the kid," he said slowly.

"Yes, I am. Yesterday, Lamar and his cousin, Virgil, took me to the Gordon's house to change clothes, then on over to the church. He's a kid, Mitch. A kid with a great story to share with his buddies. Lamar will be talkin' and then all of Maceyville will be gossiping about the black woman raped by three white boys." Kat took a deep breath. "When April 7 rolls around, those three animals will be poundin' on his door to make sure he keeps his mouth shut."

"Then why isn't Virgil on the list? You know him too, so if your theory is on target, his name should be right beside Lamar's."

Kat played with her dress hem. "Wait another five minutes then check again."

"That's not funny, Kat."

"Knowing what's going to happen is a heavy burden. The power of life over death." She looked up, her eyes sparkling with tears. "Mitch, how did you get here?"

"The door opened at 6:12 Monday night."

"I left that same morning and I know there *wasn't* a 6:12."

"Stop right there," Mitch said. "I know what you're thinking…and it's wrong."

"Let me see the name."

He stepped away, hands behind his back. "The way your mind is working you'll find a vague connection whether one exists or not."

"There was not a 6:12 when I left," she repeated. "I want to know who's in that time slot."

Mitch glanced at the list. "It's no one you know. Let it go, Kat."

"I can't let it go. *Who is it?*" Her tone was hard, demanding.

"Mr. Josephs," Mitch said quietly. "Mr. Tupelo Josephs."

Kat's face turned a shade lighter. "When I first ran into the three men, Tupelo Josephs stood up to them. He tried to make them leave me alone. And now he's dead."

"Kat, everything is turning upside down. I'm not capable of rational thought any more."

"Well, I am. The wheels all started turning with my...my rape."

"Not all the wheels. Mr. Josephs was an old man, Kat. Old people die every day because of natural causes. Who's to say that's not what happened to him?"

"That's not the case this time. His death is my fault."

"Stop saying that. Let's examine this logically. You *can't* be responsible for every new name that pops up. For example, what about this last name, Louis Smith? Are you going to claim responsibility for him too?"

"He's one of the—He's the fat one."

Mitch slapped his forehead. "Of course. I ran into that jackass at Bubba's." The realization suddenly hit home, Kat's interaction theory was right on the button. "I guess you're not the only one with connections, Kat, seems I've got two of my own, Taxi and Louis Smith."

"You skipped Kathleen Templeton."

"It ain't gonna happen."

"April 7 is going to be a lousy Palm Sunday for the Rayson family."

Mitch studied the list one more time. "Kat, did you notice the time of death and the addresses?" He sat on the end of her chair.

"Which ones?" She leaned forward.

"The last five," he ran his finger down the names.

119 Webster	04-07-63	Devore, MaximilianN	#23485	09:45 P.M.
119 Webster	04-07-63	Gordon, LamarN	#23486	09:45 P.M.
119 Webster	04-07-63	Rayson, Lettie RuthN	#23487	09:45 P.M.

119 Webster	**04-07-63**	Templeton, KathleenN	#23488	09:45 P.M.
119 Webster	**04-07-63**	Smith, Louis	#23489	09:45 P.M.

"See, Kat, they're all the same. The address is 119 Webster and the time is 9:45 P.M.," he said.

"Lord in heaven, Mitch, we're all gonna die in the Freedom Methodist Church on Palm Sunday."

Mitch took Kat in his arms, rocking her like a small child. "You're reading an out of date document, partner. We're going to make five changes in that time line."

She pulled away. "How about cutting it down to four?" she asked, her eyes hardening into crystalized honey. "Louis Smith can eat shit and die for all I care."

"As you wish, m'lady."

22

Lettie Ruth locked the front door, officially closing the clinic for the day. So many changes had taken place in just a few days. She couldn't remember the last time she or Timothy had locked the doors at the end of the work day. Before Kat came along, they may have had a little trouble with the local boys, but nothing that would have called for bolting the door shut. Nervous, without knowing why, she peeked out the window. The street was quiet, folks all inside getting ready for their suppers. She rubbed the goose bumps on her arm, then hurried out to the kitchen.

In between the afternoon's patients she'd managed to fit in a little kitchen duty. After all her huffing and puffing yesterday about cooking, she'd put together a fine supper of honey cured ham, sweet potatoes, green beans and biscuits. And to make it up to Timothy, two pecan pies. She took the ham out of the oven and slipped the pies onto the cooking rack. She double checked the oven's temperature gauge, then gave it a good hard tap with her finger. The cranky old stove overheated lately and she didn't want them to burn.

The oversized kitchen table made it difficult to move around the room, so she removed the extra leaf. Dreama and Taxi had begged off, claiming they were too tired to eat. Lettie chuckled. They might be too tired to eat, she thought, but they ain't too tired for much else.

She counted out five place settings. Once she got everybody rounded up, they could sit down for supper. Alvin and Timothy were napping upstairs, trying to make up for their sleepless nights guarding the church. Her house guests were still out back. She glanced out the kitchen window. Kat and Mitch were sharing one chair, their heads bent close together over a piece of paper. She never knew two people to do so much serious talking. It would be nice to see one of them smile ever now and then.

She pushed open the screen and called, "Supper's ready, y'all get washed." Not waiting for a response she shut the door and started for the second floor, time to wake her sleeping beauties.

Lettie Ruth could hear Alvin's snoring before she got half way up the stairs. She found him sprawled flat on his back on the bed in the first hospital room. The ceiling fan made slow lazy circles over his head. The outside shutters kept most of the late afternoon sun out of the room, but his face was sweat beaded and his damp undershirt clung to his skin.

He looked so tired she hesitated to wake him. It wouldn't be any trouble to stick a plate in the oven and let him sleep on. She'd turned away to tiptoe out when he spoke.

"Hey, Sister. Everything okay?"

"Everything's fine, honey," she said, facing him. "I came to wake you for supper."

He sat up and sniffed the air. "Something sure smells good. You make a pecan pie?"

"I made two. Thought I better try and make up for the mean way I've been treating Timothy lately."

Rayson laughed. "Shoot, he didn't pay you no mind."

"Even so, I should try to be nicer to him." She swatted his foot. "Now, get yourself together and come on down. I gotta go wake Timothy. He'd never forgive me if I let him sleep through a meal."

"Miss Kat and Mitch still here?"

Lettie Ruth stopped half way to the door, puzzled by his question. "You expecting them to be going off somewheres?"

Rayson shrugged. "I don't know what I'm expecting. It's a strange feeling I got about those two."

"What kind of feeling?" The knot she'd carried around in her stomach since yesterday's set-to in the corn cinched up another notch. She called it her worry knot, and it had a good record of letting her know when things were about to go wrong.

"If I tell you about my feeling, well...you'll be thinking I'm crazy."

"I'm your sister, Alvin, and I already know you're plum crazy. So go ahead."

"You know all those folks we been talking to about the ghosts? And that tingling feeling up and down our necks?"

"Yes."

"I get the same feeling from them."

"Those were old folk's stories, Alvin. Probably not one real ghost in the whole lot."

"Maybe yes and maybe no. You ever get a strange sense about something?"

Lettie Ruth thought of her nervousness downstairs when she locked the door. Now she felt a bad time coming on and her worry knot tightened. "I reckon most everyone has from time to time."

He watched the fan blades circle for several seconds. "Like I said, I got a feeling. And that feeling is telling me Miss Kat and Mitch ain't supposed to be here. Like they don't belong."

"Maybe you sense that because they're from another town. And don't forget, Mitch is a Yankee boy."

"It's more than coming from another town or being a Yankee, Lettie Ruth. It's like..." He paused, scratching his head. "You remember that book by H.G. Wells, *The Time Machine*?"

"I remember you reading it."

"In the book, the main character—The Time-traveler—didn't belong in the places he visited. His clothes were all wrong. The way he talked. Everything about him just didn't fit in."

Lettie Ruth laughed. "Are you telling me you believe Kat and Mitch traveled here in a time machine?"

"Of course not. But something about them isn't right."

"Like what?"

"Mitch's shoes."

"What's wrong with his shoes?"

"Take a look for yourself, then you tell me."

* * *

As soon as he heard Lettie Ruth's footsteps on the stairs, Alvin fished around under the bed until his hand landed on the slick nylon fabric. He pulled the navy blue backpack free, but left it lying on the floor. Poking around in somebody's property, without them knowing, seemed a bit sinful. But then, sometimes you couldn't avoid crossing the road. He needed answers and those answers were zipped up tight inside this bag.

When one of the men had brought it to the church Monday night, Alvin's intentions were honorable. He'd only looked inside to learn the owner's name. But what he'd found was a whole lot more than a name.

He wiped the sweat beads off his forehead and took a deep breath, before pulling the photograph out of the small inside pocket. No matter how many times he looked at it, he still couldn't control his shaking hands or the churning in his stomach. Alvin slowly unfolded the wrinkled photo. The three people, captured forever on the glossy paper, caused his heart to hammer. Father, Mother and Daughter. He turned it over, in a childish hand someone had written:

*"My family, May 14, 1983. Pop: Alvin Paul Rayson. Momma: Delores June Rayson.
And me: Kathleen "Kat" Ruth Rayson."*

"Why are you here, daughter?" Alvin whispered. "Why have you come back in time?"

* * *

Lettie Ruth dropped her napkin and bent over to pick it up. Mitch's shoes were no more than ten inches from her face. She stared hard, trying to see what got Alvin so worked up. Her guest's feet wore scuffed white leather shoes, with little blue check marks on the sides and heels. But nothing about them made her think they'd come out of a time machine. Or did they? She took a second look. They seemed a bit unusual, all that leather, but then Lettie didn't shop for men. For all she knew this was the kind of play shoes all the men in his town wore.

She grabbed the paper napkin and began to back out from underneath the table when Mitch shifted his feet. She caught a glimpse of the bottom of one shoe. The sole, carved in fancy patterns, had writing on it.

MACEYVILLE, AL. P.D.
IT'S A NEW MILLENNIUM—1/1/2000

At first the words didn't register, the meaning jumbled in her head. Then she understood.

Alvin's head poked under the table and Lettie Ruth put her finger to her lips and pointed up. They withdrew, their eyes locked across the table.

The conversation swirled around her as pieced together the scraps of information. What new things could she discover if she looked? Go slow, she warned herself, don't fancy up the facts. Stick to what you know.

What *did* she know about them? Kat, found naked in a cotton field, didn't have any clothes to examine. Other than the rape, nobody knew anything but her name. And not even the whole thing. What kind of a name was Kat? Sounded like a dang pet!

The most striking thing was how strongly she reminded Lettie Ruth of Alvin. Same eye color. Same dimples. They even displayed similar behavior characteristics. As though to confirm her theory, Lettie looked at Kat's plate, then at Alvin's. They'd both nearly drowned their meat in tarter sauce. And putting tarter sauce on ham was a disgusting habit Brother had carried over from childhood, and he'd picked it up from their daddy. How many other folks shared this trait? And another thing, Alvin always ate his biscuits dead last. Both his and Kat's were still sitting on the side of their plates.

Lettie Ruth pinched her arm resting in her lap, annoyed that she'd allowed herself to get caught up in Brother's fantasy. These might be odd coincidences, but they didn't mean a darn thing. No reason why Kat couldn't like tarter sauce as much as Alvin. And could be she wasn't saving the biscuit, maybe she just didn't much care for them.

According to Taxi Devore, Mitch was a Yankee policeman from out of town, with a colored woman friend. His shirt and pants looked fine. As for the words on the bottom of his shoes, she believed folks could write pretty much what ever they wanted. They sure didn't need Lettie Ruth Rayson's stamp of approval first. But it did seem a bit odd.

23

Lamar Gordon, suffering from a bad case of the heebie-jeebies, just had to do something when he heard the engine. He poked a finger through the kudzu and pressed his eye to the leafy peep hole. This same white stake-bed truck had rumbled past his house four times now, kicking up road dust and filling the air with black exhaust. The Confederate flag on the back snapped and flapped so hard he thought it might jump right off the broom stick.

"They still ridin' on our street, son?" Pastor Jackson Gordon's deep voice rumbled softly, like far away thunder.

Lamar glanced over his shoulder. His daddy stood in the doorway, his Sunday shirt glowing ghost-white in the fading light. "Yes, sir. This makes four times I seen them."

"How many men in the truck?"

"Three in the cab, six in back."

Pastor Gordon nodded. "You keep watch a bit longer. I got to make some phone calls."

Lamar shivered slightly at the words. If his daddy was phoning folks, he must be expecting trouble. And he truly hated this kind of trouble. In his twelve years on this earth, he'd seen lots of Negroes get bloodied for no good reason. He'd seen it too many times to count and it looked like before the sun came up, somebody in the east Hollow would be bleeding in his yard. He folded his hands and closed his eyes, sending a little prayer to Heaven. "Please God, don't let my daddy get hurt again."

* * *

Alvin Rayson hung up the receiver and turned to the four people seated in the waiting room. "We got some trouble building over at Pastor Gordon's," he said.

Timothy Biggers was first on his feet. "How long 'til it strikes?"

"Pastor said they passed by his place four times already. He figures we got ten or fifteen minutes."

"Let me lock and load."

Rayson held up his hand. "Pastor says no guns this time, doctor. He wants to talk it down."

Biggers snorted. "Talk it down? Alvin, those boys wouldn't be messin' round there if they didn't want to do some damage."

"I know. But Pastor Gordon said he's got an idea of what to do. We're supposed to come over to his house and park on the street. And, Dr. Tim, he said to tell you special, 'don't bring that rifle of yours, and no side arms or the shotgun you keep in the closet'."

"You've delivered the message, Alvin. You can go to Heaven with a clear conscious," Biggers said, getting up off the sofa. "Excuse me, but I need to get my things together." He disappeared into his apartment.

Moments later Rayson heard the whack as the bolt chambered a round from a fresh ammo clip into the M-1 Garand.

Lettie Ruth peeked out the window, her face troubled. "Is Pastor expecting problems to spill over our way?"

"He didn't say, but I'd guess most will happen on his street this time," Rayson said.

"Mind if I come along?" Mitch asked. "I handle myself pretty well around trouble. Maybe I can help cool things off."

"I know one thing for sure," Kat declared. "I *ain't* stayin' here."

"Now, Miss Kat," Rayson said. "You don't need to be steppin' into this."

"Why not? When it comes to trouble, I'm as good as that one," Kat said, pointing a finger at Mitch.

Rayson stepped closer and placed both hands on her shoulders. "This ain't the time for you to be pulling no attitude on me, girl."

Kat dissolved into laughter. "Judas Priest, it's the same old line, except now I'm hearing it before I was born!" Her own comment sent her into another fit of laughter and she collapsed on the sofa.

"Is she all right?" Rayson stared at her, wondering if he should call the doctor.

"She'll be okay," Mitch said, as he jerked Kat to her feet. "She just needs to rest. All this excitement is making her talk crazy."

"You hear him, Mitch?" She giggled. "Did you hear?"

"I heard him," he said. "*Everybody* heard everything, Kathleen."

She looked at Alvin, then at Lettie Ruth, suspicion filled their faces. "Everybody?"

Mitch nodded.

"Uh-oh."

"Uh-huh," Mitch said.

She faked swooned and grabbed Mitch's arm. "I need to lie down," she said, staggering drunkenly toward the hall, dragging him along with her.

"Don't leave without me," Mitch called over his shoulder.

Rayson watched until they'd disappeared up the staircase. "Some mighty strange goings on around here," he said quietly. "You starting to see what I been talkin' about, Sister? How things don't fit?"

"Some." Lettie Ruth waited a beat. "But the girl is not at her best tonight. Could be those things she's sayin' only sound crazy on account of—"

He didn't let her finish. "On account of nothing. You heard it, same as I did."

"But it didn't make sense, Alvin. How could she hear you tell her something before she was born?"

"Have you looked at Kat? I mean taken a *real* good look at her?"

"Yes."

"What did you see?"

"A pretty woman."

"Quit hedging, Lettie Ruth. Don't pretend you don't see that girl wearing *my* eyes and wearing *my* dimples?"

She nibbled on her bottom lip. "Well, I reckon hers are a little bit like yours. I guess."

"If I was to have a girl child someday, you think she might look like Kat?"

"Alvin Rayson! Are you talking about that time machine book again?"

"I'm talking about what my daughter might look like." The feeling he and Kat were related had been growing in him all day. So many of her mannerisms—the way she moved her hand or used certain phrases—were his way of doing things. Delores' way of doing things. Kat's eye color and dimples, that kind of sameness only ran in families. In some mysterious fashion, he believed this woman to be the child he'd have one day. The how or why she'd turned up at this particular time remained a mystery. But she'd come for a reason.

"Well, she's got enough attitude to be your child," Lettie Ruth said.

Alvin Rayson smiled, his dimples digging deep holes in his cheeks.

* * *

"Folks is here, daddy." Lamar stepped from behind the kudzu and waved to Virgil as he raced across the yard. All along Webster Avenue, the cars were parking bumper to bumper.

Pastor Gordon stood behind his son, hands resting on his shoulders. "Praise God," he whispered.

"Amen. Hey there, Virgil," Lamar said, as his cousin climbed the porch steps.

"Hey, Lamar. Evening, Uncle Jackson."

"Here's what I want y'all to do," Pastor Gordon said. "I expect those white boys to be comin' our way again. And soon as they do, you and Virgil run inside and squeeze down behind the ice box."

"Daddy," Lamar protested. "I'm not hidin' in the house like a girl."

"No, you be in the house 'cause I *told* you to be in the house."

"But I can help. I'm near as big as you."

Pastor Gordon stared into Lamar's eyes. "You've already been a big help. Without your sharp eyes I'd never known about that truck. I'm gonna need you in the days to come, son. I don't want to lose my secret weapon in our first battle."

Lamar kicked at the rough plank flooring of the porch. He didn't want to be hunkered down behind no ice box when the truck came back. No matter what Daddy said, it was still hiding. His thirteenth birthday would be here on Friday, the day after tomorrow, and to the Jewish people a boy turning thirteen meant he'd become a man. He wished he was Jewish. He bet none of their boys would be cowering behind no ice box tonight.

* * *

Mitch and Timothy Biggers rode in the back seat. Alvin, Lettie Ruth and Kat in the front.

No amount of talking could convince Kat to stay at the clinic. This was her first chance since the rape to take a step toward regaining control of her life.

Besides, she was trained for confrontational situations. In fact, she and Mitch were the only professionals in the bunch. Everyone else had a boat load of courage and good hearts, but they didn't know jack about dealing with the bottom feeders.

Biggers tapped her shoulder. "You real sure you know how to use that weapon?" he asked, referring to the .44-caliber Colt Anaconda he'd loaned her.

This was the third time he'd asked the same question in as many blocks. And for the third time she responded, "I'm an expert shot, Timothy. Tell him, Mitch."

"She's an expert shot, Timothy."

"See my trigger finger?" She wiggled her right index finger in the air. "No bandages."

"I've never seen so many cars," Lettie Ruth commented as they turned up Webster Avenue.

"I told you, Pastor Gordon has a plan," Rayson said, as they fell in line behind three cars inching along. "He told me if the street got used up, to pull into the empty driveways."

"I suggest you do something mighty fast, Alvin," Biggers said. "The headlights comin' this direction are too high to be mounted on a sedan."

They were forced to wait until the Ford in front pulled into a drive, but before Rayson got the car in gear Kat, Mitch and the doctor jumped out. He watched as they darted across the street heading for the Gordon's house. All three sure looked like they knew what they were doing. Timothy Biggers carried his rifle muzzle up, reminding Alvin of a World War II recruiting poster. Mitch and Kat's hands dropped to their sides as they cut between two parked cars, but he caught a brief metallic flicker when they trotted underneath the streetlight.

* * *

"Kat, you sure as hell better know how to use that Colt," Biggers whispered once they reached the safety of the shadows next to the house.

"Take care of your own ass and don't be worryin' so much about mine, Timothy," Kat snapped.

A curly head poked out of the window. "Hey, Miss Kat, Dr. Tim," whispered Virgil. "Y'all come to help Uncle Jackson?"

Lamar shoved his cousin out of the way and stuck his head out the window so far he nearly lost his balance. "You ought to be someplace else, Miss Kat, things don't look good around here tonight."

"I'll be fine, Lamar, don't you worry."

Biggers leaned a shoulder against the ship-lap siding next to the window. "What y'all supposed to be doing 'bout now? I don't think your daddy's want you boys hanging out the windows."

"We gonna help fight," Lamar announced.

"Going kick white butts," Virgil yelled over Lamar's shoulder.

"Is that so?" Biggers handed Kat his rifle. "Y'all boys move on out of my way." He used his arms to pull himself over the window sill. Once inside he turned and stuck his hand out the open space. "My rifle, if you will, Miss Kat."

"You gonna stay in there?" she asked, transferring the weapon to its owner.

"My young soldiers and I will battle from this position," he said.

"Good idea, could get a little dicey in there. If y'all need backup, give me a call."

Biggers nodded and disappeared inside, she heard him giving orders for the boys to move to the rear of the house.

Mitch crept to the corner. Kat followed his lead. Crouched beside the house and hidden from the street by a tangle of honeysuckle, she laid her gun down long enough to rip the splint off her left hand. She flexed her fingers, it hurt some, but the slight ache wouldn't slow her down. She picked up the Colt revolver she'd borrowed from Biggers, and rechecked the cylinder.

"Good to go, partner?" Mitch whispered.

When she saw the stake-bed truck coming down the street the white-hot flame of panic erupted in her chest and traveled up her spine. *They'll see me.* The trembling started in her hands. The gun fell to the ground.

"Kat?" The voice faint.

They'll see me. An emotion beyond fear ruled her mind and body. Kat crawled into the glowing mist surrounding the honeysuckle bush. The roaring in her ears grew louder with each heartbeat, drowning out all sounds. Deaf and blinded by absolute terror, she curled in a ball, seeking invisibility.

Hands on her shoulders. *White Hands.* She clawed at them, desperate to keep the hands from touching her again.

24

Mitch didn't know what he should do. The Gordon's front yard was about to fill up with Kluxers and his partner huddled in the shadows. Every time he tried to touch her she fought like a wild animal, and he was afraid if he forced it she would attract unwanted attention.

He eased toward the rear of Pastor Gordon's house, closer to the window Biggers had climbed through earlier. He tapped the gun barrel on the glass.

The window slid open, Biggers stuck his head out. "Problems?" he whispered.

Mitch nodded. "Kat's having a big time panic attack. She's curled up in the bushes and won't let me touch her."

"Hold on." His head disappeared. After a brief conversation with Lamar and Virgil, the doctor climbed out the window.

* * *

The pickup skidded to a stop in the middle of the street. Nine hooded men in white robes piled out carrying baseball bats and chains. Unable to reach the preacher's yard directly, they clambered over the cars parked bumper-to-bumper along Webster Avenue.

Pastor Jackson Gordon, five-foot five-inches and of slight build, waited for them on the second step, Bible in hand. "Evening," he said, once all nine men stood in his yard.

"Hear you been keepin' a jigaboo bitch here at your place," the mob leader said. "One who got herself all beat up."

"Got no woman here," Gordon answered.

"Hand her over," the leader demanded.

The preacher moved off the steps and into the yard. "Got no woman here."

"We know that niggerbitch been at your house," a man in back yelled.

"Seen her with that boy of yours," another voice called out.

"Yeah, and we don't plan on wasting no more time," the leader said. "Hand her over, preacher man."

"Got no woman here," Gordon repeated.

"You keepin' all that nigger pussy for yourself, boy?" asked the man in back.

Their rumbling grew louder and more angry. The leader moved closer, swinging the heavy chain in a tight circle, with each arc it struck the ground, kicking up a dust cloud.

* * *

"There's too many jackasses around here right now to try moving her inside," Timothy Biggers whispered.

Mitch agreed, any form of physical contact with Kat was out of the question. Especially since the doctor didn't have any better luck with Kat. In fact, he seemed to have made matters worse, because if they so much as twitched a finger, she flailed wildly in the air. Sooner or later, all this activity in the shadows would be noticed.

"We'll have to screen her from the yard," Mitch said. "I don't want her to see those robes...and I sure as hell don't want them to see her."

"We may end up on the defensive," Biggers said, studying their position.

"Damn it," Mitch muttered, his attention diverted as the mob leader closed in on Pastor Gordon. "That's Billy Lee."

"Billy Lee Mitchell?" Biggers asked, peering intently through the bushes. "You know him?"

"He's a relative."

Biggers grunted. "Nice family tree you got."

"Thanks."

"You sure it's him?"

"Do bears shit in the woods, doc? That robe can't hide his voice. Or his swagger."

"Or his brass knuckles," Biggers added, pointing to the glint off Billy Lee's hand. "Saw him rip a fella's face open with those once."

"I guarantee he won't rip anyone open tonight."

"If we have to shoot him will it cause family problems?"

"You might say that."

* * *

Their insults grew louder and more pointed as the hooded men moved into position, forming a semicircle around the preacher. The air crackled with anger. And fear.

Billy Lee Mitchell rattled his chain. "What kind of fertilizer you want us to make out of that little nigger pup of yours?"

Pastor Gordon remained silent.

"I put fifty pounds of coon babies on my cotton last year and doubled the crop," one man said.

"I mixed mine in with the hog slop. Got the best damn hams in the state of Alabama," another commented.

Billy Lee turned his back on Gordon and addressed his men, "This is by-God America, and we're by-God Americans. I say we take a vote." The men hollered in agreement.

"Who's for picaninny cotton fertilizer?" he asked.

A robust "Yes!" erupted.

"Nigger boy hog slop?"

The crowed erupted, cheering and whistling.

"Guess that's the winner. Looks like your boy's going to be chopped up for the hogs, Preacher Man. Or…" He paused dramatically, then raised his hood slightly and spit a wad of tobacco on Gordon's shoes. "Or…you could just make it easy on yourself and hand over the woman."

"Got no woman here," Gordon stated again.

Billy Lee swung the chain. The side of the preacher's head and neck burst open, releasing a flood of red. In seconds, his white shirt was saturated. The Bible in his hand was blood slick, but he stayed on his feet, his face passive.

"You got shit for brains, Sambo?" someone in the mob shouted.

"Give us the woman," Billy Lee growled.

"Got no wom—"

"That's the last fucking time those words is gonna come out of your mouth." Billy Lee swung the chain at the preacher's legs until Gordon collapsed.

Pastor Gordon struggled to his knees and slowly raised the dripping Bible above his head.

On his signal, Webster Avenue lit up like the Fourth of July. Every porch light, inside house light and car headlight along the street clicked on. Radios and television sets were turned full volume. Outside, automobile horns and car radios blared.

The hooded men turned in circles, confused and stunned by the light and cacophonous noise, then moved closer together. A pack of scared dogs.

Billy Lee whipped around, the dirt clung to the hem of his white robe. "A little bit of racket ain't gonna scare us off, nigger." He swung his chain until Gordon fell face forward on the ground.

As though someone had pulled the plug, the sound ceased. The nine men spread apart, murmuring and kicking up a mini-dust storm as they milled around the front yard.

Billy Lee bent over and shook Gordon's shoulder. "Where's the woman?"

"Got no woman here."

"Kick the living shit out of him, Billy Lee," the man in back shouted.

"Goddamn it!" Billy Lee exploded. "No names."

"Aww hell, these damn niggers don't care about no names. Half of 'em can't read or write."

"And they're deaf as bats."

"Just shut it up," Billy Lee said.

Pastor Gordon raised his head slightly until he could see the circle of men. "I can read, and I can write," he said. "And I'm good at remembering too."

Billy Lee viciously kicked at the preacher's ribs until his head dropped again.

* * *

"We've got to do something," Mitch whispered. "They'll kill him."

Biggers rested a hand on his back. "Wait up. Jackson's still calling the shots. I don't think it's a done deal yet."

"Those boys are playing for keeps. They want him dead. This is going to end real soon. And end badly."

"You Yankees are always forgetting how slow things move in the South. We're nowheres near the end of this evening's soiree. We still have time to get our hands dirty."

"You're going to sit here and let them beat the shit out of that man?" Biggers' cavalier attitude didn't set well with Mitch. His police training focused on *intervention* not *wait and see*.

Biggers grinned. "Now that ain't gonna happen." He pointed to the yard. "You watch out yonder."

* * *

Billy Lee kicked half heartedly at the preacher, then backed off. "How's your memory now, tar baby?" he taunted. "Bet you'll remember this night for a long time."

Gordon lifted his head and smiled. "And so shall you." He raised his trembling Bible once more.

Car doors opened. Passengers climbed out. People emerged from their homes and the two groups joined forces in a silent march toward Gordon's yard.

A hooded man pointed to the sidewalk. "Trouble coming."

Billy Lee glanced over his shoulder. He froze for a moment then turned to face the oncoming marchers. "You niggers stop right there," he ordered. "Stop right there I said." When they failed to obey his commands, he turned back to the downed preacher. "Tell them to git on out of here or I'll finish you off."

"You tell them yourself, you're the boss man," Gordon said.

Billy Lee swung the chain one last time before he motioned for his men to retreat. Still throwing hate filled insults and threats, the nine climbed aboard the truck and left the east Hollow.

25

From her position in the sidewalk procession, Lettie Ruth saw Timothy Biggers motion from the side of the house and left the marchers.

"Kat won't let us near her," Mitch explained when she stepped into the shadows.

"You want to give it a try?" Biggers asked. "See if you can settle her down enough so we can get her moved out of there."

Low pitched keening emanated from the huddled figure in the bushes. Lettie Ruth dropped to her knees and crawled under the drooping honeysuckle. She lay on her side, eye to eye with Kat. "Them men is gone, honey," she said softly. "Come on out now." Lettie thought she heard a slight break in the sing-song wailing. She held her hand inches from Kat's closed eyes. "Take hold of me, baby. Alvin's waitin' in the car to drive us home."

"My Pop's here?" Kat whispered, her eyes opened slightly.

"He sure is," Lettie Ruth answered, although certain she must have misunderstood the question.

"Not in the hospital?"

"No hospital. We're taking you home."

Kat reached up and grabbed Lettie Ruth's hand.

* * *

Lettie Ruth sat on the edge of the bed humming softly. Her hand made lazy circles on Kat's back. The panic attack was over, and the sedative Timothy had administered seemed to have kicked in. However, the drained shell in the bed frightened Lettie more than the huddled soul she'd found under the honeysuckle bush.

What had scared her so bad as to have put her in the state? Lettie Ruth pulled the sheet over Kat's shoulder and tiptoed out of the room. She needed to talk to Mitch and find out how it all started.

*   *   *

"How's Kat?" Mitch asked, when Lettie Ruth entered the TV room.

"She's sleeping now, ought to be better when she wakes."

"What caused the relapse? She's been acting fine."

"You just answered your own question, Mitch. Kat's been *acting* fine. Given what all happened to her, it's a wonder this didn't come about sooner."

"Will it happen again?"

"Got no way of knowin'. Sometimes panic attacks are triggered by something real specific. Sometimes not. That's why we gotta try and figure out this puzzle."

"I think the reason is obvious, Lettie Ruth. Men wearing Klan costumes. Kat's never seen anything like that except in text books."

Text books? What kind of Southern colored never saw the Klan act out? This seemed to be one more of Alvin's crazy puzzle pieces. Lettie didn't want to get into the why for's at the moment. Her main concern was fingering the cause of Kat's panic. She sat in the recliner and popped the footrest. "Kat never talked about robes or hoods being part of the rape, so it don't seem a likely cause to me. But I guess it's as good a reason as any."

"She might have recognized their voices."

"Could be. Lots of mean talk tonight. But somehow that don't feel quite right either." Lettie thought back on the scene in the Gordon's yard, trying to see the things Kat had seen. "When did she start actin' out?"

Mitch looked up at the ceiling, his brow wrinkled in thought. "We got to the house, the boys were hanging out the window and she talked to them. Everything was fine." He stood and began to pace. "Timothy climbed inside the window to be with the boys. Kat and I moved over to the corner of the house so we could monitor the action. That's when she fell apart."

"What y'all lookin' at around the corner when she got all worked up?"

Mitch shrugged. "Nothing special. The yard...Pastor Gordon standing on the steps."

"That doesn't seem enough to bring on her attack. Gotta be something we ain't thinking about."

"Let's run through it again. The house, the boys, Timothy crawling through the window."

"Pastor on the steps," Lettie Ruth said.

"And then the truck pulled up. The men got out." Mitch stopped pacing. "You think it could be the men?"

"Now we is back to the robes again."

"But everybody knew they were white underneath. And white men raped her."

"She knew the trouble would be white when we left here for the Pastor's house."

"Okay, if not the men, what about the truck itself? Could it be connected to the rape?"

Lettie Ruth nodded. It sounded reasonable to her. "I'm acquainted with that particular white truck myself."

"Is that the same white truck you and Taxi ran into on Tuesday morning?"

Lettie Ruth shivered. After what happened in the corn field the other morning, the sight of the stake-bed—full of Ku Klux Klan—had caused her own heart to beat faster. If it belonged to one of the rapists, no wonder Kat had fallen into a deep well of panic.

"That the same one, but my problems with them didn't go very far," Lettie Ruth said."Mostly the men is full of beans and hot air," she said. At her words, Mitch's face flushed and his freckles glowed. For a moment she thought he might rip the sofa pillow in half.

"Most men. But definitely not Floyd, Little Carl or Louis," he spit out each name. "They're mean as hell and enjoy causing innocent people pain. You saw the results of Kat's encounter. And tonight, the same sort of scum whipped Pastor Gordon with a chain."

"Mitch, that's the way things is around here when you're colored."

"It's wrong, Lettie Ruth. Color shouldn't matter."

"Well it does. Folks like me, Kat and even the pastor, know we got to be cautious."

*   *   *

Dr. Biggers knotted the final stitch in Pastor Gordon's head. "You ain't gonna be as pretty as you were this morning, Jackson," Biggers said. "But since I'm such a fine surgeon, the scarring will be rugged and masculine."

Pastor Gordon chuckled. "That's good news. I been worrying some about my rugged masculine appeal lately."

"You got yourself some broken ribs," Biggers said. "But they'll heal. It's your chewed up leg that's gonna require more treatment. I'm keeping you here, and off your feet, for a few days until the swelling goes down."

"I've got work to do at the church," Pastor Gordon protested.

"Alvin's capable of tending to your flock," Biggers said. "Listen to me, Jackson. The rusty chain that boy was swinging, cut clean to the bone, even nicked it in a couple of places. Infection is likely, and I don't want to see it turn into gangrene."

"What about Lamar?"

"He's welcome here. I've got plenty of room and he can help Lettie around the clinic."

"I'm afraid we're heading into a dark period, Timothy. I don't want to be carrying that kind of darkness through your doors."

"I've been on the Klan's list of favorites for a long time, Jackson. Shoot, if some good old boy didn't bust out a window or dig up my flowers every couple of weeks, I'd feel down right neglected."

"Going to be more than foolishness this time. The voter's registration and lunch counter sit-ins have got them all riled up, Timothy. They are looking for an excuse."

"In-bred pieces of crap," Biggers muttered. "Makes me ashamed to be a Southerner."

"So how come you to grow up so different from these boys?"

"I didn't grow up different. I went off to war. When you fight side by side with a man, it's a whole lot harder to see color. Especially when both of you bleed red." Biggers sat on a wooden chair in the corner of the exam room. "In the Marianas, in the South Pacific, the Negro Marine Ammunition-and Depot companies were in the thick of it along with the rest of us. Their shore parties were specially trained to move the supplies and ammo from the landing craft to the inland troops."

"Did you know Dilmer Richards? He owned that gas station east of town? He was over there too, at Peleliu I believe," Pastor Gordon said.

"Yeah, we were over there at the same time, and on occasion we'd talk. I remember how fast his company unloaded the beach craft, even under enemy artillery fire. They hauled the ammo to the front lines, then they'd turn right around and carry the wounded back to shore." Biggers leaned back in the chair until it rested against the wall, balanced on two legs. "Almost every day, round sundown, I watched little bunches of Negro Marines heading to the front lines to fight the Japs. And that was after working all day."

"Dilmer's always was a hard worker."

"I felt real bad when he died in that house fire last month."

"He was active in the voter's registration. Klan didn't like it."

"Klan don't seem to like Negroes, no matter what you folks do."

"You don't seem to have a problem liking Negroes, Timothy."

"Sure I do." Biggers laughed. "I can't stand Chester Newton."

Gordon chuckled. "Nobody cares much for Chester. White or colored."

"He's an arrogant and mean SOB. Maybe he ought to consider joining the Klan."

"You got an interesting way of thinking, doctor."

"My way of thinking about people started changing on Peleliu." He got up and started arranging the gauze dressings on the instrument tray. "When I got back home...the way folks treated the war veterans made me sick inside."

"What do you mean?" asked Pastor Gordon.

"I mean all those parades and barbecues. Good jobs handed out like Halloween candy. The folks back here couldn't do enough for the veterans. But I never saw a colored face marching in a parade or up on the stage. No medals, no cheers. And sure as hell, no jobs."

"That's the way things is down here, Timothy. You ought to know that."

"Don't make it right. It's old time thinking, that should have been buried with the War Between the States."

"Maybe this is the war that will change things," Gordon said.

"You mean this *civil rights war* Dr. King's preaching about, Jackson?"

"That's the one, Timmy. That's the one."

*   *   *

Kat smiled when Mitch stuck his head in the door. "I've been wondering about you," she said. "Come on in."

"You feeling better?" he asked, pulling the rocking chair closer to the bed and sitting down.

She sat up. "I've never been so scared in my life."

He rocked slowly. "Lettie Ruth said you had a panic attack."

"That's the damn truth." She fingered the ribbed edges of the chenille bedspread. "When I saw their truck again...I lost it. I really lost it."

"Lots of unpleasant memories must have surfaced all at once," Mitch said.

"Will I react like that every time I see a white stake-bed?" The question had been rattling around in her head for hours. "A police officer can't afford to have a panic attack every time a white truck drives past."

"There are methods of dealing with your fears, once we're home, we'll find someone to help you."

Kat shook her head. "I can't go to the department shrink. If Chief Smith gets wind of this, he'll pull me off the street."

"Then go see a private practice doctor. What Arlin Smith doesn't know, can't hurt you."

"I've discovered the opposite. What you don't know, *can* hurt you." She leaned back against the headboard. "I'm tired, Mitch. Tired of everything in this time period. It's ugly and it's dangerous."

"You're strong, Kat. I know you can make it until Sunday."

"Then what? Am I supposed to go on home and forget all this happened? Forget about Lettie Ruth?"

"Didn't we decide this afternoon to let things run their natural course? I thought we agreed that you and I shouldn't be tinkering with events."

"Knowin' what's coming around the corner makes it hard to stick my hands in my pocket and stay clear of it. I want to jump in and do something."

"I do too, but look at the changes we've already instigated. And the only thing we've done is come here."

"You ever get the feeling something greater than both of us is calling the shots?"

Mitch nodded. "It's weird. Every time I look in a mirror I half expect to have disappeared."

A foreboding sense of inevitability grabbed her heart and squeezed. "*Can we go home?*" Kat asked.

"Sure we can, in fact we're going home on Sunday."

His words didn't soothe her tumultuous feelings. And the flicker of doubt in his blue eyes confirmed her suspicions. They both knew this trip through time would end badly for one member of the Red and Black Team.

26

APRIL 04—THURSDAY

Last night events had left a gritty residue. Tiny particles worked their way into Mitch's head, slipping between the folds of his defensive barriers. Confused and uncertain as to where he fit in this new world, James Mitchell decided to go in search of his roots. Childhood memories of his early life in Alabama were yellowed with age and colored by the stories his mother shared. He wanted to dig down, get to the rock bottom truth of his past.

He parked Timothy Biggers' gold and white Ford Fairlane on Blodgett, across from Billy Lee and Pamela Mitchell's house. Counter to his memories, the small clapboard wore a fresh coat of paint and the flower beds were bursting with spring color. A twenty-foot high magnolia tree spread its green arms over the roof, protecting the little house from summer heat and winter rains. In the future, Mitch's tire swing would hang from one of its strong branches.

A pretty red haired woman, wearing a sleeveless lime green blouse and flowered skirt, came out a side door. She balanced a laundry basket on her hip as she navigated the four steps to the yard.

Mitch slid lower in the seat, in case she happened to look his direction. A lump formed in his throat as he watched the familiar movements. The way his mother's hands moved as she shook out the damp clothes, the toss of her head when a strand of hair fell out of place.

She seemed happy, or at least his interpretation of what her happiness would look like. He'd never seen his mother really happy. Even after they moved to Pennsylvania, a deep sadness remained in her eyes. As Mitch got older, he frequently wondered what Billy Lee could have done to destroy all the joy in her life. She bent over and removed a tiny pink shirt from the basket and hung it on the line. Pamela Mitchell continued to hang baby clothes until three rows fluttered in the spring breeze.

Baby clothes? Mitch searched his memory banks for any mention of his mother having cared for another child before he'd been born. He was the oldest of his cousins, on both his mother and father's side of the family, and an only child. He concluded she must be helping someone else do their laundry. Then he heard a baby cry. Pamela hurried toward the house and in a few minutes returned with a chubby red-haired infant in her arms. She spread a colorful patchwork quilt under the magnolia and sat with the child in the shade. The little girl—Mitch had decided the child must be female because of the pink hair ribbons—smiled and made happy baby sounds.

He heard the growl of the Impala's engine long before it turned the corner. Billy Lee swung it into the graveled driveway and hopped out. He frowned and walked toward his wife and child.

Mitch lowered the window another three inches so he could hear what was being said.

"What's she doing out front?" Billy Lee asked.

"I'm hanging out the laundry and Carolyn started to cry," Pamela answered.

"Won't hurt her none to cry. That's what they do."

"There's no reason to let her cry when I'm right here." Pamela lifted the baby onto her lap, wrapping her arms protectively around the small body.

Billy Lee looked around at the neighboring houses, then squatted beside the quilt. "You know my feelings on this."

"And you know mine."

Billy Lee's hand shot out like a rattlesnake and he slapped Pamela's cheek. "My own wife won't be giving me sass." In one smooth motion he jerked the baby out of her mother's grasp and stood. Carolyn dangled by one arm. "This is the last time I'm telling you. I won't have the neighbors gossiping about us. Keep her out of sight." He tucked the screaming infant under his arm and marched into the house.

Like a deflated balloon, Pamela Mitchell collapsed on the quilt. Mitch couldn't hear anything, but her body shook and he knew his mother was crying.

A sister. I had a big sister no one ever told me about. What had happened to her? What did Billy Lee do?

* * *

Mitch waited until the clinic's temporary patients and guests had settled down for the night before he tapped on Kat's door. Humiliated and angered by his father's behavior, he rode an emotional roller coaster and needed to talk it out.

Kat opened the door and he slipped inside. "Rough day?" she asked.

"In many different ways, and for many different reasons." Like two lovers in a secret rendevous, they conversed in whispers.

"Timothy told me what happened last night. He said one of your relatives was there. Is that the reason you're all worked up? Because Billy Lee was at the pastor's house?"

"He's part of it." Mitch sat on the bed and leaned over. Arms resting on knees, he stared at the floor. "Every hour that passes I feel more and more detached from reality. I'm not sure who I am any more."

"You haven't changed, Mitch," she assured him. "It's the world around us that's different."

"That's the problem. Because things *are* so different, I'm not acting right."

Kat sat on the floor in front of him. Forcing him to look her in the eyes. "I don't understand what you mean by, 'not acting right'?"

"If a mob pulled a stunt like last night's in the year 2000, what would you do?"

"Step in."

"Exactly," he said. "But I didn't. I stuck to the shadows and let my own father assault an innocent man."

"Mitch, you had to let things play out the way Pastor Gordon wanted."

"Why? Why did I have to let it play out?"

"It's the way things—"

He interrupted. "So help me God, if I hear 'it's the way things are' one more time I'm going to put my fist through the damn wall."

"Can't change the truth by molesting a wall, Mitch." Her attempt at humor failed, he didn't even crack a smile.

"I'm sick and tired of things I can't change," he said, ignoring her comment. He wanted to be angry. Wanted to take his anger out in the most physical way possible.

She smiled at him. "You're having difficulty with this concept because you're white."

"Odds are that I will remain white for a long time," he grumbled.

"Hush up, I'm tryin' to teach you something. Because you *are* white, you've never run up against racist attitudes. All this bull shit you're witnessing, I wade through it seven days a week."

He raised his eyebrows. "This is still going on? Even in our time?"

"You poor white child, the things you don't see." She held her hands out, "Help me off the floor." He pulled her to her feet and she curled up in the corner rocking chair. "Maybe we should've talked about it a long time ago."

"About what?"

"About me being black. And you being white."

"This is ridiculous," Mitch said.

"No it's not. We are friends and partners on the job, but what do you know about my private life?"

Mitch thought about her question. It was true, they'd worked together for five years and occasionally gone out to see a movie or for dinner, but beyond that, she was right. He didn't know how she spent her free time. And Kat didn't know any more about his activities. Why didn't they know?

"Have you ever wondered why our off duty relationship is so different from our on duty relationship?" she asked. "Why our friendship hasn't moved to the next level?" When he didn't answer, she continued. "It's because I'd be uncomfortable in your white world, and you'd be uncomfortable in my black world."

"That's not true."

"Honey, it's so true that if it was a rattlesnake, you'd be bit and layin' dead in the floor by now."

"We've gone places together. We see each other outside of work."

"Do we?" Kat asked. "When's the last time you called said, 'let's go get some barbeque down at Little Joe's'? Or asked if I wanted to go to a University of Alabama football game with you?"

"I didn't know you liked football."

"Stop it, Mitch. You can't make the facts disappear by ignoring the reasons behind them. Have you ever dated an African-American woman? Other than myself, do you have any black friends?"

"No, to the first question. And yes, to the second."

"What do you and these black friends do together?"

"We make music at The Blue."

"So you call these fellas and say 'hey, let's go down to The Blue, I'll drive?"

Mitch shifted uncomfortably. "Not exactly that way. We kind of drop in. It's not real organized."

"Why not? If you like makin' music together...why don't you *go together*?"

"Damn it, Kat, it just doesn't work like that. Guys don't go around making plans all the time."

"Ever come down to the east Hollow for a pick-up basketball game? The black officers play twice a week. Or do you stick to the high school gym on the west side of town?"

He didn't like the picture she painted. The longer she talked, the more he was forced to examine his life style. For someone who proclaimed to be non-racist, James Mitchell led a very white life. And to be honest, he *didn't* have any black friends, only black acquaintances.

What was Kat's status? A friend? Or an on the job partner that happened to be black? *Fair weather friend.* Grandpa Paddy's words haunted him.

"I don't know why we are having this discussion now," he said. "None of this applies to our current situation."

"You have to shake free of all preconceived ideas about race before you can get a handle on our situation. No history or sociology text book will ever be able to explain the nuances of black and white interactions in this time period."

"How am I supposed to acquire this handle if everything I've read or been taught is wrong?"

"Open your eyes, Mitch. Listen to what Lettie and Dreama have to say. Watch Taxi and Pop. They are your text books."

In Mitch's opinion, this lesson in race relations was a colossal failure. As far as his text book examples, all he'd seen Taxi do was shrink away from a confrontation and 'yes, sir' and 'no, sir' any white person he ran across. He'd listened to Dreama's angry diatribe against whites. And so far, Lettie hadn't said or done anything of note.

"My text books haven't been very enlightening," he informed her. "What about my father? Could I use Billy Lee as a model of the Southern white male?"

Kat released an exasperated sigh. "You are being purposefully obtuse, James Mitchell."

"No, I'm not. I just haven't seen anything to contradict what I've been taught. The blacks still kowtow to the whites. A few are angry and want changes, while the majority sit back and do nothing."

"You really don't see it do you?"

"See what?" His frustration level rose at a rapid rate. In what direction did his partner want this conversation to go? What did she expect from him? "Kat, I'm not black. I have never been black. And I never will be black. Given those three irrefutable facts, how can I possibly understand all the nuances?"

"It's not the nuances I want you to see and understand."

"Then what is it?"

"I want you to see black people are made of flesh and blood and bone. We are just like you."

27

APRIL 05—FRIDAY

When Mitch emerged from his room the next morning, his mood matched the stormy skies overhead. Bruised clouds, swollen by the rain they carried, turned the sunny day into a premature twilight. Thunder rumbled ominously as the dark gray ceiling lowered over Maceyville.

Lightening zig-zagged across the horizon. Fat rain drops began to fall as Mitch and Lamar Gordon spread plastic tarpaulins over the exposed lawn furniture. They raced for the back door arriving seconds before the deluge.

Lamar shook from head to toe like a dog, leaving a fine spray of rainwater on the kitchen floor. "It's gonna be a big ole storm," he said. "Hope somebody thinks to shut up our windows at home."

"If you want, I'll drive you over to the house to check," Mitch offered. Any activity was better than being stuck indoors all day. Especially given the morose mood that had infected Bigger's clinic.

"That would probably be a good idea, Mr. Mitch. I know for sure nobody thought about a rainstorm comin' in when we left last night."

"Run upstairs and see if your dad wants you to pick up anything while we're there and let the others know where we're going."

*   *   *

The streets were rapidly becoming mini-rivers and in low lying areas, water already crested over the curbs. Two blocks from the Gordon's Mitch hit a flooded intersection and the Ford gave out. He and Lamar managed to push it to the side of the road, then hiked the rest of the way to the boy's house. The umbrellas they'd borrowed from the clinic offered little protection from the wind driven slant rain. By the time they reached their destination, they were drenched and left a trail of wet footprints on the hardwood floors inside the house.

As Lamar gathered the things his father had requested, Mitch closed the windows. In some rooms the rain had already soaked the curtains. In others, the painted walls were dripping. Suddenly the thunder and lightening let loose another volley. The transformer on the corner gave a loud pop and the power went off, filling the long skinny house with shadows. Mitch repeatedly banged into pieces of furniture as he navigated through the maze to reach the back bedroom.

He found Lamar fighting with a stuck window. The rain blew through the half-open glass and puddled on the floor. The nearby bedspread was a soggy mess. "Looks like you could use a little help," Mitch said.

Lamar nodded. "This one's been stuck since February. Don't think we can get it movin'."

"Well, maybe the rain loosened it up some, what you say we try one more time?" Mitch added his muscle and together they managed to get the water soaked wooden frame to lower until only an inch remained open.

"That's surely a whole lot—" Lamar began, then abruptly stopped when the front door slammed shut.

Mitch put a finger to his lips and motioned the boy to get inside the closet. He slipped the .38 from the ankle holster and pressed his back to the wall nearest to the bedroom door. He tried to breathe shallowly, so he could hear the furtive noises coming from the front of the house. The narrow architecture of the Gordon's house precluded any offensive action. If he stood in the doorframe, he could see directly into the living room, which meant the prowlers could see him. With Lamar on the premises he didn't want a gun battle. The walls were so thin the bullet velocity wouldn't be lessened enough to prevent serious injury.

Lamar stuck his head out of the closet and his brown eyes grew wide at the sight of the weapon in Mitch's hand. Before Mitch could respond, the door snicked shut again. He heard muffled thuds from inside and a few seconds later the door opened, this time the boy held a double-barrel shotgun.

Mitch shook his head and pointed to the ground, ordering him to put it down. When Lamar stepped out of the shadowed closet, his face seemed to have aged ten years, his mouth forged into a determined line. Mitch knew there weren't enough words in the world to convince the kid to back down. There was no warrior so fierce as the one defending his loved ones and his home. But the anger he saw in the boy's eyes worried him.

Lamar grudgingly lowered the shotgun until it rested on its stock, muzzle pointing at the ceiling. His hands trembled and a wet sheen of perspiration coated his face.

Mitch nodded in approval. He gestured to an empty space next to the chifforobe, between the bed and window. This location would put the young Mr. Gordon as far from the action as possible. Following his instructions, the boy wedged himself between the chest and bed, then dropped to one knee, shotgun at the ready.

A cannon roar of thunder shook the window panes. In the silence that followed Mitch cocked his head to the side trying to determine the source of the trickling water-like sounds he heard. The storm raged outside and he assumed the old roof sprung a leak. Within seconds the odor of kerosene drifted into the back bedroom. "Never assume," he muttered, "to do so almost always makes an ass out of you and me."

Whispers and shuffling accompanied the lantern fuel smell as the prowlers moved closer. "That's all of it," someone murmured. "Ain't got no more." An aluminum can bounced through the open door.

"Let's get it done," a second voice said, as they returned to the living room.

Mitch figured once the blaze was set they'd take off. Cowards didn't usually stick around for applause. These guys would want to be clear of the house before the smoke alerted the neighbors. He looked around the room mapping out a strategy. As soon as it was clear he'd shut the door and shove something in the crack. Hopefully buying them enough time to break out the window and climb to safety.

Unfortunately he couldn't do anything about the Gordon's house. A kerosene ignited fire burned hot and fast, allowing little time for intervention techniques. Once he and the boy got out of the house, they could grab a hose and try to limit the damage to the front. It all depended on how the arsonists had applied the accelerate trail. The flames would jump if they'd doused both furniture and walls, but if they'd concentrated primarily on the floor, it would move slower.

Crackle and popping filled the house. The hungry inferno consumed the dry wooden floor. When the lazy tendrils of black smoke eased into the back bedroom, Mitch slammed the door shut and yanked the white chenille spread off the bed. On his knees he tried to poke the fabric between the floor and door, but it was too fluffy to fit snugly in the narrow space, so he ripped off his damp shirt and shoved it in the crack.

Lamar shook a bed pillow free from its case, wrapped the cotton shell around his hand and punched out the window panes, shattering the glass. Mitch used the shotgun butt to bust through the remaining wooden slats. As soon as he'd cleared a large enough opening, the boy scrambled out and he followed.

They raced along the side of the house. Suddenly Mitch hit a patch of mud, slipped and landed on his back. Lamar turned around, but he waved him off yelling, "Get a hose!" They needed to get a jump on the fire. If the kid used precious seconds to help a clumsy Irishman to his feet, the Gordon's wouldn't have a house left.

Lamar ducked under the porch and came out with a coiled green garden hose slung over his shoulder. The galvanized steel water spigot stood at one end of the porch, he knelt in the quagmire created by the rain gutter and struggled with the brass fittings. His mud caked fingers transferred gobs of clay-like soil to the nozzle threads. He spit on the casing and rubbed it clean, the two pieces slipped into each other.

Covered from head to toe in muck, Mitch slogged through the water logged yard. The rain continued to pound the earth, dark clouds swirled menacingly in the southwest and he hoped a tornado wasn't headed their way. He saw the kid almost had everything put together, so he grabbed the free end of the hose and dragged it onto the porch.

The arsonists weren't smart enough to have soaked the outside planks with kerosene and at the moment, the fire was contained within the structure itself. As soon as the water began to flow, Mitch kicked open the door.

A black cloud billowed out the door and he doubled over as his lungs filled with the acrid smoke. When it cleared slightly, he saw the living room engulfed in flames, the sofa and curtains were three quarters gone. Hoping to create a fire break, he directed the hose to the undamaged area, spraying the furniture. The orange-red flames lapped up the water like a thirsty beast. In other parts of the room the demonic glow continued to ravish the Gordon's belongings.

Suddenly glass burst through the side window, followed by a second stream of water. Then a third stream shot through the room from the opposite side. The neighborhood was answering the alarm. The glowing fingers gave one last feeble attempt to grab onto a chair, then faded into a puff of white smoke.

*   *   *

Mitch stood in the middle of the yard, allowing the rain to beat down on his body, washing the mud and soot away. His chest and arms, burned during his fire fighting, blossomed with clear blisters. He watched the tiny old woman in a plastic rain bonnet march across the driveway. She stopped in front of him, dug a handful of grayish green lard-like substance out of a crock, then slapped it on his chest without speaking. Since she barely reached his elbow, she tugged on his arm until he bent over. She then proceeded to vigorously rub the goo into his tender skin. He couldn't decide which hurt more—her treatment, or his injury.

"Hold still, sonny," she ordered. "Gotta get you greased up, don't want no more blisters."

"Thank you, Ma'am." He tried to dodge a second handful but she was too quick. "I think you greased me up enough already."

"Who's doin' all the doctoring here? You or me?" she asked, her lips smacking around the bare gums.

"You are, Ma'am."

"Then stand still."

Mitch heard a snicker behind him and glanced over his shoulder, he didn't dare move for fear the old lady would brain him with her crock. Lamar leaned against a tree, a big grin spread across his face.

"What's so funny, kid?" he asked.

"Mr. Mitch, you look like one of them pink greased pigs I seen at the county fair."

The woman chuckled. "Don't he just."

Lamar moved around to the front for a better look. "That's gonna hurt some."

"Not according to Mrs. Doctor here," he said and the woman lightly slapped his chest.

The boy gestured toward the woman. "Mr. Mitch, I'd like you to meet Mrs. Woodard. She knows almost as much as Dr. Tim about tending the sick."

Mrs. Woodard snorted. "Tim ain't but a little ole puppy when it comes to sickness."

"She worked with the doctor before Lettie Ruth come along," Lamar explained.

"Now that Rayson girl is smart," she said. "Got herself a college diploma sayin' she can doctor. I never had me one of those," she said sadly.

Mitch touched her shoulder. "You don't need one, Mrs. Woodard. You're a natural born healer."

She smiled up into his face. "Why thank you, Mr. Mitch. Those are kind words."

He slid his hands across his chest. "I feel better already, thanks to you."

Lamar waved to someone across the street. "Hey, Taxi," he shouted. "Come on over."

As Taxi Devore trotted across the flooded street, his shoes sent sprays of water squirting sideways. His black nylon shirt and khaki trousers stuck to his body, rain dripped from his hat brim onto his shoulders. "Happy Birthday, Lamar," he said. "I came by to see if you was ready for those shootin' lessons, but it don't look like a good time."

"Things been exciting around here," Lamar said, as he wiped the rain off his face.

"Ain't it kinda wet to be standin' in the yard?" Taxi asked.

Mitch pointed to the house. "It's just as wet inside."

"They tried to burn our house down, Taxi," Lamar said. "And on my birthday too."

Taxi took his hat off and smacked it against his trouser leg. "You don't say?"

"Yeah, but me and Mr. Mitch put it out," Lamar said, then covered his ears as a series of giant thunderclaps echoed off the houses.

Hat again in place, Taxi looked around the yard. "Where's your daddy, Lamar? He get hurt?"

"Daddy's over to the clinic. Been there since last night."

"What happened last night?"

"Kluxers come callin'."

Mrs. Woodard plucked at his sleeve. "Bunch a damn fools. Wearing bed sheets and pointy Halloween hats," she said. "Stood right here in this yard and beat up on the Pastor."

"He's okay," Lamar said quickly. "Dr. Tim just wants him to stay in bed a day or two. And he knew if Daddy come home he'd be off visiting folks and never get off his leg."

Mitch saw the anger swirling in Taxi's eyes and in the way he clenched and unclenched his fists. He wondered how much longer the man would sit on the sidelines. The day Maximilian Devore finally let it loose there would be one hell of an explosion, and the folks in west Maceyville would be wise to take cover.

"You know about this?" Taxi asked, glancing sideways at Mitch.

"Yeah."

Lamar hopped from one foot to the other. "You shoulda been here, Taxi. Cars all over the place, and *hundreds*, maybe even a *thousand*, colored people marching down the sidewalk. When those Klan boys seen us, they turned tail and run off."

"You put an end to it, Mitch?" Taxi asked.

"No. The preacher ran the play his way. His orders were, no violence."

Taxi dug a hole in the mud with the toe of his shoe. "No violence is gonna get somebody killed," he said.

"But it worked, Taxi," Lamar said. "Daddy stood his ground and they run off."

"Not before your daddy got hisself hurt." Taxi squatted in front of the boy. "You can't mess with the whites around here. They kill a nigger most every day just for fun."

Lamar shook his head. "I ain't afraid. Like Dr. King says, if we want things to change—"

"Did you see Dr. Martin Luther King in this yard last night?" Taxi asked, his voice harsh. "Did he take the beatin' for your daddy, Lamar?"

"No, but if he'd been here, I know he would have."

"Lamar, this is dangerous business. People are gettin' killed." Taxi gestured toward the Gordon's house. "Their places were all the way burned to the ground. All these marches and sit-ins and I ain't seen nothin' changing."

"It will," Mitch said. "It's going to take a few years, but I promise you, the old ways will die out."

Taxi got to his feet. "How you know?"

"Later on we'll talk about how I know. For the moment, I'm asking for you to accept it as the truth."

"Does you knowing things got something to do with those fancy white shoes of yours?"

Mitch looked at his filthy athletic shoes. Somebody had finally noticed.

28

"The year 2000." Taxi got up from the kitchen table and walked to the refrigerator. "The year 2000." He opened the door and stuck his head inside, moving things around on the shelves. "You got to be shittin' me," his words echoed in the near empty ice box.

Mitch poured himself another cup of coffee, he remained silent, allowing Taxi time to digest all he'd heard. He hadn't reached the decision to confide in Taxi easily. But with Kat's reliability in question—due to her unpredictable panic attacks—his back was against the wall. He needed an ally. There were too many people in jeopardy now, no way he could cover everyone alone.

After dropping Lamar Gordon off at the clinic, with a promise of double shooting lessons, Mitch had suggested they go to Taxi's place for a powwow. If they tried to have this conversation at Biggers' someone would have interrupted every five minutes. And Mitch didn't want to be interrupted. It would be a difficult tale to explain, and the listener didn't need any extra distractions.

Taxi finally withdrew his head from the refrigerator and looked at him. "You must think I'm one dumb nigger boy, Mr. Mitch." His words were as cold as the air coming out the open door.

Mr. Mitch? Good God, I'm right back where I started. "No I don't." He knew time-travel wouldn't be an easy sell when he'd started, but he certainly hadn't anticipated such a negative reaction. "You're far from dumb, Taxi."

"Then why you spinning this tale?" Taxi slammed the door. "Only some willie what just fell off the pickle boat is gonna buy into this."

"I understand your problem. Jesus, if you came up to me claiming to be from the future, I'd probably deck you and ask the questions later." Mitch waited. This deal could go one of two ways, he'd either be picking himself up off the kitchen floor or…

Taxi walked over to the table and plopped down. "Let's see if I got this right. You crossed a street and all a sudden it's a whole new year?"

Mitch nodded. "Bingo. I jumped from the year 2000 right into 1963."

"Why you want to do something like that?"

"Kat."

"Her too?"

"*Her* idea. Taxi, would a grown man be crazy enough to do something like this on his own?" Receiving no response to his attempt at humor, he pushed on. "I get the feeling you still don't believe me," Mitch said.

"Would you believe me if I was the one spinning this yarn?"

"I might. I do know I'd give it some thought before deciding you were a liar."

"Tell me about this here 2000 of yours."

"I can't do that, Taxi. Sticking my finger in the past and stirring things all around could cause major problems in my time."

"Sure makin' it hard for me to believe your story, Mr. Mitch."

He couldn't think of another way to *prove* anything he'd said. And without proof, it looked like he was dead in the water. "I'll admit it's one hell of a wild story. But I give you my word as a man, it is God's own truth."

Taxi began to pick apart a piece of bread crust left over from their lunch. After a few minutes he looked up. "How come everybody crossing that street don't go back and forth in years?"

Mitch allowed a little flicker of hope to spark. At least the man had begun to ask questions, which could mean Taxi didn't completely discount the possibility of time-travel. "I don't know how it works, but I know we're here for a reason."

"Why cain't you and Miss Kat go on back?"

"I could answer your question, but I'd rather not right now."

"If you's expectin' to be believed, Mr. Mitch. Then you just best be getting on with the answering."

Mitch worked on keeping his Irish temper under control. He couldn't allow Taxi's needling questions and attitude to push his buttons. I would be better to answer one innocuous question now, and save the fancy foot work for later. "The doorway between the years only opens when somebody dies."

"Lots folks dying every day."

"This door only works with specific people. People on a very specific list."

Taxi snorted. "You got a way to wiggle out of everything don't you? But I ain't gonna sit here and be made a fool no more." He stood and jammed the still damp hat on his head. "I'll ride you back to the clinic, after that, I don't want to be seein' or hearin' from you again."

"Wait." Mitch leaned across the table and grabbed for Taxi's arm, but his fingers slid off the slick nylon shirt. Stretched across the remains of their lunch, he didn't see Taxi's incoming fist until it connected with the side of his head. The blow knocked him off the chair and onto the floor.

Taxi grabbed the front of Mitch's shirt, yanking him upright. "I had enough of your white boy shit. Get the hell out my house." He spun Mitch around like a top and sent him stumbling toward the door.

It took all of Mitch's 250 pounds to stop the forward momentum. He spun to face his angry host. "You get one free punch," he said. "Don't try it again."

"Then you best bop on out of here, *future boy*." Taxi drew his fist back.

Mitch didn't have a choice. He grabbed Taxi's elbow, and burrowed his thumb into the tender inner flesh until the man gasped with pain. "Settle down," he said, then released his hold.

"My arm and shoulder, done gone dead," Taxi moaned.

"I just pressed on a nerve ending, you'll be okay in a few minutes."

"White folks is all the same, a nigger don't do your bidding, you cause him pain."

Mitch kicked a chair into the middle of the room. "Sit!" he barked.

"Sure, *boss*." Taxi gave him a fierce scowl, before taking a seat. "Whatever you say, *boss*."

"Shut the fuck up, Taxi. This isn't a game, I need your help."

"Don't know what help you be needin' from this boy," he said, rubbing his elbow.

"What's it going to take to get you to listen?"

Taxi stared at him for a moment then said, "Tell me somethin' that ain't yet come to be."

"Shit." Mitch's brain went blank, what could he say to solidify his position? He couldn't announce, four little girls will be killed in the bombing of the Birmingham 16th Street Baptist Church on September 15. He couldn't say, on November 22, President John Fitzgerald Kennedy will be shot in Dallas by Lee Harvey Oswald. There must be something else. Some fact less dangerous. "Commander Neil A. Armstrong will walk on the moon July 20, 1969," he blurted out.

Taxi shrugged, unimpressed. "That's a long time to wait to find out if you be tellin' the truth, Mr. Mitch. Ain't you got something in the here and now?"

"In the here and now?" Mitch closed his eyes and prayed to one of Kat's voodoo spirits for inspiration. It must have worked because an image of Billy Lee's sleek black Chevy drove into his head. His eyes popped open. "Oh, yeah, I got a here and now for you."

* * *

Kathleen Rayson Templeton felt twelve-years old again, called on the carpet to answer for her misdeeds. This time the issue wasn't whether or not she'd skipped bible class to go downtown with her girlfriends, or whether or not she'd kissed David Finder behind the chapel. This meeting had been called by Alvin Rayson to discuss the truth…the whole truth and nothing but the truth.

Her father and aunt had cornered her in the TV room shortly after Mitch and Taxi had dropped Lamar off. Now, seated in the recliner Kat dreaded the next few minutes.

Alvin Rayson threw the opening punch. "Who are you and where did you come from?"

And she countered by sidestepping. "I'm Kathleen Templeton. My folks are from New Orleans."

"I see," he said.

Kat found his ensuing silence ominous. Her father may have been thirty-seven years younger, but he'd already cultivated the tone and magnificent frown which indicated his displeasure. If this was to be a battle of wills, Kat feared she was seriously out-gunned.

"Me and Alvin is from New Orleans," Lettie Ruth said.

Great, Kat thought, another country heard from. Not only must she contend with her father's grilling, now her aunt had joined the Rayson inquisition team. And both of them were as suspicious as a pair of mice around a cheese-filled mousetrap. If she could only lead them down a false path, she might survive this impromptu family meeting.

"It's a real pretty city," Kat commented, taking the first step on the New Orleans pathway. "I especially like the area around Jackson Square."

"The Café du Monde," Lettie Ruth sighed.

"Beignets," Kat said reverently. The women looked at each other and broke into laughter.

"If you ladies are through extolling the virtues of New Orleans—"

"Men don't understand food the way we do," Lettie Ruth said to Kat.

"That's 'cause men are from Mars and women are from Venus," Kat said.

Lettie Ruth laughed. "That's the best way of explaining it that I ever heard."

"You should write a book about all the differences between men and women," Kat suggested.

"And I'll call it 'Men are from Mars, Women are from Venus,'" Lettie Ruth announced.

"Lettie Ruth!" Rayson sputtered, his exasperation showing in his tone. "I'm tryin' to be serious here. Quit interrupting with men and women differences and book talk."

"Oh for goodness sakes, Alvin. Kat's sittin' right here in front of us, she didn't run off down the road. You got plenty of time for serious talk."

Kat stood. "Actually, I do need to take care of a few things. Could we postpone this discussion for an hour or two?"

Rayson snorted and gave his sister an icy glare.

"Of course, you can, honey," Lettie Ruth said. "But don't tire yourself. When you get done, I want you to lie down and rest."

*   *   *

Kat paused for a moment outside the TV room and allowed relief to flood her system. This must be the way Daniel felt, she thought, when God sent the angel into the lion's den. Her aunt Lettie Ruth had shut Alvin's mouth just as surely as the angel shut the lion's mouth.

The enormous crash of thunder rattled the entire house and Timothy Biggers stuck his head out of his office door. The way his hair stood on end and the rumpled white doctor coat, Kat assumed he'd been sleeping on the office sofa before the thunder alarm went off. He'd spent another night guarding the Webster Avenue church and looked like he needed an extra twelve hours in a real bed.

The hallway lights flickered. "Is the power gonna hold?" she asked, a cold chill spread up her arms.

Biggers shrugged. "This is an old building. Sometimes the wiring gets cranky when a storm this size blows in. I better hunt down the candles just in case."

"Don't you have a back up generator?"

"We used to, until somebody dumped a pound of sugar in the tank a couple of days ago. So it's doubtful it will do us much good."

Kat shivered. Would his generator have been tampered with if she wasn't here? She nodded to the doctor and hurried down the hall to her room. She wanted to check the damnable list again, just in case someone new had suddenly appeared.

*   *   *

Mitch pointed to the black Impala half way down Blodgett Street. It was parked back end first in the driveway of the clapboard house. "I own that car in the year 2000. And I guarantee, if you push her to 65 mph she'll die and roll belly up on the road."

"So says you."

Mitch opened the car door and climbed out. "Give me five minutes and I'll prove it to you."

"Where you goin'?"

"Going to make a temporary appropriation. Be ready to hop in when I pull along side."

"You expectin' me to leave my car here?" Taxi asked, eyeing the white neighborhood nervously.

"It will be all right. Nobody's out in this storm and besides, what would they want with an old 1946 De Soto?"

Taxi frowned. "She may be ugly, but she's paid for," he said indignantly.

"No offense meant. Believe me, your ride will be fine parked here for a half hour."

Taxi looked angry, and far from convinced, but he nodded. "Not much street traffic this afternoon, I reckon she'll be waitin' when I comes back."

Mitch nodded and shut the door. He trotted down the sidewalk, grateful the weather had created a false twilight. The thunder and lightening were still battling in the skies as the rain continued to fall in heavy gray sheets.

He jogged past Pamela and Billy Lee Mitchell's house once to get a feel for the situation. He had no desire to run into his father, especially since he planned on liberating the Chevy. All the drapes were closed in the front, apparently his parents were riding out the storm indoors. He crept along the side and chanced a quick look inside the first undraped window. He saw the back of a man's head, the hand on the chair arm held a can of beer. The TV on, volume turned up high. He remembered his father's favorite past time—other than running moonshine—had been watching televison. The noise from the program, plus the storm, should mask the Impala's growling engine.

Mitch pulled his car keys out of his pocket and unlocked the Chevy, he was about to slip inside when the front door opened. He ducked down just as Billy Lee stepped out on the small porch. His father lazily scratched his stomach, glaring at the darkened sky. Suddenly a noise from inside caused him to spin around and yell, "Goddamn it, Pam. Shut that brat up, she's louder than a pack of hounds." He hawked up a wad of phlegm, spit over the rail and stomped back inside.

Crouched behind the Chevy, Mitch doubled up his fist and slammed it into the driver side door, denting the rolled steel. Torn between stealing his father's toy and breaking into the house and beating the living hell out of him. Mitch punched the panel again. *I had a sister.* The memory of the innocent baby dangling from Billy Lee's hand caused him to tremble with rage. If I don't do something, he thought, that little girl will die again.

He stood, eager to battle the evil ogre hiding within the clapboard walls. He saw his mother peek out the kitchen window and stepped away from the car, prepared to bolt down the street if she raised the alarm.

Suddenly Pamela Mitchell smiled. "Take it," she mouthed and waved her hand. "Go!"

Mitch grinned, if his mother gave him permission to steal the SOB's play thing, what jury would convict him? Besides, a Southern gentlemen was raised with better manners than to ever argue with his momma.

In less than thirty seconds he and Taxi were headed for the open road.

* * *

The black Impala sailed down the slick highway, a plumes of rainwater trailing in its wake. The throbbing engine vibrated the floorboards and caused the plastic hula dancer hanging from the rear view mirror to shimmy provocatively.

"Taxi, you asked for a here and now." Mitch pressed the accelerator and the speedometer needle climbed steadily. "And this is it. When we hit 65, I predict this vehicle will do the following in this precise order: One, she'll backfire twice. Two, the engine will begin to sputter and the exhaust will turn black. And Three, she'll die deader than Robert E. Lee within thirty seconds."

As predicted by 'future boy' Mitchell, when the speedometer reached the magic number 65, Billy Lee's car went through the opening sequences and conked out. Taxi grudgingly admitted that might be proof. "Not very good proof, mind you," he said, "but proof none the less."

They'd pushed the very dead Chevy a quarter mile further before spotting the open barn. The Impala currently occupied the lower level. The men reclined in the fresh smelling hayloft and waited out another rain squall.

"I've been meaning to ask you something for several days," Mitch said.

"Uh-huh."

"How does a person go from being a Maximilian to being called Taxi?"

"Used to drive a taxi cab."

"That's it? No elaborate story?"

"Nope, just me in a yellow cab." Taxi rolled onto his back and pulled his hat over his face. "Gonna get me some sleep here."

"Think again, pal," Mitch said. "We're going to start our conversation from the very beginning."

"Don't believe there is much to say 'tween us."

"Looks like we'll be in this barn for a long time. Might as well pass the time talking to each other."

Taxi tipped his hat brim up enough to see Mitch. "This gonna be another time-traveling conversation?"

"Yes. I'm from the future," Mitch announced. "Yes, I know you're not 100 per cent convinced I'm telling the truth. But it doesn't matter. If we don't work together, people will die," he paused, debating whether or not to continue along this road.

To enlist Taxi's support he needed the Mother of all motivators. Would knowing he was scheduled to die in two days motivate Maximilian Devore? Or would it have the opposite effect and fuck him up so completely he'd become more hindrance than help?

Mitch took a deep breath and began, "Kat crossed over Park Street." Taxi rolled his eyes and Mitch kicked his leg. "Stop screwing around and listen. She crossed because on April 5, thirty-seven years ago, Lettie Ruth died."

"Lettie Ruth is gonna die *today*?"

Some of the tension went out of Mitch's shoulders. Taxi had focused on the problem, not the time-travel issue. "That's the way it originally went down thirty-seven years ago. But not now."

"What happened to her?"

"I don't know for sure."

"You got to know how things happened if you gonna stop 'em."

"I know the when, the where and the time. Is that enough information for you?"

Taxi rolled over on his stomach. "How you know all that?"

"We have a list of victims, from the 1963 Maceyville Police Department files."

"And Lettie Ruth is on that dead list of yours?" he asked.

"Yes. But now everything's gone to hell in a hand basket."

"What you mean?"

"The Arson/Fatality list. The damn thing keeps adding on names. And switching dates."

"Arson?" Taxi's eyes narrowed. "This is some story you be weavin'."

"Stay with me here, pal. The day Kat got here, there were only twelve victims listed. Then yesterday, four additional names popped up. Now we have sixteen dead people."

"This has gotta be the biggest pile of horse shit in the whole wide world." Taxi stood, angrily brushing the hay off his clothes. "You don't be respectin' me. No sir, no respect."

"I respect you."

"Like hell," Taxi roared. He swung over the edge of the hayloft and quickly descended the ladder. When he reached the bottom, he looked up at Mitch. "You been playin' with my head for long enough, Mr. Mitch. I'm going back and get my car. You do what you want."

"Kat and I know all the new people on the list," Mitch said, in a last ditch effort to redirect the conversation. "We've met them since we got here…in 1963. Something we've done, or are doing, is causing the changes."

Taxi paused near the door. Without turning around he asked, "Who be named? Who's new on that list of yours?"

"Lamar Gordon, Kat Templeton, Louis Smith…and Maximilian Devore."

"So I got my name on that dead list now?" Taxi slid the heavy wooden door open and walked out into the rain.

Mitch lay back on the hay and covered his eyes with his arm. He doubted the breech between them could ever be mended. Distrust ran deep between the races in the South. Trust was hard won and even harder to keep. Once you betrayed that confidence, there was no going back. He'd made a major mistake disclosing this crazy time-travel business. What made him think any man in his right mind would buy into this nonsense? Hell, he *was* an active participant and at least once every hour he questioned whether or not he was dreaming.

"Now what?" he asked the empty barn. "I've alienated one of the few friends I've made here. By the time I get back to the clinic, I'll probably find myself without any friends." He wearily swung over the edge and climbed down the ladder.

He got as far as the barn door, then returned. There was a Biblical scale rainstorm going on outside and he figured God owed him one. He climbed inside the Impala and turned the key. The black monster roared to life. At least he wouldn't have to walk back to town in the rain.

Mitch backed out of the barn and pulled a U in the yard, keeping his fingers crossed the tires didn't get stuck in the mud. When he reached the highway he wondered if Taxi would accept a ride back to his De Soto. "I could be ready to bite someone's head off," he told the wiggly hula dancer, "but if they offered me a lift in a torrential downpour I'd say yes."

Less than a quarter mile down the road he saw a drenched Maximilian Devore despondently hunched on the shoulder. His hat had soaked up so much rainwater it hung around his face like a woman's head scarf. He looked like a drowned puppy.

Mitch stopped the car and leaned across the seat, he opened the door and silently waited. In less time than it took to sneeze, Taxi was sitting beside him.

29

APRIL 05—FRIDAY

The Arson/Fatality list remained the same as yesterday. Kat's tensed body sagged with relief. She folded the paper into a small square and shoved it in the pocket of her borrowed jeans. Like an American Express card, she never left home without it. She'd become paranoid, believing if she didn't check every few minutes the list would undergo dramatic alterations.

Her greatest fear—that a random act would set up another catastrophic run of events—colored her every action. Short of locking herself in this room until Sunday, she couldn't figure out how to avoid changing the past. A conversation with a neighbor, a grocery store purchase, who could predict the ramifications of such simple acts? A prime example, was the terrible death monster she'd conjured by just talking to Lamar Gordon. The attack on Pastor Gordon lay squarely on her shoulders. Because she talked to his son, the Klan had paid them a visit.

She opened the door and stepped into the third floor hallway, then, as an afterthought returned to her room. She rummaged in the night stand searching for a pain pill. She'd never admit it to anyone, but her body was in revolt against the punishment it received. She felt as stiff and achy as an ancient grandma.

Kat pulled aside the window shade at the sound of an engine. The rain beating against the glass distorted her view somewhat, but she could still recognize the De Soto. "It's about time," she muttered. Mitch and Taxi had been gone for hours. She was anxious to talk to her partner, she'd hurt his feelings last night and wanted to clear the air between them.

* * *

Pastor Gordon rolled over, wincing as the sheet snagged on his bandages. He swung his legs off the side of the bed and gingerly tested his weight. He dreaded the walk to Timothy's fancy bathroom at the end of the hall, but the doctor had ordered leg soak therapy three times a day in his whirlpool. It seemed to Gordon the distance had doubled with each trip. Moving with the speed of a giant tortoise, he hobbled down the corridor.

Since the second floor bathroom faced the secluded back yard, Biggers' had installed a large plate glass window above the sunken tub. The top of the rose trellis peeked over the ledge and Gordon saw the bright red buds being washed by the storm. Fat raindrops pounded against the pane, and he thought he heard small bits of hail tapping on the glass.

He dumped a couple of handfuls of Epsom salts into the tub, turned on the faucet and sat on the tiled edge as it filled. With a groan, he set about the task of unwrapping his wounded leg for the second time today. The chain Billy Lee Mitchell used had opened a deep chasm in his upper and lower right leg. By comparison, the gaping hole in his left leg looked minuscule.

Being a modest man, the preacher lowered the Venetian blinds over the big window before disrobing. He gritted his teeth and stepped into the water.

* * *

Lettie Ruth finished cleaning the last exam room just as the green De Soto parked in front of the clinic. She gave it a cursory glance out the front window, pleased to note Taxi and Mitch had managed to show up in time for supper. Their timely arrival didn't surprise her, men were most always on time when it came to eating. She continued down the short hall leading to the kitchen, her mind on Lamar's birthday supper Kat had put together. The three layer chocolate cake sitting on the table looked real pretty with the white frosting and decorations from the five and dime. She peeked in the oven, the meat loaf sure did smell good. Lettie felt like a woman of leisure today, not having to juggle cooking and patients had been a rare treat.

* * *

Lamar Gordon snuggled into the blue and yellow blanket, humming *Happy Birthday*. His thirteenth birthday had been pretty exciting. He wondered what the whole next year would be like. His mind began to wander and the images flickering on the TV screen melted into scenes from his own life. Men in robes and hoods, his daddy bleeding on the ground, a Bible held high above his head. Lamar felt bad about last night, wishing he could have been braver. But those men scared the bejesus out of him. When they started hollering and beating on his daddy, he and Virgil quit peeking out the window and followed Dr. Tim to the back of the house.

He'd been just as scared in the fire today, but this time he didn't run and hide. Him and Mr. Mitch done good. And everybody in the neighborhood said his house would be okay once they painted and fixed up the burned parts.

But what about those men? They'd come sniffing around again, this battle wasn't no where near over. In fact, Dr. King kept on preaching about colored folks standing up together and how things wouldn't get better until people started changing and started caring. Maybe I ought to do a little changing in the way I handle things, he thought.

Lamar tiptoed to the door and looked down the corridor. He heard Dr. Tim rustling papers in his office and the bubbling sound from the big tub meant Daddy was in there again. Assured he wouldn't be observed, he scurried down the hall to his room. He'd sneaked the shotgun and a box of shells out of the house after the fire, wrapped in a bundle of clothes. Next time those Kluxers came visiting he planned to show them how much this colored boy had changed. He shoved a handful of ammo in each pocket and carried the gun back to the TV room.

First he tried to hide the shotgun behind the curtain, but it was too heavy and kept falling over. Next he shoved it in back of the cabinet TV, but the stock stuck out. When he heard the floorboards creak and steps coming his way, he stuffed it behind the sofa cushions and jumped on top of it. He threw the blanket around his shoulders to camouflage the bulge.

* * *

Timothy Biggers hurriedly finished the last of his paperwork in his office, lured by the delicious aroma of meat loaf. From the kitchen smells he figured

Kat must be as good a cook as Lettie. As he passed the bathroom he heard the muted rumble of the water jets, noting with satisfaction that the pastor had followed his orders.

He waved to Lamar and received a sparkling smile in return. The boy was curled up in front of the TV, a brightly crocheted blanket wrapped around his shoulders. "Anything worth watching?" he asked.

"I like them soap operas," Lamar said. "You white people sure are funny, Dr. Tim."

Biggers laughed and continued down the hall. The boy's resilience had impressed him. Witnessing his father's beating by the Klan, the next day his house set on fire and the kid could still smile. He was tough, and would grow into a fine man—if he lived long enough.

He saw two silhouettes through the stained-glass front door as he reached the bottom step, and assumed it to be Mitch and Taxi. As he moved to let them inside, the door exploded inward.

The concussion force propelled him backwards. He landed near the foot of the stairs. Colored glass fragments and splintered wood sprinkled down on him, smoke shrouded the foyer and hallway.

Through the fog like haze he saw four men enter the clinic. They wore street clothes, but their faces were hooded. Biggers scrabbled across the foyer, his goal to reach the rifle stowed under the false panel behind the lobby desk. A fit of coughing slowed his progress and he bumped into a pair of legs. He looked up and said, "A step closer and the blast would have blown my face off." A heavy work boot smashed into his cheek.

*   *   *

The tallest man tossed a length of rope to one of the others, pantomiming tying Biggers' hands. He didn't want to speak, the doc knew his voice. He glanced around the waiting area, disappointed there weren't any bloody niggers lying in the floor. He'd hoped to take out two or three with the dynamite.

Satisfied the doctor was neutralized so no one would be shot to hell and gone this time, he headed toward the kitchen. Even through all the smoke and sulphur he smelled meat loaf.

A smile filled the inside of his muslin hood when he found Lettie Ruth Rayson cowering beneath the kitchen table. Rather than crawling after her, he gripped the table's edge and heaved it upwards. The heavy oak furniture toppled over on its side like a wounded elephant and the birthday cake landed upside down on the floor.

"Hey, girl. Whatcha doing down there?" he asked, not caring whether or not she recognized his voice. In the long run it wouldn't matter, because dead folks made lousy witnesses. He prodded her balled up figure with his foot. "Get on up."

As she got to her feet, it pleased him to see her tremble. At least one nigger in this town had enough brains to be afraid of the West Central Alabama Ku Klux Klan. He reached out to brush a smudge of flour off her cheek, when she flinched he felt a slow heat building below his belt.

"You and the doc the only folks home?" he asked.

Lettie Ruth nodded.

"Sure about that, nurse nigger?"

"Check on upstairs if you don't believe me."

He didn't care for her insolent response and especially didn't like the fact she'd stopped shaking all over. He took a long hard look in her eyes. He didn't see fear. The only thing staring back at him was anger.

"Let's you and me *both* check the upstairs," he said, allowing his tone to deliver the unspoken part of his message. He grabbed her upper arm and piloted her out of the kitchen.

*   *   *

Pastor Gordon's first thought when the explosion rocked the clinic was of his son. He had to find his boy and get him to safety. Forgetting the seriousness of his injuries, he popped out of the water like a cork. Caught off guard when his leg buckled, and he landed face down in a swirling eddy of Epsom salts. He wiggled around until he could sit upright, but in the process he cracked his head on the chrome handle of the spigot. The water immediately turned a murky pink. He grabbed the wash cloth and held it to his forehead fighting the dizziness and nausea threatening to overpower him. He needed to get out of the tub right now.

He knew those responsible for the explosion would search the building, and the idea of being caught naked as a jay bird in the bathtub held little appeal for Jackson Gordon. He used the tiled rim for support as he exited the tub, the gashes on his legs were open and bleeding freely. As he stepped onto the light-blue bath mat, an ugly red stain spread around his feet. He grabbed the nearest hand towel, pressed it over the deepest wound on his left leg, securing it in place with the gauze bandage he'd removed earlier.

He dug through the dirty laundry hamper until he found a pair of trousers and a shirt. Luckily the pant leg slipped over the bulky towel and gauze bandage. Within seconds the exposed wounds on his other leg bled through the cotton fabric, but he didn't have time to hunt for another bandage.

He stepped toward the door and the trousers fell around his hips. Since Timothy was a good six inches taller and thirty pounds heavier, Gordon couldn't keep the pants up around his waist so he yanked the cord off the Venetian blinds and threaded it through the belt loops.

*   *   *

As though his daddy's shotgun was Aladdin's magic lamp, Lamar Gordon rubbed his hand across the smooth wooden stock. "I wish," he stopped and nibbled on his lip. If he only got three wishes, he wanted to be sure they were good ones. There were so many things. He wanted to swim in the city pool. Use the downtown library. Eat at a fancy lunch counter. Ride the bus to school instead of walking. He vigorously rubbed the stock. "I wish—" The explosion rattled the window panes and caused small pieces of plaster to fall from the ceiling. His hand closed around the shotgun and he yanked it free of the sofa cushions.

Lamar squeezed his eyes shut and whispered, "I only got one wish and I wish I knew how to shoot this thing." He'd been hunting with his daddy, but he'd never been allowed to fire the weapon. Taxi had promised him a full day of learning how to shoot for his birthday, but he needed to know how to shoot now. He tried to remember how to load the shotgun. Fumbling with the shells, he finally succeeded in awkwardly shoving them in the breech.

He sat very still and listened. He knew better than to walk around, this old building had more creaks and groans than his grandma's rocking chair. Even though he heard no voices, he knew folks were downstairs. And they were white, because Negroes had more sense than to blow up Dr. Tim's clinic. The eerie quiet gave him a tingly feeling all the way down to his toes. He looked around. Even if he hunkered down behind the sofa they'd find him in a Dixie second. The closet, crammed full of doctor stuff, didn't leave any room for a thirteen-year-old boy.

Lamar slid off the sofa and knelt on the floor. "Daddy says to trust in you, Lord, and I do. So if you're not too busy, could you look down here on this colored boy and help out a little? Amen."

The ceiling creaked suddenly. Someone was walking around overhead. He smiled. He'd plum forgot all about Miss Kat sleeping upstairs. But God had remembered and sent her to help. Being a policeman and all, she knew about guns and shooting. "Thank you, Lord."

* * *

Kat dry swallowed the pill at the same instant the front door exploded, and nearly choked to death on the white tablet. Coughing and fighting the tears clouding her vision, she retrieved Timothy's Colt from the top shelf in the closet. She checked the cylinder—fully loaded, but it held only six rounds. Each bullet must strike the intended target. She had no room for a wild shot.

Luckily her the third floor location gave her a slight edge over the male guests and patients currently residing in what Lettie Ruth had dubbed the 'Second Floor Boy's Dormitory'. She ran a mental inventory of those downstairs right now—second floor: Pastor Gordon and Lamar. Lettie Ruth and Timothy were probably still on the ground floor. Mitch and Alvin were gone.

The ones who blew up the door would be searching from the bottom to top. Kat had no time to relocate to the lower floor so she could protect the Gordons. All she could do was to find a strategic post that could be defended. Preferably a position which would allow her to pick off the bad guys one by one as they ascended the staircase.

The U-shaped layout of the floor offered little in the way of cover. She envied the cowboys in the old Saturday matinees. They always had a big boulder to duck behind.

Sans a boulder, Kat decided her best bet was the bathroom. It faced the stairs and she could use the cast iron tub for protection. It would be tricky, she'd have to shoot through an open door, but it could be done. Must be done.

30

When Mitch turned the corner and saw the empty stretch along the curb on Blodgett Street his guts squirmed like a nest of rattlesnakes. Thank God. He'd dropped the still angry Taxi at home with the promise to return with his car. Mitch didn't feel up to the inevitable tongue lashing because the De Soto, a piece of green shit if he ever saw one, had vanished. He doubted anyone really wanted the car, much less have bothered to steal it. The fact that it *was* gone worried him. What had happened? If no one wanted it and no one stole it, where did it go?

His questions dissipated like a puff of smoke when he saw the red-haired woman carrying a baby stagger down the steps of the small clapboard house. He hit the brakes so hard the Impala skidded several feet past Pamela and Carolyn Mitchell before the brakes caught. Leaving the car in the middle of the street, engine running and door open, he reached his mother just as her knees buckled. He scooped her and the baby up in his arms and carried them to the Chevy.

His mother trembled so hard her teeth chattered. Mitch took off his damp windbreaker and wrapped it around her shoulders, then removed his plaid sports shirt to cover his shivering little sister. Carolyn's tiny arms were a mass of purple black fingermarks, and her bottom lip swollen. Pamela's bruised face and blackened eye told the rest of the story. Mitch swallowed his angry words. These two didn't need another Mitchell raising hell.

Without speaking, he closed the passenger door, went around to the driver's side and got in. He looked at Pamela, when she didn't protest, he shifted into drive and pressed the accelerator. His only goal, to put as much distance between his family and the son-of-a-bitch that had beaten them.

After several minutes' Pamela spoke, "I saw you from the kitchen window earlier. You were standing beside this car."

"Yes, ma'am. It was supposed to be a joke on...on your husband. I'm sorry if my silliness caused—"

"None of this is your fault," she interrupted. "Billy Lee had finished with the hitting long before he discovered the car to be missing. There's something you need to know, all this," she touched her face, "is because...is all my fault. I aggravated him."

"What set him off?"

She lowered her head and a curtain of red hair fell across her face. "The baby is teething and crying a lot more than usual. It really bothers him."

"You can't let him get away with it."

"If I hadn't argued with him, things wouldn't have gotten this rough," she said, then raised her head. "But I will never allow him to leave his mark on the baby. I was just protecting Carolyn, not trying to make Billy Lee mad."

"A man shouldn't hit his wife and child. No matter how angry he gets."

"You're the only one around here that feels that way." She angrily brushed the hair from her eyes. "This is the South. Men beat their wives and children."

Mitch curbed the Chevy and turned off the engine. He pushed the seat back so he could turn sideways and face his passengers. "It doesn't matter where you are—South, North, East or West—assault is illegal. You can have him arrested and take him to court."

Pamela looked at him, her blue eyes defeated. "That never happens down here. Wife beating is a sport, not a crime."

"Then leave him. Go back to Pennsylvania."

She stiffened and Carolyn began to whimper. She crooned to the baby, rocking back and forth on the seat. Once the child had settled she turned to Mitch. "How do you know about Pennsylvania?"

He stared out the front window, watching the wipers sweep the heavy rain off the glass. He'd spoken without thinking. A habit Kat had tried to break for five years. Now what do I say? he wondered. Unless he came up with a plausible explanation, Pamela Mitchell would jump out of the car and run screaming down the street.

"Your accent," he said. "I'm from Pennsylvania and I guess I recognized a fellow Yankee."

"Not too many like us in Alabama." She held out her hand. "I'm Pamela Mitchell and this is my daughter, Carolyn."

Mitch grasped her hand desperately trying to think up an alias. Why did names like Vito Correlone, Forrest Gump and Rocky Balboa keep popping into his head? He needed something that remotely resembled the Pennsylvania Dutch names. "I'm Han Solo."

"Hans?" she asked. "Like in the children's book, *Hans Brinker and the Silver Skates*?"

"Almost, it's just Han. There's not an '*s*' on the end. They forgot to put it on my birth certificate. My mother picked the name because she used to read a lot. She always loved fairy tales. You know, the 'lived happily ever after' stuff."

"I love to read, or at least I did before I married. When I attended the University of Alabama, I majored in English Literature." She sighed. "Billy Lee says reading is a waste of time for a woman."

"Well *Billy Lee* is way off base. He's trying to control you, make you as stupid as he is."

"He's not stupid, Han."

"Okay, he's not stupid. But he is acting like an ogre, and I learned a lot about ogres from my own father." Mitch started the engine.

"Your dad was a hitter?"

"A champion hitter."

"Did your mother leave him?"

His heart skipped a beat. That was a Catch-22 question. Another look at his mother's face and the baby's purple arms settled the issue. "Yes, she did. Only not soon enough," he said. "She waited too long and it cost her a child."

"Oh God." Pamela trembled and hugged Carolyn. "Your father hurt—"

"Not hurt, Pamela," Mitch said. "He *killed* my little sister."

"Your poor mother. Knowing if she'd only left him sooner…what a terrible thing to endure."

"Given the chance again, I'm certain she'd leave him the first time he hit the baby."

"I wish I had the courage. Sometimes Billy Lee gets so angry it scares me, and I'm afraid if I stay, something bad will happen to both of us." She kissed the top of Carolyn's head.

"Sounds to me like you've already made the decision. Maybe you're stronger and braver than you think."

"My whole life would change."

"Yes, and it would probably be a good change."

Mitch kept his eyes on the road, afraid Pamela would see the shine of tears in his eyes. He knew her life would be so much better if she left Billy Lee now. She was young enough to find a man to love her and Carolyn the right way.

Wonderful things lay ahead, if he could only convince his mother to leave Billy Lee Mitchell. Of course, if he succeeded there would be another change.

"Where to, m'lady?" he asked, praying she didn't tell him to take her back home.

Pamela shrugged. "I don't know. I haven't made many friends in Maceyville, I'm a little *too Yankee*."

He chuckled. "I think we're both *too Yankee* for this place. But, I do have friends in Maceyville. I'm sure they wouldn't mind if you stayed with them."

"I don't know."

"Do you know Dr. Timothy Biggers?" When she nodded, he continued. "I'm staying at his place and he's got plenty of extra rooms."

"What about Billy Lee? He'll come looking for us."

"Maybe not."

Mitch knew what the end result of this confrontation with his father would be, and had no qualms about moving his chess piece that direction. This woman deserved more happiness than she'd known, and he wanted her little girl to live. He held the power to ensure a better life for his mother and sister. And he intended to do just that, regardless of the consequence.

31

Lettie Ruth saw the bloodied doctor leaning against the check-in desk. He raised his head high enough to meet her gaze. He may have been hurt some, but the fury in his eyes told her he would be all right. She figured the first chance to come his way, Timothy would be running the show down here.

Her escort gave her a rough shove, then twisted her arm behind her back. She didn't fight his iron grip because she would be no use to the others if he started in on her. Once upstairs, and away from the other three men, she'd get down to business. Dreama Simms may have taken all those classes on nonviolent resistance, but Lettie Ruth Rayson had taken different classes. A girl didn't grow up in the streets of New Orleans without learning how to take care of herself.

As they cleared the landing, she saw the bathroom door inch open. In case the Pastor or Lamar hadn't seen them, she thought it best to make their presence known.

"Let go of me you redneck jackass!" she shouted. She jerked her arm free and swung wildly at her captor's head. She felt a burst of satisfaction when she connected with his nose. A second later, a red blossom of blood stained the muslin hood.

"Stupid nigger." He grabbed a handful of hair and slammed her head into the wall. "You best learn to mind your manners."

She shook her head, clearing the stars swimming in front of her eyes. It could've been worse, she thought. He could of taken a baseball bat or a chain…Her thoughts faded as she looked him over. This particular Klansman didn't carry anything in his hands, no weapon that she could see. Of course he might have a gun tucked in his belt, but then again, he might not.

* * *

    Lamar heard the confrontation in the hall and knelt behind the couch, the shotgun resting across the back cushion. He took slow breaths and tried to control the trembling in his hands. Right now the gun wiggled so much he wouldn't be able to hit anything. He laid his cheek against the stock and sighted down the barrel, his finger curled around the trigger.

    He didn't know if he could pull the trigger. *'Thou Shalt Not Kill'*. That was the sixth commandment. No matter how mad he got at those Egyptians, even old Moses knew better than to break that rule. And Lamar didn't like the idea of spending eternity in the fires of Hell. On the other hand, he didn't much care for people exploding Dr. Tim's house and beating up on the people inside.

    When Lettie Ruth stumbled through the door, followed by the hooded man, all of Lamar's earlier doubts and nervousness disappeared. He felt ice cold. His hands steady. It took several seconds for the situation to register on the white man, but Lettie Ruth was quicker. She immediately dropped to the ground, giving Lamar a clear shot.

    He held his breath and pulled one hammer back on the double-barrel shotgun. He jerked the trigger.

* * *

    Lettie Ruth opened her mouth to tell the boy to stop, but when she saw the murderous rage in the Kluxer's eyes she fell to the floor. If Lamar missed, the man would kill him.

    The shotgun roared like an angry fire breathing dragon bent on destruction. A wide section of doorframe vanished as the dragon took its first bite. The recoil knocked the boy backwards and he disappeared behind the sofa.

    The man jumped over Lettie Ruth and clambered across the flowered cushions. Within seconds he reappeared, with Lamar in one hand and the shotgun in the other. He twisted the boy's arm behind his back and shoved him toward the center of the room.

    "You ought to know better, pickaninny." He held the gun over his head, then threw it into the hall like a javelin. "Your pop toy ain't no match against mine."

Lettie Ruth's fears came to pass when he pulled a handgun from inside his shirt. She figured Lamar had about thirty seconds to live if she didn't do something. The TV room didn't stock a supply of weapons, so her resources were limited. Other than a few magazines and jigsaw puzzles, there wasn't anything of use. While the man toyed with Lamar, she eased a hand down her leg until she touched her shoe. A size eight, white nurse's oxford, probably wouldn't be the ideal weapon for defense, but under the circumstances it seemed pretty damn good.

Slipping the shoe off her left foot, she gripped the toe end. Plotting her moves like a choreographer, she brought her arm around in a sweeping arc at the same time shifting from a prone position to kneeling. Sensing her movements, the man turned toward her, which left his groin vulnerable. Lettie Ruth rammed the one and a quarter inch rubber heel into his testicles.

He screamed and doubled over. In a second he lay moaning in the floor, curled in the fetal position. He still clutched the gun near his head and she kicked his wrist with her right foot, the heavy oxford sent the gun sliding across the hardwood floor and underneath the sofa.

"Get it, Lamar," she told him. The boy slithered under the sofa and soon emerged with the weapon. "Point it at him," she instructed. "And if he so much as blinks an eyelash, you shoot." With a final glance at the fallen man, she moved toward the door. The shotgun lay in the hall. If she could reach it in time.

*   *   *

The lightening flashed like a strobe, and thunder rumbled ominously. The storm hovered over Maceyville like a dark and evil spirit bent on revenge. Kat fidgeted in the cast iron tub. Fueled by adrenalin she found it difficult to remain still. When another volley of thunder roared through town, she stood.

Standing, with one leg outside the bathtub, she froze when the shotgun blast echoed throughout the three-story structure. Who'd fired? she wondered. And who got shot? Her next action depended upon the answer. If the wounded party was one of the invaders, hurrah for the good guys. If not, one of her new friends needed help. Suddenly someone screamed.

The high-pitched wail of agony penetrated Kat's adrenalin armor and the white-hot flames of fear began. "Oh, no," she whispered. People needed her help, she couldn't let this happen again.

She fought against the clawing hands of terror, but lacked the strength to break free. The prickly sensation moved through her body and nothing seemed real. She seemed to float down into the bathtub where she curled in a small trembling ball. Mixed up images filled the screen behind her closed eyes. The cotton field, men in robes, white pickups. Mitch, Lettie Ruth. The pictures rotated with such speed she felt nauseous. Somehow, in all this insanity Kat knew she was in the midst of another panic attack. She struggled with the raw surge of emotions, fiercely battling the demons of fear. "God, help me," she whispered.

* * *

The three men rushed from the waiting area to the foot of the stairs when the shotgun exploded. After a murmured conference, one climbed to the second floor.

A haze floated in the air and the smell of burned gun powder caused him to sneeze. Slivers of wood and chunks of plaster littered the hall. He hesitated, nobody had brought a weapon except Billy Lee, and he was still downstairs. So who pulled the trigger?

He eased over to the wall and pressed his back against the plaster. His eyes swept back and forth with each sideways step toward the first open door. It was too quiet and not to his liking. After the front door blew apart, the folks inside ought to have been running around and making noise.

First an eye, then his whole head poked around the door frame. The room appeared empty, but he couldn't see behind the door. "Floyd?" he whispered. "You in here?" He stiffened when something hard and round pressed against his back.

"Get on in there," a deep male voice commanded, followed by increased pressure from the weapon.

The second nudge enraged him. Who in the hell did these niggers think they were messing with? No stupid jungle bunny could order him around. He faked a step into the room, pivoted, his foot swung around, connecting with a pair of legs.

Preacher man hit the deck with a thud, the rubber end of the toilet plunger he held above his chest, waved in the air like a funeral daisy.

The man bent over, butt sticking into the TV room, his hood gently swayed. "My daddy always told me coons was dumber than a stump. What you gonna do with that, boy?" He thumped the black rubber. "Plannin' on—"

"This ain't no plunger," the woman behind him said. This time he heard the distinctive click as she cocked the gun hammer.

Preacher man scrambled to his feet, using the stair railing for support. Blood ran down his leg and pooled on the floor. "Back into the room, real slow," he ordered.

The white knight complied, his mind racing to find a way out. He walked backwards until his legs bumped into the sofa.

"Sit," the preacher said.

This will not do, he thought. I can't let a couple of niggers get the drop on me. He bent his knees in preparation to sit, then spun around. His attack pulled up short by the double barrel shotgun in his face.

* * *

Within the safe darkness, Kat heard voices. They were so faint she couldn't make out all the words. As she concentrated, the trembling gradually lessened, the hot flashes cooled and she opened her eyes. The bathtub glowed in the strange afternoon light, rain beat against the narrow window pane.

The smell of burned gunpowder drove a spike of reality into her foggy mind. *Get up, Kathleen.* This time the words were crystal clear. A calm and controlled strength began to push her panic aside.

Although still lightheaded and terrified of another panic attack, she stepped completely out of the tub. She crept to the door, then to the head of the stairs. The stillness grated on her nerves. When things were noisy, you couldn't pick apart each tiny little sound and conjure all sorts of interpretations as to the relevancy. You simply went about your business, and met things head on.

She heard the floorboards creak at the bottom of the landing. Someone was moving around on the second floor.

* * *

Timothy Biggers had reached the end of his tolerance. Blowing up the front door had been annoying, but not worth getting his brains beat out. But now, the two idiots were ransacking his exam rooms. They'd already destroyed several expensive instruments and seemed bent on inflicting the same punishment on the remainder of his medical equipment.

He continued his on slow, but steady, route to the desk. Over the past ten minutes he'd inched his way from the foyer to the waiting area on his stomach. Another two feet would put him within grabbing range of his rifle. He paused to catch his breath and mulled over the anatomical areas in which he intended to shoot the men. Due to a rip-roaring headache, and an aching jaw from the boot kick, Biggers didn't feel up to performing any lengthy surgeries this afternoon.

The wounds should incapacitate the fools, he thought, not necessarily kill them. Although, if they busted up his new defibrillator, so help him God, he'd shoot them right between their eyes. He ducked when an otoscope came flying out of exam four, disintegrating upon impact. On his feet, he covered the remaining distance in record time.

Biggers pressed his palm against the false panel on the desk. The fully loaded M1-Garand felt good in his hands. He assumed a rifleman's kneeling stance and waited.

* * *

Mitch stopped several hundred yards short of the clinic when he saw Taxi's De Soto. Now he knew the whereabouts of the car, and most likely who took it. He should have known Billy Lee would recognize the green junker after their run-in early Tuesday morning.

Mitch's list of stupid mistakes continued to grow. At his insistence, Taxi had left his car parked near the Mitchell's house. And when the Chevy turned up missing, Billy Lee made a connection. However, he'd connected the wrong dots.

"Is your husband still at home?" he asked Pamela, hoping his postulations were incorrect.

"I don't know. I guess he could have come back to the house. He'd only left a few minutes before you picked us up. Why?"

He pointed down the street. "A friend of mine left his car on your street. And now it's here. I think Billy Lee may already be inside Dr. Biggers' clinic."

"Why on earth would he come all the way to the east Hollow?"

"What I think is, Billy Lee may be looking for some payback because of the Impala."

"How would he know to come over here?"

"On Tuesday, Billy Lee and some of his pals paid a visit to Dr. Biggers'." Mitch pointed to the painted over clinic sign that read: DR. NIGGERS

CLINIC. "That car was parked out front. Then later, there was a second run-in downtown."

Pamela chewed on her fingernail. "You're saying Billy Lee believes that the owner of the green car is the same person who took his Chevy this afternoon?"

"Bingo. And if I'm right, there could be trouble inside." Mitch cut the engine and opened the door.

"Would you like me to talk to him? See if I can calm him down?"

Her offer momentarily stunned him. He'd always believed his mother to be strong, but this went beyond strength. This was courageous. "No, that would be a very bad idea, Pamela. I want you and Carolyn to stay in the car until I come back."

She nodded, then handed him the plaid shirt he'd placed over the baby earlier.

"What's this for?"

"Han, you shouldn't walk into trouble without a shirt."

The comment was so silly he laughed. "Is that similar to the clean underwear rule?"

She blushed then began to giggle. "I suppose it is."

Mitch pulled on the shirt and buttoned it, then leaned over and kissed her on the cheek. "Thanks, Mom, I appreciate the advice. Now remember what I said. You stay here." He climbed out of the car and hurried down the sidewalk.

The heavens put on another lightening and thunder show, then the clouds split wide open pelting Mitch with pea-sized hail stones. As he cut through the yard next to the clinic, ice particles slowed his progress as he tried to avoid slipping.

He closed in on Biggers' clinic from the side, figuring a backdoor entry less risky than a full frontal assault. He didn't know what was going on inside, but given Billy Lee's temperament, it couldn't be anything but bad. He checked the cylinder on his Smith & Wesson. Fully loaded. He pushed through the tall juniper trees screening the perimeter of Biggers' property.

The screen was closed, but the wooden door stood open. He quickly ascended the four steps and cautiously entered. The unmistakable odor of explosives and gunpowder sent a chill down his spine. Something bad had gone down. The kitchen table had been flipped onto its side, plates and silverware scattered across the floor. A smashed birthday cake lay amidst the wreckage. He scanned the area, looking for bloodstains. Or bodies. None found, he allowed a pin prick of relief. Although someone had trashed the room, no one appeared to have been wounded or killed. At least not in the kitchen.

He paused next to the door.

*　　　*　　　*

"Hey, jackasses, y'all come on out here," Timothy Biggers yelled. Locked, loaded and ready, he waited for the two men.

They sauntered out of the exam room bent on kicking his butt. When they caught sight of his rifle, their body language altered dramatically. Instead of the cocky walk with doubled up fists, they slumped. It reminded Biggers of the scene in *The Wizard of Oz*, when the wicked witch began to melt.

"Take a seat." Biggers inclined his head toward the sofa, the rifle barrel remained steady. "Oh, and I'd appreciate if y'all would remove those silly god-damn hoods."

Billy Lee Mitchell and Louis Smith jerked off their white muslin hoods and threw them in the floor. Eyes on the doctor, they slowly moved across the foyer and into the waiting area, stopping inches from the sofa.

"I said SIT!" Biggers roared. When the men plopped down on the cushions, he smiled. "Don't y'all think it would've been easier to use the doorbell?"

"Fucking nigger lover," Billy Lee snarled.

"That's *Doctor* fucking nigger lover to y'all," Biggers corrected.

"Think you could maybe point that rifle of yours another direction?" asked Louis.

"Don't worry about where it's pointing, Louis. You ought to worry about whether or not I'll pull the trigger."

"He ain't gonna shoot nobody," Billy Lee said. "That would be cold-blooded murder, cause none of us got a gun."

"I don't care if you have a damn gun or not, Billy Lee. I got every right to defend my property, it's in the Constitution."

"Fuck the Constitution."

"That was down right ugly, son. And un-American."

"What's ugly and un-American is you socializin' and *livin'* with a nigger bitch."

The Garand in Biggers' hands exploded, the deafening sound reverberated off the walls. The bullet went through Billy Lee's right arm. Ping! The ejected cartridge case bounced off the wall and hit Louis in the forehead.

"If I was you, Billy Lee," Biggers said calmly, "I'd close my fucking mouth before something vital gets shot off."

* * *

The sound of additional gunfire brought Kat down the stairs to the second floor. She rounded the corner of the second floor TV room, her .45 in the lead. Two men sat in the floor, hands bound with venetian blind cord, Pastor Gordon held a shotgun on them.

Kat glanced over her shoulder to make certain the hallway remained clear, then walked closer. She reached down and jerked off the first hood. Floyd's malevolent black eyes stared up at her. Hand trembling, she removed the second white hood. Little Carl.

Lettie Ruth touched her arm and Kat nearly pulled the trigger.

"Move on back, honey," her aunt said. "We're in charge here. No need for you to get all worked up."

Kat nodded, too shaken to speak. Until this moment she'd believed the horrible events in the field were buried in a deep hole in her mind. Memories destined to never see daylight again. But here they were, less than two feet away. She could feel their eyes…like hands…undressing her with each blink. Raping her with each glance.

Kat cocked the hammer and pulled the trigger.

Floyd twitched once, then his eyes closed.

32

Mitch had tensed at the sound of gunfire, but with the second shot coming so soon, he charged through the door. In an aerobatic maneuver reminiscent of his New Orleans Saints days, he dropped to the ground. His shoulder hit first and slivers of glass from the front door cut through his shirt as he rolled. Rising to a crouch he aimed his .38 into the waiting area. Timothy Biggers had two men in his rifle sights.

"Those must hurt like a bitch," Biggers said, referring to the glass shards embedded in Mitch's shoulder. "When things settle down a bit I'll take a look."

Mitch pointed to the shattered front of the building. Hard driving rain came in through the gaping hole and the entire foyer was fast becoming a small lake. "Looks like you have lake front property now, Timothy."

"Damn fools tried to blow my place up." The two men seated on the couch glared at the doctor and Billy Lee bared his teeth. But neither moved an inch.

"Is it safe to assume they now have second thoughts?" Mitch asked.

"Ain't none your business, Yankee boy," Billy Lee snarled.

"Well hell, if it ain't a small world," Mitch said. "Hello, Mr. Mitchell."

"I shoulda known you'd be rubbin' noses with Dr. Nigger."

"I'm confused, maybe you can clear things up, Billy Lee. You and your pal did a job on the door, right?"

"Yeah, so?"

"I mean, you had the dynamite and the balls to blow this place to kingdom come. Right?"

"Yeah," Billy Lee said warily.

"So why are you two sitting on the sofa with a gun in your faces?"

"Fuck you, Yankee boy."

Mitch turned to Biggers. "I just love the Southern gentry. Such a classy way of speaking."

"We take pride in our boys down here," Biggers said. "They can go anywhere in the world and be immediately recognized as a racist jackass."

"Fuck you, Dr. Nigger," Billy Lee snarled.

"A limited vocabulary," Mitch said. "But for a jackass, I guess it's impressive."

"Best if you shut up right now," Billy Lee said. "And even better if you'd high tail it North, 'cause I ain't gonna be here much longer."

Mitch laughed harshly. "Truer words were never spoken, old man. But I have a couple of people to tend to before my time's up."

Billy Lee jerked his head around and looked out the window. "Goddamn it! That's my car out there and my—"

"And your wife and daughter."

Before Billy Lee could respond to Mitch's taunting, Lamar barreled down the staircase. He nearly went head first into the wall before he performed a skidding about-face on the wet hardwood. His saucer eyes panned across the group in the waiting area. When he saw Billy Lee's bloody arm, his face turned gray.

"Mr. Mitch," Lamar wheezed. "She done went and killed him."

Mitch and Biggers exchanged glances. "We better get up there," Mitch said.

"First we have to lock those sons-a-bitches in the closet," Biggers said, "key's in the door."

"I'm bleedin' to death here," Billy Lee complained. "You can't lock me up like this."

Biggers picked up a wet roll of gauze dressing from the floor. "Wrap this around your arm," he said, throwing the sopping mess across the room.

"This ain't even dry. Or clean," Billy Lee complained, as he squeezed the water from the gauze roll.

"Then you better pray you don't get gangrene," Biggers said.

Mitch ended their conversation with a couple of prods from the business end of his .38. "Get up and move, *slowly*, over to the exam room."

"That nigger loving son-of-a-bitch ought to fix my arm. He's the doc—"

"Billy Lee, if I was in your shoes, all shot up and bleeding, I'd keep my mouth shut," Mitch advised.

"But he—"

"And I'd shut it right now." Mitch opened the closet and forced them inside. It was a tight fit, barely enough room to breathe, but it would hold them for a few minutes. "Get your pal to help you with the bandage. I hear he's good at tying people up." He slammed the door and turned the key, then tossed it on the exam table.

* * *

The second floor could have been mistaken for a mausoleum. The silence heavy and foreboding. Rain ticked against the big bathroom window, green leaves and red rose petals clung to the glass. Biggers and Mitch turned right at the top of the stairs then stopped.

"You wait here, Lamar," Mitch said.

"That's what I'm gonna do. I don't ever want to go back in there," the boy said. "I already seen too much blood."

"Go sit in my office, son," Biggers said. "I'll come fetch you in a bit."

Lamar nodded and quickly walked away.

"Ready?" Mitch asked. Biggers nodded and they cautiously approached the corner room.

Mitch took point and entered first. Lettie Ruth and Pastor Gordon stood to his left, in front of the television set, their faces were mirrors of the horror they'd witnessed. Kat sat against the wall to his right, near the door. Her revolver, held in a two-hand grip, pointed toward a shaken Little Carl seated on the sofa.

"What's going on, Kat?" Mitch asked, his voice low and level. When Biggers tried to go around him, he held up a hand. "Wait up," he whispered.

"Got one of 'em," she said, her voice devoid of all emotion.

The blank look on her face made Mitch think twice about walking in front of the loaded weapon. He didn't know if she was fully cognizant of her surroundings, or if she even recognized him.

"Okay if I take a look?" he asked. When Kat nodded her permission, he crossed the room. From the front, Floyd looked as though he were sleeping, but closer inspection of the back of his head told an entirely different story.

"Crazy nigger bitch blew Floyd's head off," Little Carl bleated. He sat erect on the sofa, a thin white rope looped around his wrists. Mitch doubted it would hold for more than two seconds if he really wanted to escape.

The .45 sounded like an indoor thunderclap. The bullet dug into the sofa, hunks of cushion foam floated in the air. Kat's face remained impassive, as though her actions were controlled by an outside force.

"Hey, partner," Mitch said, hoping his voice and words could shake her out of the trance-like state and back into this reality. "That one hit a little close to me."

"Sorry," she mumbled. "I'm just gettin' so damn tired of being called a nigger."

Mitch walked over and squatted beside her. "I think you've got these boys pretty much in line. Want to hand over your weapon?"

Kat shook her head.

He took a deep breath, trying to maintain an even keel. She was so close to the edge she might as well have already jumped off. "What's next?" he asked, eyes on her trigger finger, anticipating the next twitch. "You plan on taking both these guys out?"

Her eyes shifted in his direction. In the brief flicker of inattention, Little Carl, ropes flying, launched himself across Floyd's corpse. Kat nailed him in mid-air.

Too late, Mitch rammed his shoulder into her, knocking her sideways. He wrenched the gun from her hand.

"That's two," she said coldly.

This time Biggers didn't stop at the door. He knelt beside Little Carl, trying to staunch the blood gushing from his mid-section. Lettie Rose flung open the closet and grabbed several boxes. In a few seconds she and the doctor were working like a well-oiled machine.

The discarded medical supplies and bloody bandages multiplied rapidly. To Mitch's untrained eye it seemed they were losing the battle.

"That's it," Biggers said, after a few more moments of frantic activity. "Nothing more to be done for him."

Mitch closed his eyes. Two dead men. Make that two dead *white* men, he thought, killed by a black woman. Jesus H. Christ, things had gone wrong. And then some. Nothing made sense to him anymore. The past was fast becoming the future and vice versa. Dear God, he wanted to go home.

Kat pulled the Arson/Fatality sheet out of her pocket and unfolded it. She looked up and smiled. And it frightened him more than anything he'd ever seen.

"See?" she said, pointing to the paper.

He leaned over. "See what, partner?" He would rather stare at the damn list for the rest of eternity than look in her dead eyes or see that ghoulish smile again.

"Everything's all right again. Lettie Ruth is still alive."

"What?"

"Just look."

So he did.

MARCH-APRIL 1963 ARSON/FATALITY

2789 10th	03-02-63	Pauley, GladysN	#23476	01:25 A.M.
4721 Riverside	03-05-63	Richards, DilmerN	#23477	12:11 A.M.
801 Mt. View	03-07-63	Carpenter, AliceN	#23478	01:03 A.M.
5429 Park	03-10-63	DeCarlo, MattieN	#23479	01:30 A.M.
109 Blodgett	03-17-63	Beason, Harold	#23480	06:50 P.M.
900 Grant	03-29-63	Peterson, Abel	#23481	02:15 A.M.
7643 Elm	04-01-63	Jefferson, TyroneN	#23482	04:05 A.M.
6780 South	04-01-63	Josephs, TupeloN	#23483	06:12 P.M.
654 Azalea	04-02-63	Spencer, LeroyN	#23484	05:20 A.M.
3449 Brook	04-05-63	Smith, Louis	#23485	06:45 P.M.

At first Mich didn't understand what he saw. It was true, all the newest entries for April 7 were gone. But Floyd and Little Carl weren't on the list. Why not? If Kat's theory was to be believed, she was the eye of the hurricane and that particular hurricane had just blown away two full-grown men. So why didn't their names show up.

The list now ended with Louis Smith.

Kat looked at her watch. 6:44 P.M.. "We can go home in one minute," she said.

Louis Smith! He'd left him locked in the downstairs closet with Billy Lee. And he hadn't searched either one. Mitch felt incredibly stupid, of course his father would be carrying, his type always did.

He jumped up and started running. He took the stairs two at a time, halfway down his foot slipped on the explosion debris and he tumbled to the bottom. Dazed, he lay motionless outside the exam room.

Inside, the sound of gun fire.

Back on his feet, he skidded around the corner and grabbed the skeleton key off the exam table. He fumbled with it, but it wouldn't fit in the lock. Frustrated, Mitch flung open cupboards and drawers until he found a red handle screwdriver. Returning to the closet he shoved it between the door and the strike plate. The old wood cracked and he yanked the closet open. Louis Smith tumbled out. Thrown off balance, Mitch struggled with the body.

Revolver cradled in the palm of his hand, Billy Lee Mitchell swung. Mitch didn't have time to duck, the blow struck him in the temple and he fell backwards. Through a red curtain he saw his father race from the room.

* * *

Lettie Ruth secured the square gauze pad over the stitches in Timothy's cheek with surgical tape, then leaned over and whispered in his ear, "What are we goin' to do?" She didn't want the Gordon's or Alvin to hear any more than necessary. In fact they already knew more than she liked.

Biggers shook his head. "I'm not thinking clear enough just yet."

She stole a glance at the three bodies laid out in the exam room floor. "Folks is gonna look for those boys," she said, a slight tremor in her voice.

He inclined his head toward the waiting area. Through the open door she saw Kat lying on the sofa, knees drawn up to her chest. "And that one's not in too good shape either."

"Maybe it's best," she said. "That child's faced more than her share of troubles, that's for sure. How much can a person be expected to bear?"

Biggers lightly touched his bandaged cheek. "Get me a handful of aspirin and help me into my quarters."

"Your quarters? Why?"

"I'm hurting," he said as he got to his feet. "And I need to make a few *private* calls."

When she returned from getting him settled, Lettie Ruth found Lamar sitting on the front porch steps. She stepped outside, the heavy rain had moved on a little while ago and now hardly more than a drizzle fell. Everything smelled clean and fresh. All the leaves were shiny green and drops of water clung to the flower petals. She wished all the dirty ugliness inside the clinic could be washed away as easily.

"Hey, Lamar, what's goin' on out here?" she asked, sitting beside him.

"Just waitin' on Mr. Mitch." He pointed to a black Chevy Impala parked down the street. "He told me to stay here 'cause he was gonna to talk to that lady."

Lettie Ruth squinted, but couldn't make out the woman in the dark. "He give you her name?"

"Nope."

To the best of her knowledge, Mitch didn't know anyone in Maceyville except the folks in the clinic, Dreama and Taxi. She was glad Alvin couldn't be here to see this, he'd surely make a mountain out of a mole hill. Brother would be ranting about time machines and getting everybody all worked up.

She patted Lamar on the back. "Why don't you come inside and we'll put together another birthday cake for you."

He leaned over, elbows on his knees. "I don't feel much like having a birthday no more."

"Can't say I blame you. But maybe if we work at it we can still make something good out of this day."

"I reckon." He squinted through the twilight at the black Impala. "Wonder what they's talkin' about for so long."

Curiosity overruled her good manners and she started to rise. "Maybe I ought to go see if anything's wrong."

Lamar shook his head. "Better not, he said stay to here, and he meant it Miss Lettie. He looked real serious, didn't smile or nothin'."

Lettie Ruth sat back down, but never took her eyes off the car. Or the woman inside.

33

Mitch leaned his head back against the car seat and let the rain scented breeze coming through the window cool his face. He could see a few stars peeking through the scattered clouds. Only a light drizzle fell now, the fierce storm had moved on. He hoped the human storm would move through as quickly.

"I've been watching it rain and wondering," Pamela said.

"Wondering what?"

"Wondering why you entered my life at exactly the right moment. When I needed help."

"My grandfather told me when fortune smiles you should always smile back."

"That's a nice piece of homespun wisdom, Han. But it provides little insight." She turned to face him. "Do you really know Billy Lee? Or did you fabricate the fact to make me more comfortable."

"No fabrication, I've known him for years. But it *was* pure luck that I happened to drive by your house earlier."

"There's something special about you, and I can't explain it. From the first moment I trusted you. And given my history with men, that's an extraordinary feat. You're helping me and yet ask nothing in return. Why?"

"Because you need me. You certainly don't need another man making demands."

"Billy Lee demands a lot of things."

"How did you end up with him?" This was a question Mitch had never asked his mother, although he'd come close so many times.

"Well, let's say Carolyn is older than our marriage."

"That's a good answer," he said. In fact it's the best damn explanation he'd ever heard for how a nice woman got stuck with a genuine asshole.

"Han, you saved our lives today. Thank you."

"You are most welcome, m'lady. Now it's my turn to confess. Things occurred in the clinic this afternoon that will most likely affect your future with Billy Lee." Right or wrong, he gave her an abridged version of recent events, beginning with Kat's rape and ending with the three dead bodies in the clinic. He wanted her to know the truth, and not be taken in by the elaborate tale Billy Lee would surely weave.

"Did he mean to kill Louis?" Pamela asked, after a prolonged silence.

Mitch shook his head. "Probably not on purpose. I'd guess Billy Lee tried to shoot the lock off and the bullet ricocheted."

"And the others? Your friend is the one that—"

"I'm not saying she did the right thing, but under the circumstances her actions are understandable."

"Oh, I think she did the right thing," Pamela said. "Those men were animals."

"Our legal system is set up to take care of men like that," he argued. "The courts and juries decide—"

"Not in Alabama, Han. There's no legal system if the victim is colored. They'll hang her before they let those boys spend one night in jail."

The bitterness in her voice surprised Mitch. He'd never heard his mother speak so forcefully or offer such a strong opinion. "You're probably right about the jail. But killing them is still stepping over the line. And she killed two men."

Pamela's mouth curved in a tiny cryptic smile. "That's the only way she could guarantee punishment for their crimes. Without the closure, she wouldn't be able to move on in her life. You'd understand if you were a woman, Han."

"How so?"

"Women spend most of their lives being told what, where and when. It begins with our fathers, then a husband, on down to the grocery clerk or the gas station attendant. Men treat us like children if we're lucky, or as second class citizens if we're not so lucky. Han, in this world there are many different kinds of niggers. And being a woman is one of them."

"I'd hate to think you're right."

"Someday," Pamela said. "In some far off future day, men and women will evolve to the point where they've learned to appreciate each others strengths."

"Does Billy Lee appreciate your strength?" Mitch asked, redirecting the conversation back to the main issue.

"Not hardly." She angrily flipped the hair off her shoulder. "All he appreciates is a cold beer. Which I'm supposed to deliver to his hot little hand with a smile and a curtsy."

"How much longer are you going to allow him treat you like a nigger?"

Pamela wouldn't meet his eyes, she busied her hands by straightening Carolyn's little pink and blue check dress. Finally she spoke, "While you were inside I thought about what you'd told me, about how your mother waited too long to leave. And the terrible price she paid." She looked up and captured his cornflower-blue eyes with her own cornflower-blue ones. "So, if you wouldn't mind driving us to the Greyhound station, Carolyn and I will be leaving Maceyville, Alabama. Tonight."

Mitch felt lightheaded, like he'd downed too many shots of whiskey. This was the first time since Lisa had died that he felt this good. "What about clothes? You'll need baby things."

"I keep extra clothes in the trunk for Carolyn, in case of accidents." She giggled. "But I guess mostly because it really irks Billy Lee."

"Stuff from your home?"

"There's nothing in the house that can't be replaced. Don't worry, Han, we'll manage."

"What about money for the tickets?"

Pamela grinned. "Money? She rooted around in the diaper bag and pulled out a wad of bills the size of her fist. "Billy Lee never figured out why I fed him beans and cornbread three times a week."

Mitch laughed, remembering his mother's intense dislike for beans and cornbread. In fact, until he'd attended the University of Alabama, he'd never tasted cornbread. He reached into his shirt pocket and pulled out the cowboy boot pin he'd given Kat once upon a time. "If it's all right, I'd like to give Carolyn a present."

"Of course it's all right, Han."

He attached the pin to the baby's dress. Her chubby fingers played with the shiny piece of jewelry. "Someday, when she's older, will you tell her the pin is a reminder she may have to kick down a few doors to get what she deserves."

* * *

APRIL 06—SATURDAY—2:00 A.M.

Waiting for the bus to depart, Mitch never once questioned his decision, and it perplexed him to some degree. He'd expected doubt, regret, maybe even fear to dump all over him. But the only emotions to pay him a call was joy and incredible peace. Apparently convincing Pamela to leave Billy Lee was more than the right decision, it was *meant to be.*

In the past year since Lisa's death, he'd lived like a monk. Celibate and isolated from the world. Nothing and no one waited for him in the year 2000. His grandparents were gone and since the stroke, his mother didn't recognize him anymore. She wouldn't miss a son she couldn't remember.

Whatever you called it, karma or kismet, the die had been cast. By choosing this path, he'd save one person from a life filled with sadness and regret. And to another he'd give a life. It was a good night.

Mitch waited to leave until the bus had pulled out of the station and he couldn't see his mother waving from the back window any longer. He got as far as the parking lot before the reality of his situation hit. Mixed emotions flooded his system. Happiness for his mother and sister's bright future warred with a strange sense of loss. In a few hours he would permanently change people's lives, but they would never know. And they wouldn't remember that once upon a time, a ginger-haired man had loved them.

* * *

Taxi Devore studied the three bodies, then pulled out a tape measure. In a few minutes, his calculations were completed. He turned to Timothy Biggers. "Gonna be a squeeze, but my old car's got a good size trunk. I reckon we can bend 'em here and there and shove."

Biggers nodded. "You sure about doing this? It could turn out to be a dangerous load."

"Being colored is a dangerous load, Dr. Tim. And it ain't killed me yet."

"In that case, we'll load up in an hour or so, I want to make sure the streets are empty."

"What about the other folks? They gonna take part in this?"

Biggers shook his head. "Just you, me and maybe Mitch if he gets back here in time. Alvin, Pastor Gordon and Lamar shouldn't be involved. Same goes for the women."

"Lettie and Miss Kat ain't gonna sit by, they's not that kind of women."

"They'll sit by if they don't find out what's going on. And I'm not tellin'. Are you?"

"No, sir. My mouth is shut tight." Taxi peeked through the blinds. "But somebody's sashaying up the walk and her mouth ain't never shut."

Biggers hurried out of the room to meet Dreama Simms at the door. "Evening, Dreama."

"It's startin' to rain again," she announced, shaking the water off her umbrella.

"What brings you out this late and in the rain?"

"Lettie called and said y'all could use a hand, cleaning up the messes around here."

He stepped out on the porch, in an attempt to stop her from entering. "I appreciate the offer, but most all the work is done. We're goin' to bed now."

Dreama's eyes narrowed and her hands rose to her hips. "Timothy, me and you can stand on the porch till sunup, and *not* talk about what you got inside. Or we can take care of business."

"You're not coming inside, Dreama," Biggers said, his voice hard. "No need for somebody else to—"

"I came to help." She ducked under his arm and walked into the foyer. "Now where y'all keeping the bodies?"

Biggers whirled around and watched open mouthed as Dreama entered the first exam room. "Jesus Christ!" he exploded. "Lettie Ruth! Lettie Ruth, get your butt down here!"

"Three ugly sons-of-bitches, ain't they?" Dreama said, as she passed the door.

He saw Lettie Ruth paused at the top of the landing. "Did you call that woman?"

"Stop hollerin' at me."

"Get on down here," Biggers growled.

"Not 'til you stop all that hollerin'," Lettie Ruth said. "You got some temper, Timothy Biggers."

"I haven't lost my temper…yet," he said. "Now get down here."

"Timothy, you got to understand about all this. It's not your business."

"Come down here, please."

Lettie Ruth moved slowly down the steps. "This is colored business."

"Ain't no color in my house," he said quietly.

She reached the last step and stopped, placing her hand on his shoulder. "I know that, probably better than any person on earth. But what's layin' on our floor is still colored business. And I want you to back down and let me handle it."

He patted her hand. "You can't handle it alone. It's gonna take everyone in this house, colored and white, to pull it off. Three men don't up and disappear without somebody, somewhere, knowing something. And I'm afraid we're that something."

"Because of Billy Lee Mitchell?"

"He won't be a problem," Mitch said as he walked through the front door. "I've decided to take him on as my special project."

"That boy is crazy," Lettie Ruth warned. "Crazy mean."

"And he won't ever change," Mitch said. "That's why I'm devoting my energy to dealing with his personality flaws."

"You think he'll keep quiet after you deal with his flaws?" Biggers asked.

Mitch nodded. "I guarantee nobody will hear a peep out of him."

"Do you know where he is?"

"No, but I know where he'll end up. You take care of the others and I'll handle Billy Lee."

*   *   *

Kat sat up and rubbed her eyes. The full impact of her actions settled like a steel blanket around her shoulders. Because she'd flipped out, her family and friends were in trouble. She needed to find a way to defuse all this before everything hit the fan. Maybe if she and Mitch put their heads together, they could come up with a workable solution.

She found Timothy and Lettie Ruth in the kitchen. "Hello," she said hesitantly, remaining in the doorway. Earlier they'd talked about what happened upstairs and Kat felt they understood why she reacted in such a violent manner. But the facts still hung in the air between them, she'd killed two men. How could they ever forget?

"Hey, honey, come on in. I just put up a pot of coffee," Lettie Ruth said, as though nothing out of the ordinary had occurred.

"Are you sure?" Kat asked, looking at Timothy.

"Of course," he said. "We can always use another pair of hands. Grab a broom and get busy."

Grateful for their acceptance she went to work. In a short while they finished and were seated at the table with cups of steaming coffee.

"Have you seen, Mitch?" Kat asked.

"He and the woman took off little while back," Lettie Ruth said.

"What woman?"

"The one that's been sittin' out front in that shiny black car."

Kat thought for a minute, the only other woman Mitch knew in Maceyville was his mother. After all his lectures about interacting with family members would, he dare to contact Pamela? "Did he say anything about her? A name?" she asked.

"He seemed a bit secretive if you ask me."

"Mind your own business, Lettie," Biggers said. "He's a grown man and if he has a lady friend, good for him."

Lettie Ruth sniffed. "A lady friend, with a baby?"

"A baby?" Biggers grinned. "Maybe she's a real good lady friend."

"I don't think you ought to be making light of this. A woman with a baby got no business messin' with single men."

"You've misjudged him," Kat said defensively. "Mitch has family in the area. She's probably a cousin or something."

"Both of you take it easy," Biggers said, picking through a plate of burnt meat loaf. "Her name's Pamela. I delivered that baby girl eight or nine months back."

"Well why didn't you say so?" Lettie Ruth asked.

"It's more fun listening to you make up stories."

Kat's stomach knotted up. Mitch hadn't *accidently* run into his mother. He'd gone looking for her. And now her partner was interfering with the past. She thought about the things they discussed about his early years, trying to figure out what he could be up to. She knew Pamela left Billy Lee when Mitch was five or six years old, but he'd never mentioned a sister. If Kat were given a choice of one thing from his past that would push him into this insane action, she'd pick the sister. Something obviously happened to her and it appeared her partner was going to try and stop it from occurring.

"Do you know where he went?" Kat asked.

"Not for sure, but I'd guess he took them home," Lettie Ruth said.

"Then you expect him back soon?"

"Mitch is gonna be tied up for a while," Biggers said. "He has a couple of things to tend to this morning."

"Like what?" Kat's blood seemed to slow in her veins.

"He took Pam and Carolyn to the bus station—"

"How come you know so much?" Lettie Ruth interrupted.

Biggers raised his eyebrows. "Men talk to each other, just like women. Mitch told me."

"Then why is he takin' her?"

"That's his business. None of mine, and most certainly none of yours."

"You said he had a couple of things to do," Kat said. "What else?"

"He's planning on spending some quality time with Billy Lee Mitchell."

Kat's hand trembled as she placed her cup on the table. "Timothy," the doctor looked at her and she tried to keep the panic out of her eyes and voice, "what did he say?"

"He told me, Kat," Biggers said, staring into her eyes. "He told me."

"Everything?"

"Everything. And I found it to be a damn interesting discussion."

"What you two talkin' about?" Lettie Ruth asked in an annoyed tone.

"Like Alvin says, Lettie Ruth, it will all come out in the by and by," Biggers said.

Kat nodded. "For now, let's get back to Billy Lee."

"He said we didn't have to worry 'bout that boy," Lettie Ruth said, obviously pleased to be included in the conversation again.

Kat bit her bottom lip. "Why don't you have to worry?"

"Mitch is going to convince him to keep quiet," Biggers said.

"And he said no need for us to get all worked up, 'cause Billy Lee wouldn't never talk about what went on today," Lettie Ruth said.

Kat's eyes filled with tears and they ran down her cheeks. "He's going to kill himself," she whispered.

Lettie Ruth took her hand. "No, honey, Mitch will be just fine. He's going to take care of Billy Lee."

"If he does that, then he won't be…"

"Won't be what?" Lettie Ruth asked.

"He won't ever be." Kat knew her words didn't make sense to her aunt, but it didn't matter. She had to find her partner before he did anything stupid. Killing Billy Lee Mitchell in 1963 would guarantee James Andrew Mitchell would not be born in 1965.

Excusing herself, Kat raced to the second floor. She stood in the middle of the T.V. room, her heart hammering in her chest as the fear grew. The room had been cleaned, all signs of the earlier violence erased. She remembered looking at the Arson/Fatality list right before Louis was shot downstairs. Where did she put it? She turned her pockets inside out—nothing. She bent down and peered under the furniture. Where was the damn list?

"Lookin' for this?"

She jumped when the male voice spoke from behind her. Alvin Rayson stood in the door, the crumpled sheet of paper in his hand.

"I found it in the hallway earlier. Didn't look familiar, so I figured it belonged to you or Mitch."

Kat held out her hand. "Yes, it does. Thank you, Pastor Rayson."

He looked at the list. "Interesting piece of paper you got here. Did you know it changes from time to time?"

She sat on the sofa. She didn't have an answer for this man. Should she explain to him about time-travel and future daughters? "I know," she whispered. Rayson sat beside her, his scent so familiar she could barely keep from throwing her arms around him.

"Care to talk about it?"

"Some things are for the knowing and some for the telling."

He held up the list. "This one is for the telling, Kathleen. Peculiar things been happening since you arrived and I'm wanting explanations."

"You don't want these explanations, sir, and someday you'll thank me for being so evasive." She held her hand out. "May I please have it?"

"What interests you on this peculiar list?" Rayson asked, still holding on to the paper.

"If you won't return my property, will you at least read the last entry out loud?"

He ran his finger down the names. "Says here, Louis Smith."

Kat sagged against his shoulder, her breathing ragged. "Then there's still time," she whispered.

"Don't be so sure, it read different a few minutes ago."

She sat up and stared at him, her eyes hard. "How different? What did it say?"

"Said Billy Lee Mitchell. But that name's gone now and I want to know why."

"Ask me again in 37 years, Pop." Kat snatched the paper out of his hand and raced from the room and down the stairs.

"You can count on it," Rayson shouted.

34

APRIL 06—SATURDAY—4:00 A.M.

Mitch realized his original plan of simply blowing his father to kingdom come wouldn't work. That approach would cause even more problems for Tim Biggers and the clinic. He needed to figure out a way to draw suspicion away from his east Hollow friends.

And to make sure Kat got to Park Street at the right time.

He parked the Impala on Webster Avenue and went inside the Waffle Shop. The smell of fresh coffee and maple syrup filled the narrow building. He took a seat at the end of the chrome trimmed counter and motioned for the waitress. "Double order of waffles, bacon, ham, eggs and hash browns," he told her. His last breakfast should be really good and really big. "Oh, and leave the coffee pot."

As his stomach worked on the enormous meal, his brain worked on the enormous problem. Permanently removing Billy Lee Mitchell posed no difficulty, just one bullet. His father's reputation as a bad boy wiped out many plausibility problems regarding his imminent demise. The police wouldn't closely scrutinize the death of one more moonshine runner. But leaving a trail, in case the police zeroed in on the clinic, pointing to a clear-cut reason for Louis, Floyd and Little Carl's disappearance required a delicate touch.

He *what-if'd* several scenarios before hitting the jackpot.

* * *

Kat would have preferred to leave the phone booth door open, but the rain was getting harder and blowing in on her. Enclosed in the humid glass rectangle, she thumbed through the tattered and dog-eared white pages until she hit the *M* section. She ran her finger down the list, searching for a Billy Lee Mitchell.

"There it is," she muttered. "B.L. Mitchell, 752 Blodgett 555-1256."

Now she needed transportation. No sooner had the thought entered her mind than a car turned the corner. Since she was still in the east Hollow Kat thought it would be safe to flag it down and hitch a ride. The teenage driver didn't want to go to west Maceyville, especially at four in the morning, so she turned on the charm. When that failed, she pulled the .45.

* * *

Kat cautiously peeked in the window at the back of the house. Although the place was quiet and dark, she didn't want a confrontation with Billy Lee. Surely if Mitch were inside, he would have let her know by now. She stood under the eaves and watched the water spill out of the rain gutter trying to decide her next move.

Her gut instinct told her Mitch would turn up here. But what-if she missed him? What-if he'd already been to the house? *I have to find him before it's too late.* Kat pulled the wet sweater off and dropped it in the trash can, then trotted down the alley.

* * *

Mitch pulled the black Impala into the driveway and cut the engine. Rain drummed on the car roof and the windows immediately fogged over. He rummaged in the glove box until he found a piece of paper to write on.

He chewed on the end of a pencil, thinking it through. His note must clearly convey his message. On the other hand, the wording must be vague enough so police suspicions weren't aroused. Because if they tracked it back to the clinic, Mitch would have defeated his own purpose.

"You want what I took? 6:00 A.M. at 5429 Park Street."

He left the note face up on the dash and got out of the Chevy.

* * *

Lettie Ruth Rayson couldn't recall ever feeling such absolute terror before. The terror completely engulfed her as the Ford closed the distance between vehicles. Its headlights blinked several times, then it slowly pulled around the

De Soto. The man behind the wheel didn't bother to look over as he passed them.

In the last two hours this had been the only vehicle she'd seen, but it generated enough fear that it might as well have been loaded with a whole regiment of Alabama State Troopers. She thought carrying dead white men in the trunk gave a whole new meaning to the slogan, 'Watch out for the other driver'.

She leaned forward and tapped Taxi on the shoulder. From the way he jumped she figured he was watching out for the other driver too. "How much longer?" Lettie Ruth asked.

"We be gettin' into the bayou's in about ten miles."

"You sure you can find this place?"

"I been huntin' gators down here since I been tall enough to hold a shotgun. I won't have no problem."

Lettie Ruth sank back, only slightly eased. She glared at the back of Dreama's head, recalling how hard headed she'd acted earlier. After coming over to the clinic and agitating the situation, she had a lot of nerve to be sleepin' at a time like this. Everybody's always talking how *northern agitators* stirred things up, well they ought to be more worried about *southern agitators*. Lettie fumed over the tacky way her friend had behaved…

Lettie sat in the chair while Timothy Biggers and Taxi studied a road map spread on the check-in desk, working out the safest route.

"You expectin' my man to drive all the way down to bayou country with dead Kluxers in the back of his De Soto?" Dreama asked, coming into the room.

Taxi frowned. "You stay out of this."

"I know one colored man better stay out of it," she said. "You can't be haulin' white bodies all over the county, Taxi."

"We mapped out a safe route, Dreama, it won't be a problem," Biggers assured her.

"Oh, and I suppose you be ridin' along with him?"

"No, I won't be going," the doctor said quietly.

"Why not? It happened in your clinic, Timothy."

Biggers gave her an exasperated look. "You're not lookin' at the whole picture here. Somebody needs to stay in town and douse the rumors. I expect to have a waiting room full of Maceyville policemen by noon."

"And where's Mr. Mitch during all this hauling and talking? I don't see him working to fit no bodies in his car."

"He's handling other business," Biggers said.

Dreama's chest heaved and her anger grew. "And Kat? Where's the woman what started all this? How come we the only ones here?"

"Kat's lookin' for Mr. Mitch," Taxi told her.

"Taxi offered to take care of the bodies, Dreama. Nobody asked him," Biggers said. "And I'll talk to the police—"

"So you gonna be here all alone and you gonna do all the explaining?" Dreama interrupted.

Lettie Ruth had kept her peace up to this point, but the implied meaning of the question was too ugly to let pass. "You are going in the wrong door, girl. Best back off."

"I want to know what your white doctor plans on tellin' the white policemen, Lettie Ruth."

"If you got something on your mind, Dreama," Biggers said, "quit dancing around the edges."

Lettie Ruth heard the anger bubbling underneath Timothy's words. Everybody knew where Dreama was going with this line of thought. Without actually coming right out with it, she'd just accused Timothy of selling them out.

Brown poison shot out of Dreama's eyes. "Why would you side up with a nigger girl that went and killed two white men?"

"Because it's my clinic and my business. I take full responsibility for what happens within these walls. I won't be jumpin' in bed with the local law."

"That mean you'll be saying you pulled the trigger? Leave Kat completely out of it?"

Taxi grabbed her by the arm. "You said enough, Dreama. We don't need extra aggravation right now."

Dreama jerked her arm away. "You best be worryin' about a whole lot more than aggravation. It won't never be his white ass swingin' from a tree branch, Taxi. You think he'll give up doctoring for a nigger?"

Biggers turned and stomped out of the room, his face a dangerous shade of red.

"I wonder if you listen to your own mouth sometimes," Lettie Ruth said, keeping her voice low. "Don't give me that look," she said when Dreama rolled her eyes and pursed her lips. "How could you say those things about Timothy?"

"How could I?" Dreama tapped her foot. "He's makin' the plans, telling Taxi where to dump the bodies. But he ain't comin' along, Lettie. And if he don't get his hands dirty, what's to keep him from talking? The law boys will be all over him and this place and they ain't known for being nice. Honey, your doctor will be giving out the whole story soon as they start hittin'."

"You don't know Timothy."

"Don't matter. No white man ever put himself through misery on account of coloreds." She flapped her hands in the air. "If he tells them about the shootin', all's gonna happen is a little ole bitty article in the newspaper. He tells where the bodies got dumped, it's another article in the paper. But if he tells them a colored girl shot those boys, who's gonna get put in jail for murder? Ain't gonna be the white doctor. And if he talks about the colored man what got rid of the bodies, who they be lynching?"

"And you figured out a way to stop all this from happening?" Lettie Ruth asked.

"No, it's too late for figuring. We made a mistake long time ago by lettin' a white man get too close. You may like him, and work for him, and live with him...but he won't give it all up for Lettie Ruth Rayson."

"Don't be so goddamn sure, Dreama Simms." Timothy Biggers marched through the door and slammed his rifle down on the desk. "If you're through running your mouth, get your ass in gear and help me load them boys."

"Here comes another one," Taxi said.

Biggers ducked down as the oncoming headlights lit the inside of their car. In a second it was behind them and Lettie Ruth released a rush of pent up air.

"Dr. Tim, we gonna see more cars closer it gets to sun up," Taxi said. "About time for you to get out?" They'd decided before leaving the clinic that Biggers would ride with them until sunrise, then get out and hunker down in the bushes until after everything was finished. It wouldn't do any good to have Taxi pulled over by a Trooper because of a white man riding in his back seat.

"I suppose so," Biggers mumbled.

Lettie Ruth looked at Timothy, his jaw was swollen twice its normal size and a purple bruise covered half his face. She knew he must be feeling bad, but he never complained. Mile after mile he just stared out the windows, the only time he moved was when cars passed them.

Taxi steered the car off the road. "We be back in ten or fifteen minutes, Dr. Tim. You stay low."

Biggers remained in the back seat. "This is foolish. I've come this far, no reason not to see it out."

Lettie Ruth touched his hand. "Timothy, if we get stopped on account of you..."

"I want to help, Lettie Ruth."

"You helpin' by letting us gets on with it," Taxi said.

Dreama stirred and turned around. "Your hands are dirty enough, Timothy. Get on out of the car now."

Before he could respond, a car pulled in behind them, the light bar on top of the police cruiser flashing. The Alabama State Trooper got out of his vehicle, adjusted his hat and holster, then marched toward them, stopping several feet away from the De Soto. Without speaking he pantomimed rolling down the window.

"What y'all doin on the road this early?" The trooper asked, capturing Taxi in his flashlight beam.

"My boy here is driving me, I'm Dr. Timothy Biggers." He opened the door and stepped out onto the shoulder.

"What happened to you?" the trooper asked, studying the doctors face.

"A tree branch blew off during the storm yesterday, caught me full on," Biggers explained. "That's why he's driving. My jaw hurts like a bitch."

The trooper played the light over Dreama and Lettie Ruth. "What about these other niggers?"

"The one in back is my nurse and the other is learning to be a nurse."

"Why ain't you in a white man's car?" the trooper asked, his tone suspicious.

Biggers laughed. "My boy always drives when I need to take a nurse." He leaned closer and whispered, "Well hells bells, you think I want a bunch of niggers smellin' up my Fairlane?"

The trooper laughed. "I sure wouldn't. Where y'all headed?"

Biggers pointed down the road. "Back to Maceyville."

"Y'alls pointing the wrong way."

Biggers snorted. "My goddamn nigger ain't got no sense of direction. I fell asleep in the back and next thing I know here we are. By the way, *where* is here?"

"Shit, y'alls getting real close to the Mississippi state line."

"Mississippi? I shoulda known better than to bring three of 'em along," Biggers grumbled. "Well, since we're this close maybe I'll keep going and have breakfast over there."

"There's good place about twenty miles ahead, called Bubba's."

"Bubba's you say? We got a bar in Maceyville called Bubba's Julep Junction, I hope this place is better."

"It is." The trooper shined his light on Taxi again. "You best learn to read a map, boy."

"Yes, sir.

Biggers climbed back in the De Soto, his eyes on the floor. "Y'all understand why I did all that don't you?" he asked.

Dreama waited until the Trooper's tail lights disappeared over the ridge then she jumped out of the car and ran around to the back door. She yanked the handle, reached inside and planted a wet kiss on the startled doctor's mouth.

"Of course we do, Timothy," she said, between smacks. "You was as good an actor as that Gregory Peck."

35

Kat waded through the flooded intersections, and with each successive block her mood darkened. Defeated, she sat on the curb and allowed her tears to mix with the rain on her cheeks.

Dangerous for you. Stay away. Don't cross. The warning from the disembodied telephone voice mocked her despair. Arrogance and her refusal to listen had led to this disaster. Six days ago she'd embarked upon a great time-travel adventure which ended up a nightmare. Only now the nightmare extended beyond her own person. Mitch, seduced by the malevolent power of foreknowledge, would move heaven and earth to right what he perceived to be wrongs. Regardless of the outcome.

Not once in the last five years had he mentioned a sister. And for one to suddenly appear, caused her nerves to dance. Mitch's sister was another Lettie Ruth mystery. Whether by accident, or on purpose, something had happened to the child. And that something was the catalyst that started this crazy scheme bubbling in Mitch's head. He believed getting rid of his father would save the baby.

But he'd overlooked one thing. Getting rid of Billy Lee also got rid of James Mitchell. She buried her face in her hands as a strange emptiness filled her heart. Overcome by sadness she didn't hear the approaching footsteps until the person was only a few feet away.

Her heart rate increased tenfold as she raised her head. Turning slightly toward the sidewalk, her muscles tensed, ready to take flight at the slightest hint of danger. Her ginger-haired partner strolled toward her, head down and unaware of her presence. She waited until he was an arm length away before standing. His startled expression made her laugh.

"For a cop you sure don't pay much attention to what's going on around you," she scolded.

Mitch grinned and shrugged. "Too damn wet outside for the bad guys."

"Where's your ride?"

"Delivered back to the original owner," he said, sitting on the curb.

She brushed a clump of matted leaves off a section of curb and sat beside him. "That's not too smart, considering the weather forecast. You realize we gotta walk all the way back to the clinic now."

Mitch shook his head and pointed to the street sign: PARK STREET. "This is as far as we're going, kid."

Kat didn't want to go where he was leading, but she also knew she didn't have a choice.

"I bet it's not even raining on the other side of the street," he commented. "Why don't you walk over there and check."

"Not without you."

"Kat, I won't be crossing."

Once he'd said the words, reality set in and a piece of her heart died. She stood and stared across the street. "Then I'm not going either. We'll just stay here and make a new life."

"You've got to go back and take care of your Pop. He's expecting you."

"He'll be fine. In fact, I can guarantee that Lettie Ruth is taking care of him right now."

"Then you completed a successful mission." He stood and gathered her in his arms. "Now it's time for you to go home."

She held onto him, afraid if she let go he would disappear in a puff of smoke. "Come with me."

"I can't do that. Someone needs my help here."

"The baby?"

He leaned back until he could see her face. "You know about Carolyn?"

"Lettie Ruth saw a woman and a baby with you in the car. And after what you told Timothy about the bus station, well, I just put two and two together."

"And came up with my mother and sister?"

"Yes."

"I always said you were an observant cop."

"Are they gone?"

"They're on a bus to Pennsylvania."

Kat's heart skipped a beat. "Then everything is okay. You can come with me."

"No. If I don't change the past…Carolyn will never grow up."

"Maybe you've already done enough."

He shook his head. "No, I've only made matters worse for them by convincing Mom to leave him today. Billy Lee knows about me but he's connecting all the wrong dots."

"He thinks you and your mother are…"

"Bingo. And he'll hunt them down and probably kill them both this time. So I have to see this thing through."

She swallowed the lump in her throat. Arguing would be futile. He'd already set the wheels in motion. It was only a matter of time. "When?" she asked.

"In a few minutes. When he gets here you've got to cross, Kat. It's going to get messy real fast."

"What about you? What will happen?"

"Don't worry about me. Just cross."

Kat reached up and brushed the hair out of his eyes, her fingers lingering for a moment on his freckled forehead. "I always meant to tell you just how much you remind me of Howdy Doody," she said.

Mitch laughed and tugged on one of her curls. "And you've always made me think of Shirley Temple."

"This is too hard." Her eyes filled with tears and she blinked rapidly, fighting the enormous wave of sadness threatening to sweep her away. "My heart hurts."

"I know," he whispered, "mine too. But the hurt won't last forever."

"Mitch, I don't want to forget you."

"Even if you forget in your head," he touched her chest with one finger, "you will always remember in here."

Kat placed her hand over his and squeezed. "There are so many things I wanted to say to you and…should have said."

"Kathleen, each time I looked in your eyes I heard all those things. Our friendship's been special from the beginning, because deep inside, we both knew it wouldn't last very long. And because we sensed the ticking clock, I think we crammed an entire lifetime into each day."

"Three hundred sixty-five time five…that's one thousand eight hundred and twenty five days."

"Not days," he said. "One thousand eight hundred and twenty-five lifetimes."

The Impala swung around the corner, capturing them in its headlights. Mitch leaned over and kissed her lips so gently it felt like butterfly wings brushing across her mouth.

"It's time," he said. "You know what to do?"

"When you...when Billy Lee..." The words stuck in her throat.

"When I pull the trigger, you cross that center line. Don't stop, and don't look back until you reach the other side of Park."

"I can't—" The rest of her sentence was cut off as Billy Lee Mitchell climbed out of the black Chevy.

Mitch gave her a smile and a shove, then walked toward his father.

36

YEAR 2000

APRIL 06

Kathleen Templeton stopped near the curb, turned and looked back across Park Street. "You're right, partner. It's not raining." She closed her eyes and his wonderful freckled face floated inside her eyelids. It took all her strength to keep from returning. She didn't want to be in this place...in this time without her friend.

Suddenly dizzy, she staggered and leaned against a Tupelo tree for support. A kaleidoscope of images filled her head. Events from her life, events she'd never experienced were suddenly very real. My past has changed, she thought, the life I knew never existed.

She opened each new memory with the excitement of a child on Christmas morning. For 29 years she'd been living in an alternate time line. What other wondrous surprises would she discover? She saw birthdays and holidays with a family which now included Lettie Ruth.

But the joy was tempered by a sense of loss. Kat frowned. As her new past settled in, something else seemed to be slipping away. "I have to hang on to the memories," she said.

✷   ✷   ✷

Although it was only 6:00 in the morning Kat raced down the hospital corridor, ignoring the visiting hours rules. Nothing would keep her from seeing her Pop, she'd bust down the CCU door if they tried to stop her. Luckily no one interfered and she slipped into his room.

The robust figure in the bed stirred and opened his eyes. "Kathleen." He held his arms out.

She held him tight and buried her face in his neck. "I'm so sorry I wasn't here for you."

"Don't be worrying about that, you were a long ways off. Lettie Ruth took good care of me."

Kat raised her head and looked at him. "Lettie Ruth?"

He gestured to an unmade cot in the corner. "Sister, won't go home. She's been sleeping here since Friday evening."

"Where...where is she now?"

"Stepped down the hall. She'll be glad to see you again. It's been a long time."

Unsure whether or not he remembered the way things were *before*, she remained silent. Did he remember once upon a time Lettie Ruth had disappeared?

When her aunt walked into the room, emotions flooded Kat's system. Her harrowing visit to 1963 whirled before her eyes in vivid technicolor. The spinning increased until she felt like she was falling through time.

Cotton field. White pickup. Ku Klux Klan. Blood. A ginger-haired man. Rain.

"Help me get her on the cot. Lettie."

"Lay back down, Alvin. I can lift her just fine."

"Wake her up, Lettie."

"She'll come around on her own. Give her a minute."

"What happened?"

"She's been trying for almost a week to get back here to you. The child is exhausted."

"She's still got the bruises."

"I would imagine so."

"You think she knows?"

"Hush, Brother, she'll hear you."

"Hear what?" Kat asked, her mind foggy and heavy.

"Don't worry yourself, child," Rayson said. "It will all come out in the by and by."

Lettie Ruth insisted Kat remain on the cot for an hour before allowing her to leave the hospital, and only then if she promised to go directly home and get in bed.

"But I'm supposed to go to choir practice this evening," Kat argued. "I have a solo tomorrow."

"You can sing next week," Lettie Ruth said. "I'll smooth it over with Dreama."

"She'll blow a gasket." The choir director's legendary temper still caused Kat to tremble, after 29 years.

"I'll handle her. And if I have trouble, I'll let Taxi take over."

"I wish you could fix it with my congregation," Rayson said. "Do you know who's doing the preaching tomorrow morning?"

"Webster Avenue will be joining us at Hope and Glory," Lettie Ruth said. "Lamar Gordon's in the pulpit."

"Didn't he just have a birthday?" Kat asked, surprised that she even knew this information.

"Yes, he did," Lettie Ruth said with an odd smile. "I made him a chocolate cake."

"But he never got to eat it," Rayson grumbled.

"That was some birthday," Lettie Ruth said, her voice taking on a far away quality.

Kat shook her head. There they go again, she thought. Old folks always remembering the past.

"It sure was," Rayson said. "I remember when he—"

37

APRIL 08—MONDAY

When Kat walked into the Daisy Wheel café, she saw her partner already seated in the back booth. As usual, Carolyn Mitchell's ginger-red hair, piled haphazardly on top of her head, threatened to tumble down at the slightest breeze.

As Kat slid into the booth she looked up and grunted. Carolyn didn't function well before noon.

"Did you read this article?" Carolyn asked, shoving the newspaper across the table.

"Which one?"

Carolyn pointed to the front page. "'MYSTERY SOLVED AFTER 37 YEARS'. Seems three men from Maceyville—Oh, just read it for yourself," she said, yawning. "It's way too early."

"One of these days you'll learn to go to bed before the sun comes up."

"It's hard to get away sometimes."

"So stop spending all your time at The Blue playing the piano."

"I can't. It's in my blood."

"Hush. I'm reading now," Kat told her partner.

MACEYVILLE SUN TIMES
April 8, 2000

MYSTERY SOLVED AFTER 37 YEARS

On April 5, 1963 Floyd Barnes and (Little) Carl Patterson vanished without a trace. Yesterday the county coroner positively identified remains found in a swamp near the Mississippi state line as Barnes and Patterson. They'd been wrapped in logging chains, and shoved under a stone outcropping.

At the time of their disappearance an intensive search of the area turned up negligible results. Since both were known to be active in the Ku Klux Klan, many speculated they'd offended the powerful organization. Weather also contributed difficulty to the investigation. Long time residents recall a big storm on April 5th which kept people indoors most of the day thus limiting possible eye witnesses.

Dr. Timothy Biggers told this reporter he'd been near the Mississippi state line that evening and didn't see anything unusual. "Nobody was out that night," said Biggers. "I'm sure if anyone had seen anything suspicious they'd have contacted the police."

The early sixties were turbulent in Alabama. In June, Medgar Evers, field secretary for the National Association for the Advancement of Colored People, was assassinated. September 15th, four young girls died in the bombing at the 16th Street Baptist Church in Birmingham.

Maceyville also had its share of tragedies. A spate of house fires, linked to Barnes and Patterson, plagued the east Hollow, claiming numerous black lives. It was this atmosphere of violence that fueled the men's racist attitudes. They were responsible for the arson fatality of Dilmer Richards and Tupelo Josephs, but, before legal action could be taken they had disappeared.

"It was like they fell through a crack in the earth," Robert Trewsman said of the missing men. "I liked those boys. They come in my bar, Bubba's Julep Junction, all the time and never caused no trouble."

In an interview, Pastor Lamar Gordon (Webster Avenue Methodist Church) implied the two men had participated in KKK harassment at his home when he was thirteen-years old. The alleged visit occurred three days prior to their disappearance. Gordon's neighbors also reported seeing the men set a fire that nearly destroyed Gordon's home.

Another murder on this same date is believed connected to the disappearances. In the early morning hours of April 6, moonshine runner Billy Lee Mitchell's body was found in the middle of Park

Street, shot twice in the head with a .38 caliber handgun.

When the officers responded they discovered Louis Smith, (father of police chief Arlin Smith), shot and his body stuffed into the trunk of Mitchell's black 1962 Chevy Impala. A note found at the crime scene implied Mitchell and Louis Smith may have had a falling out.

Barnes and Patterson's involvement in this dispute is not known, but all four were seen together earlier in the day.

The bodies may have been found, but the mysterious 'why' remains. Why did four young sons of the South meet such violent deaths? "If anyone knows the answer, they aren't talking," said Chief of Police Arlin Smith.

Kat looked up.

"Billy Lee Mitchell is my daddy." Carolyn's cornflower-blue eyes twinkled mischievously. "God, no wonder Mom took off for Pennsylvania. You think it's too late to change my name?"

"Nothing's wrong with your name. Be proud. The sixties were just bad down here. Lots of mean stuff going on, you're lucky your mother took you away."

"You ever wonder what it must have been like back then?"

"I don't have to wonder. I know."

"Oh, that Black-Awareness thing?"

"More or less."

"Want to hear something weird? The day all this happened is the very same date Mom and I left Maceyville. The story goes Billy Lee beat the shit out of both of us and from nowhere this wonderful man, kind of a guardian angel, appeared. He rescued us and talked Mom into leaving town. We'd probably both be dead if he hadn't come along." Carolyn opened her police jacket and folded back the lapel, reveling a copper and brass cowboy boot pin. "My angel gave me this pin. He said the boot was a reminder that sometimes I might have to kick the door in."

"He was right about the door, partner."

Carolyn touched the little cowboy boot. "I always wished I knew his name."

"Call him Elvis." Kat blinked back tears. "You would have loved him."

"I think I always have."

0-595-28980-0

Printed in the United States
34694LVS00006B/23